A COMPANION TO E.M. FORSTER

Volume–2

Sunil Kumar Sarker

ATLANTIC

PUBLISHERS & DISTRIBUTORS (P) LTD

Published by

ATLANTIC

PUBLISHERS & DISTRIBUTORS (P) LTD

B-2, Vishal Enclave, Opp. Rajouri Garden,
New Delhi-110027
Phones : 25413460, 25429987, 25466842

Sales Office
7/22, Ansari Road, Darya Ganj,
New Delhi-110002
Phones : 23273880, 23275880, 23280451
Fax : 91-11-23285873
web : www.atlanticbooks.com
e-mail : info@atlanticbooks.com

ISBN 81-269-0748-7 (Vol. 1)
ISBN 81-269-0749-5 (Vol. 2)
ISBN 81-269-0750-9 (Vol. 3)
ISBN 81-269-0751-7 (Set)

Printed and bound in India at Syndicate Binders, Noida

DEDICATED TO

*The memory of my dear mother, **Nilima Sarker**, and my dear younger brother, **Subarna Kumar Sarker**, both of whom had seen the manuscript of this book, while in preparation, but before the manuscript could actually turn into this book, they suddenly departed from this earth.*

Preface

Edward Morgan Forster is one of the most read, most difficult, most controversial, and most discussed front-ranking twentieth century English novelists. Is he a modern novelist or a Victorian? Has he, in fact, written only a single novel and not six? Is he really difficult to read? Is he plain-speaking or enigmatic? Are his novels realistic, or is he fantasying in them as in his short stories? Does he have any message to deliver through his novels or is he just an entertainer? These are some of the questions that have been variously answered by critics, and this has made him all the more interesting. His novels apart, Forster is one of the major short-story writers of the twentieth century as well, astonishingly having not more than some two dozen extant pieces. In his short stories he is exactly fantastic as in his novels he is starkly realistic, and this should point to his wide range of literary peregrination. This is not all, Forster is a worthy and wise critic, commanding respect from other critics, writers and readers.

This book may be treated as an easy guide to Forster, the man, the novelist, the short-story writer, and the critic. After having read the works of a writer, hundreds of questions about the man that the writer is lurk behind us, and so to seek the answers to some of such questions about Forster in it I have dealt with his biography at a length that may seem to some readers rather inordinately expatiated, but then readers are not all of the same kind. For the biographical informations, frankly, I have heavily drawn on the official biographer P.N. Furbank's *E.M. Forster: A Life* and Nicola Beauman's *Morgan: A Biography of E.M. Forster*. I have narrated (or, rather, re-narrated) the starkly bare stories of all the five most popular novels of Forster—*Where Angels Fear to Tread, The Longest Journey, A Room with a View, Howards End, Maurice* and *A Passage to India*—again at some length, as I thought that for an understanding of a novel the bare story of it, which we can rarely recall in details after a lapse of time, particularly if we are voracious readers of fictions, is undeniably of some help. For the like reason, I have also narrated the 'stories' of his short stories. Forster is no less renowned as a critic and a theorist of the novel than as a novelist or short-story writer; as a novelist he can well compare with Henry James or Virginia Woolf, for instances, and as a short-story writer with Edgar Allan Poe or Katherine Mansfield, and, likewise, as a critic and theorist of the novel he stands in comparison with the novelists-cum-theorists-of-the-novel Henry James, Virginia Woolf and Percy Lubbock. It is for this reason that here I have discussed his *Aspects of the Novel,* freely quoting from the text.

I claim not even the least originality in this book, and no observation on, or criticism or appreciation of, Forster, here, is mine (except in a very few cases, and those only by the way); what I have done here is an orderly collocation of materials relevant to Forsteriana. This book may seem to be encumbered with quotations, at places even with long ones, but instead of paraphrasing them, instead of selling others' ideas and views as my own, I preferred to honestly do as I have done. Again, repetitions are here at places, but I have not shunned them keeping in mind the convenience of the reader. I have always had an eye not so much to the quality of my setting forth as to the quantity of materials essential to understand Forster.

My sons, Dr Suman Sarkar and Dr Sutanu Sarkar, had perseveringly collected books on Forster from diverse sources for me, without which certainly I could not have written this book, and my wife, Smt Manju Sarker, has typed the whole manuscript of it. My affectionate thanks I extend to them all. Lastly, I am grateful to Dr K.R. Gupta, Chairman, Atlantic Publishers and Distributors (P) Ltd., New Delhi, for publishing this book.

SUNIL KUMAR SARKER

Contents

VOLUME 3

Where Angels Fear to Tread 6

1

INTRODUCTION

Nicola Beauman, in his *Morgan: A Biography of E.M. Forster,* has made a very striking comment about Forster and his first novel *Where Angels Fear to Tread:* "His first novel was in some ways the first modern novel; and it arrived ten years before the first modern poem, Eliot's 'The Love Song of J. Alfred Prufrock'" (Beauman, 164). When actually Forster began to write his first completed and published novel *Where Angels Fear to Tread* we do not for certain know, but this we for sure know that he finished it in 1904, at Harnham—the place where, curiously, he also completed his other novels, though they were began elsewhere. Nicola Beauman writes in this regard: "In the late autumn of 1904, at Harnham, Morgan [i.e. Forster] finally finished his first novel: how appropriate that although he made beginnings in other houses, other rooms, the house where he was to write all of his six works of fiction was the one where he completed his first" (Beauman, 162). Forster wrote this novel with a very facile pen, for he finished it within the space of only a couple of weeks; and, yet, after completing the first draft of it he found that the novel only needed a few minor correctional touches. It was so because while writing the novel he was most confident about all the episodes and other elements of it, and also about its whole course, from the beginning point to the end. But Nicola Beauman, though he trusts to the facility of Forster in writing this novel, is a little cautious about his conclusion in this regard: "There is no way of knowing whether he polished

Where Angels Fear to Tread a great deal and copied it out, or whether he wrote it straight off. Yet the few weeks it took him to write, and the feat that at the same time he was writing three short stories and continuing with 'New Lucy,' suggests the latter, and it [this novel] has a certain *elan,* an unforced quality, that perhaps comes from something approaching spontaneity. There were, naturally, some changes (the kind that nowadays, with word processors, can no longer be traced) but they were minor. The overall impression is of a novel written with confidence and ease, as though Morgan [i.e. Forster] knew exactly where he was going and what he was doing" (*op. cit.,* 163).

When Forster was writing this novel, along with the 'New Lucy' novel and three short stories—which included 'The other Side of the Hedge' and 'The Purple Envelope'—Forster was merely twenty-six years of age, and yet, astonishingly, he "had *nothing more to learn* about prose style, narrative, characterisation, insight and all the other qualities that need to be part of a great novel" (*ibid.*). The first novel of Forster, *Where Angels Fear to Tread* is astonishingly considered by some critics as 'one of the most perfect novels of the twentieth century' (*ibid.*).

Where Angels Fear to Tread is, to an extent, autobiographical; and this is so very naturally, for the very first novel of an author tends to be autobiographical, oftentimes inspite of himself. The central character of this novel is Philip Herriton, who is, characteristically, hardly at variance with Forster himself. Nicola Beauman writes: "Morgan [Forster], like Philip, had found that the way to avoid confrontation with the tragic, unbearable aspects of life was to laugh at them, to be deflationary: he transmuted the self-deprecating quality that had been his carapace throughout life into his art" (*op. cit.,* 164). This is but only one point of similarity or *vraisemblance* between Forster and Philip, and there are a few others, minor though they be. Forster himself said that *Where Angels Fear to Tread* aimed at 'the improvement of Philip,' i.e. perhaps, at subplanting the Sawston (Tonbridge) culture of Philip (i.e. of Forster's school life) with the culture of

Monteriano (i.e. San Gimignano); or, rather, aimed at replacing the mechanistic culture with the humanitarian culture. But this novel is much more than just that; its scope is not simply the persona of certain single person, or his or her self-improvement; its canvas is much more wider, that provides space for consideration of cultural or value-related differences between the English suburbia, with its lukewarm sensibility and inhibitory mores, and Italy, with its warm sensibility and aesthetic freedom. Nicola Beauman writes about this novel in this regard: "*Where Angels Fear to Tread* is, however, far more than Philip's growth in self-knowledge: it is about the inhibited values of [English] suburbia versus the warm lack of inhibition of Italy, and yet is subtle enough to show the strength as well as the flaws of both; it is about the importance of the bodily and the intellectual and the spiritual" (*ibid.*).

The basic story of *Where Angels Fear to Tread* Forster found from over-hearing a bit of conversation 'at Siena or that sort of place.' Forster himself wrote about how he came by the basic story of *Where Angels Fear to Tread* and how he utilised it in the fabric of the fiction: "'I overheard an English lady talking to another English lady about a third English lady who had married an Italian far beneath her socially and also much younger, and how most unfortunate it was. This story bit of twaddle stuck in my mind. I worked at it until it became alive and grew into a novel of contrast. On the one hand was the English suburbs with the grey inhibited life that I knew only too well, and on the other hand was Monteriano, a romantic hill town which I established in Tuscany on the basis of San Gimignano'" (Beauman, 124). P.N. Furbank says almost the same thing: "The plot originated in a scrap of *pensione* gossip, overheard by him [Forster] some time during the previous two years [previous to the year in which Forster wrote down the novel, i.e. previous to 1904], about an English tourist who had a *mesalliance* with an Italian" (Furbank, I, 109). But Furbank has hazarded another source of the story of *Where Angels Fear to Tread:* "Another conceivable source might be an incident in the Trevelyan family. In 1890 an aunt of the Trevelyan brothers, Florence

Trevelyan, being then middle-aged, married a Sicilian doctor named Salvatore Cacciola and settled in Taormina—to the great disapproval of her family apart from G.M. Trevelyan, who used to pay her friendly visits in Sicily. It seems very possible that G.M. Trevelyan should have mentioned the story to Forster" (*ibid.,* f. n.). Furbank further writes that "Echoes of Maimie Aylward's second marriage were probably also in his [Forster's] mind" (*ibid.*).

According to Nicola Beauman, the plot of *Where Angels Fear to Tread* is similar to that of Henry James's *The Ambassadors* (1903), which was published two years before the publication of *Where Angels Fear to Tread.* In James's *The Ambassadors,* 'Stretcher is sent to Paris to bring home Chad, said to be entangled with a less than respectable female'; and in Forster's *Where Angels Fear to Tread* Philip and Caroline are sent to Monteriano to rescue the child of Lilia and Gino, but the rescuing falls through and it is revealed that Philip has fallen in love with Caroline, and Caroline has fallen in love with her social inferior, the slovenly Gino Carella. The plot of *The Ambassadors* is, in brief, as follows. "Lambert Stretcher is sent to Paris by Mrs Newsome, a wealthy widow, to persuade her son Chad to return to Massachusetts and his responsibilities as head of the family business. Stretcher's success as an ambassador will ensure his marriage to Mrs Newsome when he returns. *En route* to Paris, he meets Maria Gostrey, an expatriate American whose witty and sympathetic observations introduce him to the pleasure of European life. In Paris he finds Chad an assured and sophisticated young man who is not eager to return to America. Stretcher is introduced to Madame de Vionnet, a charming French woman who has clearly been the refining influence on Chad's life. "Stretcher's letters to Mrs Newsome reveal his declining enthusiasm for his embassy, and she sends further ambassadors—her daughter Sarah and Sarah's husband and sister-in-law—to appeal to Chad. They receive little help from Stretcher, and their lack of success with Chad estranges Stretcher from Mrs Newsome. In the ensuing action Stretcher makes two discoveries: that Chad's liaison with Madame de Vionnet is an intimate one, and that his own sympathies rest with Chad. He remains detached, however, content to observe life rather than participate in it, and ultimately returns to his life as a widower in Massachusetts" (Ousby, 22). And the plot of *Where Angels Fear to Tread* is, in brief, as follows. Lilia Herriton, a widow in her early thirties, is urged to spend a year in Italy by her brother-in law, Philip, who believes that the experience will purify and ennoble her. Accompanying a younger but less impulsive neighbour, Caroline Abbott, Lilia departs. All goes well until news reaches the Herritons in Sawston that she intends to marry again. Mrs Herriton, a domineering social snob, dispatches Philip to prevent the catastrophe but he arrives too late. On reaching Monteriano he discovers that Lilia has already married Gino Carella, several years her junior and a dentist's son. Philip returns with Caroline to England.

The marriage fails and Lilia dies in childbirth. Mrs Herriton and her equally unsavoury daughter, Harriet, eventually decide to retrieve the baby from its father's dubious influence. Philip is again dispatched, this time with Harriet, and Caroline Abbott, guilt-ridden over her part in Lilia's downfall, determines to adopt the child herself. All three meet in Monteriano (where Forster supplies a delightfully comic description surrounding a performance of the opera *Lucia di Lammermoor*) and Philip and Caroline begin to succumb to the charm of Italy.

"Gino proves to be a devoted father and the mission is more or less abandoned. Harriet refuses to admit defeat however, and attempts to steal the baby. The carriage in which she, Philip and the baby are travelling is involved in a collision. It overturns and the baby is killed. Gino assaults Philip and the three English characters retire. On the journey home, Philip discovers that he has fallen in live with Caroline, she with Gino; her future seems to hold spinsterhood and charitable works" (*op. cit.,* 995).

Besides the similarity between the two stories or plots of the two novels, there is another semblance between the two fictions, on the point of theme. In both the novels the fundamental fictional problematic is social cultural diversity, congruence and contradiction. *Where Angels Fear to Tread* has also thematic identity with Forster's short story, 'The Eternal Moment': in the short story Miss Raby imagines that during her earlier visit to Vorta her porter Feo Ginori fell in live with her (this is but her wistful day-dreaming) and she with him, consequently, inspite of the fact that Feo was far below her in social status, and cultural refinement, due to their belonging to two contrasting cultures of differing grades of refinement, Miss Raby belonging to the superior culture and superior status of the English society and Feo to the inferior culture and inferior status of the Italian society, as Lilia in the novel fell in love and married Gino Carella, a person far below her in social status and a stoutly young nincompoop *sans* all refinement (one may notice the partial similarity between the two names: Feo Ginori and Gino Carella).

At first Forster called his first novel to be published 'Monteriano,' but on the publisher's suggestion chose two alternative titles for it, out of which two the publisher finally selected the present title of it—*Where Angels Fear to Tread*. P.N. Furbank writes that in 1905 Forster "had completed his 'Gino' novel, and had sent it off, on a speculation, to Blackwoods. He sent a copy at the same time to H.O.M. [Hugh Meredith, Forster's class-mate at Cambridge, who had a tilt towards high-falutin and intellectual romanticism and who exerted considerable intellectual influence on his homosexual lover—Forster], who was much impressed and told him it was a 'great' work. 'I do not mink it will ever seem so to me,' Forster remarked to himself soberly, 'it is not more than careful and praiseworthy.' By March [1905] he had heard from Blackwoods that they would publish it, though not on very generous terms. They told him he must change the title, as the present one would decrease the 'already very doubtful' chances of sale; and having no ideas himself, he consulted Dent [Edward Joseph Dent, Forster's friend], whose novel in so many ways it was. Dent supplied a whole list of suggestions, and from these he [Forster] selected *Where Angels Fear to Tread* and *From a Sense of Duty*. Blackwoods to his [Forster's] mother's disgust, chose the former" (Furbank, I, 123). So we may say that naming the novel *Where Angels Fear to Tread* was rather a joint enterprise of Forster and his friend Edward Joseph Dent. Forster too was not happy with the title, and wrote to his mother about Blackwoods's selection of the title: "'it was perhaps unwise to accept it [the title *Where Angels Fear to Tread*]'" (*ibid.*).

Forster sent the manuscript of *Where Angels Fear to Tread* to Blackwoods actually for favour of its being published in their magazine, in installments, but very fortunately for Forster, Blackwoods decided to publish it in book form. The terms of the publications were not comfortable for Forster, neither were they rather honourable for him, and, nevertheless, he accepted the terms because it was his maiden venture, his *debut,* in the arena of publishing novels. According to the terms of Blackwoods Forster would get "nothing on the first 300 copies, 10 per cent on the next thousand, 15 per cent up to 2500 and one shilling a copy thereafter [according to Nicola Beauman, one shilling of 1905 is equivalent to 2.50 Pounds of 1993]" (Beauman, 174). Forster was rather indifferent to the publication of *Where Angels Fear to Tread,* because he would like to get the manuscript of it published by Methuen or Heinemann, but as the manuscript was almost instantaneously accepted by Blackwoods, he accepted Blackwoods terms only lukewarmly.

Why Forster did choose the title *Where Angels Fear to Tread* out of a whole list of titles sent to him by Dent, on his request, for the first novel of his, is not very clear to us, but we may at least discover some potential clue in his being a member of the 'Conversazione Society.' When Forster was at Cambridge, he was elected to the secret society called 'Apostles' or 'Conversazione Society.' The number of the members of the Society was generally limited to 7 or 8, and in the case of an outsider desirous of becoming a new member of the Society, an old member had to resign from it in order to make room for the new-comer. But even after his resignation, the old member could attend the meetings of the Society as an 'angel', i.e. the old members of the Society used to be called 'angels.' On the other hand, those members who resigned their memberships not for entry of new members but for their disaffections with the Society were called 'fallen angels.' The title *Where Angels Fear to Tread* might have been chosen by Forster for the association of the word 'Angels,' in the title of the novel, with the appellation awarded by the Society to a member resigning for the entry of a new member—the appellation of 'angel.' The 'Conversazione Society' was almost strictly guided by the moral philosophy of G.E. Moore, as we have already said, and Forster was, through the Society, much influenced by Moore's philosophy of life, or, rather, his moral philosophy. The fundamental principle of Moore's moral philosophy was that truth, beauty, and personal relation were to be regarded as the three only exclusive values of life. Forster, we repeat, admired, and incorporated into himself, Moore's ideal vision of life, that eschewed the Victorian hypocritically mechanical concept of life and society, and rejected the Victorian concept of social stratification—all that the Clapham Sect, to which the Forster family associated itself, stuck to. The influence of Moore's moral philosophy on *Where Angels Fear to Tread* is deeply ingrained, and, as a necessary corollary, that of the 'Conversazione Society' as well. Now, some have hazarded that the title *Where Angels Fear to Tread* might have been chosen by Forster as an 'Apostolic joke' or 'angelic joke'—a 'joke,' because what the 'angels' thought to be right they perhaps would shirk the performance thereof; but Lilia did not evade performance. She became 'angelic' by breaking through the cultural divide between herself and Gino, by rejecting her Sawstonian (Tunbridgean) middle-class tradition, and by ratifying, by her act of marrying her social inferior Gino, the 'angels's' cardinal moral ideals of truth, beauty and personal relation.

This might have been the reason behind Forster's selecting, for his maiden novel, the title *Where Angels Fear to Tread* (and another title: *From a Sense of Duty*) from a whole list of possible titles supplied by Edward Joseph Dent. But the question remains: from where did Dent procure this title? The title was taken from line 625 of Alexander Pope's *An Essay on Criticism* (1711). In Part III of this work, Pope speaks about 'mad, abandon'd critics' who are 'bookful blockhead, ignorantly read.' Such critics, says Pope, must poke their noses into any piece of literary work, even though these may be beyond their intellectual calibre, and without understanding them well will make wild critical comments on them. Pope says that no literary work is safe from their obtrusive and blunt probings, that they do never trepidate, never fear to enter into a literary arena that is a *caviere* for them:

> No place so sacred from such fops is barr'd,
> Nor is Paul's church more safe than Paul's church-yard:
> Nay, fly to alters; there they'll talk you dead:
> For fools rush in where angels fear to tread,... (625)

Lilia, in *Where Angels Fear to Tread,* is as dare-devil, blunt, irresponsible and brisk as those blunt critics who foolishly rush into superior and very complex creative works which even worthy, and so angelic, critics quaver to consider. This may have been another and perhaps more potential reason why Forster chose the title *Where Angels Fear to Tread.*

All the novels of Forster have been very popular, perhaps except *Maurice;* and all his novels have been filmed, except *The Longest Journey,* and all the film versions of his novels have received warm and echoing acclaims from the public. In 1991, *Where Angels Fear to Tread* was filmed under the direction of Charles Sturridge. In Sturridge's film, Helena Bonham Carter (who acted in four out of five Forster films) acted as Caroline Abbott; Rupert Graves appeared as Philip Herriton; and Judy Davis acted as Harriet Herriton. There are some noticeable departures in the film from the novel. "For instance, in *Where Angels Fear to Tread* [the novel itself] both Philip and Caroline are described as tall, an important marker of their class positions and aspirations, whereas both Bonham Carter and Graves are burgerishly short" (Tambling, 220). But the film mostly corresponds with the novel, not only as regards the essentials but also as regards details. For instance, Forster fictionally created Monteriano—the 'topoi' of the principal episodes—on the model of the real topoi San Gimignano, and Sturridge, in his film, took San Gimignano to be the Monteriano of the novel, because San Gimignano much resembles Monteriano.

The principal characters or 'people' (the term is Forster's) of *Where Angels Fear to Tread* are the following:

Lilia Herriton (nee Theobald; had been wife to Charles Herriton, but now a widow, aged 33)

Philip Herriton (brother to Charles Herriton and Harriet Herriton, and Lilia's brother-in-law)

Mrs Herriton (mother to late Charles, Philip and Harriet, and Lilia's mother-in-law)

Harriet Herriton (daughter to Mrs Herriton and sister to Charles and Philip)

Caroline Abbott (neighbour to the Herritons, later fiancee to Philip)

Gino Carella (Lilia's second or Italian husband, later fiance to Caroline)

The minor characters include: Mrs Theobald (Lilia's mother); Mr Kingcroft (Lilia's sympathiser to whom she tilted a little in affection after the death of her husband Charles); Irma (Lilia's little daughter by late Charles, aged around nine), and Perfetta (Lilia's handmaid in Italy).

The locales of the episodes or incidents of *Where Angels Fear to Tread* are the following:

Sawston (fictional place modelled on Tunbridge, where the Herritons lived, and where the Herritons bought a house for Lilia to live in with Irma)

Yorkshire (where Mrs Theobald lived)

Monteriano (fictional place modelled on San Gimignano, where Lilia had gone to be 'purified' but rashly married Gino Carella).

The novel runs upto about 160 pages and is divided into ten chapters or sections of more or less equal length.

2

THE STORY

Lilia Herriton was going to Italy, being accompanied by Miss Caroline Abbott, ten years younger than she, as her chaperone of sorts. Mrs Herriton (Lilia's mother-in-law), Philip Herriton (Lilia's brother-in-law, and a barrister by profession), Mrs Theobald (Lilia's mother), Mr Kingcroft (for whom a little passion grew in Lilia after her husband Charles Herriton's death in the recent past) and Irma (Lilia's little daughter) arrived at Charing Cross (near London) to see Lilia and Miss Caroline off. Lilia had been married to Charles Herriton, after their dating for long ten years, in the recent past, and a daughter, Irma, was born to them. Charles suddenly died, and after his death Mrs Herriton suspected a little but growing warm passion going between Lilia and a gentleman named Kingcroft. To placate intensification of that passion and to provide Lilia with an opportunity for mental change, Mrs Herriton was bent on parcelling out Lilia to Italy with the conviction that the Mediterranean air of Italy 'purifies and ennobles.' After Charles' death Lilia wanted to live with her mother, Mrs Theobald, at Yorkshire, keeping Irma, a girl around nine years old, with herself. Mrs Herriton, however, found a compromise formula between Lilia's spirit of freedom and her own sense of dignity: she bought a house for Lilia, at Sawston, and Lilia was living there with Irma for three years. But Mrs Herriton, a 'domineering social snob,' was not at peace with her compromise formula, she was always apprehensive of the honour of the Herriton family being dashed to the ground by the incipient but fast growing epistolary intercourse between Lilia and Kingcroft. She believed that Lilia, being merely thirty three and a widow, must be suffering from oppressive libidinal demands, and a journey to Italy and a stay there for a year would save Lilia, for Italy 'purifies and ennobles'.

Italy till then retained the images of the Middle Ages. Reaching Italy, Lilia and Caroline put up at Monteriano and visited Florence, Rome, Santa Deodata and some such other refreshing and invigorating places. Lilia did never snap her connection with the Herriton family in England and, as a reward, she continued to receive financial largesses from the Herriton family regularly. She frequently wrote assuring letters to Irma and Mrs Herriton, and less frequently to Mrs Theobald.

On a sudden, one day, an astonishing and enervating letter arrived from Mrs Theobald to Mrs Herriton, breaking the news that Lilia was engaged with an Italian. Mrs Herriton and Charles' younger brother Philip were alarmed that by marrying for the second time, (and that in an alien and less refined country), Lilia would have insulted them all. Mrs Herriton pronounced her verdict on Lilia. "'If Lilia marries him she insults the memory of Charles, she insults Irma, she insults us. Therefore I forbid her, and if she disobeys we have done with her forever'" Mrs Herriton promptly telegraphed to Lilia to know more about her engagement, particularly to know if she was engaged with a man at or below her social status. And soon a reply telegram from Caroline Abbott came to announce to the consternation of all: 'Lilia engaged to Italian nobility. Writing. Abbott' (section 1).

To rescue Lilia from her impending catastrophe of getting married to the Italian far below her in social status and refinement, Mrs Herriton sent Philip (without being accompanied by anybody) to Monteriano where Lilia and Caroline (an almost passionless and equianimous woman of twenty-three years) had been excursioning, and where Lilia revived her amorous drive. Philip liked and loved Sawston the most as he hated Italy the most. He loved Sawston because he believed in the individual's conformity with the society, culture and tradition and did not believe in individualism, let alone ideosyncracy. And he hated Italy because whatever he hated—individualism and romancing and all that—were there in Italy, and whatever he loved the most—conformity and tradition—Italy lacked in. However, reaching the hotel, Stella d' Italia at Monteriano, where Lilia and Caroline were putting up, the first news that Philip received was that Lilia had not only fallen in love with Gino Carella, twelve years younger than herself, within the inconceivably short space of her first eleven days of staying at the hotel, but, apprehending troubles to her proposed marriage with Gino on somebody's arrival from Sawston, Lilia had hastily married him. Caroline told Philip that Signor Gino was "'Very good looking. All his features are good, and he is well built—though I dare say English standards would find him too short.'" Philip learned from Caroline that Gino was a son of a dentist, and his social status was such that he deserved to be addressed as 'signor.' Even the first impression of Italy was disgusting to Philip, for he abhorred the deformed beggars and the 'Authorised Guides' there. At the dinner table, when Gino sat opposite him, Philip saw Gino to be markedly swarthy and saw him abominably spit on the floor. Only one grace Philip discovered in Gino. Gino was proficient in pallone—a sort of lawn tennis. Philip could not stand the abominable behaviour of Gino, and told Lilia about him: "'he is probably a ruffian and certainly a cad.'" But Lilia would not be persuaded that her marriage was an act of stupidity, nor would she be ready to snap her nuptial relation with Gino at any cost. During a conversation with Philip she once burst forth: "'For once in my life I'll thank you to leave me alone. I'll thank your mother too. For twelve years you've strained me and tortured me, and I'll stand it no more. Do you think I'm a fool? Do you think I never felt? Ah! when I came, to your house a poor young bride, how you all look me over—never a kind word—and discussed me, and thought I might just do; and your mother corrected me, and your sister snubbed me, and you said funny things about me to show how clever you were! And when Charles died I was still to run in strings for the honour of your beastly family, and I was to be cooped up at Sawston and learn to keep house, and all my chances spoilt of marrying again. No, thank you! No, thank you! 'Bully'? 'Insolent boy'? Who is that, pray, but you? But, thank goodness, I can stand up against the world now, for I've found Gino, and this time I marry for love!'" Inspite of so much from Lilia, Philip presages that "'this engagement [between Lilia and Gino] will not last.'"

Philip also earnestly tried to dissuade Gino Carella from the marriage: "'Signer Carella, I will be frank with you, I have come to prevent you marrying Mrs Herriton, because I see you will both be unhappy together. She is English, you are Italian; she is accustomed to one thing, you to another. And—pardon me if I say it—she is rich and you are poor.'" Philip also promised Gino to offer him 'a thousand lire' in case he did not marry her, because Philip did not know that Gino and Lilia by then had already been married, promptly and secretly though. The offer only incensed Gino, who, in an unguarded moment of heat, generated out of their firy conversation, pushed Philip on to the bed in order to slam him, and disclosed to Philip the truth that on the intelligence received that Philip had been coming to them, he and Lilia got married in utter haste. Now, understanding that his mission of rescuing Lilia quite fell through, Philip was preparing to return to Sawston. Caroline, in her shattering bewilderment, cried out and told Philip: "'I daren't to stop here. You will have to take me with you!'" And they came back to Sawston (section 2).

After their marriage, Lilia persuaded Gino to buy a particular muddy and tiled brick house of her choice, and that Gino gleefully did. Lilia was quite happy in that house "with nothing to do except give orders to smiling workpeople, and a devoted husband as interpreter." She wrote a letter to Mrs Herriton describing her happiness. Mrs Herriton did not answer that letter, but Harriet did. The recently bought house of Lilia was situated opposite the Volterra gate of Monteriano. "The house is bigger than it looks, for it slides for two storeys down the hill behind, and the wooden door, which is always locked, really leads into the attic." In the house, "There are several rooms, some dark and mostly stuffy—a reception-room adorned with horse-hair chairs, wool-work stools, and a stove that is never lit—German bad taste without German domesticity broods over that room; also a living-room, which insensibly glides into a bedroom when the refining influence of hospitality is absent, and real bedrooms; and last, but not least, the loggia, where you can live day and night if you feel inclined, drinking vermouth and smoking cigarettes, with leagues of olive-trees and vineyards and blue-green hills to watch you." "It was in this house that the brief and inevitable tragedy of Lilia's married life took place."

The relation between Lilia and the Herriton family soon began to sour. When Lilia was departing from Sawston to sail for Italy, Harriet Herriton offered her a trinket of an 'inlaid box' for keeping it with her as a memento, and for keeping in it handkerchiefs and collars. But as now Lilia had married Gino, Harriet wrote to Lilia asking to return the same to her and thenceforward to make further communications not with anybody of the Herriton family but only with their solicitor. By this time, Lilia began to treat her husband clearly as her inferior: "She always treated him as a boy, which he was, and as a fool, which he was not, thinking herself so immeasurably superior to him that she neglected opportunity after opportunity of establishing her rule. He was good-looking and indolent; therefore he must be stupid. He was poor, therefore he would never dare to criticise his benefactress. He was passionately in love with her, therefore she could do exactly as she liked." Above all, she thought Gino better than Charles, and so she deemed her second married life a substitute for heaven.

Before his death, Charles, in his will, had left a good sum of money and property for Lilia to prevent her possible second marriage, which he at least faintly suspected. So long good amounts of money were being regularly sent to Lilia by the Herritons, according to the will of Charles, but now the solicitor of the Herritons asked Lilia to "disgorge a large sum of money for Irma." Gino did not want to lose a portion of the sum received regularly from the Herritons, and so he suggested that "Irma had better come out and live with them." "But Lilia had not the courage even to suggest this to the Herritons, and an unexpected terror seized her at the thought of Irma or any English child being educated at Monteriano." However, Gino was much depressed at the demand of the solicitor, and began to spend whole days "in the loggia leaning over the parapet or sitting astride it disconsolately."

Gino was a man who loved to keep himself within himself, and so needed no friends, and, in fact, he had none. When Lilia decided to throw a tea-party, she asked Gino to invite his friends, but he said that he had none that might be invited. Lilia asked him not to keep himself cooped up within the house but to make friends. Gino only naively told her: "'I want to see no one but you.'" And then he "spat on to an olive-tree." Lilia loved his silliness, and even confessed before him that "she loved him just for his silly self." Lilia was impatient to receive Gino's people—his friends and acquaintances—but Gino, after imaginatively ferreting out for friends and acquaintances, ultimately found only one lady to whom in the past he was introduced for matrimonial purpose. Though she asked Gino to make acquaintances, Lilia advised him not to mix and parley with lowly people for fear of lowering their dignity: "'But, Gino dear, if they're low class, why did you talk to them? Don't you care about your position?'"

Gino was a happy soul now, more or less; the only two things that he now care about were 'idleness and pock-money.' He used to lie "full length on the parapet, and began to smoke and spit under the silence of the stars." Lilia somewhat gradually got used to the Italian style of life. She discerned that "Italy is such a delightful place to live in if you happen to be a man [and not a woman!]. There one may enjoy that exquisite luxury of Socialism—that true Socialism which is based not on equality of income or character, but on the equality of manners. In the democracy of the *caffe* or the street the great question of our life has been solved, and the brotherhood of man is a reality." But Italy was not all good; women were, for instance, considered inferior to men and were under threats of being robbed of their honour and ornaments. So for the first time in his life Gino realized that he had some responsibilities towards Lilia. Lilia sometimes used to take solitary walks; Gino prevented her from walking alone in the streets, and asked her to take Gino's cousin Perfetta with her, and she smilingly accepted his advice. Though Gino posed before Lilia as her guardian, he knew that she was older than he and so secretly held her as his superior. The couple thus continued to be an ideal one. But, yet, Lilia was getting gradually bored, being friendless and rather lonely.

Gino had at least one friend, and that in Spiridione Tesi who is older than Gino and 'more full of experience,' and a waiter by profession. On hearing about Gino's sudden marriage, Spiridione took a fancy to see Gino and Lilia on his way to Siena. Spiridione asked Gino about Lilia: "'But tell me more.

She is English. That is good, very good. An English wife is very good indeed. And she is rich?'" Gino told him that Lilia was 'immensely rich' and blonde, and also that he was very happy with her. Everybody said that Gino deserved such a blonde and rich wife. Spiridione asked the age of Lilia, and Gino said, 'thirty-three.' Spiridione further asked if Lilia was simpatica (Forster says in parenthesis that nothing will translate that word.) Spiridione explained the term 'simpatica' thus: "'The person who understands us at first sight, who never irritates us, who never bores, to whom we can pour forth every thought and wish, not only in speech but in silence—that is what I mean by simpatico.'" Simpatico is a quality generally found in children, Gino told Spiridione. Gino now told Spiridione that Lilia was 'Sufficiently so,' i.e. she was sufficiently simpatica. He also told Spiridione about Lilia: "'She is rich, she is generous, she is affable, she addresses her inferiors without haughtiness.'" Gino further told Spiridione, who was older than himself, that Lilia was not a Catholic like himself, and that he was not a devoted or active Catholic, because he did not go to church. He told this to say that inspite of their religious difference, nominal though that was, they were a happy couple.

Gino took Spiridione, inspite of the letter's mild resistance, to Lilia, because she asked him to bring to her his friends and acquaintances. Spiridione was a 'dashing young fellow', a waiter. Lilia was delighted to see Spiridione. "Spiridione's manners were very agreeable. He kissed her hand on introduction, and as his profession taught him a little English, conversation did not flag." Spiridione loved music passionately and so Lilia played on the piano 'very badly' and then Spiridione sang 'not so badly.' When Spiridione was returning from Gino's house, he advised Gino, as a friend, not to bring to his house friends and acquaintances, as, Spiridione obliquely indicated, the attractiveness of Lilia was precious and so it should be jealously guarded because it was Italy and no other place (section 3).

Lilia's happiness of married life soon began to wear away; Gino, on the other hand, renewed his interest in travelling, particularly over such places as Empoli, Siena, Florence, Bologna, etc. Lilia now oftentimes reflected upon the state of her married life, and was sometimes "seized with a vulgar fear that she was not 'married properly' and that her social position in the next world might be as obscure as it was in this." Being tormented by such thoughts, she joined the Roman Catholic Church or what she called 'Santa Deodata's', under the advice of Spiridione and with the concurrence of Gino. Lilia took to this course perhaps because she was gradually being so to say ostracised by the Herritons as well as by her own mother, Mrs Theobald. The Herritons "would not even let her write to Irma, though Irma was occasionally allowed to write to her." In this her pathetically insulated life she once found a whiff of fresh air in a letter to her written by Mr Kingcroft affectionately enquiring about her. Lilia was inchingly going away from Gino. Gino, who on the surface was a docile being, had "plenty of brutality deep down in him." Struggle for dominance ensued between Lilia and Gino; sometimes over flimsy matters the two engaged in bitter altercations. For instance, one day there was a verbal duel between them over whether Lilia might walk alone or being accompanied. She said: "'I always do it in England.'"

"'This is Italy.'"

"'Yes, but I'm older than you, and I'll settle.'"

Gino pleaded he was her husband and so her overlord. Lilia took up her monetary weapon: "'And I have got the money.'" Actually their skeleton family was sustained by the regular inflow of money from the Herriton family and so Gino was horrified at the veiled warning of Lilia. By now Lilia well realised that Gino married her only for her money, but yet she was not to succumb to him—she asked him impolitely to mend his manners.

Lilia's discovery of Gino's infidelity—that he had no affection for her and that he entered into the nuptial tie with her only because of her money—almost shattered her self: "She broke down utterly, and sobbed and cried in Perfetta's arms." She now knew that "there was no one who would receive her now." However, after closely scanning Gino's inner mental structure, she came to the conclusion that if she could give birth to a son, Gino would turn to be a loving and affable husband: "'if I have a child he will be different. I knew he wants a son.'" Earlier the couple sometimes created awkward spectacles when the husband and the wife fought against each other for paramountcy, but now Lilia abruptly modified herself, mellowed herself, realising that it was a sort of fault on her part not to have borne a son for Gino. Of course Lilia neither loved Gino nor hated him, albeit the changed Lilia was now a delight to her husband. He was overjoyed and over buoyed as to say: "'Ah, one ought to marry! Spiridione is wrong; I must persuade him. Not till marriage does one realize the pleasures and possibilities of life.'" Contrarily, Lilia was gradually growing indifferent towards Gino, and, all at the same time feeling a pull towards Sawston in England. One moonlit night she came down to the road and walked upto where "a great cypress interrupted the monotony of the girdle of olives" and where "she had sat with Gino one afternoon in March, her head upon his shoulder." She could not join her past with her present, and, sentimental as she was, she began to cry perhaps in self-denunciation. A diligence was passing by her through the road that led to the Siena gate, "from which the road to England started." She, without deciding anything, called after the diligence: "'Vengo! Vengo!'" But as the driver of the diligence was loudly singing he could not hear Lilia. The carriage went a considerable distance. To catch it Lilia took a short-cut scabrous path, but fell down in the thick dust. So long her wits did not work, but as she now came to her senses, she thought Gino would have been very angry for her absence, and so dragged herself slowly back to her 'captivity'.

Gino was really very angry against Lilia, and when she returned, he threw a barrage of abusive words at her, but this did not make her cower, rather she discovered her strength to fight back, "for as he spoke she was seized with indignation and feared him no longer, and saw him for a cruel, worthless, hypocritical, dissolute upstart, and spoke in return." However, the domestic and nuptial battle was soon over, and the impending tragedy turned into a laughing comedy, at least in its externalities. Gino found his own behaviour with Lilia devoid of civility, *outre* and absurd, and so crushed it with a hearty guffaw and a gentle touch on her shoulder. The bickerings between them was not in fact due to any incongruence between the two personalities. "No one realized that, more than personalities were engaged; that the struggle was national; that generations of ancestors, good, bad, or indifferent, forbade the Latin man to be chivalrous to the northern woman, the northern woman to forgive the Latin man. All this might have been foreseen: Mrs Herriton foresaw it from the first."

Lilia was feeling wretched, and in her misery she wrote a letter to Irma, perhaps because Irma's absence now oppressed her, and in writing a letter to her daughter Lilia's sorrow found an escape route. In the letter she wrote about "the causes and growth of her misery"; but, yet, though Mrs Herriton perused that letter, she did not find it necessary to answer it. Irma could not even know that her mother had written to her. Only Harriet sent a note to Lilia asking her not to make further communication with Irma. When Harriet's note arrived, Lilia and Gino were sitting on the loggia. "He often sat with her now, watching her for hours, puzzled and anxious, but not contrite." Gino asked her about the content of Harriet's letter. Lilia just replied "'It's nothing'" and went away to write a very short letter not to the Herriton family but to Mr Kingcroft. The gist, of the letter was "'Come and save me.'" Lilia herself went to the post office to drop the letter. But as the postman was Gino's friend, due to some pre-arranged negotiation between Gino and the postman, Lilia's letter did never reach Mr Kingcroft. Receiving no reply from her forlorn hope, Mr Kingcroft, Lilia became hopeless and then ill. On the other hand, Gino was distracted because his only desire to become the father of a man like himself was not fulfilled, because his hope of being immortal through a son was not materialised. Love itself he did not count so much; he did not hold love above "a mere physical triviality, like warm sun or cool water." Wishing a child Gino sometimes himself went to Lilia and "prayed the crude uncouth demands of the simple", and he offered candles to Santa Deodata. Sometimes he would assure her of his love: "my dearest Lilia! Be calm. I have never loved anyone but you." Lilia knew Gino only wanted a boy from her, and so in reply she made a tender joke of him: "'You are a boy yourself, Gino.'" No, Gino needed not be a boy to Lilia, for she gave birth to a 'beautiful boy.' But, alas! she died after giving birth to that boy. (section 4).

When Lilia died, Philip Herriton was just twenty-four years of age. "He was a tall, weakly-built young man, whose clothes had to be judiciously padded on the shoulder in order to make him pass muster. His face was plain rather than not, and there was a curious mixture in it of good and bad. He had a fine forehead and a good large nose, and both observation and sympathy were in his eyes. But below the nose and eyes all was confusion, and those people who believe that destiny resides in the mouth and chin shook their heads when they looked at him." He was aware of the defects, of the weakness, of the lack of the manliness that is expected of a virulent personality, in his face, and sometimes in his young days would remonstrate about this to his image in the looking-glass. But he had two enviable natural gifts: sense of beauty and sense of humour. "The sense of beauty developed first. It caused him at the age of twenty to wear parti-coloured ties and a squashy hat, to be late for dinner on account of the sunset, and to catch art from Burne-Jones to Praxiteles." His penchant for beauty drove him as far as Italy, when he was just twenty-two. The romantic Italy quite changed Philip. "He came back with the air of a prophet who would either remodel Sawston or reject it." The Sawstonian Philip was converted into an Italian Philip. But Sawston was more potential than Italy, for, before long, Philip's verve for aesthetics left him. He was now under the influence of his second gift—laughter. He laughed that in Italy there was not only beauty, but there were also "avarice, brutality, stupidity—and, what was worse, vulgarity." His enthusiasm fizzled out after he saw Lilia, 'a silly woman,' married Gino, 'a cad'.

Philip Herriton did not like the idea of breaking the news of Lilia's marriage and of her death to the little Irma. But he did not favour secrecy, for he believed that any dishonesty on the part of parents or guardians did positively ruin the morals and manners of a child. Inspite of the Herritons, Irma came to know of her mother's death, and wept profusely. But now what would the Herritons do with the baby son of Lilia? Mrs Herriton openly showed her insouciance to the baby, saying: "'This baby's quite beside the point.'" It was also clear that Mrs Theobald, Lilia's mother, was not at all concerned about the baby. Only Philip could persuade the Herriton family to see a newly opened channel for economic back-flow, agreeing to hushing up the matter about the baby. The family would claim that as Lilia was now dead (and she left no issue), the money that would go to her from it must hence remain with it as the guardian of Irma (earlier Lilia acted as her guardian). Harriet Herriton agreed to Philip's proposal delightfully: "'Good. So those are our tactics—to tell no one about the baby, not even Miss Abbott.'" And Mrs Herriton, too. Philip told his mother that hence they were going to begin a new life, and the mother accorded, because hence they all would be at accord.

As told, Irma could no longer be held in darkness about the death of her mother; she knew it and wept loudly. Caroline also came to know that Lilia died at childbirth, and "broke down utterly." Meanwhile, affection began to grow between Philip and Caroline, particularly on a travel they made from Sawston to Charing Cross. Philip now discovered a few agreeable qualities in her that he earlier did not notice. By this time Philip forgot everything about Lilia. He said: "'Let the dead bury their dead.'" But Caroline felt partially guilty for the tragic life of Lilia, thinking that she perhaps could forestall the marriage between Lilia and Gino. She told Philip: "'You never knew how much I was to blame.'" She recalled that it was to a great extent due to her suggestion that Lilia, after falling in love with Gino, married him. However, temperamentally also Philip and Caroline came closer to each other. Philip's trip to Italy, previously, reformed him, so that he was no longer a foolhardy Sawstonian, and the same thing happened to Caroline when she accompanied Lilia to Italy.

Caroline told Philip: "'I hated Sawston, you see.'" Philip replied: "'So did and do I.'" Caroline, like Philip, after their trips to Italy, learnt to hate the Sawstonian psychology: the idleness, the stupidity, the respectability, and the selfishness of the people of Sawston. She told Philip about Sawston: "'I had got an idea that everyone here spent their lives in making little sacrifices for objects they didn't care for, to please people they didn't love; that they never learnt to be sincere—and, what's as bad, never learnt how to enjoy themselves. That's what I thought—what I thought at Monteriano.'"

Caroline told Philip that she admired Gino, frankly. "'And Gino, I thought, was splendid, and young, and strong not only in body, and sincere as the day.'" She once again confessed her sense of guilt for the tragic life of Lilia: "'Lilia is dead and her husband gone to the bad—all through me.'" Caroline told Philip that it was while she was negotiating between Lilia and Gino that she for the first time in her life tasted 'real life'—the life of 'splendour and beauty.' Philip ratified her actions as an intermediary and justified her notion of 'real life': "'Society *is* invincible—to a certain degree. But your real life is your own, and nothing can touch it. There is no power on earth that can prevent your criticizing and despising mediocrity—nothing that can stop you retreating into splendour and beauty—into the thoughts and beliefs that make the real life—the real you.'" Philip and Caroline were conversing about all these things on the train, and as the train reached Charing Cross they got down and proceeded towards their individual destinations. But the most astonishing thing was that even after that cordial conversation, to Caroline "the gulf between herself and Mr Herriton [Philip], which she had always known to be great, now seemed to her immeasurable."

Irma was kept in darkness of the tact that she had a 'lital brother' (little brother) there in Monteriano, but she was receiving picture post-cards from time to time from Monteriano, presumably from Gino. One day she was inordinately delighted to receive a picture postcard from Monteriano, subscribed 'from your lital brother.' "Stupid Harriet caught her, boxed her ears, and tore the postcard into fragments, Irma howled with pain, and began shouting indignantly,' Who is my little brother? Why have I never heard of him before? Grandmamma! Grandmamma! Who is my little brother? Who is my—'." Mrs Herriton edified Irma about the existence of her little brother, not wholly, but partially—beguiling her as far as she should and might be beguiled. The edification blurred Irma's memory of her mother, but ingrained in her heart an intense longing to see her brother in person. Irma was interested even in her 'new father,' i.e. in Gino. She asked if she could pray for her little brother and her 'new father.' Harriet told her that Gino was a devil, and this was a clear hint to Mrs Herriton to consider Harriet too harsh for Irma. Mrs Herriton therefore managed to send Harriet to Tirol for six weeks, so that she could decide upon what to do with Irma after consultation only with Philip. Mrs Herriton was apprehensive that Gino, whom she imagined to be a man without probity, might be corrupting the morals of Lilia's little son. She was thinking of Miss Abbott, for some help she might put in solving the moral problem of the baby of Gino, but Miss Abbott's life now "was devoted to the dull acts of charity." Philip showed no interest in the baby saying: "'The child is no relation of ours.'" But Mrs Herriton was quite concerned about the baby. She tried to convince Philip of the necessity and responsibility of looking after the baby through the channel of sympathy: "'Poor Lilia was almost a daughter to me once.'"

Philip found that Miss Abbott took an 'unexpected interest' in the baby. She told him that "'The child came into the world through my negligence'" and so "'It is natural I should take an interest in it.'" Mrs Herriton tried to persuade her not to worry over the baby: "you must not brood over the thing. Let bygones be bygones. The child should worry you even less than it worries us. We never even mention it. It belongs to another world." But she would not be refomed: she rather showed 'colossal impertinence' to the Herritons in rejecting their indifference to the child, outright. Philip quite understood this, and so he cautioned his mother about Miss Abbott: "'If we won't do anything she's going to raise a scandal—that we neglect our relatives, etc., which is, of course, a lie.'" Philip concluded that Miss Abbott had become virtually mad, and that she showed signs of her madness while in Monteriano. Mrs Herriton agreed with her son that Miss Abbott had shown impertinence to them, but she could not stand the idea that the child grew up in Monteriano and under the evil influence of Gino: "'Ought the child to grow up in that place—and with that father?'" She grudged that Miss Abbott demonstrated before their eyes her responsibility towards the child. She became impulsive in divulging her plan of rescuing the child from Monteriano, adopting it, and bringing it up. Philip throughout his life was virtually a puppet of his mother, and so he dared not contradict Mrs Herriton's several decisions. He could not understand to what purposes Mrs Herriton was going to employ "her diplomacy, her insincerity, her continued repression of vigour." "Mrs Herriton's policy only appeared gradually. It was to prevent Miss Abbott interfering with the child at all costs, and if possible to prevent her at a small cost. Pride was the only solid element in her disposition. She could not bear to seem less charitable than others." She justified her intention of rescuing the child from the grip of that 'horrible man', Gino also by thinking that Irma would be delighted to get her brother.

Whereas pride worked behind Mrs Herriton's motive of rescuing the child, what worked behind Miss Abbott's similar motive was her sense of 'sacred duty' towards it. Miss Abbott suddenly developed an amount of contempt for Monteriano, and Sawston, to her newer view, wore a layer of gloss. She thought "Monteriano had become a magic city of vice, beneath whose towers no person could grow up happy or pure. Sawston, with its semi-detached houses and snobby schools, its books, teas and bazzars, was certainly petty and dull; at times she found it even contemptible. But it was not a place of sin, and at Sawston, either with the Herritons or with herself, the baby should grow up." As soon as Mrs Herriton decided to bring the child from Monteriano and adopt it, she "wrote a letter for Waters & Adamson to send to Gino—the oddest letter", expressing therein that she was desirous of adopting the child, "provided that Gino would undertake never to come near it, and would surrender some of Lilia's money for its education." Philip predicted to his mother that Gino would part with the child if it was profitable to him, that is, if the expenditure on account of the child exceeded the money Gino continued to receive from time to time from Sawston. His prediction about Gino's crassly practical attitude originated in his disgusting experiences in Italy. He told his mother that he grew 'Weary, weary, weary' of Italy, and that Sawston was a 'kind, pitiful place.' And then he went to Miss Abbott's to meet her. Philip told Miss Abbott that his mother was endeavouring to bring Lilia's son, and to that effect had already written to Signor Gino Carella. Both Philip and Miss Abbott 'uttered fervent wishes' for the success of Mrs Heniton—Philip's mother—which meant that they wanted Lilia's son brought to England, Miss Abbott being most anxious to see the child brought to England, particularly because she thought Gino to be "'a thoroughly wicked man.'" But her crass comment about Gino seemed to have a double entendre.

Meanwhile Gino replied to Mrs Herriton's letter fervently asking him to agree to bringing Lilia's child to England (to Sawston). "Gino could not accept the generous offer. His parental heart would not permit him to abandon this symbol of his deplored spouse." Mrs Herriton concluded that "For some perverse reason he will not part with the child." She went to seek help from Miss Abbott, but she returned disgusted with Miss Abbott: she called Miss Abbott a 'beastly woman' and was exasperated at Miss Abbott's daring to interfere into matter of Lilia's child (perhaps Miss Abbott expressed her close psychological connection with the child and with Gino, not obtusely but abstrusely). However, being jealous of Miss Abbott's interest in the child, Miss Herriton instantaneously ordered Philip to go to Monteriano, needless to say to fetch the child. Philip told his mother that as he hated Italy he would not go to Monteriano. Miss Herriton, as if, warned him that if he did not go, Miss Abbott would surely go. Nay, she told him that Miss Abbott was going to Monteriano that very evening. She further told him: "'Stop that nonsense, Philip. I will not be disgraced by her [Miss Abbott]. I will have the child.'" Philip told her mother Miss Abbott should be left free to do what she liked to do, and that Gino "'will marry her [Miss Abbott], or murder her, or do for her somehow. He's [Gino is] a bounder, but he's not an English bounder. He is mysterious and terrible.'" But Mrs Herriton would not hear even a single word of Philip: he would have to go to Monteriano. Not only this, Mrs Herriton also irrevocably decided that her daughter, Harriet "'shall go too. Harriet, now, will be invaluable!'" (section 5).

Philip and Harriet reached Italy for the 'expedition' of rescuing the baby of Lilia. Philip observed that Miss Abbott's interest was more keen than theirs, and yet he apprehensively predicted that "the expedition promised to be highly comic." He was indifferent to the rescuing of the baby, and only interested in the humours surrounding the whole matter. The two were travelling by train for thirteen hours from Tirol to Verona where the heat of the sun was oppressive. "And on the second day the heat struck them, like a hand laid over the mouth, just as they were walking to see the tomb of Juliet. From that moment everything went wrong. They fled from Verona. Harriet's sketch-book was stolen, and the bottle of ammonia in her trunk burst over her prayer book, so that purple patches appeared on all her clothes. Then, as she was going through Mantua at four in the morning, Philip made her look out of the window because it was Virgil's birthplace, and a smut flew in her eye, and Harriet with a smut in her eye was notorious." However, from Verona they went to Florence and there they bought two tickets for Monteriano, and it was in Monteriano that they met Miss Abbott who went there singlely, beforehand. Buying the two tickets was, as if a hard physical trial for Philip in the narrow slit, and so he made the contemptuous remark: "'Italy was beastly, and Florence station is the centre of beastly Italy.'" But immediately afterwards "he had a strange feeling that he was to blame for it all; that a little influx into him of virtue would make the whole land not beastly but amusing. For there was enchantment, he was sure of that; solid enchantment, which lay behind the porters and the screaming and the dust. He could see it in the terrific blue sky beneath which they travelled, in the whitened plain which gripped life tighter than a frost, in the exhausted reaches of the Arno, in the ruins of brown castles which stood quivering upon the hills. He could see it, though his head ached and his skin was twitching, though he was here as a puppet, and though his sister knew he was here. There was nothing pleasant in that journey to Monteriano station. But nothing—not even the discomfort—was commonplace."

Philip told Harriet that he would first keep her at the hotel Stella d' Italia, and then find time to go to Santa Deodata to read a book in the freshness and coolness of the place. Harriet accused philip of losing the interest in the baby—the only reason of their coming there. "Philip acknowledged her reproof to be true. He did not care about the baby one straw. Nevertheless, he meant to do his duty, and he was fairly confident of success. If Gino would have sold his wife for a thousand lire, for how much less would he not sell his child? It was just a commercial transaction." Then Philip took a view of the beautiful tower of the Collegiate Church of Santa Deodata. The 'lengo' ultimately drew up at the hotel Stella d' Italia, and they got down, and were promptly received by the landlady. Harriet reminded Philip that they went there only to get the baby, all the while remaining somewhat pugilistic. There they found out Miss Abbott. Philip was exasperated at the sight of Miss Abbott, because, he thought, it was too much for her to try to take the baby back to Sawston, as he and Harriet were endeavouring to do the same. But soon Philip "had an inspiration." He asked Harriet to talk to Miss Abbott and himself proceeded to meet Gino. While he was walking towards the residence of Gino, Philip was 'meditating' that Gino might have by that time jocularly sold the baby to Miss Abbott. Reaching Dogana, the place where Gino resided, Philip asked men where Gino Lived, and a little girl sprang up and led him through mule-track, and in about half a minute showed him Gino's house. A certain man shouted at the house, and Perfetta, Gino's maidservant appeared high up on the loggia."

Philip asked Perfetta if Gino was in, and got the reply that "She did not know. He was away on business. He might be back this evening, he might not. He had gone to Poggibonsi." As she heard the name Poggibonsi, the girl, on the spur of the moment, sang the song that her foremothers had sung seven hundred years back—*Toggibonizzi, fatti in la,/Che Monteriano si fa citta*! And then the little girl begged a halfpenny to Philip, which he gave her. Philip shouted from below that he wanted to leave a message for Gino. Perfetta, therefore, went inside the upper storey to bring and lower a basket with strings to pull up the message. Philip was waiting for Perfetta, below, avoiding the stink from drain and gazing at the 'frightful spotty blouse' of Lilia hung above. Earlier Philip did not forget to request Perfetta to show him Lilia's baby son. Perfetta brought the baby and exclaimed: "'Beautiful as an angel!'" Philip enquired of Perfetta if an young lady, "pale, large, tall" had earlier come there, but as she was a little hard of hearing, he could not receive any satisfactory answer from her, and so, in a huff, retired to the hotel Stella d' Italia, where Miss Abbott mysteriously beckoned to him. He followed her and she closed the door. Miss Abbott told Philip that Harriet knew nothing about her corming there. Philip asked Miss Abbott: "'In what capacity have you come to Monteriano—spy or traitor?'" Miss Abbott said that his mother much misbehaved with her, that she 'never wanted the child' and that nevertheless she was too proud to let the child go to herself (Miss Abbott). She said that she could not trust Philip's mother, and "'So I have come here alone—all across Europe; no one knows it; my father thinks I am in Normandy—to spy on Mrs Herriton.'" She further told him: "'If you are here to get the child, I will help you; if you are here to fail, I shall get it instead of you.'" Philip asserted that he and Harriet were there to get the child, and that his mother had "'fixed no money limit whatever.'" But he also said that he did not approve of the plan of getting the child anyhow, because it was absurd, even though Harriet approved it.

Philip asked Miss Abbott to "'take charge of the entire rescue party.'" He told her that he had already arranged a meeting with Gino. Philip suspected that earlier Miss Abbott had met Gino, but Miss Abbott exclaimed and said: "'Eighteen months ago I might have done such a thing. But I trust I have learnt how to behave by now.'" "Philip began to see that there were two Miss Abbotts—the Miss Abbott who could travel alone to Monteriano, and the Miss Abbott who could not enter Gino's house when she got there. It was an amusing discovery." In fact, Miss Abbott had earlier met Gino, accidentally though. She had come here in Monteriano a day earlier than Philip and Harriet. She went to the Rocca to enjoy the sunset, and there talked to Gino. She told Philip about the meeting: "'It was very awkward for me. But I had to talk: he seemed to make me. You see he thought I was here as a tourist; he thinks so still. He intended to be civil, and I judged it better to be civil also.'" She said that Gino was 'perfectly disgusting' and that he pretended that he had loved Lilia, and that he had offered her to show Lilia's grave—'the grave of the woman he has murdered!' Philip corrected Miss Abbott; he told her that the Italians were honest, and that they were "'essentially dramatic: they look on death and love as spectacles.'" Eighteen months ago Philip came to Monteriano, before Lilia's death, and then Gino misbehaved with him. When Miss Abbott mentioned it, Philip said that Gino had said he had been sorry for that. So Gino did not seem so bad to Philip, after all.

In the sweat company of Miss Abbott, Philip forgot the business for which he had come here—to get the child. "What did the baby matter when the world was suddenly right way up? Philip smiled, and was shocked at himself for smiling, and smiled again. For romance had come back to Italy; there were no cads in her, she was beautiful, courageous, lovable, as of old. And Miss Abbott—she, too, was beautiful in her way, for all her gaucheness and conventionality. She really cared about life, and tried to live it properly." He no more mentioned the baby, and Miss Abbott, as before, ran her fingers over the 'delicate curves' of the baluster. "He watched her in silence, and was more attracted to her than he had ever been before." Miss Abbott desired the closeness to Philip, after the beautiful view of Rocca. She told him: "'I wish I was Harriet,' throwing an extraordinary meaning into the words." And then she called him to see the great towers through the Gothic window. They "remained together at the window because it was a little cooler and so pleasant. Philip found a certain grace and lightness in his companion which he had never noticed in England. She was appallingly narrow, but her consciousness of wider things gave to her narrowness a pathetic charm. He did not suspect that he was more graceful too. For our vanity is such that we hold our own characters immutable, and we are slow to acknowledge that they have changed, even for the better."

Miss Abbott noticed an opera-bill, and told him that it was "*Lucia di Lammermoor*. By the Master Donizetti. Unique representation. This evening." He told her that the Italians knew how to live boisterously, and that "'Italians don't love music silently, like the beastly Germans. The audience takes its share—sometimes more.'" Miss Abbott proposed to go to the opera with him, but he reminded her that they went there to rescue the child. The limitless joy of Miss Abbott, grown out of the idea of going to the opera, suddenly reached its nadir, and she became once again Miss Abbott of Sawston—'most appallingly dull'. Philip and Miss Abbott, really, had had a very excellent interview, suffused with all goodwill, and it seemed they were flirting. Harriet on a sudden appeared right in the middle of the romantic scene, but created no commotion, no grudge on the part of Miss Abbott, particularly. She told Philip: "'You see him [Gino] tomorrow at ten, Philip. Well, don't forget the blank cheque. Say an hour for the business. No, Italians are so slow; say two. Twelve o'clock. Lunch. Well—then it's no good going till the evening train. I can manage the baby as far as Florence—'" Philip asked her not to be so much in hurry. Miss Abbott intervened; she cautioned the other two that Gino might not accept the cheque against losing the child, that he might refuse the offer. Harriet quipped: "'I don't know the meaning of the word ['refuse'].'" She divulged the plan of rescuing the child. A particular woman would carry the baby to the hotel [Santa d' Italia] and

Philip was to tip her for it. Harriet asked Philip to take away Lilia's silver bangles, the 'inlaid box' she lent to Lilia, etc. along with the baby, but Philip told her that he was interested only in the baby and in nothing else.

Philip told Harriet that they—himself and Miss Abbott—were feeling tired, and so would go to the opera, the romantic *Lucia di Lammermoor* by Sir Walter Scott (1771-1832). The three went to the opera: Philip, Miss Abbott and Harriet. The two ladies felt ashamed as they thought of their mission of rescuing the child and of enjoying the opera—an odd combination indeed. Many years ago Philip had gone into the theatre, in which they were now sitting, to enjoy the performance of *La Zia di Carlo*. The theatre was given, later on, a great face-lift, for which reason Philip exclaimed: "There is something majestic in the bad taste of Italy; it is not the bad taste of a country which knows no better; it has not the nervous vulgarity of England, or the blinded vulgarity of Germany. It deserves beauty, and chooses to pass it by. But it attains to Beauty's confidence." Philip tried for tickets for a box, but failed, and so they were to remain content with 'stalls.' "Miss Abbott was pleasant, and insisted on praising everything; her only regret was that she had no pretty clothes with her." In the theatre, Philip "saw a charming picture, as charming a picture as he had seen for years—the hot red theatre; outside the theatre, towers and dark gates and medieval walls; beyond the walls olive-trees in the starlight and white winding roads and fireflies and untroubled dust; and here in the middle of it all, Miss Abbott, wishing she had not come looking like a guy." Miss Abbott liked it all awfully.

The drop-scene of the opera was raised amidst chaos and cries, and "the chorus of Scotch retainers burst into cry. The audience accompanied with tappings and drummings, swaying in the melody like corn in the wind." Harriet was annoyed and Miss Abbott felt tired, but Philip "grasped the principle of opera in Italy—it aims not at illusion but at entertainment." Soon "Families greeted each other across the auditorium. People in the pit hailed their brothers and sons in the chorus, and told them how well they were singing. When Lucia [the heroine, or the bride of Lammermoor] appeared by the fountain there was loud applause, and cries of 'Welcome to Monteriano!'" Now, "Lucia began to sing, and there was a moment's silence...and as she sang the theatre murmured like a hive of happy bees." "Miss Abbott fell into the spirit of the thing. She, too, chatted and laughed and applauded and encored, and rejoiced in the existence of beauty. As for Philip, he forgot himself as well as his mission. [As if] He was not even an enthusiastic visitor. For [as if] he had been in this place always. It was his home." Even Harriet lost her natural inhibition; and Miss Abbott, who never took a drop of wine, was oddly swaying with the drunk audience.

"Violent waves of excitement, all arising from very little, went sweeping round the theatre. The climax was reached in the mad scene. Lucia, clad in white, as befitted her malady, suddenly gathered up her streaming hair and bowed her acknowledgements to the audience. Then from the back of the stage—she feigned not to see it—there advanced a kind of bamboo clothes-horse, stuck all over with bouquets. It was very ugly, and most of the flowers in it were false. Lucia knew this, and so did the audience; and they all knew that the clothes-horse was a piece of stage property, brought in to make the performance go year after year. None the less did it unloose the great deeps. With a stream of amazement and joy she embraced the animal, pulled out one or two practicable blossoms, pressed them to her lips, and flung them into her admirers. They flung them back, with loud melodious cries, and a little boy in one of the stage-boxes snatched up his sister's carnations and offered them. 'Che carino!' exclaimed the singer. She darted at the little boy and kissed him. Now the noise became tremendous. 'Silence! silence!' shouted many old gentlemen behind. 'Let the divine creature continue!' But the young men in the adjacent box were imploring Lucia to extend her civility to them. She refused, with a humorous expressive gesture. One of them hurled a bouquet at her. She spumed it with her toot. Then, encouraged by the roars of the audience, she picked it up and tossed it to them. Harriet was always unfortunate. The bouquet struck her full in the chest, and a little *billet-doux* fell out of it into her lap."

In exasperation Harriet "moved down the gangway, and compelled Miss Abbott to follow her." Philip "was drunk with excitement, then heat, the fatigue, and the enjoyment had mounted into his head." "He deserted his ladies and plunged towards the box. A young man was flung stomach downwards across the balustrade. Philip handed him up the bouquet and the note. Then his own hands were seized affectionately. It all seemed quite natural." Philip was feebly trying to disengage himself when some amiable youths, who knew Philip to be Gino's friend, invited him to enter their boxes. At this moment Gino himself emerged from somewhere among the boxes and shouted that Philip was more than his friend—Philip was his relative, nay, his brother "'A relative! A brother! Fra Filipp [Mr Philip], who has come all the way from England and never written.'" Philip said he had certainly written to him. Gino, then, shouted at him: "'Come in to us.'" "The next moment he [Philip] was swinging by his arms. The moment after he shot over the balustrade into the box. Then the conductor, seeing that the incident was over, raised his baton. The house was hushed, and Lucia di Lammermoor resumed her song of madness and death." At the end of the opera Philip told Gino that he wanted to speak to him next day at ten o'clock, sharp, and Gino laughingly agreed: "'Certainly!'" Miss Abbott was waiting for Philip, but Harriet perhaps "had gone straight to bed." Philip told Miss Abbott about Gino: "'He's a perfectly a charming person, and so are his friends. I'm his friend now—his long-lost brother. What's the harm? I tell you Miss Abbott, it's one thing for England and another for Italy. There we plan and get on high moral horses. Here we find what asses we are, for things go off quite easily, all by themselves.'" Philip said that Gino was no 'porky' father and that he was the least concerned about the baby.

That day, like Philip, Miss Abbott also had a 'wonderful evening.' She could not go to bed for overmuch of her happiness. But suddenly she was engulfed by a tide of shame as she remembered that she came there to rescue the baby, and thereby "to champion morality and purity, and the holy life of an English home." Yet "all night long she was troubled by torrents of music, and by applause and laughter, and angry young men who shouted the distich out of Baedeker:

> *Poggibonizzi, fatti in la,*
> *Che Monteriano si fa citta!*

Poggibonsi was revealed to her as they sang—a joyless, straggling place, full of people who pretented. When she woke up she knew that it had been Sawston" (section 6).

At about nine o'clock, next morning, Miss Abbott knocked at the door of the house of Gino, and she was called decorously in by Perfetta, and was shown a seat in the drawing-room. There a picture of Lilia was seen hung, flanked by a 'little piece of black drapery' to show mournful respect to the departed soul. There were two tables nearby, on one of which was Baedeker's *Central Italy* (which belonged to Lilia as her guide-book), and on another was Harriet's inlaid box. Miss Abbott did not sit, but kept her calm all the while, because "only if she was very calm might her behaviour be justified." That is, nobody could suspect her of having the intention of stealing Gino's baby. "She had broken faith with Philip and Harriet: she was going to try for the baby before they did. "Miss Abbott reasoned thus: Harriet 'would bluster and be rude' and Philip would take the stealing of the baby to be a great joke, and so both would needs fail, and so everything depended only on herself. She knew that Gino was 'terribly strong'—so strong that in the previous year she was almost conquered by him—and so Harriet and Philip would not be able to cope with him. She had written to Philip telling him all this. Meantime, Miss Abbott developed a soft corner in her heart for Philip: "she had got to like Philip a good deal after their last strange interview."

At last Gino came in "singing fearlessly from his expanded lungs, like a professional," but unlike Englishmen "who always have a little feeling against music, and sing only from the throat, apologetically." Gino padded upstairs, looked into the reception-room, where Miss Abbott was waiting for him, but did not notice her. The room "was in a shocking mess. Food, bedclothes, patent-leather boots, dirty plates, and knives lay strewn over a large table and on the floor. But it was the mess that comes of life, not of desolation." Gino first called out for Perfetta, then turned and saw Miss Abbott but remained in affable for her, and albeit she was intently watching him. He lit a cigar and puffed out a heavy ring of smoke that girted her, and she screamed in tear. He brought wine for her, which of course she refused, and asked why she was trepidating. "He, too, was frightened, and perspiration came starting through the tan. For it is a serious thing to have been watched. We all radiate something curiously intimate when we believe ourselves to be alone." However, Miss Abbott eventually told him that she was there on some most important business with him. He again poured out a glass of wine and offered it to her, and this time she accepted it. And as she drank, she became self-conscious, and asked him: "'Perhaps you are engaged'". Gino replied he was not, and then told her: "'Now I see what frightened you.'" Gino, next, took her to his living room and showed her his baby son. She saw the baby "lying asleep on a dirty rug," and this sight disconcerted her. She felt an urge to kiss the eight months old 'remarkably fine child,' and said: "'What a fine child, Signor Carella.'" Gino simply smiled.

As the room seemed untidy to him, Gino proposed they should go to the loggia, where it was cool. "Miss Abbott picked her way to the chair. He sat near her, astride the parapet, with one foot in the loggia and the other dangling into the view. His face was in profile and its beautiful contours drove artfully against the misty green of the opposing hills." Miss Abbott saw him and murmured to herself: "'A born artist's model.'" They engaged in a conversation that verged on cordiality. Gino treated her as his friend, and she told him that this time she had come there as a friend that, in her earlier tour, she had been. Miss Abbott asked Gino: "'Do I understand that you are proposing to marry again?'" Gino nodded 'yes.' He said he wanted to marry another woman. Miss Abbott forbade him to marry for the second time: "'You have ruined one woman; I forbid you to ruin another. It is not a year since Lila died. You pretended to me the other day that you loved her. It is a lie. You wanted her money. Has this woman money too?'" She became irritated: marriage without love she could not approve of, and he had no love in his heart. She thought she could have left the room sweepingly if the baby could have been stolen right away. Gino told her that the woman, whom he liked to marry, loved him passionately. She said expletively, though: "'Then God help her!'" Gino stamped impatiently. She asked if he was wanting his proposed wife to be his housekeeper, his slave, or something like those. He said he would want his future wife look after the baby. He told her in a single breath: "'You meant that we could not always be together yet, she and I. You are right. What is to be done? I cannot afford a nurse, and Perfetta is too rough. When he was ill I dared not let her touch him. When he has to be washed, which happens now and then, who does it?—I. I feed him, or settle what he shall have. I sleep with him and comfort him when he is unhappy in the night. No one talks, no one may sing to him but I.'"

Miss Abbott suggested that instead of marrying a new wife, for the reason of baby, he could seek help from his relatives in Empoli. Gino replied he would rather prefer England than Empoli. She said England would be better, for the boy had a grandmother there. He said the boy had a grandmother also in Empoli, but he would not seek help either from his mother or from his father, because they would create a cleaveage between his son's thoughts and his. Miss Abbott wondered at Gino: "This cruel, vicious fellow knew of strange refinements. The horrible truth, that wicked people are capable of love, stood naked before her, and her moral being was abashed. It was her duty to rescue the baby, to save it from contagion, and she still meant to do her duty. But the comfortable sense of virtue left her. She was in the presence of something greater than right or wrong." A little while afterwards, he commanded the sleeping baby to wake up, and "lifted his foot and trod lightly on its stomach." She cried in fear: "'Oh, take care!'" "He stood with one foot resting on the little body, suddenly musing, filled with the desire that his son should be like him, and should have sons like him, to people the earth. It is the strongest desire that can come to a man—if it comes to him at all—stronger even than love or the desire for personal immortality. All men want it, and declare that it is theirs; but the hearts of most are set elsewhere."

The baby woke up, but Gino did not greet it; he rather continued to describe the woman he was thinking to marry: "'This woman will do exactly what I tell her. She is fond of children. She is clean; she has a pleasant voice. She is not beautiful; I cannot pretend that to you for a moment. But she is what I require.'" Gino suddenly became agile to wash the baby while Miss Abbott was thinking that perhaps her plan of stealing the child was going to be a flop. So she was turning to go, while he was arranging hot water, soap, etc. to wash the baby. But, completely denuding the baby, he asked her to hold the baby that seemed 'a little kicking image of bronze.' Tears began to roll out from her eyes—"wrong tears," because she was going to steal the child. On the other hand, looking at the child, Gino prided himself: "'Who would have believed his mother was blonde? For he is brown all over—brown every inch of him. Ah, but how beautiful he is! And he is mine: mine for ever. Even if he hates me he will be mine. He cannot help it; he is made of me; I am his father.'"

Miss Abbott asked Gino if she could help him in washing the baby, and he gave her the baby without speaking. Then both of them began to wash the baby like a ritual, deriving from their individual services immense joy and happiness. Alter the washing, Gino was searching for a soft towel, but found none, and so Miss Abbott produced her 'clean handkerchief' for the purpose of drying him. The baby now seemed a 'copper vessel.' Miss Abbott then sat on a chair "with twenty miles of view behind her," and then Gino "placed the dripping baby on her knee" and sat beside them. The three—Miss Abbott, the baby and Gino—as if made the picture of "the Virgin and Child, with Donor." It was just at this moment that Philip entered into their presence and saw that divine picture. He whispered into Miss Abbott's ear that he wanted her help in their common mission. She did not say even a word, but went away, 'weeping bitterly' and disappeared 'among the trees.' Philip asked Gino if Miss Abbott told him of some business, Gino said she had not told him of any business. At this moment Perfetta returned from outside, "loudly complaining of the size of Monteriano and the intricacies of its streets." Gino now gave Philip a cigar, and then the two "proceeded to the business" (section 7).

Harriet Herriton saw no sign of the success of their mission of saving Lilia's baby son, and she arrogated the failure of the mission or the delay of the success of the mission to Miss Abbott. She told Philip that Miss Abbott had a two-fold purpose in coming to Italy: to try to defeat the mission and to see the Italian (Gino). Philip assured her that their mission as yet should not be taken to be a failure. He told her: "'I've not got the baby, Harriet, but at the same time I haven't exactly failed. I and Signer Carella are to have another interview this afternoon, at the Caffe Garibaldi. He [Gino] is perfectly reasonable and pleasant.'" He told her that Gino desperately needed money, but at the same time he had "certain affection for the child." But Harriet would not be persuaded to cool down. She only accused Miss Abbott of 'intolerable duplicity' and only sobbed. But Philip would not think ill of Miss Abbott: "The access of joy that had come to him yesterday in the theatre promised to be permanent. He was more anxious than heretofore to be charitable towards the world." He advised Harriet to count on Miss Abbott's help for the success of their mission.

Just before midday, when in the intense heat streets were clearing, Philip stood in the centre of the Piazza. "The Piazza, with its three great attractions—the Palazzo Pubblico, the Collegiate Church, and the Caffe Garibaldi, the intellect, the soul, and the body—had never looked more charming." From the Piazza, Philip entered Santa Deodata's "to continue his mission." He asked the sacristan: "'Is there an English lady here?'" The sacristan "nodded cheerfully towards a kneeling figure. In the midst of this confusion Miss Abbott was praying." Philip was not surprised because he expected a spiritual breakdown for Miss Abbott. She told him that she could no more help him in his mission, because she had changed her mind. He demanded nothing from her but only the promise that she would not divulge their plan to Gino. She consented. Philip stuck to Miss Abbott even though he had nothing more to tell her: "But he did not move, for it was an increasing pleasure to him to be near her, and her charm was at its strongest today. He thought less of psychology and feminine reaction. The gush of sentimentalism which had carried her away had only made her more alluring. He was content to observe her beauty and to profit by the tenderness and the wisdom that dwelt within her." "It was the first time she had ever praised him." The saintliness of Miss Abbott was supplanted by something not less desirable than the original.

Philip told Miss Abbott that that afternoon he was going to have another interview with Gino, but he was mostly deficient about the interview. He was expecting an 'honourable failure.' She did not like 'honourable failure,' and persuaded him first to decide whether he was going to leave the baby with its father or take it away, and then to act. She confessed she felt herself muddle-headed. She did not like he be inert, 'dead.' 'She came up to him, and then her mood suddenly changed and she took hold of both his hands. 'You are so splendid, Mr. Herriton, that I can't bear to see you wasted. I can't bear—she has not been good to you—your mother.'" Philip was not much swayed. He told her: "'Miss Abbott, don't worry over me. Some people are born not to do things. I'm one of them; I never did anything at school or at the Bar. I came to stop Lila's marriage, and it was too late. I came out intending to get the baby, and I shall return an "honourable failure." I never expect anything to happen now, so I am never disappointed. You would be surprised to know what my great events are. Going to the theatre yesterday, talking to you now—I don't suppose I shall ever meet anything greater. I seem fated to pass through the world without colliding with it or moving it—and I'm sure I can't tell you whether the fate's good or evil. I don't die—I don't fall in love. And if other people die or fall in love they always do it when I'm just not there. You are quite right; life to me is just a spectacle, which—thank God, and thank Italy, and thank you—is now more beautiful and heartening than it has ever been before.'" But the emotional discourse they entered into could not alter them phenomenally.

Discontentment prevailed among the three members of the rescue-parry. Harriet called Miss Abbott a turn-coat, and asked Philip to arrange a carriage for herself and Philip for the evening train, for the return-journey to England. Miss Abbott also wanted to come back home. Harriet goaded Philip to somehow fetch the baby before half past eight in the evening—before she leaves for England. But Philip showed no interest in the baby, and consequently he failed in the interview with Gino at the Caffe Garibaldi—Gino could not be persuaded to part with the baby. Philip broke the news of his returning to England to Gino, along with his plan to come to Italy next year. Gino shook hands with him most cordially, and offered him to become the god-father of his next baby expected out of his near future marriage. He requested Philip to tender his love to Irma. Harriet ended her packing and made a brown paper cover for her new Baedeker. "The carriages came round at a quarter past eight. It was not raining much, but the night was extraordinarily dark, and one of the drivers wanted to go slowly to the station. Miss Abbott came down and said that she was ready, and would start at once." But Harriet was not to be found anywhere. Philip entered into her room and found it empty. "All that was left of her was the purple prayer-book which lay open on the bed. Philip took it up aimlessly, and saw—'Blessed be the Lord my God who teacheth my hands to war and my fingers to fight.'"

It was now half past eight. "All the luggage was on, and still Harriet had not appeared. 'Depend upon it,' said the landlady, 'she has gone to Signor Carella's to say goodbye to her little nephew.' Philip did not think it likely. They shouted all over the house and still there was no Harriet". Soon "A man came up the street with a note. Philip read, 'Start at once. Pick me up outside the gate. Pay the bearer. H.H.'" Philip asked the man who it was that sent the note, and from where it was sent. The landlady told Philip that the man was an idiot and could not speak. Yet Philip understood that the note was from his sister Harriet. But he could not discern the place where she was waiting for him. The landlady suggested that she would be waiting outside the Siena gate. The carriage went a distance but Harriet was not to be found. The train was about to be missed; it was too late. Philip now shouted in the darkness; "Harriet! Harriet!'" And he saw Harriet "waiting for them in the wet, at the first turn of the zigzag." Philip saw a bundle in Harriet's hands; it was the baby. "She would not let him talk. The baby, she repeated, was asleep, and she put up an umbrella to shield it and her from the rain." Philip conjectured that Gino perhaps submitted to the persuasiveness of Harriet and handed over the baby to her. He also conjectured that the carriage of Miss Abbott by then "must be descending the darkness some mile or two below them," because she started earlier.

Monteriano was drowned in the darkness, and they "could see nothing but the occasional wet stem of an olive, which their lamp illumined as they passed it." "They travelled quickly, for this driver did not care how fast he went to the station, and would dash down each incline and scuttle perilously round the curves." Philip wanted to see the baby and so lit a match under the shelter of Harriet's umbrella, and saw that the baby was not asleep but awake. The little light of the match went out. Philip said the face of the baby indicated that all went wrong with him. Philip lit another match, which went out soon; but with its light Philip could see that the baby was crying. Harriet would not believe it, because had the baby cried she could hear it; but when she touched the face of the baby she felt the baby bathed in tears. Harriet supposed the baby cried because of the 'night air' or the 'wet of the rain.' But Philip conjectured that it cried because it was somehow hurt. He said that it was too uncanny that the baby cried but its crying was not heard. Harriet asked him to keep quiet, because, she thought, the baby wanted to sleep. "She crooned harshly as they descended [as the carriage descended], and now and then she wiped up the tears which welled inexhaustibly from the little eyes. Philip looked away, winking at times himself. It was as if they were travelling with the whole world's sorrow, as if all the mystery, all the persistency of woe were gathered to a single fount. The roads were now coated with mud, and the carriage went more quietly but not less swiftly, sliding by long zigzags into the night." Their carriage now reached the cross-road to Poggibonsi, where one could have the last view of Monteriano.

Philip was feeling sorry for Gino because of his great loss of the baby. Harriet suddenly asked him to strike matches to have a look of the baby. The first and the second matches blew out immediately, but the third match caught fire. They 'contemplated' the face of the baby in the little trembling light of the match. "Then there was a shout and a crash. They were lying in the mud in darkness. The carriage had overturned." The accident occurred in the wood where the darkness was more opaque. Philip was a good deal hurt, but was steady. Suddenly Harriet screamed full-throated: "'The baby—the baby—it slipped—it's gone from my arms! I stole it!'" Philip fainted, but soon recovered; but the confusion persisted all around. Harriet was now screaming like a maniac: "'I stole it! I stole it! I stole it! It slipped out of my arms?'" The driver shouted: "'Keep still!'" And then he began to search for the baby. He lighted a match and found the bundled baby among divers things of the carriage. It had fallen into a rut. Harriet burst out laughing: "'I stole it! I and the idiot—no one was there.'" Philip cautioned every one not to move lest the baby got trodden, and all obeyed. He took the baby and laid it on his knees, and was cleansing its face of mud, rain and tears. "He was listening—not for a cry, but for the tick of a heart or the slightest tremor of breath." Miss Abbott's voice was heard. The accident was due to the collision of Philip's carriage with that of Miss Abbott. Miss Abbott called out to Philip: "'Where are you?'" With a lighted lamp she was approaching Philip. Philip shouted: "'Silence!'" "He shook the bundle; he breathed into it; he opened his coat and pressed it against him. Then he listened, and heard nothing but the rain and the panting horses, and Harriet, who was somewhere chuckling to herself in the dark." Miss Abbott took the bundle from him—the bundle that embraced the baby. The baby was dead! (section 8).

The crime of stealing the baby must belong to Harriet, but how did she commit the crime? "It was clear that she had gone prepared for an interview with Gino, and finding him out, she had yielded to a grotesque temptation." And this temptation was to steal the baby. "But how far this was the result of ill-temper, to what extent she had been fortified by her religion, when and how she had met the poor idiot—these questions were never answered." However, after the death of the baby, Philip thought it almost his religious duty to inform Gino of the death of his son, and so he ordered the driver of the injured carriage to go back to Monteriano, and "after a two hours' absence" Philip came back to Gino's house. Gino was out. Perfetta welcomed him, seated him on a horsehair chair, and went out to call Gino home from Caffe Garibaldi. She did not yet know that she had lost the baby. Gino heard of Philip from Perfetta, and entered into the house crying out to Philip: "'So you are back! How glad I am! We are all waiting—'" He did not yet receive the shock of his son being dead. "Philip had seen too much to be nervous. In low, even tones, he told what had happened; and the other [Gino], also perfectly calm, heard him to the end. In the silence Perfetta called up that she had forgotten the baby's evening milk; she must fetch it."

Philip confessed the saddest incident was due to his cowardice. He said that Harriet was ill and that Miss Abbott was guiltless. He begged they be excused. Gino "was feeling the place where his son had lain. Now and then he frowned a little and glanced at Philip." Philip shouted at him: "'Break down, Gino; you must break down. Scream and curse and give in for a little; you must break down.'" Gino became agitated, roamed across the room, touched everything of the room except Philip, and at last accosted him. Gino's "face was that of a man who has lost his old reason for life and seeks a new one." Gino came nearer to Philip, and "Philip stood his ground." Philip told Gino with all frankness: "'You are to do what you like with me, Gino. Your son is dead, Gino. He died in my arms, remember. It does not excuse me; but he died in my arms.'" Gino gripped Philip by his broken elbow, and then dealt a blow at him with all his strength. Then the two engaged themselves in bouts of mutual physical violences punctuated by brief periods of peace for mustering energies. At one point of time Gino gripped Philip's windpipe, when at first Philip "was glad, for here, he thought, was death at hand." Philip shouted at Gino: "'But your son *is dead,* Gino. Your son is dead, dear Gino. Your son is dead.'"

Meanwhile, Miss Abbott arrived on the spot. She held Gino by the shoulders and held him down in a chair, and then told him: "'What is the good of another death? What is the good of more pain?'" "He too began to tremble. Then he turned and looked curiously at Philip, whose face, covered with dust and foam, was visible by the stove. Miss Abbott allowed him to getup, though she still held him firmly. He gave a loud and curious cry—a cry of interrogation it might be called. Below there was the noise of Perfetta returning with the baby's milk." Philip suffered much, physically, from Gino's blows, and now fell down awkwardly, shouting "'Help! help!'" After a moment, while in the arms of Miss Abbott, Gino shouted, indicating Philip: "'Kill him! kill him for me.'" Miss Abbott insisted both Philip and Gino to stop the matter there. Gino saw Perfetta with milk and asked her to "Put the milk on the table'", because it would no more be needed. The climax of the episode ended there with Gino submitting to Miss Abbott: "The peril was over at last. A great sob shook the whole body, another followed, and then he gave a piercing cry of woe, and stumbled towards Miss Abbott like a child and clung to her. "All through the day Miss Abbott had seemed to Philip like a goddess, and more than ever did she seem so now. Many people look younger and more intimate during great emotion. But some there are who look older, and remote, and he could not think that there was little difference in years, and none in composition, between her and the man whose head was laid upon her breast. Her eyes were open, full of infinite pity and full of majesty, as if they discerned the boundaries of sorrow, and saw unimaginable tracts beyond. Her hands were folded round the sufferer, stroking him lightly, for even a goddess can do no more than that. And it seemed fitting, too, that she should bend her head and touch his forehead with her lips. "Philip looked away, as he sometimes looked away from the great pictures where visible forms suddenly became inadequate for the things they have shown to us. He was happy; he was assured that there was greatness in the world, there came to him an earnest desire to be good through the example of this good woman. He would try henceforward to be worthy of the things she had revealed. Quietly, without hysterical prayers and banging of drums, he underwent conversion. He was saved." "Miss Abbott said the milk intended for the baby should not be wasted, and asked Gino to take some of it. She also asked Gino to persuade Philip to drink of the milk. Both Gino and Philip obeyed" (section 9).

The rescue party consisting of Philip, Harriet and Miss Abbott was to come back to England. Philip now quite forgot Gino's beastly behaviour, and now thought him to be his friend. He told Miss Abbott that while he was ill, after the physical violence on him by Gino, Gino nursed him with a dedicated soul. He said Gino also tied for him "at the inquest, and at the funeral", obviously to save him from punishment. Miss Abbott told him, when he would write to Gino, from England, to tender him her "kindest regards", Gino, from his end, wrote to Philip imploring him 'to marry Miss Abbott, even if her dowry's small'" and to regard her as his "refuge from domestic difficulties." The rescue party was standing "in the corridor of the train, slowly ascending out of Italy towards the San Gotthard tunnel." Philip expressed his plan to see Gino's new wife next spring. Miss Abbott told him that Gino was heartless; he had quite forgotten the baby. Philip corrected her and said that Gino was unhappy for the baby and that he was really inconsistent in his behaviour, but he liked him the more for that reason. Miss Abbott showed no interest in going to Italy next spring. By this time Philip had fallen in deep love of her: "By this time he loved her very much, and he could not bear to be puzzled. He had reached love by the spiritual path: her thoughts and her goodness and her nobility had moved him first, and now her whole body and all its gestures had become transfigured by them. The beauties that are called obvious—the beauties of her hair and her voice and her limbs—he had noticed these last; Gino, who never traversed any path at all, had commended them dispassionately to his friend."

But it was a puzzle to Philip why Miss Abbott always avoided himself as well as Gino. Philip became mentally and physically broken down after his days in Italy; but Harriet, after her brief illness was her former self. Philip thought he could no more live at Sawston—in England. On the other hand, Miss Abbott felt she could go back to Sawston, live there and work. She would look after her father and remain engaged in "hundred ties". Philip suddenly exploded: "'You're too good—about a thousand times better than I am—I want to see you often—again and again.'" He asked her not to go back to her old mode of life, but, implicitly, to a new one, because, as he said, "'Too much has happened'": "'Not only pain and sorrow, but wonderful things: that tower in the sunlight—do you remember it, and all you said to me? The theatre even. And the next day—in the church; and our times with Gino.'" Miss Abbott responded: "'All the wonderful things are over.'" But Philip was aggressive: "' I don't believe it. At all events not for me. The most wonderful things may be to come—'" They were conversing in the running train, which was by this time "crawling up the last ascent towards the Campanile of Ariolo and the entrance of the tunnel." Philip saw a riddle in Miss Abbott and told her: "'I thought I understood you, and I don't. All those two great first days at Monteriano I read you as clearly as you read me still.... And now you're frank with me one moment, as you used to be, and the next moment you shut me up.'" He told her that she was everything to him: "'You see I owe too much to you—my life, and I don't know what besides.'" He further told her that she had become mysterious, whereas she herself once warned him not to be mysterious. Philip concluded by telling her that she would no more be able to adjust with the life of Sawston.

Philip at last seemed to win her. She murmured: "'It is tempting—'". She meant that it was tempting to her not to be mysterious. Philip thought his hope came to be realised, and so became overjoyed. She confessed she was feeling lonely. "'The train seemed to shake him towards her. He was resolved that though a dozen people were looking, he would yet take her in his arm'". Philip also said he felt lonely. Now suddenly Miss Abbott sprung a shattering surprise to him. She said she loved Gino, and then burst into tears, and murmured 'Gino! Gino! Gino!' Philip, finding nothing else to say, said: "'Rather! I love him too!'" She thought her love for Gino was not quite clear to him, and so she repeated: "' I am in love with Gino'". She said she fell in love with him like Lilia did before her. She continued: "'I dare tell you this because I like you—and because you're without passion; you look on life as a spectacle; you don't enter it; you only find it funny or beautiful. So I can trust you to cure me. Mr Herriton, isn't it funny?'" She gave out the reason of her love for Gino: "'He's not a gentleman, nor a Christian, nor good in any way. He's never flattered me nor honoured me. But because he's handsome, that's been enough. The son of an Italian dentist, with a pretty face.'" She further said, almost deliriously: "'I love him, and I'm not ashamed of it, I love him, and I'm going to Sawston, and if I mayn't speak about him to you sometimes, I shall die.'" Philip indifferently asked if it all was her "passing fancy". She said, definitely no. Philip developed malice against her. "Here was the cruel antique malice of the gods, such as they once sent forth against Pasiphae. Centuries of aspiration and culture—and the world could not escape it." Hatefully, Philip asked if there was anything common between herself and Gino, and received the answer that there was nothing common between them that could grow affection, except the times in which they met. Philip again asked: "'Which—which times?'" Miss Abbott answered: "'The time I thought you weak and heedless, and went instead of you to get the baby. That began it, as far as I know the beginning. Or it may have begun when you took us to the theatre, and I saw him mixed up with music and light.'"

Philip told her that she fell in love of Gino through his fault. Miss Abbott said there was no fault in him, through which she was 'refined' or 'transfigured'—through which she was converted from a Sawstonian to an Italian. "As she spoke she seemed to be transfigured, and to have indeed no part with refinement or unrefinement any longer. Out of this wreck there was revealed to him something indestructible—something which she, who had given it, could never take away." She was not satisfied with what she said to him, and so further told him: "'I say again, don't be charitable. If he had asked me, I might have given myself body and soul. That would have been the end of my rescue party. But all through he took me for a superior being—a goddess. I who was worshipping every inch of him, and every word he spoke. And that saved me.'" Philip thought Gino was Endymion, the extremely and perpetually beautiful youth, to Miss Abbott, nothing less. But she also held Philip so high in estimation that "without regret he could now have told her that he was her worshipper too." Philip said nothing to her but only "'Thank you for everything.'" "She looked at him with great friendliness, for he had made her life endurable." All this happened while Harriet was sleeping comfortably in her carriage in the train which now entered the San Gotthard tunnel. Philip and Miss Abbott anxiously "hurried back to the carriage to close the windows lest the smuts should get into Harriet's eyes."

3

DISCUSSION

(i)

Robert Langbaum is not far from truth when, in his *The Modern Spirit,* he writes: "Actually, Forster has written two masterpieces—his last novel [*A Passage to India*] and his first, *Where Angels Fear to Tread*" (Langbaum, 128). According to Nicola Beauman,we may recall, *Where Angels Fear to Tread* was not only Forster's first novel but also "in some ways the first modern novel; and it arrived ten years before the first modern poem, Eliot's 'The Love Song of J. Alfred Prufrock'"

(Beauman, 164). But what is a modern novel? Where lies the modernity of a modern novel? To answer this question we cannot do better than quote the following. In her essay 'Modern Fiction' (that appeared in her *Collected Essays,* vol. ii: 1966), which may be deemed as the manifesto of the modern novel, Virginia Woolf said that in contrast to the conventional or 'old' novel, which was 'materialistic,' in the sense that it interested itself only in the externalities, the episodes, the 'body', if we like, the modern novel is interested in the internality, in what happens in the consciousness, in the soul, in the spirit, in the wholeness of life. She said that the proper stuff of the novel refuses to be confined in such a vestment as the traditional novel had been. She said the proper stuff of the novel is not something palpable, three-dimensional and orderly, but atomic and scattered. It is fleeting like life, or it is life that is fleeting; it is semi-transparent, mystical. Woolf writes in that essay: "Look within and life, it seems, is very far from being 'like this.' Examine for a moment an ordinary mind on an ordinary day. The mind receives a myriad impressions—trivial, fantastic, evanescent, or engraved with the sharpness of steel. From all sides they come, an incessant shower of innumerable atoms; and as they fall, as they shape themselves into the life of Monday or Tuesday, the accent falls differently from of old [as in 'old' or conventional novels]; the moment of importance came not here but there; so that, if a writer were a free man and not a slave, if he could write what he chose, not what he must, if he could base his work upon his own feeling and not upon convention, there would be no plot, no comedy, no tragedy, no love interest or catastrophe in the accepted style, and perhaps not a single button sewn on as the Bond Street tailors would have it. Life is not a series of gig-lamps symmetrically arranged; life is a luminous halo, a semi-transparent envelope surrounding us from the beginning of consciousness to the end. Is it not the task of the novelist to convey this varying, this unknown and uncircumscribed spirit, whatever aberration or complexity it may display, with as little mixture of the alien and external as possible? We are not pleading merely for courage and sincerity; we are suggesting that the proper stuff of fiction is a little other than custom would have us believe it" (Lodge, 88-89). Woolf further writes: "...the problem of the novelist at present, as we suppose it to have been in the past, is to contrive means of being free to set down what he chooses. He has to have the courage to say what interests him is no longer 'this' but 'that': out of 'that' alone must he construct his work. For the moderns 'that,' the point of interest, lies very likely in the dark places of psychology. At once, therefore, the accent falls a little differently; the emphasis is upon something hitherto ignored; at once a different outline of form becomes necessary, difficult for us to grasp, incomprehensible to our predecessors" (Lodge, 90).

Where Angels Fear to Tread is not a conventional novel in so far as it is not at all preoccupied with the externalities of the characters as such but what happen in the consciousnesses of the principal characters, particularly in the consciousness of Philip, the externalities being treated as mere projections of the states of the consciousnesses. So it may be said that the novel is not concerned with, to use the words of Virginia Woolf, the 'body' but with the 'spirit' of the principal characters, especially with that of Philip. The theme of the novel is spiritual, for it evaluates the two cultures, that of England and that of Italy, by juxtaposing the two contrasting cultures, and strives to suggestively show preferability of the one than the other. The novel, therefore, is indubitably modern, both as regards its subject matter and as regards its treatment. It "is a perfect little comedy of manners" (Langbaum, 128). But if it is a comedy of manners, it has a shade of the tragic too. Lilia could not enjoy her newly gained spiritual freedom in the open and 'authentic' culture of the south (Italy) but for a while and then died in childbirth; Philip, being transformed, like Lilia, by the open, resuscitating and invigorating culture of Italy, strongly loved Caroline Abbott, but she had already fallen in love of Gino; and Caroline, also transformed by the freeing spirit of Italy, was infatuated by the regular contour of Gino's physique and fell in love of him, but he had already announced his banns with a girl, immediately after Lilia's death. Lilia, Philip,

Caroline—all of them—failed to achieve their aspirations, and so all the three are, at least partially, tragic characters. In fact, not only in *Where Angels Fear to Tread* but in all other novels Forster has shown us the universal tragic incongruity between man's aspiration and his achievements.

Forster had very few themes for his fictions, and so sometimes we come across repetitions of the same or similar themes in his fictions. Thus James Buzard, in his article 'Forster's Trespasses: Tourism and Cultural Politics' has found parallelism between Forster's short story 'The Eternal Moment' and his novel *Where Angels Fear to Tread.* According to him, both the short story and the novel upholds a culture where the spiritual and the beastly are commingled in a proportionate and balanced way, and where any violation of this equilibrium or balance leads to punishment. Buzard writes: "In 'The Eternal Moment,' Miss Raby's 'ugly and withered' body expressed the corruption of the new [civilized and urbanised] Vorta that she had helped to create; in *Where Angels Fear to Tread* the bodies of Sawston representatives also suffer for the sins committed against Monteriano. Forster makes the bigoted Harriet endure a variety of minor physical ailments throughout the novel—someone steps on her corns, she gets smuts in her eyes, and *so* forth" (Tambling, 24).

Forster has written two Italian' novels: *Where Angels Fear to Tread* and *A Room with a View.* Both these novels are based on Italian tours, and very expectedly there are resemblances between them. But, as in *A Room with a View,* in *Where Angels Fear to Tread also* the tour *per se* is not of any considerable consequence, the emphasis of the novel falling on the distance between the English (Sawstonian) culture and the Italian culture. The novel, therefore, may have some sociological interest. Robert Langbaum writes about the novel: "...*Where Angels Fear to Tread* compares only two cultures—England, standing for will and order, and Italy, standing for emotion and erotic love. By reference to comic stereotypes, Forster quickly sketches in the manners of Sawston, upper middleclass suburbia, and throws them into comic juxtaposition to the manners of San Gimignano (here called Monteriano), the almost perfectly preserved thirteenth-century town near Siena" (Langbaum, 129). The English culture is inordinately stretched on the line of the rational, and so, as if pathologically, suffers from an absence of affectivity, of emotionality. The Italian culture, as represented by Gino in the novel, on the other hand, is a happy blend, as Forster would like to say, of the rational and the emotional, in the very appropriate proportions the emotional comprising a sense for 'Beauty, evil, charm, vulgarity, mystery.' The Italian culture is therefore, as Forster would like us to understand, humane, and so desirable.

Forster believed that the weak and anaemic English culture should have been invigorated and sanguinised with a dose of the vitality of the Italian culture. In *Where Angels Fear to Tread,* he has very authentically demonstrated the snobbishness of the English culture. English culture is so frowningly snobbish that it could never stand the idea of being improved upon by its exposure to the salubriously modifying influences of any alien culture. In the novel *Where Angels Fear to Tread* both Philip and Caroline, like Mrs Herriton, had been overly contemptuous of the culture of Monteriano, till they exposed themselves to the salubrious influence of the alien culture, and this was the most potential ground behind their ardent striving to retrieve Lilia's child from Monteriano. But after their exposure to the culture of the Mediterranean warm Italy they themselves were spiritually transmogrified, and they could realise that not the cold English but the warm Italian culture should one adulate, and that the English culture would only benefit from its exposure to the Italian, though the Italians were rather wicked, uncouth and brutal. Caroline, for instance, after her unintentional exposure to the culture of Monteriano, learned "the terrible truth that wicked people are capable of love", which was earlier quite unbelievable to her. In *Where Angels Fear to Tread*, Forster is clearly on the side of the Mediterranean (Italian) culture—a culture where the head and the heart keep a balance, unlike the English culture where the head is always bent upon repressing the heart. The laconic, radical and myopic English (Sawstonian) culture is all 'spiritual', and so regrettably fails to understand that for the birth and growth of a whole man both spirituality and materiality, which are available around the Mediterranean, are essential. In the novel the English tourists to Italy have had the education that materiality or sensuality, like spirituality or aestheticism, is a desideratum for making our life happy and perfect. James Buzard writes about this edification that Forster has canvassed for in all his novels: "What the dwellers in Forster's tourist world cannot escape is the materiality of culture, the mundane and unaesthetic living body on which the touristic fantasy-versions of places are constructed. Forster urges a view of culture as including, on equal terms, dentists and frescoes, physical urges, material needs, and aesthetic pleasures: a view of culture as 'a whole way of life', not held in solution for visitors to admire and 'appropriate'" (Tambling, 25).

(ii)

Forster's novels are so complex that it is not at all easy to identify the foundation stones, the themes, upon which the fictional structures are erected. The themes are multi-faceted or chameleon-like, so that different facets of the same theme yield different perspectives; no one perspective can capture the totality of the significance of a particular theme. From one perspective what appears to be the theme of *Where Angels Fear to Tread* may be expressed by the single word 'saving,' or by the single term 'being saved.' After Lilia died leaving the neonate behind her, Mrs Herriton became frantic to rescue the little baby from the hold of its 'despicable' (she thinks so) father Gino, not so much for its own sake of being saved as for the sake of saving the honour of the Herriton family. Before this, Mrs Herriton had been anxious to baulk Lilia's marriage with Gino with the same end in view—to save the honour of the Herriton family. There are also spiritual savings of Philip and Caroline from their Sawstonian narrow concept of culture with which they had been growing up with incomplete personalities. Their contact with the warmer culture of Italy (Monteriano) widened their view of culture: after the contact they could realise that both aestheticism and materialism, both rationalism and emotionalism, and both idealism and realism are necessary for the complete life of a man, for his complete personality. Philip's and Caroline's Italian experience, therefore, saved them from being fragmentary personalities.

But 'saving' is not the only possible theme of *Where Angels Fear to Tread;* there may be the important eternal issue of good and evil in the novel. We may recall here that, when in contact with the Bloomsbury group, Forster was mightily influenced by the moral philosophy of G.E. Moore, according to whom 'good and 'evil' are irreducible and intuitive concepts central to social life, and according to whom 'goodness' is the bed-rock of ideal human life—goodness, that manifests through friendship and sense of duty. All Forster's novels, except perhaps *Maurice* and *The Longest Journey,* are distantly concerned with the ideas of goodness and evil. In all his novels, except *Maurice* and *The Longest Journey,* Forster has shown us the conflict between goodness and evil through the jarrings between two sets of values: in *Howards End* between the values of the Schlegels and those of the Wilcoxes; in *A Passage to India* between the English (or Tonbridgean) values and the Indian values; and in *A Room with a View* and *Where Angels Fear to Tread* between the English and the Italian values. In *Where Angels Fear to Tread,* the basic ethical question, ineluctably blended with the theme, is which one of the two value systems is good and which evil—the Sawstonian and the Monterianonian? No, Forster does not explicitly takes side with any one of the two; he only urges us to understand that both are incomplete in isolation from the other, and therefore both are severally evil, and that the ideal value system must be a blend of the two. A subsidiary theme of the novel may be the sense of duty. In the novel, Philip and Caroline went to Italy (Monteriano) to rescue Lilia's baby from a sense of duty, which is akin to goodness. This point should not be undervalued because Forster first gave the novel the title 'From a Sense of Duty'.

According to D.S. Savage *Where Angels Fear to Tread* is based on not one, but two related themes: the theme of 'personal salvation' and the theme of the concern for good and evil. Philip and Caroline had had their personal salvation by escaping the narrow English culture, and they re-oriented their notion of good and evil, and thereby reformed their ethical concern. Savage's interpretation of the theme of the novel is agreed upon by Trilling. But Trilling adds that in *Where Angels Fear to Tread* there is also an additional theme: the theme of the conflict between the English sense of respectability and the Italian drive for paganism—between the Englishman's ideal of beauty and the Italian's ideal of masculinity. Rex Warner holds a different view about the theme of the novel. He says that the theme of the novel is the concern about the Englishman's under-developed heart. Philip and Caroline, before their contact with the liberating air of Italy, were brain-all beings, having no warm and genuine passion. They thought it below their dignity even to wear their minimal passions on their sleeves. They were drawn to the sham social customs and mores which required that passions must only be privately felt and that very minimally, and in no case should they be publicly visible. They respected the head and denounced the heart. But human instincts can neither be denied nor be repressed. When Philip and Caroline exposed themselves unawares to the salubrious and impassioned atmosphere of Italy, they could clearly realise that the head is not everything and that the heart meant much. They could understand that the life that is predominated by the head is an incomplete life, and that the heart has to intervene in the course of life to make it into a whole. In Italy, they did not only see with their head the nasty beggars but they did also see the beautiful and amorous statues, and they became complete, whole. According to Rex Warner, this is the educative value of this novel and its thematic core.

(iii)

The plot of *Where Angels Fear to Tread* is rather simple. Plot may be thought to be well-ordered and logical sequences of actions, which constitute a more or less autonomous structure through which the story (and the other elements) of a novel manifests itself. In *Where Angels Fear to Tread,* Forster has introduced two locales, Sawston (England) and Monteriano (San Gimignano in Italy), and two cultures, juxtaposedly, to explore the related issues of cultural incompatibility, completeness or wholeness of human personality, personal salvation, goodness *versus* evil, and the development of the human heart (passion). The novel is structurally based on the antagonism between the English culture and the Italian culture and on the salubrious and ameliorating effect of the commingling of the two cultures on the two characters: Philip and Caroline (besides Lilia). However, A.S. Collins, in his *English Literature of the Twentieth Century,* has drawn the plot of the novel as follows: "In *Where Angels Fear to Tread,* on the one side is Forster's suburbia, Sawston, where Mrs Herriton lives armoured in convention and snobbery; on the other is Italy, where her widowed daughter-in-law, Lilia, has become engaged to a vulgar Italian, Gino, some years younger than herself. Lilia must be rescued, for the sake of the Herriton's social standing, to appease their outraged gentility, and for the sake of her Herriton daughter born of her first marriage. So Mrs Herriton sends her son Philip to Italy to try and buy off the Italian, only to find they are already married. When Lilia dies in childbirth, another deputation is sent, this time to rescue the baby. Unable to understand the vulgar father's love for his child, Philip's narrow-minded sister Harriet kidnaps it, and as a result of her bungling stupidity the child dies. So at the expense of two deaths Sawston closes this scandalous chapter, but not with total success, for Philip and Caroline Abbott, a spinster friend of the Herritons who has taken it upon herself to show an active interest in the proceedings in Italy, have learned a lesson. They now know that there are human values that Sawston ought to recognise. Caroline reverences the wonderful love of Gino for his baby—indeed, she falls in love with him, with his elemental naturalness. Philip, who had long loved Italy, has been won over to a deep admiration for Gino, and after Gino, in his agony at the death of his baby, tries to murder him, Philip is again reconciled to him. Philip and Caroline return to England at least with their souls awakened from the death-in-life of

Sawston, but Harriet has lost her soul too many years before and nothing can save her" (Collins, 197-98).

(iv)

The major characters of *Where Angels Fear to Tread* are Lilia Herriton (*nee* Theobald), Signor Gino Carella, Philip Herriton, Miss Caroline Abbott, Mrs Herriton and Miss Harriet Herriton. The novel may be thought, for convenience, to consist of two parts: part one comprising the first four chapters, and part two the rest six chapters. The first part of the novel is dominated by the ebullient caprices and waywardnesses of Lilia, under the influence of her unquenched romantic thirst for life. Lilia's character occupies the beginning five chapters of the novel, and then she dies in childbirth.

Forster, like Aldous Huxley and William Golding, had the penchant for naming his fictional characters significantly, keeping in view some salient aspects of the characters or the roles they play. The name 'Lilia' was perhaps derived from the term 'Lily,' which refers to a species of flower which is thought to be a symbol of innocence or purity. In *Where Angels Fear to Tread,* Lilia is an innocent young widowed lady, variously tortured by the Herriton family. In Monteriano, she fell in love of Gino innocently, and then she died. In her character, what is the most obvious and essential is her mighty innocence, and so, we may say, her name Forster has employed very significantly. Her extremely romantic and flambuoyant life-style notwithstanding, she is surely innocent in a liberal-humanist sense.

After the death of her husband, Charles Herriton, Lilia had been living in the Herriton family in Sawston along with her only daughter, the little Irma. Mrs Herriton, her mother-in-law, soon found her intolerable and so bought a house not far away from the Herriton house, where she was staying. But then Mrs Herriton's suspicious mind found another cause of anxiety: she thought Lilia was in incipient love with one Mr Kingcroft. Hastily, therefore, Mrs Herriton transported Lilia to Monteriano in Italy for the reason of Lilia's 'purification' or her 'transfiguration', like that of the Goths long long ago. Lilia was then just 32, but there was no sign of her passions waning or of her prettiness fading. Nine years ago, Charles Herriton was won over by Lilia's beauty. She was rather overly passionate, for no sooner had Charles died than she was growing a fancy for Mr Kingcroft, and, not long after that, she fell headlong in love with Gino within an inconceivably short time, and that in a hotel in Italy.

In the very beginning chapter of *Where Angels Fear to Tread*, Philip tells us that, like Mr Kingcraft, Lilia had "the knack of being absurd in public." The truth of Philip's opinion about Lilia we may at least partially discern in her too hasty marriage with Gino with whom she was not even enough acquainted. This hasty marriage of hers only arrogate to her sensuality in the extreme, and yet she possessed some comfortable knowledge of the Pentateuch, or the five Books of the Old Testament, and she once used to discuss it with Mr Kingcroft. But Philip, younger brother of the deceased Charles Herriton, did not find any religious sentiment in her, inspite of all that; he rather took her to be a varitable Philistine (chap. 1). She was "wilful and silly" (chap. 1) and always went "with her clutches after pleasure" (chap. 5). She "had something of the slattern in her nature, and there was no need to keep up appearances [she thought]" (chap. 3). As the Herriton family was rich, money was no problem to Lilia; nevertheless she did not enjoy a happy married life with Charles, and thought that she was not "married properly" (chap. 4). That she was not 'married properly' is true, for after her marriage with Gino, she told Miss Abbott that she had married Gino "'and this time I marry for love!'" (chap. 2). She was not at all happy in the cribbed and over critical atmosphere of the Herriton family. She told Miss Abbott: "And when Charles died I was still to run in strings for the honour of your beastly family, and I was to be cooped up at Sawston and learn to keep house, and all my chances spoilt of marrying again'" (*ibid.*). She was rash, as may be understood from her marriage with Gino within so short a time and without the least consideration of the pros and cons of such a serious matter. Irma, her own daughter, she was not so very fond of for reasons not known, but perhaps because her amour was more powerful and pressing than her filial affection. She fell in love with Gino not so much for anything else as for the beautiful masculine contour of his musculature. This indicates the sensual nature of Lilia's love. She had really "no great sense of beauty, but she was sentimental" (*ibid.*). And this precipitated her marriage with Gino.

After her marriage with Gino, Lilia changed a lot. She became suave and gentle, and she lost her earlier sauciness and superciliousness. Gino, after his marriage with Lilia, told his dear friend Spiridione Tesi about her: "'She is rich, she is generous, she is affable, she addresses her inferiors without haughtiness'" (chap. 3). He told Spiridione that she was 'simpatica' (the narrator tells us that "Nothing will translate the word:" *ibid.*). Lilia was 'simpatica' (sympathetic) without being religious. Gino was a Catholic but she was none, and yet she had enough catholicity, espicially after her marriage with him (*ibid.*). That after her marriage with Gino, Lilia changed considerably is beyond doubt. While Lilia had been in England, Mrs Herriton saw only negative qualities in her—Mrs Herriton saw she was beyond the buckle—but Gino fully domesticated her: "As Mrs Herriton had often observed, Lilia had no resources. She did not like music, or reading, or work. Her one qualification for life was rather blowsy high spirits, which turned querulous or boisterous according to circumstances. She was not obedient, but she was cowardly, and in the most gentle way, which Mrs Herriton might have envied, Gino made her do what he wanted" (chap. 4). But though Lilia was docile to Gino, her relation with him was to an extant perplexing: "He was particularly kind to her when he hardly ever saw her, and she accepted his kindness without resentment, even with gratitude, so docile had she become. She did not hate him, even as she never loved him; with her it was only when she was excited that the semblance of either passion arose. People said she was headstrong; but really her weak brain left her cold" (*ibid.*). In short, Lilia was "a very ordinary woman" (*ibid.*) with "clutches after pleasure" (chap. 5). Her sensualness is quite obvious, and in the matter of sensualness she could be rash and impudent, as is clear from her quick marriage with Gino whose regular physical contour she was quite drawn to.

Lilia's second husband, Signor Gino Carella, was the son of an Italian dentist, who had been practising in a "minute provincial town" (chap. 2) Gino had "a tiny tot of a brother" (*ibid.*), and was very good looking, as we gather from Miss Caroline Abbott who was infatuated by his physical beauty. Miss Abbott tells us about the physical beauty of Gino: "'All his features are good, and he is well built—though I dare say English standards would find him too short'" (*ibid.*). He had "square shoulders" and his "face [was] without refinement," "but not without expression" (*ibid.*). He wore a moustache, and was indolent (chap. 3), but he could play Pallone excellently (chap. 2). He was not blonde like Lilia, but possessed, as we have said, an excellently carved figure which magnetically drew Miss Abbott to him. He was absolutely honest and sincere. It was for all these treasures of Gino that Miss Abbott consented to Lilia's marriage with him. Miss Abbott said about Gino: "'And Gino, I thought, was splendid, and young, and strong not only in body, and sincere as the day,'" (chap. 5). She once mused about him: "He's charming, but he's no fool; he conquered me last year, he conquered Mr [Philip] Herriton yesterday, and if I am not careful he will conquer us all today.... He is terribly strong; Lilia found that out, but only I remember it now'" (chap. 7). But strong though he was, he was innocent and simple too, and Lilia loved his innocence and simplicity—the innocence and simplicity which can be found only in a little boy. In fact, Lilia used to treat him as a boy, and tell him: "You are a boy yourself, Gino'" (chap.4). Gino was really "a charming boy" (*ibid.*).

Gino was a Catholic, though he did not go to church; he was religious only in a crisis. For instance, when he wanted a son, by Lilia, but could not produce one, he gave candles to Santa Deodata: "Gino was distracted...he wanted a son. He could talk and think of nothing else. His one desire was to become the father of a man like himself, and it held him with a grip he only partially understood, for it was the first great desire, the first great passion of his life. Falling in love was a mere physical triviality, like warm sun or cool water, beside this divine hope of immortality: 'I continue.' He gave candles to Santa Deodata, for he was always religious at a crisis—" (*ibid.*). But his love for Lilia was constant and unalloyed and intense, inspite of the fact that he had decided to marry only to become immortal through a son. He confided to her: "... I have never loved anyone but you" (*ibid.*).

Though Gino prefered to keep himself within himself, at best within the four walls, he could, if he would, make friends easily, and best ones at that. He had one very close friend—Spiridione Tesi. Spiridione was impressed by Gino and wished him well. He told Gino. "'But you, Gino, deserve your good fortune [Lily], for you are a good son, a brave man, and a true friend, and from the very first moment I saw you I wished you well'" (chap. 3). Not only Spiridione, but everyone of the neighbourhood, as the narrator tells us, was of the opinion that Gino deserved a lady—rich and 'simpatica'—as his wife. Everyone really loved him (*ibid.*). Gino was fond of journeys as he was fond of friends, a few that he had. To his close friends be was a precious object. "There were, of course, the times when he [Gino] was away altogether—at Empoli, Siena, Florence, Bologna—for he delighted in travel, and seemed to pick up friends all over the country. Lilia often heard what a favourite he was" (chap. 4).

Forster has given us a clear picture of the look and manners of Gino in chapter 2 of *Where Angels Fear to Tread.* For some reason or other, Gino showed in his mien the marks of the heaviness of existence. When he married Lilia, he was only 21 while she was 33, but even at this rather young age, Miss Abbott told Philip, Gino seemed to be much older. He was not rich like Lilia; he was rather worse off. He had just finished his military service as a private in a crack regiment. He "received a solid education" and could quote from Dante's *Inferno,* and yet he could not be called a gentleman, because he was swarthy, as it was Philip's first impression of him. He was brutal, and nasty too—he spat, for instance, on the floor.

Philip's opinion about Gino was that "he is probably a ruffian and certainly a cad," though his father was "courtesy itself" and his uncle was a priest and his cousin was a lawyer at Rome. (chap. 2). Gino was not fair like Lilia, but was brown, (chap. 7). He loved his son as much as he did Lilia. However, Philip's opinion about the character of Gino was quite contrary to that of Miss Abbott: Philip saw Gino as a 'bounder,' as a dissolute. He said that Gino was "'mysterious and terrible. He's got a country behind him that's upset people from the beginning of the world'" (chap. 5).

Peter Burra has found parallels of the character of Gino in the characters of Stephen (*The Longest Journey*) and George (*A Room with a View*). Burra writes: "Gino, Stephen, George—these are heroes. They represent the same elemental quality as Mrs Woolf's Percival in *The Waves*. But whereas Percival is presented as an adored, desired opposite, a symbol of the unattainable, Mr Forster brings in these characters to make a clash, to conflict with the other side" (Bradbury, 69). Burra further writes: "Gino and George Emerson are very different people, but they represent the same athletic honesty. Gino was 'majestic; he was a part of nature.' 'Centuries of aspiration and culture' were defenceless against the impulses he aroused" (*op. cit.*, 68).

The character of Philip Herriton is no less important than the character of Lilia or that of Gino; rather, in a sense, the character of Philip is of the greatest importance in the novel. In fact, *Where Angels Fear to Tread* may be called a treatise on the Sawstonian Philip's re-education in the Italian school, because the all-intellect, quite 'mechanicalised' and 'de-sensitised' and tradition-bound Philip, when he got himself refreshed by the fresh and free air of the tradition-free Italy, was psychologically reformed or re-educated—he came to know that the Sawstonian way of life was not the only way of life, and that there was another way of life to lead, which was superior to the former—far superior. Forster used the name 'Philip' very significantly: the name Philip "incorporates the Greek word for love and for friend" (Beauman, 24, f. n.). In Italy Philip saw the countenance of real, unrestrained, unstinted and free instinctual love in Miss Caroline Abbott, she being psychologically converted to the Italian humanism under the influence of the Italian climates--natural and social. In the novel, Forster has deliberately forced Philip to swap the life of Sawston with that of Monteriano (Italy), which was one of the principal objectives of the novel. Philip, son to Mrs Herriton, is "the cleverer of the family" of the Herritons (chap. 1). The E.M. Forster-like Philip was a Bar-at-law, but then he was a veritable do-nothing popinjay fellow. He was a book-worm (chap. 2) and had been abundantly tetchy, sentimental, till he was reformed by the open air and naturalness of Italy (chap. 6). After he had fallen love of Miss Abbott, he gave her an assessment of himself: "'Some people are born not to do things. I'm one of them; I never did anything at school or at the Bar. I came out to stop Lilia's marriage [two months ago], and it was too late. I came out intending to get the baby, and I shall return an 'honourable failure'. I never expect anything to happen now, and so I am never disappointed. You would be surprised to know what my great events are. Going to the theatre yesterday, talking to you now—I don't suppose I shall ever meet anything greater. I seem fated to pass through the world without colliding with it or moving it—and I'm sure I cant tell you whether the fate's good or evil. I don't die—I don't fall in love. And if other people die or fall in love they always do it when I'm just not there. You are quite right; life to me is just a spectacle, which—thank God, and thank Italy, and thank you—is now more beautiful and heartening than it has ever been before'" (chap. 8).

Philip was a pampered child of Mrs Herriton, and "All his life he had been her puppet" (chap. 5). He was the younger brother of Charles, the deceased husband of Lilia. He was only one year older than Miss Caroline Abbott, and when Lilia died in Italy of childbirth he was twenty-four years of age. At the beginning of chapter 5, Forster has devoted about a whole passage describing Philip's physical features: "He was tall, weakly-built young man, whose clothes had to be judiciously padded on the shoulder in order to make him pass muster. His face was plain rather than not, and there was a curious mixture in it of good and bad. He had a fine forehead and a good large nose, and both observation and sympathy were in his eyes. But below the nose and eyes all was confusion, and those people who believe that destiny resides in the mouth and chin shook their heads when they looked at him." Philip was quite aware of social stratifications and "social differences" (chap. 2). He hated Italy from the very core of his heart, of course till he visited that country for the second time, this time with Miss Abbott: "Italy was beastly, and Florence station is the centre of beastly Italy" (chap. 6). Philip was of 'imaginative' character and had enough 'enthusiasm' (Tambling, 23). He was an 'aesthetic eunach' (Langman, 131), and 'a keenly sensitive passanger through life' (Tambling, 24). However, in *Where Angels Fear to Tread,* there is no character, besides that of Miss Abbott, that has undergone more changes—the character that has been more reformed in Italy, than the character of Philip. In fact, Philip is the central character of the novel, and not Lilia or Gino or any other character, and the novel's principal concern is the 're-education' of Philip. He was a great Sawstonian conformist at the beginning of the novel, but at the end of it we find that he "appears at least capable of understanding that Sawston is not the world, that it has deficiencies" (Tambling, 23).

Miss Caroline Abbott comes only next to Philip Herriton to be reformed and re-educated in the open-air humanist-liberal atmosphere of Monteriano and thereby get saved from the atrophying and stultifying tradition of the cribbed corner of Sawston. She was the daughter of a widow, intelligent and up-beat. In the very first chapter of *Where Angels Fear to Tread*, Forster gives us a brief description of Miss Abbott: "a tall, grave, rather nice-looking young lady." She was 10 years younger to Lilia, i.e. she was about 23 years of age when she went to Monteriano with a view to saving Lilia's son. In chapter 2 of the novel, Forster provides us with a frame of Miss Caroline Abbott's mind: "She was good, quiet, dull, and amiable, and young only because she was twenty-three: there was nothing in her appearance or manner to suggest the fire of youth." In the same chapter, Forster further tells us about her:

"All her life [upto age 23] had been spent at Sawston with a dull and amiable father, and her pleasant, pallid face, bent on some respectable charity, was a familiar object of the Sawston streets. Why she had ever wished to leave them was surprising; but as she truly said, I am John Bull to the backbone, yet I want to see Italy, just once. Everybody says it is marvellous, and that one gets no idea of it from books at all." The irony is that this hard-boiled Sawstonian was completely converted into an enthusiastic romantic Monterianonian by the touchstone of the spirit of Italy when she visited that country with the mission of rescuing Lilia's child.

That Miss Abbott possessed some winsome physical and mental qualities is attested by the fact that even Philip, the 'aesthetic eunach' was attracted to her: "Miss Abbott, between Sawston and Charing Cross, revealed qualities which he [Philip] had never guessed her to possess. Without being exactly original, she did show a commendable intelligence, and though at times she was gauche and even uncourtly, he felt that here was a person whom it might be well to cultivate" (chap. 5). Mrs Herriton, Philip's mother, noticed, and told Philip, that Miss Abbott "has a mind of extraordinary delicacy" (*ibid.*) and Philip, for himself, knew that "her nature was in the main generous and upright" (*ibid.*). Her financial condition was not of course cozy, for she used to borrow or receive money from Philip and his mother, from time to time, as aids. She went to Monteriano, at first, as a chaperon to Lilia, and picked up some Italian, which sometimes helped her in her works as a dragoman or interpreter between Lilia and Gino, and thereby helped love grow between them (chap. 2). But, even during this same time she was irresistibly attracted by the regular physical beauty of Gino, as is obvious from her comment on Gino's physical charm: "'A born artist's model'" (chap. 7).

Miss Abbott had a wonderful and rather awe-inspiring sense of obligation or duty; duty she counted as sacred. We may recall here that Forster first chose the title 'From a Sense of Duty' for this novel, and arguably he chose this title keeping in mind Miss Abbott's mighty sense of the duty on her part to rescue Lilia's child (and the consequent surprising changes in her character and in the character of Philip). In the novel itself Forster writes about Miss Abbott's sense of duty: "The child's [Gino's or Lilia's child's] welfare was a sacred duty to her, not a matter of pride or even of sentiment" (chap. 5).

Where Angels Fear to Tread is a story of change of attitude towards life not only of Philip but also of Miss Abbott. When she went to Italy, along with Philip, for the second time, she was irresistibly drawn to the regular curvature of the musculature of Gino's physique, and consequently her Sawstonian hangover left her along with her innate reticence and reserve. The weather and the social milieu of Monteriano (a fictitious place supposed to be in Italy) spiritually or mentally converted her (on her second visit) into an uncouth and firy romantic, like Lilia earlier had been. Her brisk conversion to romanticism had so great an initial impact upon her that she immediately felt infatuated by the personal beauty of Gino. After returning to England from Monteriano, she narrated to Philip Gino's physical attractiveness: "'Very good-looking. All his features are good, and he is well built—though I dare say English standards would find him too short'" (chap. 2). And when Philip asked if she liked him, she blandly replied: "'As far as I have seen him, I do'" (*ibid.*).

In a sense, Miss Abbott was a queer soul—she would have been inordinately drawn to the beautiful and the strange. In Monteriano, on her second visit, and before her attempt to steal Gino's son, Philip once put before her a very piquant, ascorbic and brief question: "'In which capacity have you come to Monteriano—spy or traitor?'" And without a moment's hesitation she answered: "'Spy!'" And immediately afterwards she was running her finger over a part of the gothic window of the hotel: "with her finger she was following the curves of the moulding as if they *might feel beautiful and strange*" (*emphasis added,* chap. 6). It was also her penchant, or rather insuperable romantic drive for the beautiful, and the strange or the *outre,* that pushed her towards loving Gino. Her love for Gino was deep and genuine. While on her second visit to Monteriano, she told Philip that Gino was "'charming, but he's no fool; he conquered me last year'" (chap. 7).

Miss Abbott believed that of all the members of the 'rescue party' it was "she alone [who] could do battle with Gino, because she alone understood him" (*ibid.*).

Miss Abbott certainly went to Monteriano for the second time quite on her sense of duty, and "not as a matter of pride or even of sentiment"; she thought that in Monteriano, the "magic city of vice", Gino's son could not "grow up happy and pure" (chap. 5) and so it was obligatory upon herself to fetch that child to England, by hook or crook, to save it. But, quite unexpectedly, she was torn away from the Sawstonian [English] tradition, root and branch, and was initiated into the mystery of romanticism—Italian romanticism. She was totally metamorphosed, spiritually. She was newly educated, like Philip, by the naturalness and naivete of Monteriano. She learnt the Italian mentality and manners, and also liked them. When, for instance, Philip suggested that she might enter into Gino's room with the view to stealing the child, she retorted: "'Eighteen months ago I might have done such a thing. But I trust I have learnt how to behave by now'" (chap. 6). Miss Abbott was so changed by Italy that Philip was struck by her alteration. He noticed her changes quite clearly: "And Miss Abbott—she, too, was beautiful in her way, for all her gaucheness and conventionality. She really cared about life, and tried to live it properly" (*ibid.*).

Harriet Herriton was a young lady "pale, large, tall," as Perfetta described her in chap. 6 of *Where Angels Fear to Tread*. She had "burly obtuseness" (chap. 7) and a "gloomy peevish creed" (chap. 5)—she always remained gloomy, and exhibited manicurism and fatuousness in everything, particularly in her moral and religious concerns. She had been in excellent relationship with her mother, Mrs Herriton, "though they had not a great deal in common" (chap. 1). "Harriet's education had been almost too successful [in the traditional English sense]. As Philip once said, she had 'bolted all the cardinal virtues and couldn't digest them'. Though pious and patriotic, and a great moral asset for the house, she lacked that pliancy and tact which her mother so much valued, and had expected her to pick up for herself. Harriet, if she had been allowed, would have driven Lilia to an open rupture, and, what was worse, she would have done the same to Philip two years before, when he returned full of passion for Italy, ridiculing Sawston and its ways" (chap. 1). Harriet was a radical or conservative Sawstonian. Her portrayal in the novel may remind one of Adela Quested of *A Passage to India;* she, like Adela and unlike Lilia, Philip and Miss Abbott, could not acclimatise in a foreign land, and so she, again like Adela and unlike Lilia, Philip and Miss Abbott, had to have some symbolic sufferances, for instances, "smuts flew in her eyes" on her rail journey to Italy (chap. 6) and after she reached Italy she was struck by the heat of the sun "like a hand laid upon her mouth" (*ibid.*). There may also be found at least a non-serious similarity between Harriet and Honeychurch of *A Room with a View,* for both of them went to Italy with Baedeker's book *Central Italy* (*ibid.*).

Forster has described the character of Mrs Herriton mostly in chapter 5 of *Where Angels Fear to Tread,* looking at her principally through the eyes of Philip who saw her from very close quarters, and wondered: "Her life, he saw, was without meaning. To what purpose was her diplomacy, her insincerity, her continued repression of vigour? Did they make anyone better or happier? Did they even bring happiness to herself? Harriet with her gloomy peevish creed, Lilia with her clutches after pleasures, were after all more divine than this well-ordered, active, useless machine" (chap. 5). The essence of Mrs Herriton's character, of course if we trust to the truth of Philip's observation, is greatly revealed through the above observation of Philip about his own mother. Mrs Herriton had not so compassionate a heart as to bring back from Italy Lilia's son after her death, but she was agile to bring the child only grudging Miss Abbott's genuine sense of duty. In this regard she was to an extent hypocritic. However, it is interesting to note that Mrs Herriton's desire to save Lilia's son is prefigured in her wish to save all the peas from birds, described in just the beginning chapter of *Where Angels Fear to Tread.*

(v)

Fantasy and prophecy are, according to Forster, two vital and enlivening components of novel, like plot, characters, etc. He tells us that whenever the novelist transmutes reality into a good novel, something 'extra' is introduced into the translation—something that is not real but fantastical. There is something angelic or ghostly in a fiction which may be compared, says Forster in his *Aspects of the Novel,* with the side-shows in an exhibition which are an 'extra' of the exhibition. Fantasy is something like the supernatural—unreal and eerie—but having an uncanny connection with the reality. In chapters 6 and 8 (about the middle of the novel) of *Where Angels Fear to Tread,* Forster has introduced two 'supernatural' or eerie or uncommon episodes or situations of Italy, one touching Philip, and the other Miss Abbott, both of whom, incidentally, were transformed in Italy.

In chapter 6, we find Philip's vision glued to the tower of the Collegiate Church of Santa Deodata, inspired as he was by the appealing attraction of Miss Abbott, and forgetful as he remained of his duty of rescuing Lilia's child: "One of the towers, rough as any other, was topped by a cross—the tower of the Collegiate Church of Santa Deodata. She was a holy maiden of the Dark Ages, the city's patron saint, and sweetness and barbarity mingle strangely in her story. So holy was she that all her life she lay upon her back in the house of her mother, refusing to eat, refusing to play, refusing to work. The devil, envious of such sanctity, tempted her in various ways. He dangled grapes above her, he showed her fascinating toys, he pushed soft pillows beneath her aching head. When all proved vain he tripped up the mother and flung her downstairs before her very eyes. But so holy was the saint that she never picked her mother up, but lay upon her back through all, and thus assured her throne in Paradise. She was only fifteen when she died, which shows how much is within the reach of any school-girl. Those who think her life was unpractical need only think of the victories upon Poggibonsi, San Gimignano, Volterra, Siena itself—all gained through the invocation of her name; they need only look at the church which rose over her grave. The grand schemes for a marble facade were never carried out, and it is brown unfinished stone until this day. But for the inside Giotto was summoned to decorate the walls of the nave. Giotto came—that is to say, he did not come, German research having decisively proved—but at all events the nave is covered with frescoes, and so are two chapels in the left transept, and the arch into the choir, and there are scraps in the choir itself. There the decoration stopped, till in the full spring of the Renaissance, a great painter came to pay a few weeks' visit to his friend the Lord of Monteriano. In the intervals between the banquets and the discussions on Latin etymology and the dancing, he would stroll over the church, and there in the fifth chapel to the right he has painted two frescoes of the death and burial of Santa Deodata. That is why Baedeker gives the place a star." In chapter 8, we see that Miss Abbott had had a vision in the precinct of the Santa Deodata where she met Philip: "For lo! she had a vision: the head and shoulder of St Augustine were sliding like some miraculous enamel along the roughcast wall. It is a gentle saint who is content with half another saint to see her die. In her death, as in her life, Santa Deodata did not accomplish much."

The hypnotically working operatic influence upon Miss Abbott (in chapter 6), who grew up in the mechanised Sawstonian culture, due to which she was radically reformed into a 'natural' and warm human being may also be taken to be a supernatural phenomenon. Philip, Harriet and Miss Abbott went to the opera *Lucia di Lammermoor* (by Sir Walter Scott). The ebullient dithyrambic spirit, generated during the performances, shook off the ennui and inertia from the soul of Miss Abbott, and she rose up to the occasion, as if in a trance. The narrator tells us: "So the opera proceeded. The singers drew inspiration from the audience, and the two great sextettes were rendered not unworthy. Miss Abbott fell into the spirit of the thing. She, too, chatted and laughed and applauded and encored, and rejoiced in the existence of beauty" (*Where Angels Fear to Tread*, chap.6).

The prophetic "is a tone of voice", says Forster. Unlike fantasy, prophecy is humourless, serious and visionary. In his *Aspects of the Novel,* he writes that fantasy and prophecy "are alike in having gods, and unlike in the gods they have." Fantasy belongs to the mysterious world of the middle ages, and prophecy "transcends our abilities" (*Aspects of the Novel*) and shows us the direction we should move to or imparts us a new knowledge about life. The prophetic element of *Where Angels Fear to Tread* works as a morale that presents itself through Philip's and Miss Caroline Abbott's new knowledge acquired in Italy that only materialism and discipline would not suffice for making a man or a woman complete and contended without at least a touch of 'spirituality' and naturalness, and that not only cohesion, that requires discipline, but also chaos, which is prompted by individuality, is salubrious to us, nay is essential for us. They learned that the Sawstonian 'refinement' destroys the soul of man whereas the 'unrefinement' of Monteriano preserves it. So, Miss Abbott was magnetically drawn to Gino, and was reformed by him, and Philip was saved by the real love that took birth in his heart in his closeness to Miss Abbott. This is the morale—the edification or prophecy—of the novel, with which Forster has ended it. At the end of the novel, we see that Miss Abbott intensely felt her love for Gino and so failed to requite Philip's love for her, and admitted that now she was not on the side of the Sawstonian 'refinement.' She politely tells the befuddled Philip: "'...Get over supposing I'm refined. That's what puzzles you. Get over that.'" And "As she spoke she seemed to be transformed, and to have no part with refinement or unrefinement any longer. Out of this wreck there was revealed to him something indestructible—something which she, who had given it, could never take away." What is this 'something' that is 'indestructible'? It is what Forster valued the most—love: it is Miss Abbott's love for Gino. She tells Philip at the fag end of the novel about Gino and about how she was 'saved': "'...If he had asked me, I might have given myself body and soul. That would have been the end of my rescue party. But all through he took me for a superior being—a goddess. I who was worshipping every inch of him, and every word he spoke. And that saved me.'"

(vi)

Two other aspects of the novel, according to Forster, are its 'pattern' and 'rhythm.' He borrowed the term 'pattern,' from the discipline of painting, and the term 'rhythm' from that of music. Pattern is related to the plot and through its relation to the plot is also related to the material of the novel. Pattern adds beauty to the plot, and is more durable than the plot. Forster tells us that once we have finished the novel, the plot departs but the pattern remains in our memory. The pattern is like symmetry, which Forster, in his *Aspects of the Novel,* explains with the help of Henry James' *The Ambassadors* where Chad and Strether change their original places or positions, making a figure like an hour-glass. Forster was much influenced by Henry James, and perhaps this is the reason why the pattern of *Where Angels Fear to Tread* has been like an hour-glass, due to Philip and Caroline Abbott changing their places, being reformed by the Italian influence. The rhythm in novel is like the rhythm in music, as Forster tells us in his *Aspects of the Novel:* "in music fiction is likely to find its nearest parallel." He says that rhythm is "repetition plus variation." In *Where Angels Fear to Tread* we come across a few things which recur, but they recur with variations. Lilia marries for the second time but her second marriage is different from her first; Philip and Miss Abbott go to Italy twice, but their second journey brings for them quite different experiences; etc.

(vii)

The plot of *Where Angels Fear to Tread* is built on a tour, on the interface between two divergent cultures—one of England, another of Italy. This is not unique of the novel, for, in fact, the plots of all the novels of Forster are built upon cultural relations, or on cultural conflicts or incongruities. Immediately after leaving Cambridge in 1900, Forster unexpectedly got an opportunity to visit Italy, and he visited that country. This tour, for the first time, gave him the shocking experience that cultures are seldom homogeneous and that cultures are conflicting. This may be obvious from the fact that his ever first completed and published fictional production, the short story 'The Story of a Panic', an essentially Forsterian output, was written not very later than his coming back to England from Italy. Before this Italian visit, he was feeling uneasy in the crippling cultural climate of the English middle class, and after that tour he had been fantasying physical and spiritual escape from that climate, and this escape-wish of his is noticeable both in 'The Story of a Panic' and *Where Angels Fear to Tread*. For, we see that in the short story Eustace escapes into the homosexual world of Gennaro to save himself, and likewise, in the novel, Lilia, actually, and Philip and Miss Caroline Abbott, imaginatively, enter into the world of Gino. An instance of cultural conflict between England and Italy Forster has shown us in *Where Angels Fear to Tread* through a minor bickering between Lilia and Gino (chapter 4) where the narrator tells us about the couple: "His [Gino's] wife was a very ordinary woman, and why should her ideas differ from his own? No one realized that more than personalities were engaged [in the bickering or 'struggle' between Lilia and Gino]; that the struggle was national; that generations of ancestors, good, bad, or indifferent, forbade the Latin man to be chivalrous to the northern woman, the northern woman to forgive the Latin man." Forster has suggested that cultural incongruence can be resolved only with "kindness and a little attention" (*Where Angels Fear to Tread,* chap. 4)—only with love—and this he has also told us through his introduction of the episode of Gokul Ashtami festival in *A Passage to India*.

In *Where Angels Fear to Tread,* as in his other novels, Forster has shown cultural conflict through interactions among divers characters. The cultural conflict is actually the clash between two systems of morality: that of England and that of Italy which is 'akin to Nature.' Peter Burra writes in his article 'The Novels of E.M. Forster': "In *Where Angels Fear to Tread* the clash is between the world of conventional morality and a world more akin to Nature. To heighten the contrast the conflicting elements are vested in England and Italy. 'More than personalities were engaged...the struggle was national.' It is between North and South, between Culture and Beast" (Bradbury, 64-65). On the one hand, Philip, Harriet and Miss Abbott are given to the conventional morality that demands conformity to the English tradition of rationality predominating over emotion, of uniformity and discipline; and, on the other hand, Gino, the Italian, is 'akin to Nature,' is emotional and unconventional.

Forster believed that as there may be cultural conflicts on the national level, so there may be cultural conversions on the individual level. In *Where Angels Fear to Tread* he suggests cultural conversion of Philip and Miss Abbott through tourism, through a connection between rationality and emotion. Their tour was not so much geographical as psychological—their tourism was what James Buzard calls 'tourism from within' (Tambling, 14), i.e. they moved from one cultural climate to another, and swapped their original English culture for the Italian culture. Philip, for one, was born and grew up in the tradition-bound mechanical culture of England. He was imaginative and enthusiastic, and yet life to him was 'just a spectacle' (*Where Angels Fear to Tread,* chap. 8). He told Miss Abbott about himself: "I seem fated to pass through the world without colliding with it or moving it—and I'm sure I cant tell you whether the fate's good or evil. I don't die—I don't fall in love..." (*ibid.*). But he was completely reformed by the warm Italian cultural climate, he was saved from the cool of the English cultural climate. He confessed to Miss Abbott his conversion: "'...You are right; life to me is just a spectacle, which—thank God, and thank Italy, and thank you—is now more beautiful and heartening than it has ever been before'" (*ibid.*). Lilia, earlier, had been so reformed by the Italian culture, and so was reformed, almost simultaneously with Philip, Miss Abbott, and, again so was reformed Adela Quested, though partially and possibly temporarily, by the warmer cultural climate of India in *A Passage to India.* One great factor contributing to cultural conversion is romantic love which, Forster believed, is possible between two persons of two different and distant cultures. At the beginning of chapter 30 of *A Passage to India,* Forster writes: "Between people of distant climes there is always the possibility of romance".

(viii)

Who is the hero of *Where Angels Fear to Tread,* if we may ask the question? Complex as Forster's novels are, it is difficult to identify the heroes of his novels. Further, Forster did not believe in the concept of hero. However, Peter Burra, in his article 'The Novels of E.M. Forster', takes Gino to be the hero of *Where Angels Fear to Tread,* like, according to him, Stephen is the hero *of The Longest Journey* and George *of A Room with a View* (Bradbury, 69). But James Buzard, in his article 'Forster's Trespasses', calls Philip Herriton the "reluctant hero" of *Where Angels Fear to Tread* (Tambling, 20), and perhaps Buzard is right. For, Gino is too passive to be the hero. On the other hand, the Sawston-trained but imaginative and enthusiastic Philip's attitudinal changes in the warm Italian climate is the intended message of the novel, and so Philip should be regarded as its hero. Earlier, to Philip, as we have already said, life was "just a spectacle" but his Italian experiences taught him that "Sawston is not the world, that it has deficiencies" (*op. cit.,* 23). He was purified and ennobled by the warm Italian climate: "...Italy really purifies and ennobles all who visit her" (*Where Angels Fear to Tread,* chap. 1). Only after his reformation or conversion could he recognise the beauty of human beings and things. In the novel, the narrator tells us that in Italy Philip "underwent conversion. He was saved" (*op. cit.,* chap. 9) and that then he recognised the beauty of Miss Abbott and spiritually fell in love of her: "He had reached love by the spiritual path: her thoughts and her goodness and her nobility had moved him first, and now her whole body and all its gestures had become transfigured by them. The beauties that are called obvious—the beauties of her hair and her voice and her limbs—he had noticed these last" (*op. cit.,* chap. 10). Miss Abbott, on the other hand, had been seeking for 'real life' in Italy and she got it through her recognition of 'beauty and splendour'. On her second visit to

Italy she told Philip about her awareness of romance during her first visit to Italy: "'it's the only tune I've ever gone into what my father calls real life'.... All that winter I seemed to be waking up to beauty and splendour and I don't know what; and when the spring came, I wanted to fight against the things I hated—mediocrity and dullness and spitefulness and society. I actually hated society for a day or two at Monteriano" (*op. cit.,* chap. 5). If we may, therefore, accept Philip as the hero of *Where Angels Fear to Tread,* we may regard Miss Abbott as its heroine. The novel is, in fact, created around the story of Philip and Miss Abbott though their story seems to be overshadowed by that of Lilia and Gino.

(ix)

James Buzard, in the same article of his, says that Forster, who believed in the necessity of the body, in man's corporeality in addition to his spirituality, was always ready to punish those of his fictional characters who denied the right of the body. He believed that man, to be a whole man, needs to respond to both the call of the spirit as well as that of the body. In his opinion, the Sawstonian spirituality only desiccates man to his death, and for the best nourishment of the human being both spirituality and bestiality are desiderata. Sawston provides only with spiritual nourishment, and so, after being reformed by the air of Italy, Miss Abbott in *Where Angels Fear to Tread* (chap. 5) confesses to Philip: "'I hated Sawston, you see.'" However, Forster would not tolerate sin against the body but seek vengence for the sinner In 'The Eternal Moment' he punished Miss Raby by soon making her body ugly and withered, and, likewise, in *Where Angels Fear to Tread* he obviously punishes Harriet, Philip and Caroline Abbott (incidentally all unmarried like Miss Raby). James Buzard writes in the same article of his: "In 'The Eternal Moment', Miss Raby's 'ugly withered' body expressed the corruption of the new Vorta that she had helped to create; in *Where Angels Fear to Tread* the bodies of the Sawston representatives also suffer the sins committed against Monteriano. Forster makes the bigoted Harriet endure a variety of minor physical ailments throughout the novel—someone steps on her corns, she gets smuts in her eyes, and so forth. The characters with more initial promise, like Philip and Lilia's companion Caroline Abbott, bear greater physical burdens for their complicity in the Sawston onslaught. Philip surfers a broken arm in the carriage accident, followed by a dark parody of the anti-tourist's goal, 'true contact' with the alien—the grief-stricken Gino beats him nearly to death" (Tambling, 24). Miss Caroline Abbott also heavily suffered. She fell headlong in love of Gino, after Lilia's death, but before the love could turn into marriage, she came to learn about Gino's second settled marriage elsewhere. Forster valued the life of the goddess Pasiphae who fell in love with a bull, meaning he upheld the conjunction of the body and the soul, and the satisfaction of both.

(x)

From *Where Angels Fear to Tread,* we may gather Forster's impression of Italy. According to him, the people of Italy are natural and warm. In chapter 3 of *Where Angels Fear to Tread,* he has satirically given a glimpse of some aspects of the life in Italy as he saw it to be. He has written: Italy is such a delightful place to live in if you happen to be a man. There one may enjoy that exquisite luxury of Socialism—that true Socialism which is based not on equality of income or character, but on the equality of manners. In the democracy of the *caffe* or the street the great question of our life has been solved, and the brotherhood of man is a reality. But it is accomplished at the expense of the sisterhood of women. ...All your lives you will meet under the open air, the only roof-tree of the South, under which he will spit and swear, and you will drop your h's, and nobody will think the worse of either. "Meanwhile the women—they have, of course, their house and their church, with its admirable and frequent services, to which they are escorted by the maid. Otherwise they do not go out much, for it is not genteel to walk, and you are too poor to keep a carriage. Occasionally you will take them to the *caffe* or theatre, and immediately all your wonted acquaintance there desert you, except those few who are expecting and expected to marry into your family. It is all very sad. But one conclusion emerges—life is very pleasant in Italy if you are a man." Another aspect of the Italian life may be found in the 'Opera scene' of *Where Angels Fear to Tread* (chap. 6) where we find a pandemonium: "But soon the boxes began to fill,... Families greeted each other across the auditorium. People in the pit hailed their brothers and sons in the chorus, and told them how well they were singing. When Lucia appeared by the fountain there was loud applause, and cries of 'Welcome to Monteriano!'" There was 'bamboo clothes-horse' on the stage. At one time Lucia advanced to the clothes-horse and created an awkward spectacle: "With a scream of amazement and joy she embraced the animal, pulled out one or two practicable blossoms, pressed them to her lips, and flung them into her admirers. They flung them back, with loud melodius cries, and a little boy in one of the stage-boxes snatched up his sister's carnations and offered them. 'Che carino' exclaimed the singer. She darted at the little boy and kissed him. Now the noise became tremendous. 'Silence! silence!' shouted many old gentlemen behind. 'Let the divine creature continue!' But the young men in the adjacent box were imploring Lucia to extend her civility to them. She refused with a humorous expressive gesture. One of them hurled a bouquet at her. She spurned it with her foot. Then, encouraged by the roars of the audience, she picked it up and tossed it to them" (*ibid.*). Such pranks and coquettishness of the women of Italy is also referred to by Shakespeare in *Othello* (III, iii, 229-231) where Iago tells Othello:

> In Venice they do let heaven see the pranks
> They dare not show their husbands; their best conscience
> Is not to leave't undone, but keep't unknown.

But everything of Italy is not despicable, says Forster: "There is something magestic in the bad taste of Italy; it is not the bad taste of a country which knows no better, it has not the nervous vulgarity of England, or the blinded vulgarity of Germany. It observes beauty, and chooses to pass it by. But it attains to beauty's confidence" (*ibid.*).

In chapter 6 of *Where Angels Fear to Tread,* Philip tells Miss Abbott that "Italians are essentially dramatic: they look on death and love as spectacles." And lastly, there may not really be many *views* of Italy—geographic or scenic—in *A Room with a View,* but there are many in *Where Angels Fear to Tread.* Philip asked Miss Abbott, "'The view from the Rocca—wasn't it fine?'" and she gently answered, "'What isn't fine here?'" meaning, in Italy (chap. 6). Such fine views are galore in *Where Angels Fear to Tread.*

(xi)

Where Angels Fear to Tread is written in the vein of Jane Austen (1775-1817), but then there is a difference between Austen's technique and Forster's. Austen had her preformed moral and social standards with which she strove to judge her characters and correct their inadequacies, but Forster had 'lack of valid standards,' for which reason he could not decide the rightness or wrongness of the behaviour of his characters, and so he had no choice but to judge his characters with 'shifting and inadequate standards' or by situating them in two different cultures so as to make the readers capable of judging the characters for themselves according to their individual tastes. Thus we find that in *Where Angels Fear to Tread* Forster has situated the principal characters, excepting only Gino, alternately in two different cultures—the English and the Italian—to bring into relief their essential attributes, and to help the readers judge the characters with their individual standards.

The influence of Henry James (1843-1916) on this novel is not to be overlooked, at the least in so far as it shows cultural contrast between the Sawstonians and the Italians. James' concern in his novels was to bring into relief the cultural differences between the older civilization of Europe and the newer civilization of America, and also the influence of the older civilization upon the newer civilization. His most famous novel *The Portrait of a Lady,* for instance, 'is a study of various American characters transplanted into a European environment.' Likewise, in *Where Angels Fear to Tread* Forster is concerned with the cultural contrast, nay, conflict, between the English culture and the culture of Italy, and has shown how the cold English culture may be replaced, subplanted, by the warm Italian culture when an Englishman comes in contact with the latter.

(xii)

Peter Burra, in his article 'The Novels of E.M. Forster', says that Forster has written his novels with many 'clues and chains' for the ease of the reader in following the course of the narrative (Bradbury, 61-62). Burra calls the clues 'ruses'. He says that with the help of the 'clues' Forster has been able to weave the different incidents of a novel into a neat and complete plot. By the clue Burra means saying something much earlier that happens much later on. Burra says that the mechanism of the clue unites the earlier incident, where the fore-knowledge of the later incident was given through oblique reference or innuendo, with the later incident, and this process of unification runs through all Forster novels, including *Where Angels Fear to Tread.* Burra, by way of explaining his point, has given an example of the clue he found in *Where Angels Fear to Tread:* "Philip is asking Caroline about her conversation with Gino. 'And of what did you talk?' 'The weather—there will be rain, he says, by tomorrow evening...' etc. The torrential storm which results in the carriage accident in which Gino's child dies is thus prepared for seventy pages before it occurs" (Bradbury, 62). This is something like the making of the prophecy of the witches in *Macbeth* 'Fair is foul, and foul is fair' and the materialisation of the prophecy much later.

However, Forster is well-known for his frequent uses of the word 'muddle' or its variants and for his repetitious employments of the tricks of journeys and tea-parties in his fictional works, and these things are to be found in *Where Angels Fear to Tread.* We read about tea or tea-parties in this novel, for instance, four times in chapter 3 alone, and come across Forster's fond words 'muddle,' 'meddle,' 'muddle-headed' and 'muddling' at least six times in chapter 6 and 8. And, to say the least, tour or journey is, as if, the matrix out of which Forster's story unfolds itself, and in this regard *Where Angels Fear to Tread* is no exception. Interestingly, Forster's another ploy in plot-construction—'sudden death'—is also not absent in *Where Angels Fear to Tread:* Charles Herriton, the first husband of Lilia, dies suddenly.

(xiii)

One may find many parallels between Forster's first novel, *Where Angels Fear to Tread* and his last—*A Passage to India.* For one thing, as a certain critic has remarked, Forster novels are repetitious, or he has really written only a single novel, for the themes and the myths of his various novels are essentially variants of a single theme or a single myth. However, some of the points of similarity between Forster's first and last novels are the following. Firstly, in both the novels Forster deals with two divergent cultures or races and their interactions. In *Where Angels Fear to Tread,* the two cultures are the Sawstonian or English culture and the Italian culture, and, in *A Passage to India,* the two cultures are the English and the Indian cultures, or, the two races involved are the English and the Indian peoples. Secondly, in *Where Angels Fear to Tread,* Philip and Miss Abbott, not to speak of Lilia, were reformed in Italy, but Harriet stuck to the English culture inspite of her journey to Italy. In *A Passage to India,* likewise, Mrs Moore was orientalised or Indianised, but not any other English people. Thirdly, Harriet despised the Italian culture, in which, as in the cult of Pasiphae, the soul as well as the body are equally respected, suffered retributions implicitly for 'sinning' against the body (at the hand of Forster). For instance, at the beginning of chapter 6 of *Where Angels Fear to Tread* we hear that when Philip and Harriet were touring by train over Verona, the scorching heat of summer struck them "like a hand laid over the mouth" (recall that Adela Quested felt something like a hand ("naked vile thing") over her mouth in the heated interior of the fatal cave she entered into with Aziz). Then, "Harriet's sketch-book was stolen, and the bottle of amonia in her trunk burst over her prayer book, so that purple patches appeared on all her clothes." Then, as she was going through Mantua at four in the morning, Philip made her look out of the window because it was Virgil's birthplace, and "a smut flew in her eye, and Harriet with a smut in her eye was notorious." Adela Quested, also, after she nervously ran out of the fatal cave and was running helter-skelter was bleeding for pricks of thorns. Fourthly, in chapter 10, or the last chapter, of *Where Angels Fear to Tread* we see the reformed Philip and Miss Abbott, when they were travelling by train back towards England, jolted towards each other by the jactitation of the train—a symbol of unconsumated union: "The train seemed to shake him towards her. He was resolved that though a dozen people were looking, he would yet take her in his arm." In *A Passage to India* also we find that Adela imagined in the fatal cave that Aziz was intending to jolt against or collide with herself. Again, when the car of the Nawab was bumped Miss Derek collided with him inside the vehicle. There is, again, a similarity between the satirical 'opera scene' of *Where Angels Fear to Tread* (chap. 6) and the satirical 'trial scene' of *A Passage to India* (chap. 24). Further instances of similarities may be found, but, perhaps, so far is enough. Similarities between *Where Angels Fear to Tread* and 'The Eternal Moment' have already been spoken of; only this needs to be said that, interestingly, the name of the central character of the short story, Ginori and that of the novel, Gino, ring alike. Again, as has already been suggested, there is also a considerable similarity between Lilia and the central character of Henry James' *The Portrait of a Lady* Isabel Archer. Both the characters have been drawn against the background of alien cultures.

(xiv)

The reaction to *Where Angels Fear to Tread,* soon after its publication in 1905, was mixed. "The first review [of the novel] appeared on 29 September [1905] and it was in *The Times Literary Supplement,* in seventy-five words it found the novel original, well-written and sometimes witty" (Beauman,

177). "*The Manchester Guardian* disliked the title [of the novel] because it found the book 'not mawkish or sentimental or commonplace' as the title suggested, but approvingly compared Morgan [Forster] with George Meredith; the *Glasgow Herald* thought it the most enjoyable book we have read for many a day'; and so it went on until, just before Christmas, the *Spectator* published a 1000-word unsigned review of such sensitivity and such perception that Morgan must have been almost surprised that he had been so well understood. When he read that 'the dominant impression left on the mind of the present writer is that under the stress of opportunity primitive instincts reassert themselves in the most carefully educated and studiously repressed natures'...he would never need to feel that he was speaking into a void" (*ibid.*).

In the modern world of criticism, criticism of *Where Angels Fear to Tread* has been both extreme and moderate. A.S. Collins, in his *English Literature of the Twentieth Century,* writes about the novel: "Told at no great length, with an agreeable irony, the novel makes its points clearly, and its rather inconclusive ending is natural enough. There is, however, something naive in the way in which Forster depicts his products of Sawston, making Harriet so black and Caroline so open-eyed in her wonder at elemental human nature. The characters indeed are types conceived by a witty young moralist, whose sense of humour is sometimes shut off by his moral preoccupation" (Collins, 198).

One of the front-ranking critics, who has dealt at length with all the novels of Forster, is John Sayre Martin. Martin, in his *E.M. Forster: The Endless Journey,* has critically evaluated all the six novels of Forster (as well as his short stories). He, in that book, has begun his discussion on *Where Angels Fear to Tread* with a shattering attack on the novel, saying that the novel deals with an unbelieveable story and that very melodramatically: "The most patently melodramatic of the six [novels of Forster], *Where Angels Fear to Tread* is as laced with implausibility as an Elizabethan tragedy and, like the latter, requires of the modern reader a generous suspension of disbelief. No modern family—and probably few Edwardian ones—would assume the proprietary interest in a widowed daughter-in-law and her child that the Herritons assume in Lilia and Irma. No modern daughter-in-law would for one minute tolerate such an interest. And if she chose to remarry, whether foreigner or otherwise—the choice, she would firmly insist, would be her own business. That her former in-laws, moreover, would actually try, after her death in childbirth, to 'rescue' her baby from its foreign father, even to the point of kidnapping it, is hard enough to believe. But grant the kidnapping and the consequent accidental death of the infant, what are we to think when the child's grief-stricken father not only refuses to report the crime to the police but almost immediately forgives the kidnappers?" (Martin, 13). Frankly, Martin's comments cannot be gainsaid, and yet he is not unhappy about the 'implausibility' of the story, because he understands that Forster only needed a semblance of a story for his moral allegory that the novel, in fact, is. Martin writes: "the novel's implausibilities, however, are not simply attributable to a cavalier disregard for realism. Rather they stem from Forster's instinct for allegory. In traditional allegory the clash of simplified characters embodying absolute moral values almost inevitably leads to far-fetched incidents. And so it is in *Where Angels Fear to Tread,* where the supporting characters and settings generally express clear-cut moral alternatives" (*ibid.*).

Martin reinforces his claim that the novel is allegoric by referring to the symbolism Forster has pumped into it. Martin writes: "Forster heightens the novel's allegorical dimension by means of several symbolically suggestive features. The smuts that afflict Harriet's eyes are an obvious symbol. The St. Gothard tunnel recalls innumerable romantic passageways between two worlds, one generally more desirable than the other. On the Italian side of the tunnel stands the Campanile of Airolo, an ironic emblem of aspiration that seems to Lilia, when she first sees it, to presage the future" (Martin, 21). Martin has found symbolism also in the town of Monteriano:

"Symbolically viewed Monteriano is a halfway house between hell and heaven. Its towers, its church, its patron saint combine to suggest its celestial aspirations; yet its life, as the novel so clearly shows, is capable of tapping demonic springs" (*ibid.*). Martin has also found an impress of Dante's *Divine Comedy* in the novel: "If Montenano is a purgatory, the little wood at the base of the hill on which the town is set recalls Dante's 'selva obscura', the dark forest in which the poet is lost at the beginning of *Divine Comedy*" (Martin, 22).

It generally happens that the first novel of a writer proves to be autobiographical, and Forster's first novel *Where Angels Fear to Tread* is no exception, for in it Philip's character has been drawn following Forster's own nature. John Sayre Martin, in a foot-note in his book *E.M. Forster: The Endless Journey,* writes: "In the MS of the novel in King's College Library, Cambridge, there is a long sentimental passage in which Forster reminisces about some of the friends he made in Italy. He then remarks, 'So it was with Philip, my true and tried acquaintance: who on this occasion, as on so many others, feels and behaves as I do.' "In his interview for the *Paris Review* (Spring 1953) Forster confesses to the resemblance between Philip, Rickie Elliot, Cecil Vyse, and himself" (Martin, 15). Philip is a romantically coloured idealist, like Forster, but unlike him he is sentimental. This sentimentality has to an extent marred the beauty of the novel. Martin writes: "The strain of romantic idealism that Forster, when he wrote his first novel, shared with Philip sometimes betrays him into sentimentality—into a tendency to inflate a subject beyond the limits of its nature. Of Gino he asserts that 'he was that glorius invariable creature, a man' (...) and of Lilia, unhappy in her marriage, he declares—perhaps half facetiously, but only half—that 'not Cordelia nor Imogen more deserves our tears'" (Martin, 25). However, the simple but suspending romantic story, the well-knit plot, the gentle satire, the salubrious comedy, the coruscating and crisp language and wit and light-hartedness of the novel are simply unforgetable. Despite his critical points against the novel, Martin has much of commendation for it. He writes: "Despite the seriousness of its theme and the violence and suffering with which it deals, *Where Angels Fear to Tread* is a comic novel, infused with wit and gaity" (*ibid.*).

The Longest Journey

7

1

INTRODUCTION

This novel is the most autobiographical among all the six novels of Forster. Forster "claimed to have put a good deal of himself into Rickie in *The Longest Journey*" (Beauman, 1), Reckie Elliot being the hero of the novel. Nicola Beauman writes that "Rickie 'more than any' represented his creator" (*op. cit.,* 15). Perhaps this was why this novel was Forster's 'favourite' (*op. cit.,* 46). Nicola Beauman himself is of the opinion that the novel is 'strongly autobiographical' (*op. cit.,* 59). Beauman's—and many others'—claim that the novel is 'strongly autobiographical' is not unsubstantial, for there are a good number of suggestions and innuendoes in the novel itself to the point that it is very much autobiographical. For one thing, Rickie, the hero of the novel, we learn, was a student of Cambridge (or, rather, King's College) where Forster in fact studied; and Cambridge is also the setting of the novel. Secondly, "Lily [Forster's mother], after all, was, like Mrs. Elliot in The Longest Journey" (*op. cit.*, 101)—'afraid of intimacy.' Thirdly, Rickie was lame in one foot (as the hero of Somerset Maugham's autobiographial novel *Of Human Bondage* was a stammerer) and, being a homosexual, Forster also was, so to say, psychologically lame. Lastly, John Sayre Martin says that "Rickie's search is also Forster's. Rickie too wants to write, and as a Cambridge undergraduate has in fact written some mythological tales like some of Forster's" (Martin, 27). Martin says that "Forster's second novel, *The Longest Journey,* is the most personal of the five [novels of his]" (*op. cit.,* 26).

Forster admitted that the novel was inspired by the *genius loci* ('the spirit of the place') of Figsbury Rings, Wiltshire. Nicola Beauman writes about the inspiration of Figsbury Rings behind the writing of *The Longest Journey:* "As with Ravello, he [Forster] would later attribute his 'inspiration,' the 'sacred and mysterious... process of writing,' to the spirit of the place, the *genius loci.* Figsbury Rings, ever afterwards sanctified in Morgan's [Forster's] mind as being the birthplace of *The Longest Journey,* is indeed a magic spot. Two miles north-east of Salisbury, 'a hill fort of the early Iron Age, consisting of a bank and outer ditch enclosing about 15 acres,' it is a beautiful, grassy hillock with views all around; when the sun shines and the wind blows gently in the long grass, the Rings still seem mystic and timeless. Here Morgan [Forster] exchanged a few words with a lame shepherd boy, and would claim that it was he who crystallised his dormant thoughts about half-brothers and landscape. In a curious way, too, for Morgan [Forster] the novel itself gave birth. 'There was reciprocation... I received, I created, I restored, and for many years the Wiltshire landscape remained haunted by my fictional ghosts.' In other words the scenery became an image of Morgan's [Forster's] emotional state; then through the act of writing 'a whole landscape is charged with an emotion, permanent as its origins were transitory'" (*op. cit.*, 151-52). P.N. Furbank writes about the impact of Forster's meeting with that lame boy, in Figsbury Rings on his consciousness: "Forster met a lame shepherd boy there [Figsbury Rings] and got into conversation with him. The boy was friendly, did not call him 'sir,' and offered him a smoke of his pipe; and when Forster offered him sixpence as they were parting, he refused it. This apparently trivial incident took on peculiar significance for Forster. He decided that the boy was one of the most remarkable human beings he had ever met. 'What strikes me even more than his offering me his pipe to smoke is his enormous wisdom,' he wrote in his diary" (Furbank, 1, 116-17). It was perhaps due to his gratitude to Figsbury Rings, for being the inspiration behind his *The Longest Journey,* that in the last phase of his life Forster, in June 1964, along with William Golding, visited Figsbury Rings for the last time (Furbank, II, 318).

The Longest Journey was published on 16 April, 1907, but we do not for sure know when actually Forster wrote the novel. Queer it is that while we find in Forster's diary traces of his workings on his five other novels, there is no mentioning, even for once, of his engagement with *The Longest Journey*. Only once, while the process of publication of *Where Angels Fear to Tread* was going on, did Forster tell his mother, "'Should I ever write another book it will be called "The Longest Journey"'" (Beauman, 178). Of course, alter his death one loose sheet of paper was found among his numerous papers, which may point to his plan of working on *The Longest Journey*. The sheet of paper is headed: "'A "Plot" 17/7/04'" (*ibid.*). Nicola Beauman writes about the sheet of paper, assuming that the "Plot" is nothing else than the plot of *The Longest Journey:* "This [the "Plot"] has as its central theme a young man who 'found happiness at Cambridge' and then made a misguided marriage; his wife 'gradually detached Humphrey from his friends'; he finds he has a brother and wishes to accept him. His wife 'naturally objects, and their dissension begins.' Finally the two men die together, the epilogue reveals that 'Humphrey's book successful'" (*ibid.*). Though there is no Humphrey and no epilogue in *The Longest Journey,* the story in the sheet of paper, may suggest that it was the acorn of the oak that is the complicated long story of the novel. We cannot be above doubt as to the period of time of the writing of the novel; and, yet, we may hazard that the novel was begun sometime in the summer of 1905 and was finished sometime in the winter of 1906. Long afterwards, to be exact in 1960, Forster himself could not recollect exactly when he began the novel and when he finished it. He only said: "I can remember writing it [*The Longest Journey*] and how excited I was and how absorbed" (*op. cit,* 179). He further said that only the matter of this novel came to him when he was as if unaware about it: "it [*The Longest Journey*] is the only one of my books that has come upon me without my knowledge" (*ibid.*). Carola M. Kaplan, in his article 'Absent Father, Passive Son: *The Longest Journey*', writes: "the most unconscious and personal of Forster's published novels,

The Longest Journey was, in Forster's words, the one he was 'most glad to have written'" (Tambling, 52). However, Kaplan says that the manuscript of this novel underwent "many revisions" before getting published (*op. cit.*, 60).

The central theme *of The Longest Journey* is a sense of loss of friendship, intellectual awareness and happiness, which Forster intensely experienced around 1903. In that year he went to Greece and stayed there for sometime, when, living away from his bevy of Cambridge friends, he was feeling unhappy due to loss of friendship, and consequent loss of intellectual awareness. Nicola Beauman writes in this regard: "His [Forster's] month in Greece in the April of 1903 was what turned Cambridge into his lifelong touchstone of friendship, intellectual awareness and happiness. It was at this period in his life that the loss of King's [King's College, Cambridge University] came to be as important as the loss of Melcombe Place, of Battersea Rise, of Rooksnest; and that the idea for *The Longest Journey,* which mourns this loss, first entered his imagination" (Beauman, 131). Months afterwards, back home, Forster saw the central idea of loss develop into the plot of another Anglo-Italian novel, which he entered into his diary of 17 July, 1904. The diary entry runs thus (Furbank, I, 118):

"A 'Plot' 17/7/04

1. Renee and Mr. Aldridge—a practical, unsuccessful man—paid a visit to Humphrey—in his second year. They are old friends: but R. for the first time 'realises' him—that he [is] clever in the first place, & that something might be 'made' of him. She disapproved of his effeminacy, & of his friends—notably the brainy uncouth undergraduate, soaked with idea of mutability, Ford, and of a don who wished to run him also.
2. H. found happiness at Cambridge after a querulous childhood, and obscure life at school. Spirits and intelligence both improved. Literary powers developed. After the departure of the visitors, he, Ford, & three or four more swore eternal friendship one evening by the rifle butts.

3. During the year of cramming for the C.S. [Civil Service], R's interest in H. increased. He got H.C. [Home Service], F. taking I.C.S. [Indian Civil Service] in order that he might have it.
4. Soon after F's departure for India, R.& H. got engaged.
5. Uncle Basil and his household at Ponte Molino.
6. R. & H. came there for their honeymoon. Pasquale; whom Uncle B., for the sake of seeing what would happen, reveals to H. as his brother. H. wished to accept him. R. naturally objects, and their discussion begins.
7. R. gradually detached H. from his friends. Her behaviour at her father's death revealed him their dissimilarity, and the Italian brother was a constant source of discord.
8. Ford, broken down, returned to England, having stayed in Italy on the way. The first meeting with R. & H. giving up H.C. to reside in Cambridge.
9. Struggle between Ford & R. began.
10. Death of Uncle Basil, releasing Pasquale.
11. Ford & H. took holiday.
12. Ford met Pasquale: who knew he was H's brother but kept silence.
13. The fire: death of P. & H.
14. Epilogue: H's book successful."

As we have said, Forster designed the above plot for another Italian novel, besides *Where Angels Fear to Tread,* but when the plot was actually bodied forth, it was an English, and not an Italian, novel: *The Longest Journey.* This second novel of Forster may be said to be an inclusive novel, in the sense that "the novel encapsulates all the themes that Morgan [Forster] was in the process of making so thoroughly his own: truth and loyalty versus convention and self-interest, the English countryside versus suburbia, the constriction of bourgeois marriage, the aesthetic impulse versus the worldly, and, as well, the tragic result of ignoring the 'symbolic moment.' Morgan [Forster] believed that if one fails to take an opportunity suddenly offered, one's life, as a result, may be fatally flawed. 'We accept it, at whatever cost, and we have accepted life. But if we are frightened and reject it, the moment, so to speak, passes; the symbol is never offered again'" (Beauman, 179-80). In *The Longest Journey,* Forster has put forth much of his philosophy of life which grew out of his experiences of life itself, and for this reason the novel was 'always his favourite among his novels.' He admitted that he had been a little sentimental in this novel but he did not feel uneasy for that. The theme of the novel was so much of a part of his life and sentiment that he earlier dealt with nearly the same theme in his short story 'The Other Side of the Hedge'. Both the short story and the novel end in the protagonist's meeting with his newly discovered brother, and this may be taken to be a pointer to the fact that the theme of the novel and that of the short story are identical.

Forster took the title of *The Longest Journey* from P.B. Shelley's poem 'Epipsychdion,' the most outspoken poem of the English language appealing for fully human love that is absolutely free from the instincts of possession and jealousy. A part of the poem Rickie recites to himself loudly in section xiii of Part I of *The Longest Journey*. The lines of the poem read aloud by him are the following:

> I never was attached to that sect,
> Whose doctrine is, that each one should select
> Out of the crowd a mistress or a friend,
> And all the rest, though fair and wise, commend
> To cold oblivion, though it is in the code
> Of modern morals, and the beaten road
> Which those poor slaves with weary footsteps tread,
> Who travel to their home among the dead
> By the broad highway of the world, and so
> With one chained friend, perhaps a jealous foe,
> The dreariest and *the longest journey* go.
>
> (italics mine)

The term 'longest journey' occurs in the novel perhaps only once, and that in section xxxiii of Part III of the novel. We will not be surprised if Forster, while choosing a title for this novel, in addition to Shelley's poem 'Epipsychidion' also kept in mind the following two lines of Kent in Shakespeare's *King Lear* (III, iii): "I have a journey, sir, shortly to go. My master calls me; I must not say no." But the journey of the title is no ordinary journey but the journey of Rickie Elliot's life and so the novel has been like a pagenantry of the life of Rickie Elliot. John Sayre Martin writes: "Rickie Elliot's longest journey is the journey of his life, taking him from the suburb in which he was born and where, during his childhood, his parents die to public school and on to Cambridge University; from there to a public school in Sawston (Forster's recurrent and repressive suburb), where he serves as an assistant master, and finally to Cadover, his Aunt Emily Failing's estate in Wiltshire, not far from which he falls victim to sudden and accidental death" (Martin, 26).

The Longest Journey is a novel of social criticism, that criticises the early twentieth century society in England "In this novel Forster is primarily concerned with the story of a sensitive young man and the problems he encounters on his introduction to the world. The author is somewhat satiric as he views his characters but, as usual, he does not present the world as a completely dreary and uninteresting place. Men, in general, are portrayed as rather weak individuals who are fighting against superior forces, but the reader is not meant completely to lose his love and respect for them. Here, in a novel which is probably autobiographical in part, we see several characters who try without success to live happily in a world of weak and misguided ideals" (Magill, 2091). *The Longest Journey* is a 'dark novel' (Martin, 27), but, like *Where Angels Fear to Tread*, it sold well: "1500 copies in the April and May of 1907 and 500 more after the June reprint" (Beauman, 189).

The Longest Journey is divided into 3 Parts, each Part having several sections: Part I is entitled 'Cambridge,' Part II 'Sawston,' and Part III 'Wiltshire.' Part I runs from section I to XV; Part II from XVI to XXVIII; and Part III from XXIX to

XXXV. His principal character or 'people' (the term is Forster's) of the novel are the following:

Frederick Elliot (nickname: Rickie): (student of Cambridge)
Miss Agnes Pembroke: (Rickie's friend at Cambridge)
Herbert Pembroke: (Agnes's brother and Rickie's friend)
Stewart Ansell: (Rickie's friend at Cambridge)
Mrs. Emily Failing: (Rickie's aunt or father's sister)
Stephen Wonham: (Mrs. Failing's nephew, and son of Rickie's mother but not of Rickie's father, and so Rickie's half-brother).

The minor characters of the novel include Gerald Dawes (an 'athletic marvel' and finance to Agnes), Miss Herriton, Mrs. Orr, Robert (who fell in love with Agnes after her marriage with Rickie), Mrs. Aberdeen (Rickie's bedmaker at Cambridge), Hornblower, Widdrington, Mr. Elliot (Rickie's father), Mrs. Elliot (Rickie's mother), and others.

There is a brief summary of the story *of The Longest Journey* in *Master Plots* (15 vol.), edited by Frank N. Magill, which will help us in following the course of the narrative of the novel. It runs as follows:

"Frederick Elliot, who was a student at Cambridge and almost alone in the world, had finally attained some degree of contentment in his life after a rather unhappy childhood. He had been born with a lamed left foot which kept him from most of the normal activities of children, and he had grown up virtually without friends. Early in his life his father had begun to call him Rickie because of its close similarity to rickety, and the name stayed with him. Besides his deformity there was another, more serious, difficulty. He found out quite early that his father and mother did not love each other and that he was loved not at all by his father and only little by his mother. Both his parents died when he was fifteen, leaving him comfortably well off so far as finances were concerned but without anyone who wanted to give him a home.

At Cambridge he had shown himself to be a capable student but one without any scholarly pretensions. He had made several friends among the non-athletic group and spent much of his time in long discussions on topics of literary or philosophical interest. One day, during such a discussion, he was interrupted by the arrival of his old friends. Agnes and Herbert Pembroke, whom he had invited for the weekend. In the meantime he had completely forgotten about them. Because these two people were part of that very small group which took an interest in Rickie's career, they spent a great part of their time at Cambridge encouraging him to decide on a particular course for his life, even if he did nothing more than write, the only thing he admitted having an interest in. They pointed out that money was not important as long as he met a certain standard of ideals.

At Christmas of that same year Rickie saw his friends again. He had stayed several days with Stewart Ansell, a friend from Cambridge, but felt it was necessary to spend a part of his vacation with the Pembrokes as well. He rather dreaded this part of his vacation because Agnes' finance, a man whom Rickie had known at public school, was to be there. Rickie not only disliked Gerald Dawes but he also hated to witness the lovers' happiness; he felt that such happiness was forever to be denied him because of his lame foot which he considered a hereditary disorder. During this time Gerald was killed while playing football, and it was Rickie who was able to offer the most comfort to Agnes by convincing her that she should suffer since her love for Gerald had been the greatest thing she could ever experience.

Two years later, when she came again to visit him at Cambridge, Rickie realized that he was also in love with Agnes, although he still felt that he could never marry because of his deformity. She convinced him, however, that they should be married. Rickie was about to finish his work at Cambridge, but they felt a long engagement was necessary for him to settle himself. Ansell immediately opposed the marriage because he sensed that Agnes was not a sincere person. She laid constant claim to honesty and forthrightness, but Ansell could not be convinced that these qualities revealed the true Agnes. He knew immediately that she would force Rickie into a dull and conventional life, convincing him at the same time that he was taking the proper step.

Soon after his engagement Rickie and Agnes visited his aunt, Mrs. Emily Failing, at her country home. Rickie had never particularly liked his aunt, but since she was his only known relative he had Agnes felt that they should go to see her. Mrs. Failing was a woman who liked people to do what she wanted and she was never happier than when they were obviously uncomfortable while carrying out her desires. While there they also saw Stephen Wonham, a young man whom Rickie had met before but whose relation to Mrs. Failing had never been made clear. However, after Rickie had been so bold as to engage in an argument with his aunt, she informed him that Stephen was actually his brother. It was not until later that Rickie found out that Stephen was the son of his mother, whom he had loved very much, and not of his father. Not even Stephen himself knew who he was, but the matter had never greatly concerned him.

After their marriage Rickie and Agnes went to live with Herbert at Sawston School. The arrangement had been worked out between Herbert and Agnes because Herbert needed help in his duties as a house master. Although Rickie soon realized that Herbert was basically stupid and that they disagreed on many points, he adapted himself to whatever course Herbert and Agnes chose. His marriage, in which he had hoped to find certain spiritual ideals, never reached a very intimate level, and before long his life became a shell. Ansell would have no more to do with him and he was cut off from the one intellect at the school because of Herbert's feelings and aspirations.

Two years later, after Rickie had apparently succumbed completely to the forces playing on him, Stephen Wonham again entered his life. It became apparent immediately that Agnes, who had kept up a connection with Mrs. Failing , had been instrumental in having Stephen thrown out of her house, all because of her desire to inherit the money from the estate. Rickie was furious but again he submitted. Stephen, who had finally been told the truth about himself, came to Sawston expecting to find the kind of love which he had never known before. But when Rickie refused to see him and Agnes offered him money never to say anything about his parentage, he left immediately.

Stephen wandered around London for several days doing jobs and supporting himself as well as he could. Before long he had saved enough money for a drunken spree. During his drunkenness, determined to wreck Rickie's house, he returned to Sawston. In the process he might have killed himself if Rickie had not saved him. By this time Rickie, under the influence of Ansell, had began to see how foolish he had been. Now he decided to give Stephen a home. Although Stephen would have none of this idea, he managed to convince Rickie that they should go away together.

Thus Rickie began the regeneration of his soul. Unfortunately it was of short duration. On a subsequent visit to his aunt, at which time Stephen insisted on accompanying him, he again saved Stephen's life but lost his own. Stephen, who had promised not to drink, got drunk and collapsed on the railroad crossing. Rickie managed to get him off, but he himself was killed. Just before he died he realised that he had been betrayed a second time by his belief in the individual" (Magill, 2091-93).

2

THE STORY

Part I: Cambridge

A tea-party was proceeding in the evening in Rickie Elliot's room at Cambridge, where a tricky philosophical question was being debated by, among others, Stewart Ansell, an empiricist, and Tilliard, a rationalist. The question was whether the objects of our perception are real or are created by our subjectivity, whether, for instance, the cow was there or it was a hallucination. Ansell contended the cow was there, Tilliard denied. The day was joyous for Rickie: in the morning he read Theocritus (the Greek pastoral poet: c 310-250 B.C.) whom he 'believed to be the greatest of Greek poets', then 'walked with people he liked'; now he finds his room full of friends, making a 'symposium'; and soon he would go to dine with his favourite Ansell. "A year ago he had known none of these joys. He had crept cold and friendless and ignorant out of a great public school, preparing for a silent and solitary journey, and praying as a highest favour that he might be left alone. Cambridge had not answered his prayer. She had taken and soothed him, and warmed him, and had laughed at him a little, saying that he must not be so tragic yet awhile, for his boyhood had been but a dusty corridor that led to the specious halls of youth. In one year he had made many friends and learnt much."

Suddenly a 'tall young woman' arrived among the young philosophers who constituted the 'symposium'—and it was Miss Agnes Pembroke. She came there to seek her brother, Herbert, who was really not there. Soon Ansell went out after the hot debate on the cow had subsided. Rickie told Agnes that Ansell was not a gentleman, that his father was a draper and his uncles were farmers, and also that he had entered Cambridge due only to his cleverness—'just on account of his brains.' Rickie went out to order dinner, and Agnes began meditating on the athletic qualities of her lover Gerald Dawes, her 'splendid lover.' She thought Gerald was physically more strong than any of the young men inside the room. She imagined Gerald "could have knocked all these unhealthy undergraduates into a cocked hat." Agnes was gentle—her nature was kindly, and yet she was ill at ease in the prolonged quietness of the room. She was recalling how glad she had been when Gerald presented her with a pair of ear-rings at the time of proposing to her and when Gerald kissed the blood-stain in her handkerchief with which she sopped the blood in her ears after they were pierced for those rings. She was now pacing across Rickie's room, running her eyes along the four walls. She saw brown Madonna and a picture of Rickie's mother on the wall and dirty teacups and Omar Khayyam on the table. She saw that the two shoes of Rickie were not the same size and concluded that he 'was slightly deformed.' She was disgustingly excited at the sight of the deformity which she thought was hereditary. She shut the door and "recalled the perfect form of Gerald, his athletic walk, the poise of his shoulders, his arms stretched forward to receive her. Gradually she was comforted."

Mrs Aberdeen, the bedmaker, arrived, and from her Agnes came to know that Rickie had bleeding nose and had brothers-like friends and no real brothers. Mrs Aberdeen also told her that Rickie always wanted to avoid troubles: "'His one thought is to save one trouble.'" Mrs Aberdeen said Rickie was a gentleman. Meantime, Agnes' brother, Herbert, a young man nearly twenty, came in. He was 'older than his sister' but 'had never been as handsome.' He "was not at all the person to knock into a gutter, for though not in orders, he had the air of being on the verge of them, and his features, as well as his clothes, had the clerical cut." When Herbert enquired of Agnes about Frederick—Frederick Elliot—Agnes, in abomination fumed and asked Herbert not to call Rickie by the name of Frederick but simply by the name of Rickie. Her meeting with Rickie was 'her first great contact with the abnormal.' At this time, Agnes heard Rickie's 'uneven tread upon the stairs.'

During dinner Agnes asked Rickie to say 'something pretty' about Gerald, both of whom belonged to the same group at school. Rickie only said—and that very shyly—that he knew very little about Gerald, and then 'began to muddle with the coffee.' Agnes told Rickie that Gerald was 'a kind of athletic marvel' and that he reminds one of one in the army who dies honourably. Herbert reminded Rickie that he was twenty and that in less than two years he would be a B.A., and then asked him what he would be doing then. Rickie said he did not know. Herbert suggested the Bar, the profession of Rickie's father, but Rickie expressed his disliking for the Bar. Agnes suggested the Church. Rickie said he was thinking about writing 'little stories.' Agnes commented that Rickie was 'just the boy for poetry' and she liked the idea of writing for him. Herbert paternally advised him to stick to writing as a means of earning, because his father and mother were no more, and because if he did that he could even marry, though he had to depend solely on himself. Herbert added: "Work and drudge. Begin at the bottom of the ladder and work upwards." Rickie knew that art of writing was not bricklaying and so it could not be improved by practice, but he only said that writing did not fetch money. Herbert asked him to write not for money but for ideals. By this time night descended and the Pembrokes went to their lodgings. Rickie went to Ansell's and told him that Agnes was 'like an empress', but Ansell said that he did not see anything of an empress in Agnes, suggesting that the image of the empress that Rickie saw in Agnes was subjective, illusory, and then began to draw a square and "draw within the square a circle, and within the circle a square, and inside that another circle, and inside that another square." Rickie asked if the squares and the circles were real. Ansell replied: " The inside one is—the one in the middle of everything, that there's never room enough to draw" (section I).

The Pembrokes went away from Rickie's room. It was a blessed Monday. Rickie went out for a walk with three friends: Ansell, Widdrington and Tilliard. They entered a dell and were conversing among themselves leaning each against a tree. Rickie shuts up his Keats. "Scarcely ever was he without a book." During the conversation, Rickie expressed his opinion: "'I maintain that one can like many more people than one supposes.'" But he was protested: "'And I maintain that you hate many more people than you pretend.'" Ansell asked Rickie if he hated his father, but Rickie did not reply, for he was disgusted at asking such a question about his dead father. Then, when Widdrington asked Rickie whether he hated his mother, he turned crimson.

Rickie spent his life uptil now in the suburb, walking on asphalt paths. His father (who was now dead) was a barrister, and resembled his son "being weakly and lame with hollow little cheeks". He had "a broad white band of forehead, and stiff impoverished hair. His voice, which he did not transmit, was very suave, with a fine command of cynical intonation. By altering it over so little he could make people wince, especially if they were simple or poor. Nor did he transmit his eyes. Their peculiar flatness, as if the soul looked through dirty window-panes, the unkindness of them, the cowardice, the fear in them, were to trouble the world no longer." Rickie's father and mother could not make a happy and durable home, and soon his father left his mother and began to live in a town far away from home. His father lived in a three-room house which was full of books, pictures and flowers.

The young Rickie realised that "his father and mother did not love each other, and that his mother was lovable. He discovered that Mr. Elliot [Rickie's father] had dubbed him Rickie because he was rickety, that he took pleasure in alluding to his son's deformity, and was sorry that it was not more serious than his own. Rickie's father "had not one scrap of genius", but yet he passed for a cultured man. Rickie "grew up in great loneliness" particularly because his mother did not like him to be in intimate relations with others. He "worshipped his mother, and she was fond of him." At this point the narrator gives us a pen-picture of Rickie's mother and an idea of the relation between the mother and the son: "she was dignified and reticent, and pathos, like tattle, was disgusting to her. She was afraid of intimacy, in case it led to confidences and tears, and so all her life she led her son a little at a distance. Her kindness and unselfishness knew no limits, but if he tried to be dramatic and thank her, she told him not to be a little goose." Rickie was so lonely that "the only person he came to know at all was himself." He would sometimes sob for being lonely, and somehow came to know that he would never have a brother.

When Rickie was thirteen, his father, Mr. Elliot, became invalid, and came back home leaving his residence in the town behind, and the first thing he did was sending Rickie to a public school against Mrs. Elliot's will to the contrary. There in the school too Rickie was not happy, because, as Mrs. Elliot told Mr. Elliot, "Rickie can't play games. He does not make friends, He is not brilliant." However, Mr. Elliot was growing old fast, and, when Rickie was fifteen, he suddenly died. Strange enough, Rickie's mother was glad at the death of Mr. Elliot: "She was much happier, she looked younger, and her mourning was as unobtrusive as convention permitted." Mrs. Elliot now decided to go to Rickie's father's sister, the gifted and vivacious Emily to live there in the country along with Rickie—"somewhere right in the country, with grass and trees up to the door, and birds singing everywhere." Rickie was taken back from school for ever, and a tutor was engaged for him. Extraordinarily, Rickie's mother also died, on a cold day, only eleven days after his father's death. Till her death the mother did shield the son with 'ceaseless tenderness.' "Such, in substance, was the story which Rickie told his friends as they stood together in the shelter of the dell" (section II).

Rickie spent part of the Christmas vacation in the 'plebian household' of the Ansells. The house-owner, Mr. Ansell, was 'a provincial draper of moderate prosperity' who did never interfere in the education of Stewart Ansell, Rickie's friend at Cambridge. Stewart Ansell first took up philosophy, but then decided to prepare for Civil Service. He had two sisters—Mary and Maud—none of whom fell in love with Rickie nor he with any one of the two. Nevertheless it was a happy visit for Rickie—his stay at the house of the Ansells where Miss Appleblossom was the housekeeper. From the house of the Ansells Rickie went to the Pembrokes who lived 'in an adjacent suburb' called Sawston where was situated a celebrated public school. The name of the house of the Pembrokes was Shelthrope, and the house "suggested a certain amount of money and a certain amount of taste. There were decent water-colours in the drawing room. Madonnas of acknowledged merit hung upon the stairs. A replica of the Hermes of Praxiteles—of course only the bust—stood in the hall with a real palm behind it" Rickie went to the Pembroke's by train and was warmly received at the station by Mr. Pembroke who told him that Gerald Dawes (the finance of Agnes Pembroke) "has strained his ankle slightly, and wants to keep quiet, as he is playing next week in a match" and so he could not be present at the station to receive Rickie. Gerald and Rickie knew each other. "The pembrokes had formerly lived near the Elliots, and had shown great kindness to Rickie when his parents died. They were thus rather in the position of family friends."

At this point the narrator gives us a pen-picture of Gerald Dawes' beautiful athletic stature as he one day stood near Agnes. Gerald "had the figure of a Greek athlete and the face of an English one. He was fair and clean-shaven, and his colourless hair was cut rather short. The sun was in his eyes, and they, like his mouth, seemed scarcely more than slits in his healthy skin. Just where he began to be beautiful the clothes started. Round his neck went an up-and-down collar and a mauve-and-gold tie, and the rest of his limbs were hidden by a grey lounge suit, carefully creased in the right places." Rickie could not tolerate his old schoolfellow Gerald, let alone be friendly with him. "Between Rickie and Gerald there lay a shadow that darkens life more often than we suppose." However, one day Rickie found Gerald and Agnes in an intensely amorous posture: "Gerald and Agnes were locked in each other's arms." Rickie "only looked for a moment [at the sight], but the sight burnt into his brain. The man's grip was the stronger. He had drawn the woman on to his knee, was pressing her, with all his strength, against him. Already her hands slipped off him, and she whispered, 'Don't—you hurt—' Her face had no expression. It stared at the intruder and never saw him. Then her lover kissed it, and immediately it shone with mysterious beauty, like some star." Rickie wondered at the uncanny and white-hot amorous sight, became crimson and afraid, and thought "'Do such things actually happen?'" (section III).

The suburban "Sawston School had been founded by a tradesman in the seventeenth century" to educate the poor, but now it was meant for the upper middle classes. Mr. Pembroke 'passed his happy and industrious life' here in this modernised Sawston School. The mottos of the school were organisation, custom and conformity. Mr. Pembroke believed that organisation was of utmost worth. "He organized. If no organization existed, he would create one. If one did exist, he would modify it 'An organization,' he would say, 'is after all not an end in itself. It must contribute to a movement.' When one good custom seemed likely to corrupt the school, he was always ready with another; he believed that without innumerable customs there was no safety, either for boys or men.... The school caps, with their elaborate symbolism, were his; his the many-tinted bathing-drawers, that showed how far a boy could swim; his the hierarchy of jerseys and blazers. It was he who instituted Bounds, and Call, and the two sorts of exercise-paper, and the three sorts of caning, and 'The Sawstonian', a bi-terminal magazine." "He was generally acknowledged to be the coming man."

"His last achievement had been the organization of the day-boys. They had been left too much to themselves, and were weak in *esprit de corps;* they were apt to regard home, not school, as the most important thing in their lives. Moreover, they got out of their parents' hands; they did their preparation any time and sometimes anyhow. They shirked games, they were out at all hours, they ate what they should not, they smoked, they bicycled on the asphalt." Mr Pembroke anyhow forced the day-boys into conformity with the 'innumerable customs' of the school. He showed Rickie the different things of the school—its library, its subterranean hall, etc.—and Rickie was impressed by everything. He assured Rickie that the school was nearing the ideals of the Greeks. He regarded Plato and philosophy but said that philosophy "'is the crown of a man's education, not the foundation.'" Changing the theme of the conversation abruptly, Rickie asked if Anges did take much interest in the school, and Mr. Pembroke replied that as she was engaged with Gerald she was not much interested in the school. Mr. Pembroke expressed satisfaction over his sister Agnes' engagement. To Gerald Dawes, Agnes was non-peril in all respects—"he could think of no classical parallel for Agnes" (section IV).

Gerald Dawes, Agne's finance, suddenly died of an injury received while playing football. Gerald expired just in the playground where, just before his death, Agnes arrived by bicycle. At first she could not understand the fatal injury of Gerald; she thought all was simply a great joke: "It must be a joke that he [chose] to lie there in the dust, with a rug over him, and his knees bent up towards his chin. His arms were as she knew them, and their admirable muscles showed clear and clean beneath the jersey. The face, too, though a little flushed, was uninjured: it must be some curious joke." Agnes asked,

"'Gerald, what have you been doing?'" and Gerald replied, "'I can't see you. It's too dark.'" For the last time she crept into his arms. "Only this time her grasp was the stronger. Her heart beat louder and louder as the sound of his grew more faint. He was crying like a little frightened child, and her lips were wet with his tears." But Agnes' love could not placate death but it took Gearald away in no time. "The incident was outside nature, and would surely pass away like a dream." Agnes returned home mournfully, leaving things for others.

Agnes felt an 'obscure spiritual crisis' within her soul. At this moment Rickie burst in. "He was splashed with mud, his breath was gone, and his hair fell wildly over his meagre face." She [Agnes] thought, 'These are the people who are left alive!' From the bottom of her soul she hated him. Rickie neared her, but she prayed to him to leave her alone. Nevertheless Rickie grew in stature before the eyes of Agnes. Rickie tried to console her: "'He's gone, Agnes, and his arms will never hold you again. In God's name, mind such a thing, and don't sit fencing with your soul. Don't stop being great; that's the one crime he'll [Gerald will] never forgive you.'" Yet Agnes' sorrow was not lessened; she "acknowledged that life's meaning had vanished." She began to accuse Herbert for postponing her marriage with Gerald, because had it not been postponed "She might have been a wife six months." She refused to be consoled, and yet Rickie continued to persuade her to accept the inevitable: "'I did not come to comfort you. I came to see that you mind. He [Gerald] is in heaven, Agnes. The greatest thing is over.'" Agnes now calmed down and became affable to Rickie and held out her hand to him. She told him: "You have grown up in a moment." She asked where Gerald was then and Rickie assured her that he was in heaven. Agnes wondered how could Rickie be so certain about immortality (section V).

Rickie did not wait for the funeral of Gerald but returned to the Silts, and as soon as the term opened went to Cambridge. He stayed with the Pembrokes only for a few days. "In his short life Rickie had known two sudden deaths, and that is enough to disarrange any placid outlook on the world. He knew once for all that we are all of us bubbles on an extremely rough sea. Into this sea humanity has built, as it were, some little breakwaters—scientific knowledge, civilized restraint—so that the bubbles do not break so frequently or so soon." Going back to Cambridge Rickie preferred to keep himself within the four walls. A letter came from Miss Agnes Pembroke. "She wrote like the Sibyl; her sorrowful face moved over the stars and shattered their harmonies; last night he [Rickie] saw her with the eyes of Blake, a virgin widow, tall, veiled, consecrated, with her hands stretched out against an everlasting wind." Agnes wrote in that latter that she was the most comforted by Rickie after the death of Gerald. "Rickie burnt this letter, which he ought not to have done, for it was one of the few tributes Miss Pembroke ever paid to imagination. But he felt that it did not belong to him: words so sincere should be for Gerald alone. The smoke rushed up the chimney, and he indulged in a vision. He saw it reach the outer air and beat against the low ceiling of clouds. The clouds were too strong for it; but in them was one chink, revealing one star, and through this the smoke escaped into the light of stars innumerable. Then—but then the vision failed, and the voice of science whispered that all smoke remains on earth in the form of smuts."

Next moment Rickie realised that he was going to be too unpractical. He thought: "'And what is the point of it when real things are so wonderful? Who wants visions in a world that has Agnes and Gerald?'" Rickie "turned on the electric light and pulled open the table-drawer. There, among spoons and corks and string, he found a fragment of a little story that he had tried to write last term. It was called 'The Bay of the Fifteen Islets,' and the action took place on St. John's Eve off the coast of Sicily. A party of tourists land on one of the islands. Suddenly the boatmen become uneasy, and say that the island is not generally there. It is an extra one, and they had better have tea on one of the ordinaries. 'Pooh, volcanic!', says the leading tourist, and the ladies say how interesting. The island begins to rock, and so do the minds of its visitors. They start to quarrel and jabber. Fingers burst up through the sand—black fingers of sea devils. The island tilts. The tourists go mad. But just before the catastrophe one man *integer vitae scelerisque purus,* sees the truth. Here are no devils. Other muscles, other minds, are pulling the island to its subterranean home...." Rickie did not advance any more on the line of the story, and thought "When real things are so wonderful, what is the point of pretending?" (section VI).

Rickie "believes in humanity because he knows a dozen decent people. He believes in woman because he has loved his mother. And his friends are as young and as ignorant as himself. They are full of the wine of life. But they have not tasted the cup—let us call it the teacup of experience." And like his friends Rickie is also inexperienced in the mode of life. However, at the end of his third year, Ansell got a first in the Moral Science Tripos and Rickie 'got a creditable second in the Classical Tripos, Part I' and then taking the B.A. degree read Greek Archaeology for Part II and again got a second class. Rickie really loved Cambridge. He said: "There'll never again be a home for me like Cambridge." He thought now the time was come when he was to part with Ansell to dive into the sea of the practical, professional world. "He was thinking of the irony of friendship—so strong it is, and so fragile. We try together, like straws in an eddy, to part in the open stream. Nature has no use for us [friends]; she has cut her stuff differently. Dutiful sons, loving husbands, responsible fathers—these are what she wants, and if we are friends it must be in our spare time."

Despite this observation of his, Rickie was searching within his soul for the image of a friend, and he found that the image was that of Agnes Pembroke, he found that "he loved her." Now Gerald no more occupied the brains of either Agnes or Rickie. Rickie still thought herself to be a goddess. "And on her he had fixed his eyes. He thought of her awake. He entertained her willingly in dreams. He found her in poetry and music and in the sunset. She made him kind and strong. She made him clever. Through her he kept Cambridge in its proper place, and lived as a citizen of the great world. But one night he dreamt that she lay in his arms. This displeased him. He determined to think a little about Gerald instead. Then the fabric collapsed." He thought of confiding his love of Agnes to Ansell but restrained himself thinking he would take him for a natural. Agnes, on the other hand, was always inspiring Rickie to write short stories—to engage himself in literature, without wasting life. She believed he could write something beautiful. But Rickie told her that he himself did not like his own literary productions: "'What I write is too silly.'" Agnes did not agree with him and told him: "'It does seem a pity that you don't make something of your talents. It seems such a waste to write little stories and never publish them. You must have enough for a book...'" Agnes' words thrilled him like a trumpet-blast.

Agnes and Rickie were wandering across the dell—both romantically inspired by the arboreal and pastoral scenarios where the Dryads dwelt. Rickie again took up the thread of conversation: "'But do you really think that I could take up literature?'" And Agnes enthusiastically replied: "'Why not? You can try. Even if you fail, you can try. Of course we think you tremendously clever, and I met one of your dons at tea, and he said that your degree was not in the least a proof of your abilities: he said that you knocked up and got flurried in the examinations. Oh!'" Agnes looked back to have a view of the dell behind them, and exclaimed: "'Oh, what a jolly place!'" Rickie asked her to enter into the dell if she wanted to see its beauty but "but did not offer to go with her. "His heart throbbed louder and louder, and seemed to shake him to pieces." Agnes called out 'Rickie' and the field of June, sky of June, grass of June, and the call of a bird pulled Rickie towards her and "She was sitting down with his head on her lap." The odours of summer floated by, and "She bent down to touch him with lips." Rickie was startled but told her that what she got from strong Gerald she will never get from him who was weak: "'Never forget that your greatest thing is over.... I am too weak.... What he gave you then is greater than anything you will get from me.'" Agnes was frightened at this, but then she chided him, saying he had been talking nonsense. And after that, she "folded him in her arms" (section VII).

Rickie announced before Ansell and Tilliard that he was going to marry Miss Agnes Pembroke, admitting that he had been in love of her for years. Ansell's 'opinions' about the happy marital union between Agnes and Rickie were the following: "She is happy because she has conquered; he is happy because he has at last hung all the world's beauty on to a single peg. He was always trying to do it. He used to call the peg humanity. Will either of these happinesses last? His can't. Hers only for a time. I fight this woman not only because she rights me, but because I foresee the most appalling catastrophe. She wants Rickie, partly to replace another man whom she lost two years ago, partly to make something out of him. He is to write. In time she will get sick of this. He wont get famous. She will only see how thin he is and how lame. She will long for a jollier husband, and I don't blame her. And, having made him thoroughly miserable and degraded, she will bolt—if she can do it like a lady" (section VIII).

Section IX is all epistolary, and it contains seven letters, all written within the space of only one month—in June alone. The first letter Ansell wrote from Cambridge to Rickie asking him to break off his engagement with Miss Agnes Pembroke, producing two grounds behind his so asking In the first place, Ansell told Rickie: "You are not a person who ought to marry at all. You are unfitted in body." And, in the second place, Ansell told Rickie: "You are also unfitted in soul." Ansell wrote he thought Rickie to be 'extraordinarily civilized.' Rickie replied from Sawston that Agnes might have been an 'emissary of nature,' but yet he was in love with her. He suspected want of warmth in Ansell and so urged him to read Shelley and Goethe—Goethe who wrote that 'the eternal feminine leads us on.' The third letter was fragmentary and was (supposedly) written by Ansell for Rickie from Cambridge. Ansell advised him to understand the ancient Greek playwright Euripides who said "the eternal faminine leads us a pretty dance." Ansell said that he objected to Rickie's marriage with Agnes for two reasons. Firstly, "'She is not serious.'" Secondly, "'She is not truthful.'" The fourth letter was from Rickie to Ansell. Rickie told him that though he (Ansell) might hate

Agnes, their friendship would never slacken, because "'our friendship has now passed beyond intervention.'" The fifth letter was written by Agnes to one Mrs. Lewin from Sawston, in which letter Agnes called Rickie a 'wonderful boy' and told Mrs. Lewin that Rickie had written a 'curious' short story entitled 'Nemi.' Agnes told her that if Rickie would go to Italy next year, he should have written 'something really good.' The sixth letter was from Herbert to one Mr. Silt. Herbert wrote from Sawston that he felt pleased with anything that pleased his sister Agnes, and that Rickie "must at least double his income before they [he and Agnes] can dream of more intimate ties." The seventh and last letter was from Emily Failing, sister of Rickie's father to Agnes. Emily wrote that she came to know of Agnes' engagement with Rickie, her (Emily's) nephew, but that she did not have any idea about what Rickie is like (section IX).

Not long after their engagement, Rickie and Agnes arrived at Cadover to see Rickie's aunt Emily Failing who was 'between elderly and old' and who was a writer. Cadover was the name of the house where Mrs. Failing (a widow) lived—the house which was situated in a beautiful pastoral ambiance where clouds played, rain drenched all under it, sparrows hopped, etc. Mrs. Failing was a 'complicated person'; "her forehead was wrinkled with an expression of slight but perpetual pain. But the lines round her mouth indicated that she had laughed a great deal during her life, just as the clean tight skin round her eyes perhaps indicated that she had not often cried." Her hair was beautiful, over which she wore brown silk shawl as she also dressed in brown silk. That day under the bower in a pastoral surround Mrs. Failing was writing a 'memoir' which she but only began like this: 'The subject of this memoir first saw the light at Wolverhampton on May the 14th, 1842.' Just at that moment Stephen Wonham, Mrs Failing's nephew (and Rickie's half-brother—*i.e.* son of Rickie's mother, not father), barged into her room in 'sodden ulster.' "He was a powerful boy of twenty, admirably muscular, but rather too broad for his height. People called him 'Podge' until they were dissuaded. Then they called him 'Stephen' or 'Mr. Wonham.' Stephen

Wonham tempestuously narrated to her the story of one Fleance Thompson: "'Flea [Fleance] has a girl at Wintersbridge, and I had to go with his sheep while he went to see her. Two hours. We agreed. Half an hour to go, an hour to kiss his girl, and half an hour back—and he had my bike. Four hours! Four hours and seven minutes I was on the Rings, with a fool of a dog, and sheep doing all they knew to get the turnips.'" Stephen Wonham was explaining to her the reason of his absence for so long.

Mrs. Failing had her own farm, and she liked to be there—it was her dream. She remonstrated to Wonham: "'Some day you must really take me to see it [her farm]. It must be like a Gilbert and Sullivan opera, with a chorus of agitated employers. How is it that I have escaped? Why have I never been summoned to milk the cows, or flay the pigs, or drive the young bullocks to the pasture?'" Wonham was listening. Mrs. Failing told him: "'A thing of beauty you are not. But I sometimes think you are a joy for ever.'" Wonham felt, slightly offended, and so Mrs. Failing commended his 'Large and steady feet.' She told him: "'You can knock down a man, but you will never knock down a woman.'" Her words were largely suggestive in a mischievous way. She was deploring the absence of the earlier romance in the pastures of England. She frankly confessed to Wonham: "'I dream of Arcady. I open my eyes: Wiltshire. Of Amaryllis. Flea Thompson's girl. Of the pensive shepherd, twitching his mantle blue: you are in ulster. Aren't you sorry for me?'" Wonham did not like such talks and so immersed his attention into a book, and Mrs. Failing, finding no attentive listener near her, once again began her mamoir: "'Anthony Eustace Failing, the subject of this memoir, was born at Wolverhampton.'" She saw in him the 'face of a strong man'; he seemed to her 'an Irish terrier'. "As a man he often bored her, for he was always saying and doing the same things. But as a philosopher he really was a joy for ever, an inexhaustible buffoon. Taking up her pen, she began to caricature him. She drew a rabbit-warren where rabbits were at play in four dimensions. Before she had introduced the principal figure, she was interrupted by a footman." The footman informed her of the arrival of Rickie and Agnes.

Mrs. Failing bounched up, 'left the shelter of the laurels' (she had been sitting under a bower) and entered the house where she 'changed her dress and glanced at the poems of Milton' and then went to meet her guests, Rickie and Agnes. On looking at Rickie, she bluntly told him: "'Rickie, you are so like your father.'" She also told him that his mother was not in good terms with herself, and that his father and herself hated each other. Meanwhile Wonham presented himself within the company and he was introduced to the guests. Mrs. Failing told Rickie that she "'never knew a woman who was so unselfish and yet had such capacities for life.'" She expatiated a little upon his mother: "Unselfish people, as a rule, are deathly dull. They have no colour. They think of other people because it is easier. They give money because they are too stupid or too idle to spend it properly on themselves. That was the beauty of your Mother—she gave away, but she also spent on herself, or tried to." Mrs. Failing came to know that the train Rickie and Agnes came there by had run over a child. She asked the philosopher Stephen Wonham what had happened to the soul of that dead child. Both Mrs. Failing and Agnes said they hated philosophy. Stephen did not say anything to them, he only stared at a distance through the window and half-audibly muttered that had there been an over-bridge instead of the level-crossing the child's soul would have been saved, (section X).

Cadover, not a very large house, was built about 1800 in the style of ancient Roman architecture, in a pastoral ambience having a church, a farm, a stream, etc. Cadover belonged to Mrs. Failing, author of some brilliant books on socialism. Cadover was in Wiltshire in which part of the country Mrs. Failing was not living not very happily because, as she said, of the stupidity of the populace. She therefore used to frequent literary *salons* in the township. "Rickie admired his aunt [Mrs. Failing], but did not care for her. She reminded him too much of his father. She had the same affliction, the same helplessness, the same habit of taking life with a laugh—

as if life is a pill! He also felt that she had neglected him." Mrs. Failing was Rickie's only living near relative, and this was the reason of her happiness in welcoming him and Agnes in her house. However, that day Mrs. Failing asked Rickie to 'go for a ride with the Wonham boy [Stephen]' for the whole day. Rickie did not like it for losing Agnes; Wonham did not like it, for he did not like Rickie; yet ultimately they had to go. Before his departure Agnes asked Rickie: "'Who is this Wonham, by the bye?'" Rickie told her that Mrs. Failing probably adopted him. Agnes told him she was apprehensive that Mrs. Failing might try to break their engagement. Hearing this Rickie kissed her hands, affectionately, as if to drive away her fear. Nevertheless, Rickie told her that in the Cadover house had 'the most awful feeling of insecurity.' Agnes asked the reason and Rickie replied somewhat cryptically and significantly: "'If any one says or does a foolish thing it's always here. All the family breezes have started here. It's a kind of focus for aimed and aimless scandal. You know, when my father and mother had their special quarrel, my aunt was mixed up in it,—I never knew how or how much—but you may be sure that she didn't calm things down, unless she found things more entertaining calm.'"

Agnes asked him not to talk of Mrs. Failing in her own house, like all this. Rickie expressed exasperation at disturbing country gossips and then 'flung his arms over her' saying: "'Dear—dear— let's beware of I don't know what—of nothing at all perhaps.'" Rickie's words sounded prophetic. Mrs. Failing asked Agnes how she liked Wonham and Agnes replied 'Very nice.' But Mrs. Failing was not very satisfied with her answer; she said. "'Nice! He is a hero.'" Mrs. Failing's definition of a hero was a man physically strong enough to make anybody feel small. Mrs. Failing confessed that she was impressed by Wonham, and said that her sixpenny books contained references to (Podge) Wonham. She told Agnes a fragment of the early biography of Stephen Wonham. She said Wonham was twice expelled from the school at fourteen because of stealing and kicking weakly boys and also because of robbing apples 'with unusual boys.' But Wonham's 'benefactress' was not at all worried for this; she rather 'gave him a prize.' However, Mrs. Failing asked Agnes not to address her as 'Mrs. Failing' but as 'Aunt Emily,' whereafter Agnes asked her: "'Aunt Emily, what did you think of that story Rickie sent you?'" "'It is bad,' said Mrs. Failing. 'But. But. But. But.'" "Then she escaped, having told the truth, and yet leaving a pleasurable impression behind her" (section XI).

Rickie and Wonham rode to Salisbury, conversing between them on divers subjects. They met Mr. Wilbraham who reported: "'another child dead!'" Then Rickie and Wonham were talking about Flea Thompson, when Wonham told Rickie: "'I promise you when I've a girl I'll keep her in line, and if she turns nasty, I'll get another.'" Rickie too "believed that life should be in a line—a line of enormous length, full of countless interests and countless figures, all well beloved.... He loved Agnes, not only for herself, but because she was lighting up the human world." However, in course of time they met a soldier in front of an inn. The soldier "slanged the proprietor and ragged the pretty girls", which made Rickie blush heavily. Rickie "was only used to Cambridge, and to a very small comer of that. He and his friends there believed in free speech. But they spoke freely about generalities. They were scientific and philosophic. They would have shrunk from the empirical freedom that results from a little beer." The soldier and Wonham cracked vulgar jokes in drunken condition. Returning home Wonham was browsing over the pages of Rickie's story, when the book fell down, and he saw a *resume* of the book on its back in Miss Agnes Pembroke's handwriting, 'intended for such as him': "'Allegory. Man = modern civilization (in bad sense). Girl = getting into touch with Nature.'" Wonham wondered at so much of praise of Nature in Rickie's story, and "Sighing into his pipe, he fell asleep" (section XII).

Agnes was glad when Rickie returned from riding for lunch. Mrs. Failing now could not digest the happy relationship between Agnes and Rickie. "She thought him inveterate and conventional. She was envious of his happiness." Agnes was worried and warned Rickie not to aggravate their relationship with Mrs. Failing and thus maintain peace for the remaining few days they were to be her guests. Rickie neither loved nor hated Mrs. Failing, he was simply insoucient about her, as he was also about Wonham. But he was surprised when Agnes told him: "But the Wonham boy is evidently a part of your aunt's life [Mrs. Failing's life]. She laughs at him, but she is fond of him." On Sunday, Mrs. Failing, Agnes, Rickie and even Wonham went to the church of Cadover. Mrs. Failing always and everywhere kept a thorough-bred pagan and seemed 'a cold-eyed Scandinavian' with a twist of Ibsenism in her judgement. Meantime, a quarrel grew between Rickie and his aunt as to his morning service. Rickie told her: "'If organized religion is anything—and it is something to me—it will not be wrecked by a harmonium and a dull sermon.'" Mrs. Failing believed in rituals which Rickie did not believe in, and this was the cause of the quarrel. Leighton announced luncheon and all partook of it. After luncheon Agnes asked Rickie to take a 'solitary walk' along with her and then they proceeded towards where Mrs. Failing had already walked up to for apologizing to Mrs. Failing for Rickie's quarrelling with her.

Rickie 'enjoyed his walk' as the village Cadford was charming. He walked upto the Rings and the charms of Wiltshire opened and he was overjoyed by the charms and then opened a book and read aloud a passage from a poem of Shelley, which passage he earlier had marked 'very good:'

> I never was attached to that great sect
> Whose doctrine is that each one should select
> Out of the world a mistress or a friend,
> And all the rest, though fair and wise, commend
> To cold oblivion,—though it is the code
> Of modern morals, and the beaten road
> Which those poor slaves with weary footsteps tread
> Who travel to their home among the dead
> By the broad highway of the world,—and so
> With one sad friend, perhaps a jealous foe,
> The dreariest and the longest journey go.

"Half a mile off two lovers were keeping company where all the villagers could see them. They cared for no one else; they felt only the pressure of each other, and so progressed, silent and oblivious, across the land. He [Rickie] felt them to be nearer the truth than Shelley. Even if they suffered or quarrelled, they would have been nearer the truth." Suddenly, Rickie viewed his aunt's pony carriage which was followed by Wonham, walking some way behind. Mrs. Failing asked Rickie: "'Will you walk me to the tree in the middle [of the wood]?'" And then taking his arm she proceeded towards that tree. She told him that the place was full of 'ghosties' (ghosts) and asked him to take her 'to the central tree'. She showed him the mangel-wurzels and asked if he admired them, but quite inadvertantly she said that the mangel-wurzels also belonged to Stephen Wonham: "Need I say it is your brother's?" "It was the second time she had made the little slip [of saying that Wonham was Rickie's brother]." Agnes neared them, and now they three were walking together.

And now Mrs. Failing made the third and last slip of tongue about Rickie's brother, Wonham, and this time the slip unmistakably revealed the truth that Wonham was Rickie's half-brother. Rickie nervously protested. "'Stephen Wonham isn't my brother, Aunt Emily.'" Mrs. Failing corrected herself and said that Wonham was his half-brother. Rickie was now puzzled: "'How could I have a half-brother?'" His aunt did not answer. Rickie frantically shouted in protest: "'It's a foul lie!'" And then he lost consciousness. After a while he 'woke up.' Then, "There broke from him a cry, not of horror but of acceptance. For one short moment he understood. 'Stephen—' he began, and then he heard his own name called: 'Rickie! Rickie!'" (section XIII).

On the way back Rickie told Agnes why he fainted, became unconscious. Back to his room, Rickie was 'almost hysterical.' Mrs. Failing came in trembling and asked Agnes if she knew why Rickie was upset. Agnes, with tears in her eyes, said she did. Mrs. Failing persuaded her to believe that she did not tell a lie about Rickie and his half-brother Wonham, but Agnes still believed that Mrs. Failing made a cruel fun of Rickie. Mrs. Failing was now repentent for what she divulged about her nephew, because her words might have soon be circulated even by Stephen Wonham himself, and in the case of that her own respectability would have been in jeopardy. She certainly could not tolerate the scandal about the Wonham boy, she went no further. "After all, she was growing old. And therefore, though she had no true regard for Rickie, nor for Agnes, nor for Stephen, nor for Stephen's parents, in whose tragedy she had assisted, yet she did feel that if the scandal revived it would disturb the harmony of Cadover, and therefore tried to retrace her steps." She kept silent. After a brief interval Agnes asked whether Wonham knew his own identity and Mrs. Failing told her that, only she, Agnes and Rickie knew that. She further told Agnes about Wonham: "'He realizes what he is—with a precision that is sometimes alarming. Who he is, he doesn't know and doesn't care. I suppose he would know when I'm dead. There are papers.'"

Agnes was exceedingly glad to know that Stephen Wonham did not know his true identity, his real heredity, and that he would never know it, because Mrs. Failing would never tell him about his true parentage, and so she and Rickie would not be tainted with the abominability of Wonham. Rickie asked her why his aunt did not divulge to Wonham his identity, which was the 'real thing' about Wonham. Agnes was surprised to hear the words 'real thing,' but only asked him if he was glad to know that Wonham knew nothing about his 'real thing.' Rickie replied: "'My God—no!'" He felt nervous and wanted her help. He told her: "'It seems to me that here and there in life we meet with a person or incident that is symbolical. It's nothing in itself, yet for the moment it stands for some eternal principle. We accept it, at whatever cost, and we have accepted life. But if we are frightened and reject it, the moment, so to speak, passes; the symbol is never offered again.'" He further told her that the symbol once came to him and he accepted it. Saying this Rickie began to fondle a hand of Agnes, but again he began to talk to her: "'But all my disgust; my indignation with my father, my love for—'He broke off; he could not bear to mention the name of his mother.' I was trying to say, I ought n't to follow these impulses too much. There are other things. Truth. Our duty to acknowledge each man accurately, however vile he is. And apart from his ideals' (here she had won the battle),—'and leaving ideals aside, I couldn't meet him [Wonham] and keep silent. It isn't in me. I should blurt it out.'"

Agnes tried to persuade him to believe that the 'symbolic moment' was over, because Stephen Wonham was gone off and would not ever come back to them, that Wonham was 'gone to the sea'. But Rickie told her that Wonham did not go away, whereby she felt frustrated. At this moment Wonham cried out, 'Elliot!' "Then Rickie advanced to the window. The girl [Agnes] darted in front of him. He thought he had never seen her so beautiful. She was stopping his advance quite frankly with widespread arms." Wonham again called out, 'Elliot!' There was a tension in the soul of Rickie: he wanted to answer the call of Wonham, but Agnes would not allow him to do that. The third call from Wonham, 'Elliot!.' Rickie heard it but did not respond; he thought if Wonham called him for the fourth time he must respond 'vile as he is', but Wonham did not call out once more. Rickie then determined to 'shout good-bye to him.' "And once or twice, as he [Rickie] followed the river into darkness, he wondered what it was like to be so weak,—not to ride, not to swim, not to care for anything but books and a girl." Now Rickie and Agnes embraced each other passionately. "The danger had brought them very near to each other. They both needed a home to confront the menacing tumultuous world" (section XIV).

Agnes' sense of purity and morality was predominant over herself and soon Rickie was infected by her sense of purity and morality so that they both hated Wonham. "She could not feel that Stephen [Wonham] had full human rights. He [Wonham] was illicit, abnormal, worse than a man despised. And Rickie, remembering whose son he was, gradually adopted her opinion. He, too, came to be glad that his brother had passed from him untried, that the symbolic moment had been rejected. Stephen was the fruit of sin; therefore he was sinful. He [Rickie], too, became a sexual snob." Meantime, Agnes arranged a *tete-a-tete* between Rickie and his aunt in the 'walled garden,' with a view to letting hear in detail about

Wonham. But Mrs. Failing did not want to further shock Rickie with Wonham's story. Rickie, however, with his aunt's consent, came back home from Cadover, next morning. "And so the disastrous visit ended."

Coming back home, Rickie 'met a certain poor woman, whose child Stephen had rescued at the level-crossing.' Rickie thought that Stephen Wonham had ofcourse brute force (with which he rescued the child) and that Wonham was coarse, ungrateful and irreligious. Thus Wonham's image became repulsive to him, though he himself was dogmatic and intolerant to 'all that was not Love' (especially the love for Agnes). Rickie remembered his 'Dryad manuscript' and with a view to retrieve it from oblivion went up to the attic and began to search for it in the 'strange ghostly place' that was the attic. Leighton was helping him. Rickie "was quite startled when a picture sung towards him, and he saw the Demeter of Cnidus, shimmering and grey." Ultimately he found the manuscript 'lay in a gutter, charred and smudged.' "The rest of the year was spent by Rickie partly in bed—he had a curious breakdown—partly in the attempt to get his little stories published. He had written eight or nine, and hoped they would make up a book, and that the book might be called 'Pan Pipes.' He was very energetic over this; he liked to work, for some imperceptible bloom had passed from the world, and he no longer found such acute pleasure in people. Mr. Failing's old publishers, to whom the book was submitted, replied that, greatly as they found themselves interested, they did not see their way to making an offer at present. They were very polite, and singled out for special praise 'Andante Pastorale,' which Rickie had thought too sentimental, but which Agnes had persuaded him to include. The stories were sent to another publisher, who considered them for six weeks, and then returned them. A fragment of red cotton, placed by Agnes between the leaves, had not shifted its position." Agnes told Rickie: "'I believe we're on the wrong track. Try an out-and-out love-story.'" Rickie said that he rather wanted 'to leave the passions on the fringe.' The two lovers were conversing in a London restaurant in Soho. Agnes also asked him to write his stories plainly, clearly, without making them complicated, difficult. She was now in favour of romance, imagination and poetry as against her earlier penchant for realism and truth. She told Rickie that "soul's what matters" not the body, though, ofcourse she did not understand what poetry is. "Actual life might seem to her so real that she could not detect the union of shadow and adamant that men call poetry." Nevertheless, Rickie was very pleased with her; to him 'she was incomparable'.

Tilliard unexpectedly presented himself before them from nowhere. After a little bit of conversation among the three, "Agnes put her lover safely into an omnibus at Cambridge Circus" and Rickie met the editor of the 'Holborn', 'a tall neat man of forty, slow of speech, slow of soul, and extraordinarily kind.' The editor told Rickie that his stories were not convincing, meaning they were flushed with imagination, mysteries, and the supernatural. Of course the editor did not quite object to all these, but he advised Rickie to write 'ghost stories' which, he assured him, he would at once accept. The editor's alternative suggestion was that Rickie might 'get inside life' through his stories. Rickie returned home, realising that his career of a writer was not going to be better than that of Mr Herbert Pembroke, that "his fortunes became intimately connected with those of Mr Pembroke" (section XV).

Part II: Sawston

"In three years Mr Pembroke had done much to solidify the day-boys at Sawston school." The headmaster was satisfied with Mr Herbert Pembroke's qualifications and dealings, but he was influenced by a particular demand of the parents of the boarders that the house-master, which Mr Pembroke was, 'should have a wife,' and consequently informed Mr Pembroke of the demand. The headmaster made it clear that if he did not marry, his appointment would be treated as probational, 'experimental.' To avoid disappointment, "two days later Mr Pembroke proposed to Mrs. Orr." But Mrs. Orr violently refused his proposal. Mr Pembroke "had always intended to marry when he could afford it; and once he had been in love, violently in love, but had laid the passion aside, and told it to wait till a more convenient season. This was, of course, the proper thing to do, and prudence should have been rewarded. But when, after the lapse of fifteen years, he went, as it were, to his spiritual larder and took down Love from the top shelf to offer him to Mrs. Orr, he was rather dismayed." He found that the god of love had parted with him. "Mr. Pembroke was conscientious and romantic, and knew that marriage without love is intolerable. On the other hand, he could not admit that love had vanished from him. To admit this would argue that he had deteriorated. Whereas he knew for a fact that he improved year by year. Each year he grew more moral, more efficient, more learned, more genial. So how could he fail to be more loving?"

But what he could not conceive of to have happened, happened—Mrs. Orr rejected him. He thought what the most he could have done for her he did. He thought: "... I rather suspect that it is a nobler, riper emotion that I am laying at the feet of Mrs. Orr." But his thoughts were muddled. "Mrs. Orr was quiet, clever, kindly, capable, and amusing, and they [she and Mr. Pembroke] were old acquaintances. Altogether it was not surprising that he should ask her to be his wife, nor very surprising that she should refuse. But she refused with a violence that alarmed them both. He left her house declaring that he had been insulted, and she, as soon as he left, passed from disgust into tears." Mr. Pembroke continued to pine for Mrs. Orr.

Dismayed on all sides as regards Mrs. Orr, Mr. Pembroke thought of proposing to Miss Herriton, but he reined himself in, and thought of becoming a clergyman by taking orders and then of founding a school of his own. He thought: "Agnes must marry Rickie in the Christmas holidays, and they must come, both of them, to Sawston, she as housekeeper, he as assistant-master." Mr. Pembroke immediately disclosed this plan of his to Agnes who came from Soho, but she refused to comment on the plan until she consulted Rickie. The lovers agreed that they would get married the earliest, but the plan of Mr. Pembroke was not savoury to him. However, Rickie told her that the editor of 'Holborn' wanted 'life' in his short stories. He asked her: "What does he *mean* by life?" Agnes said she could not explain what the editor meant by life; nevertheless she told him: "You ought to see life, Rickie." Rickie murmured, "'I wonder what Ansell would say,'" obviously to Agnes insistence on life. Agnes heard the murmur and ejaculated: "Oh, poor Mr. Ansell!" This was the first time the epithet 'poor' was applied to Ansell, but Rickie could not understand why Agnes used the epithet. However, Agnes told Rickie that had they earlier got married, they could avoid 'this horrible fog' (surrounding Stephen Wonham), by getting to Italy. Rickie accorded; he thought that "Perhaps life would be there"—the life the editor had been talking about. "He did not aspire to beauty or wisdom, but he prayed to be delivered from the shadow of unreality that had began to darken them." He decided he must do good to humanity, to do which as a schoolmaster he had wide opportunity. He had been thinking six months ago, when he had been at Cambridge: "To do good! For what other reasons are we here? Let us give up our refined sensations and our comforts, and our art, if thereby we can make other people happier and better. The woman he loved had urged him to do good!" But now at Sawston he lost his philanthropy, and was "preparing to work a beneficent machine." He began to work for benefits (section XVI).

Mr. Pembroke "offered Rickie a good salary, and insisted on paying Agnes as well" for their services in the school at Sawston. He said he most valued 'athletics or organization' and advised Rickie to 'adopt a frankly intellectual attitude' and to deny that he was 'an all-round man'. In course of time, Rickie was inducted into the staff of the school, and his 'new life began.' His health slightly improved, 'and he was nervous at the prospect of confronting the assembled house.' Agnes' task it was to superintend the numbering of the hats of the boys. At eight-ten Rickie went to the school on the first day, along with Mr. Pembroke who addressed the assembled boys thus: "'school is the world in miniature'." Mr. Pembroke then exhorted the boys "to be patriotic, athletic, learned, and religious", and pointing to the portraits of 'empire builders' that hung on the wall he explained "how patriatism has broadened since the days of Shakespeare, who, for all his genius, could only write of his country as—

This fortress built by Nature for herself
Against infection and the hand of war;
This happy breed of men, this little world;
This precious stone set in the silver sea.

And it seemed that only a short ladder lay between the preparation-room and the Anglo-Saxon hegemony of the globe. Then he paused, and in the silence came 'sob, sob, sob,' from a little boy who was regretting a villa in Guildford and his mother's half acre of garden." The proceeding terminated with the singing of the school anthem that voiced the limit of patriotism:

'Perish each laggard! Let it not be said
That Sawston such within her walls hath bred.'

Mr. Pembroke tried to impress upon Rickie that "Tradition is of incalculable importance, if a school is to have any status." He admitted that the Sawston school had no tradition and explained that it was due to the fact that "'sons of poor tradesmen went to it at first'". He was extremely censorious of the day-boys who were, he thought, also responsible for the traditionlessness of the school: "'Owing to the day-boys. How can tradition flourish in such soil? Picture the day-boy's life—at home for meals, at home for preparation, at home for sleep, running home with every fancied wrong. There are day-boys in your class, and, mark my words, they will give you ten times as much trouble as boarders,—late, slovenly, stopping away at the slightest pretext. And then the letters from the parents! 'Why has my boy not been moved this term?' 'Why has my boy been moved this term?' 'I am a dissenter, and do not wish my boy to subscribe to the school mission.' 'Can you let my boy off to water the garden?'" Mr. Pembroke told Rickie: "'Remember that I have been a day-boy house-master, and tried to infuse some *esprit de corps* into them. It is practically impossible.'" In fact, Mr. Pembroke wished every boy enter into a 'beneficent machine', which the Sawston school was, 'and learn the value *of esprit de corps*'. But, inspite of himself, Rickie could not grasp the spirit of the practical sermon of Mr. Pembroke.

Nevertheless, as the term wore on, Rickie "lost his independence—almost without knowing it." He began to imitate the more experienced masters, and was getting converted to their customs. He now forgot his ideal of 'personal intercourse' with the pupils and others, and substituted it with his newly learnt theory of 'personal influence'. "Originally Rickie had meant to help boys in the anxieties that they undergo when changing into men: at Cambridge he had numbered this among life's duties." But in the school he found that his duty was only to provide the boys with some simple formulae. Howbeit, Rickie, willy-nilly, was sucked into the tradition of the school—was, so to say, acculturised in the school. "In his form, oddly enough, he became a martinet. It is so much simpler to be severe. He grasped the school regulations, and insisted on prompt obedience to them. He adopted the doctrine of collective responsibility." Though as a teacher he was rather dull, Rickie somehow could not be wholly overshadowed by Herbert Pembroke because Herbert was stupid. "Not stupid in the ordinary sense—he had a business-like brain, and acquired knowledge easily—but stupid in the important sense: his whole life was coloured by a contempt of the intellect.... He came to his worthier results rather by imagination and instinct than by logic." And he was so even after coming through Cambridge. He was only after one thing success—"success for the body in this life or for the soul in the life to come. And for this reason Humanity, and perhaps such other tribunals as there may be, would assuredly reject him" (section XVII).

"Meanwhile he [Rickie] was a husband... Never again must he feel lonely, or as one who stands out of the broad highway of the world and fears, like poor Shelley, to undertake the longest journey." But "Neither by marriage nor by any other device can men ensure themselves a vision; and Rickie's had been granted him three years before, when he had seen his wife and a dead man clasped in each other's arms. She was never to be so real to him again." Nevertheless she continued to develop the happiness of the house: she looked handsomer, 'she would dart in and give him a kiss.' "The tone of their marriage life was soon set." They never mentioned Gerald's name, but Rickie thought that his name was yet dear to Agnes; and, in fact, Rickie "did not want her to forget the greatest moment in her life. His love desired not ownership but confidence, and to a love so pure it does not seem terrible to come second." Agnes loved him honestly, but she could not bear to hear him in raised voice. Rickie "valued emotion—not for itself, but because it is the only final path to intimacy." He could not stand unkindness of any sort, not even of his father. He told Agnes: "'My father found me a nuisance, and put me through the mill, and I can never forget it—particularly the evenings.'" He philosophically told her: "'It's not what people do to you, but what they mean, that hurts.'" He explained: "'Physical pain doesn't hurt—at least not what I call hurt—if a man hits you by accident or in play. But just a little tap, when you know it comes from hatred, is too terrible.'"

Rickie turned to friendship and 'general good-fellowship' and told Agnes that the boys of Sawston school "'can make strong isolated friendships, but of general good-fellowship they haven't a notion.'" He continued: "'You see, the notion of good-fellowship develops late... up at Cambridge it flourishes amazingly.'" He believed that good-fellowship did not develop in sawston school or in the boarding-house system. Rickie censored the theories of organisation and of mechanisation which were adopted in the Sawston school. He told Agnes: "'But seriously, what is the good of throwing boys together? Isn't it building their lives on a wrong basis? They don't understand each other. I wish they did, but they don't. They don't realize that human beings are simply marvellous. When they do, the whole of life changes, and you get the true thing.'" Rickie did not stop there, but went on: "'Patriotism and *esprit de corps* are all very well, but masters a little forget that they must grow from a sentiment. They cannot create one. Cannot—cannot—cannot. I never cared a atraw for

England until I cared for Englishmen, and boys can't love the school when they hate each other.'" However, the turgid emotion of Rickie soon subsided, particularly when Agnes caressed him with a kiss. Rickie might not have been very happy with the goings-on of the school but "His first morning's work had brought sixty pounds a year to their [Rickie's and Agnes'] hotel" (section XVIII).

Rickie did not go to Italy after his marriage, as decided earlier, for money was necessary and only in Endland he could earn money. So Rickie and Agnes put up in Ilfracombe, a resort, where the Jackson family also stayed. Mr. Jackson became friendly and even intimate with Rickie, and he frequently used to engage in talks with Rickie, especially on the dramas and dramatic fragments of Sophocles, and also on poetry and Greek mythology. Rickie wrote to Stewart Ansell to come to them even if for a day, but Ansell's reply was rather rude—he would not. Ansell was 'brutal' and this Rickie understood, but Rickie could not explain why Agnes was jealous. "Let husband and wife be as sun and moon, or as moon and sun. Shall they therefore not give greeting to the stars?" Agnes, though jealous of him, "began to patronize and pity Ansell." She was jealous not only of Ansell, but of many other things, including Nature. For, when one day Rickie looked through the window at the Virgilian countryside, she was jealous of Nature "as if Nature was some dangerous woman." However, Rickie resumed his duties for the next term, when everything of the school—its routine works etc.—seemed to him to be unreal. He told his wife about this, and the wife asked him to see a doctor, thinking he had been suffering from some mental derangement. But he explained that it was nothing serious, no more serious than the mental twist of one who thought that "the cow as not really there"—that everything one saw was unreal (section XIX).

In the British Museum, Ansell, who had been preparing his second dissertation, and Widdrington were conversing among high heaps of books on the sorry affairs of the Sawston school, when suddenly Widdrington changed topic and said: "'My cousin thinks Mrs. Elliot [Agnes] one of the most horrible women he has ever seen. He calls her 'Medusa in Archady.' She's so pleasant too.'" Weddrington did not agree with his cousin; he rather compared Mrs. Elliot with an electric light: "'Click! she's on. Click! she's off. No waste. No flicker.'" He asked Ansell, who could not follow his simile about Agnes, to visit her and understand the simile for himself. But Ansell said that "'she has no real existence.'" Widdrington said Rickie had his existence, which Ansell doubted. He said that Rickie's existence was so unhappy, which Ansell did not doubt. Widdrington said about Rickie: "'I'm certain he's miserable and lonely... He doesn't do any writing. He doesn't make any friends. He is so odd, too .... Yet he's not been married a year. Pembroke and that wife simply run him.'" Ansell confided to him that he knew "'not only Rickie but the whole of his history'" and that he was 'watching' in Rickie "'For the Spirit of Life.'" Ansell told him: "'You can't fight Medusa with anything else. If you ask me what the spirit of life is, or to what it is attached, I can't tell you. I only tell you, watch for it. Myself I've found it in books. Some people find it out of doors or in each other. Never mind. It's the same spirit, and I trust myself to know it anywhere, and to use it rightly.'" Widdrington failed to make out anything of what Ansell said. They began to stroll and met Tilliard who brought the news that 'Mrs. Elliot [Agnes] was expecting a child'. Ansell was bewildered. Widdrington said that he had heard the news from his cousin. Ansell began to recall their talk about the 'Spirit of Life'. Tilliard said that he was glad to know of the expected child, and that "'A child will draw them [Rickie and Agnes] even closer together. I like to see young people wrapped up in their child.'" Ansell announced that he was going to work on his dissertation. "Honest, he knew that here were powers he could not cope with, nor, as yet, understand" (section XX).

The 'glamour of wedlock' appeared to Rickie to have faded. Now he "had found light neither in work for which he was unfitted nor in a woman who had ceased to respect him, and whom he was ceasing to love." "It dawned on him, as on Ansell, that personal love and marriage only cover one side of the shield, and that on the other is graven the epic of birth. In the midst of lessons he would grow dreamy, as one who spies a new symbol for the universe, a fresh circle within the square. Within the circle another square, until the visual eye is baffled. Here is meaning of a kind. His mother had forgotten herself in him. He would forget himself in his son. "Rickie was informed that Agnes gave birth to a lame daughter. Lame, but the child would live—that was the consolation of Rickie." But, "After a short, painless illness his daughter died" (section XXI).

One day, at Dunwood House, A.C. Varden, a student-boarder was so cruelly ragged and pulled by the ear that a doctor had to be called in, and the doctor talked of an operation. Rickie consoled him saying: "'The world isn't all going to be like this. There are temptations and trials, of course, but nothing at all of the kind you have had here.'" Many letters arrived, in which the "writers declared that his illness was fulfilling some mysterious purpose, suffering engendered spiritual growth: he [Varden] was showing signs of this already." There was one very exceptional letter and that from Stephen Wonham. Wonham suggested that when Varden was being pulled by the ear, he should have physically react, without lying low: "'When they pulled your ear, you ought to have gone like this (here was a rough sketch)... I am twenty-two in April, built rather heavy, ordinary broad face, with eyes, &c.... I am not married'" (section XXII).

There was now a wide gulf between Rickie and his wife, such that to him "She, like the world she had created for him, was unreal." Agnes by now "had got over the tragedy: she got over everything." However, so far both of them had seldom mentioned Stephen, He was classed among the 'unprofitable dead.' Rickie now unexpectedly found that Agnes was more sympathetic to Stephen Wonham. But she persuaded him to be on the alert not to let Wonham know that he was Rickie's half-brother. And all at the same time she asked him to see Aunt Emily, his father's sister. Rickie was disinclined to meet Aunt Emily. Rickie and Agnes were conversing between them, but at a certain point of their conversation Rickie became enraged on the suspicion that Agnes was probably thinking of grasping the legacy of Aunt Emily who had no actual heir.

Rickie now raised his voice and objected to the mysterious suppression of the fact that Stephen Wonham was his half-brother. He asked Agnes: "'... Why shouldn't he [Wonham] know he's my brother? What's all this ridiculous mystery?'" Rickie told her that they were acting a lie [that Wonham was no brother of his]. He burst out before her: "'It's been like a poison we won't acknowledge. How many times have you thought of my brother? I've thought of him every day—not in love; don't misunderstand; only as a medicine I shirked. Down in what they call the subconscious self he has been hurting me.'" Rickie told Agnes: "'let us write, as coldly as you please, to Stephen, and tell him he is my father's son.'"

But in the evening Rickie made an hundred and eighty degree turn and kissing his wife told her that he would certainly not write to Stephen Wonham to tell him that he was his half-brother, through his father. Agnes returned the kiss. Rickie, however, could not think that his dead father had been so cruel to him as to leave behind for him a brother illegally got—Stephen Wonham: "His father, as a final insult, had brought into the world a man unlike all the rest of them,—a man dowered with coarse kindliness, and rustic strength, a kind of cynical plough-boy, against whom their own misery and weakness might stand more vividly relieved." He thought that this man, Stephen Wonham, and not he, would beget children and then would become immortal. He fell asleep and dreamt of his mother crying. From now on he was deteriorating: he lost his job, friends and child. And from now on "the spiritual part of him proceeded towards ruin" (section XXIII).

Meantime many things happened: Rickie's deterioration continued; Herbert visited Athens and Delphi; the Elliots paid a visit to England; Widdrington was stopping with the Jacksons; etc. Also meantime Stewart Ansell failed to procure a fellowship at Cambridge. However, the spiritual part of Agnes was also drying up. "... Agnes continued her life, cheerfully beating time. She, too, knew that her marriage was a failure, and in her spare moments regretted it. She wished that her husband was handsomer, more successful, more dictatorial. But she would think, 'No, no; one mustn't grumble. It can't be helped.' Ansell was wrong in supposing she might ever leave Rickie. Spiritual apathy prevented her. Nor could she ever be tempted by a jollier man. Here criticism would willingly alter its tone. For Agnes also has her tragedy. She belonged to the type—not necessarily an elevated one—that loves once and once only. Her love for Gerald had not been a noble passion: no imagination transfigured it. But such as it was, it sprang to embrace him and he carried it away with him when he died. *Les amours qui suivent sont moins involuntaires:* by an effort of the will she had warmed herself for Rickie. "She is not conscious of her tragedy, and therefore only the gods need weep at it. But it is fair to remember that hitherto she moves as one from whom the inner life has been withdrawn" (section XXIV).

Agnes, Rickie and Herbert were conversing about Stephen Wonham at supper. Agnes said that Mrs. Failing failed to properly raise up Stephen Wonham who had by then taken to drink and "now he has taken to be violent and rude." Mrs. Failing had been bringing Stephen up at Cadover since he was born, and she happened to be fond of him until he took to drinking. She was as if both his father and mother. Stephen grew up without any 'fixed principles' and he 'always followed his inclinations'. Howbeit, Rickie is remorseful because of his belief that he had somehow ruined his half-brother Stephen (assumeably, by not recognising him and thereby disinheriting him, and letting him take to drinks, etc. under the neglectful guardianship of Mrs. Failing). "A curious tenderness came over him, and passed when he remembered his own dead child." Rickie and Agnes were debating on the point of Rickie's share of responsibility in the degradation of Wonham. Herbert interposed and told Rickie: "'I have now heard both sides of this deplorable affair. You are talking most criminal nonsense. 'Disinherit!' Sentimental twaddle. It's been clear to me from the first that Mrs. Failing has been imposed upon by the Wonham man, a person with no legal claim on her, and any one who exposes him performs a public duty—." Rickie was deeply affected by Herbert's pronunciation. "Tears came into his eyes." He said: "'It is not that I like the Wonham man

[Stephen], or think that he isn't a drunkard and worse. He's too awful in every way. But he ought to have my aunt's money, because he's lived all his life with her, and is her nephew as much as I am. You see my father went wrong'" (section XXV).

Stephen Wonham very well knew that "One must be the son of some one", but he was in the dark about whose son he was, and he did never show any interest in discovering his parentage. However, there was a very cordial relation between Rickie and Wonham, nevertheless. Wonham did never believe that he was 'a blot on God's earth' and he believed that as Rickie and Agnes were thoroughly learned they would not concern themselves with 'blots': "'Rickie and Agnes are properly educated, which leads people to look at things straight, and not to go screaming about blots.'" Ansell was curiously watching the goings-on between Rickie and Wonham "forgetting that all this world, and not part of it is a stage" (section XXVI).

Wonham had came to know of his mysterious parentage and told Agnes about it: "'It's very odd. It is that I'm Rickie's brother.'" Agnes surprisedly enquired: "'Yes?'" Wonham replied: "'I'm illegitimate. Legally speaking, that is, I've been turned out of Cadover. I haven't a penny. I—'" Agnes' "face, which had been an even brown, began to flush slowly in the centre of the cheeks. The colour spread till all that he saw of her was suffused, and she turned away. He thought he had shocked her, and so did she. Neither knew that the body can be sincere and express not the emotions we feel but those that we should like to feel. In reality she was quite calm, and her dislike of him had nothing emotional in it as yet." Wonham was desperately in need of money and so Agnes, in consultation with her husband, offered him money, on the condition that he would never sue Rickie for share in his [Rickie's] property. Agnes so asked him to sign a document earlier prepared by Herbert to that effect. The document read as follows: "'In consideration of the sum of—I agree to perpetual silence—to restrain from libellous...never to molest the said Frederick Elliot [Rickie] by intruding'"—Wonham felt inordinately humiliated at this, refused to sign the document, and quickly walked out. At the corner of the road "he cleared his throat, spat into the gutter, and disappeared." Before all this, when he refused to sign the document, Agnes hotly warned him: "'...We defy you!'" Meantime Ansell and Rickie arrived, and during their conversation Ansell divulged to Rickie the shocking mystery of Stephen Wonham's birth.' "'Please listen again, resumed Ansell. 'Please correct two slight mistakes: firstly, Stephen is one of the greatest people I have ever met; secondly, he's not your father's son. He's the son of your mother'" (section XXVII).

Section XXVIII is unique, in the sense that in it the narrative does not advance even an iota; it is nothing else than just the narrator's comment on the nature and properties of the soul, particularly of the soul of Agnes. This three-paragraph very short section reads as follows: "The soul has her own currency. She mints her spiritual coinage and stamps it with the image of some beloved face. With it she pays her debts, with it she reckons, saying, 'This man has worth, this man is worthless.'" And in time she forgets its origin; it seems to her to be a thing unalterable, divine. But the soul can also have her bankruptcies. "Perhaps she will be the richer in the end. In her agony she learns to reckon clearly. Fair as the coin may have been, it was not accurate; and though she knew it not, there were treasures that it could not buy. The face, however beloved, was mortal, and as liable as the soul herself to err. We do but shift responsibility by making a standard of the dead. "There is, indeed, another coinage that bears on it not man's image but God's. It is incorruptible, and the soul may trust it safely; it will serve her beyond the stars. But it cannot give us friends, or the embrace of a lover, or the touch of children, for with our fellow-mortals it has no concern. It cannot even give the joys we call trivial—fine weather, the pleasures of meat and drink, bathing and the hot sand afterwards, running, dreamless sleep. Have we learnt the true discipline of a bankruptcy if we turn to such coinage as this? Will it really profit us so much if we save our souls and lose the whole world?" (section XXVIII).

Part III: Wiltshire

This section narrates the birth of Stephen Wonham, the son of certain Robert and Rickie's mother Mrs. Elliot (her first child, Rickie, being the second). Mr. Robert "a young farmer of some education", "came to Cadover on business and fell in love with Mrs. Elliot [Rickie's mother]." "She was there on her bridal visit, and he, an obscure nobody, was received by Mrs. Failing into the house and treated as her social equal. He was good-looking in a bucolic way, and people sometimes mistook him for a gentleman until they saw his hands." Once, when Robert was talking with Mrs. Elliot, "he was so close to her—so close that it was difficult not to take her in his arms—he spoke to Mr. Failing, and was at once turned out of Cadover." But this humiliation by Mr. Failing could not deter Robert from further loving Mrs. Elliot and thereby trying to win her. "Robert simply waited. He told himself that it was hopeless; but something deeper than himself declared that there was hope. He gave up drink, and kept himself in all ways clean, for he wanted to be worthy of her when the time came. Women seemed fond of him, and caused him to reflect with pleasure, 'They do run after me. There must be something in me. Good. I'd be done for if there wasn't.' For six years he turned up the earth of Wiltshire, and read books for the sake of his mind, and talked to gentlemen for the sake of their patois, and each year he rode to Cadover to take off his hat to Mrs. Elliot, and, perhaps, to speak to her about the crops." Then once in London Robert "chanced to see Mr. Elliot [Rickie's father] with a strange lady." Robert thought, "The time had come."

Strangely, Rickie's father was indifferent about what was going on between his wife and Robert. "And next time he saw his wife he congratulated her on her rustic admirer [Robert]." "Robert brought her an armful of sweet-peas." He also used to bring flowers for her, and would tell her that her husband was no good, and she would tell him that she was glad for he loved her. But however much did Robert cajoled her, she showed utter disgust towards him. One day Mrs. Elliot sweetly but emphatically told Robert: "'You either go now with my thanks and my blessing, or else you go with the police. I am Mrs. Elliot [Rickie's mother]... I am Mrs. Elliot, and if you make one step towards me I give you in charge.'" Just at that moment Mr. Elliot [Rickie's father] arrived there and shook hands with Robert with all urbanity. But Mrs. Elliot sternly asked her husband to drive Robert out of the house, and when her husband asked her the reason she told because "Robert said he loved her". She cried out to her husband "'Turn him out at once!'" and then told him about Robert: "'He has insulted your wife. Save me, save me!'" And after this Mrs. Elliot "clung to her husband and wept". Robert went out and afterwards he could not be traced out anywhere in London. Mr. Elliot now "began to realise that his wife could never belong to him again."

Mr. Failing got a letter from Stockholm written by a person he could not identify, but the person was none else than Robert. Robert eloped with Mrs. Elliot [Rickie's mother] to Stockholm, and from there wrote that it was due to the law of England that they had gone there, meaning perhaps that in England he could not marry Mrs. Elliot without Mr. Elliot's consent, but in Stockholm she was free to marry him. Robert wrote about himself, Mrs. Elliot and Mr. Elliot. "'I shall come back to face things: she will not come back till she is my wife. He [Mr. Elliot] must bring an action soon, or else we shall try one against him..... We are not like you or your wife: we want to be just ordinary people.... and not to be noticed all our lives.'" Robert and Mrs. Elliot did not believe in class difference. "Their love of beauty, like their love for each other, was not dependent on detail: it grew not from the nerves but from the soul." Mrs. Failing thought Robert and Mrs. Elliot could not be ordinary people, as Robert wrote in the letter, but they were "'forces of Nature!'"

However, soon "Robert had been drowned. Mrs. Elliot described how they had gone swimming, and how, since he always lived inland, the great waves had tored him. They had raced for the open sea." After this Mrs. Elliot returned. And Mr. Elliot, though he made certain stipulations, was positively glad to see her. People had began to laugh at him, and to say that his wife had run away. She had not. She had been with his sister in Sweden. In a half-miraculous way the matter was hushed up. Even the Silts only scented 'something strange'. When Stephen was born, it was abroad. When he came to England, it was as the child of a friend of Mr. Failing's. Mrs. Elliot returned unsuspected to her husband. "But though things can be hushed up, there is no such thing as beating home; and as the years passed she realized her terrible mistake. When her lover sank, eluding her last embrace, she thought, as Agnes was to think after her, that her soul had sunk with him, and that never again should she be capable of earthly love. Nothing mattered. She might as well go and be useful to her husband and to the little boy who looked exactly like him, and who, she thought, was exactly like him in disposition." Mrs. Elliot's second child, Rickie, was born in the meantime. "Her second child drew her towards her first. She began to love Rickie also, and to be more than useful to him. And as her love revived, so *did* her capacity for suffering. Life, more important, grew more bitter. She minded her husband more, not less." But the end came too soon to them. Mr. Elliot died first and then Mrs. Elliot (section XXIX).

Stephen felt frustrated, lonely, despondent, particularly after Mr. Failing, of whom he was fond, and Mrs. Elliot, died. "He was then twelve." He was in the school only for a brief period and then left it. "His parents had given him excellent gifts—health, sturdy limbs, and a face not ugly—gifts that his habits confirmed. They had also given him a cloudless spirit—the spirit of the seventeen days in which he was created. But they had not given him the spirit of their six years of waiting, and love for one person was never to be the greatest thing he knew." He became a materialist and took to drink and became "Somewhat a bully by nature." One thing that he wanted most was power. With all these connotations Stephen Wonham one day "left Wiltshire, half-blackguard, half-martyr." "Do not brand him as a socialist. He had no quarrel with society, nor any particular belief in people because they are poor. He only held the creed of 'here am I and there are you', and therefore class distinctions were trivial things to him, and life no decorous scheme, but a personal combat or a personal truce." Stephen Wonham went to the Isle of Wight leaving Wiltshire behind, and there he found employment. But neither job satisfaction nor moderate payment did he find there. "At the end of ten days he had saved scarcely anything." However, after some days Stephen went to Rickie and Agnes who were stopping at Wiltshire (section XXX).

Stephen came to Rickie to live with him. Rickie as if got a new life "For the son of his mother had come back, to forgive him, as she would have done, to live with him, as she had planned." Stephen, as told earlier, had already taken to drink, heavy drink. Rickie softly told Agnes about Stephen. "'...It makes no difference whose son he is. I mean, he is the same person. You and I and my sister stand or fall together. It was our agreement from the first I hope—No more of these distressing scenes with her, there's a dear fellow. I assure you they make my heart bleed.'" Rickie's mind was filled up with the sense of the substance of Shelley's poem 'Epipsychidion'; he asked Agnes to go to bed: "'I never did belong to that great sect whose doctrine is that each one should select—at least, I'm not going to belong to it any longer. Go away to bed.'" Rickie cursed his mother, but the philosopher Ansell advised him not to mind anything but only love, because "On the banks of the grey torrent of life, love is the only flower."

Rickie suddenly announced in the morning that Stephen Wonham must live with them at Dunwood House. He said: "'There's nothing to be done. Cadover's hopeless, and a boy of those tendencies can't go drifting. There is also the question of a profession for him, and his allowance.'" Herbert was there, and he commented: "'I foresee disaster.'" Rickie's decision wounded Agnes' delicacy. "Rickie had not kept his wife in line. He had shown her all the workings of his soul, mistaking this for love; and in consequence she was the worse woman after two years of marriage, and he, on this morning of freedom, was harder upon her than he need have been." He stuck to his decision, particularly because he had come to know that Stephen was the son of his mother, whom he loved, and not of his father, whom he hated. Stephen heard of

Gerald, but he did not know his relation with Agnes or Rickie. Stephen enquired of Gerald and Rickie told him that Gerald was the name of someone whom Agnes knew and who was then dead. Rickie told him that it was after Gerald's death that he inclined towards Agnes, trusting that she had forgotten him, as it appeared from her behaviour. However, Rickie told Stephen that Agnes was probably plotting for his ouster from that house. Knowing this Stephen rushed away from the house, when Rickie, from behind, was calling out at him: "'Come, I do mean it. Come; I will take care of you, I can manage you'" (section XXXI).

Mr. Herbert Pembroke understood that Agnes was concealing from him the fact that "Hitherto she had pretended to love her husband." On the other hand, Rickie imagined himself more to be 'his brother's keeper' than to be the husband of Agnes. Agnes was becoming less and less attentive towards Rickie; she was rather more concerned with the keeping of her dead child's memory alive than keeping Rickie lively. In fine, Rickie was drifting away from Agnes, and she from him. Rumours were afloat that a divorce between Rickie and Agnes was being stipulated. Agnes now—surprising enough—became sympathetic towards Stephen while "all her hatred were turned against Rickie." She recalled the memory of Gerald, taking cues that day from the poise of the strong shoulders of Stephen. Stephen "had reminded her of the greatest thing she had known, and to her cloudy mind this seemed degradation. She had turned to him as to her lover; with a look, which a man of his type understood, she had asked for his pity; for one terrible moment she had desired to be held in his arms." "Stephen was illicit, abnormal, worse than a man diseased. Yet she had turned to him: he had drawn out the truth" (section XXXII).

Rickie wished to visit Cadover and he started by train, and when the train stopped for shunting, "Stephen's face appeared, convulsed with laughter. With the action of a swimmer he dived in through the open window, and fell comfortably on Rickie's luggage and Rickie. He declared it was the finest joke ever known." Stephen told Rickie that he was going with him to Cadover. He did not behave quite civilly in the train; for instance, he once blew "a kiss out of the window to maidens." Rickie told him not to drink, in the names of morality and the Bible. "'There is also a thing called Morality. You may learn in the Bible, and also from the Greeks, that your body is a temple.'" After some time, "Rickie pretended to read. Over the book he watched his brother's face, and wondered how bad temper could be consistent with a mind so radiant. In spite of his obstinacy and conceit, Stephen was an easy person to live with. He never fidgeted or nursed bidden grievances, or indulged in a shoddy pride." Rickie wanted a man first and then a brother, and both the man and the brother he found in Stephen, and so Stephen was agreeable to him. "Stephen was man first, brother afterwards. Herein lay his brutality and also his virtue." He would tell Rickie: "'Look me in the face. Don't hang on me clothes that don't belong—as you did on your wife, giving her saint's robes, whereas she was simply a woman of her own sort, who needed careful watching. Tear up the photographs. Here am I, and there are you. The rest is cant.'" Rickie needed such a man who would work as a tonic on him; the believer but weak Rickie needed the help of the atheist but strong Stephen.

Rickie came to understand that civilisation meant at least four things; 'Organize', 'Systematize', 'Fill up every moment', and 'Induce *esprit de corps*.' He also understood that civilisation ignored 'personal contest', 'personal truces' and 'personal love'. And he further understood that Sawston represented civilisation. His train was running through the countryside, and so Rickie could clearly see the difference between the town and the country. He thought: "The country is not paradise, and can show the vices that grieve a good man everywhere. But there is room in it, and leisure." On the other hand, he supposed "that towns are after all excrescences, grey fluxions, where men, hurrying to find one another, have lost themselves." Rickie and Stephen were now conversing in a horse-drawn carriage. Stephen said: "I expect that some time or other I shall marry." Stephen showed his preference for romantic love or marriage. "There are men and women—we know it from history—who have been born into the world for each other, and for no one else, who have accomplished the longest journey locked in each other's arms. But romantic love is also the code of modem morals, and, for this reason, popular. Eternal union, eternal ownership—these are tempting baits for the average man. He swallows them, will not confess his mistake, and—perhaps to cover it—cries 'dirty cynic' at such a man as Stephen." Ansell once had said: "'A man wants to love mankind, a woman wants to love one man.'" In the case of Rickie and his wife Agnes, Ansell's antithesis found an exemplum (section XXXIII).

Rickie and Stephen reached the home of Mrs. Failing when she was about to prepare for dinner. Meantime Mr. Failing's posthumous book of essays was published and Mrs. Failing was pleased over it. She asked Rickie to read aloud from the particular essay 'The True Patriot' and he did that: "'Let us love one another. Let our children, physical and spiritual, love one another. It is all that we can do. Perhaps the earth will neglect our love. Perhaps she will confirm it, and suffer some rallying point, spire, mound, for the new generations to cherish.'" Rickie confessed to Mrs. Failing that Agnes, his wife, does not love him, nor he her. Mrs. Failing then cautioned him not to expect anything romantic from this earth. She told him that we could not escape conventions, and that ultimately conventions would swallow us: "'... I am not being sentimental. I say once more, beware of the earth. We are conventional people, and conventions—if you will but see it—are majestic in their way, and will claim us in the end. We do not live for great passions or for great memories or for anything great.'" Rickie could not agree with her: he said people certainly lived for great passions or for something great. Mrs. Failing asked him not to be sentimental but to go back to his wife: "'Now listen to me. I am serious and friendly to-night, as you must have observed.... My age is fifty-nine, and I tell you solemnly that the important things in life are little things, and that people are not important at all. Go back to your wife.'"

Rickie refused to concord with her: he told her: "'... people are important, and therefore, however much it inconveniences my wife, I will not go back to her.'" Rickie said that in the case of failure of marriage, the characters were to be blamed, and not the marriage; but Mrs. Failing said that in the case of that marriage itself was to be held responsible. Rickie abandoned marriage and took to literature, and he was thereby happy. Mrs. Failing asked how it was so, and Rickie replied: "'Because, as we used to say at Cambridge, the cow is there. The world is real again. This is a room, that a window, outside is the night—'" Rickie brushed aside romanticism and entered into the reality. Mrs. Failing got an insight into the essence of life itself and realised how she dealt with it. "Finding life dull, she had dropped lies into it, as a chemist drops a new element into a solution, hoping that life would thereby sparkle or turn some beautiful colour. She loved to mislead others, and in the end her private view of false and true was obscured, and she misled herself. How she must have enjoyed their errors over Stephen! But her own error had been greater, inasmuch as it was spiritual entirely." But Rickie still saw the 'mystic rose' and thought that "the earth had confirmed him. He stood behind things at last, and knew that conventions are majestic, and that they will not claim us in the end."

Stephen Wonham was bathing "working up-stream like an animal, splashing in the shallows." After bathing he proposed to walk with Leighton at night, and Leighton was pleased. At nine o'clock the two walked. Stephen promised to Rickie that he would not drink any more, and so Rickie asked Leighton if Stephen was drunk. Leighton hesitated, fumbled. Rickie ran upto where Stephen was lying on a deep settle and found him drunk. Rickie was angry because Stephen had broken his promise, and he knew that both Stephen and himself were going to be ruined, and consequently he broke down. Leighton took hold of Rickie and brought him home. On the way Rickie said: "'May God receive me and pardon me for trusting the earth.'" Agnes was certainly waiting for him, though not very eagerly, because "she was only his wife in name." Rickie was too weak. "At the level-crossing he leant on the gate to watch a slow goods train pass. In the glare of the engine he saw that his brother [Stephen Wonham] had come this way, perhaps through some sodden memory of the Rings, and now lay drunk over the rails. Wearily he did a man's duty. There was time to raise him up and push him into safety. It is also a man's duty to save his own life, and therefore he tried. The train went over his knees. He died up in Cadover, whispering 'You have been right,' to Mrs. Failing." Stephen was saved by Rickie, but there was none to save Rickie. Mrs. Failing later on wrote to Mrs. Lewin about Rickie that he was "'one who has failed in all he undertook, one of the thousands whose dust returns to the dust, accomplishing nothing in the interval. Agnes and I buried him to the sound of our cracked bell, and pretended that he had once been alive. The other [Stephen], who was always honest, kept away'" (section XXXIV).

After Rickie's death Stephen and Mr. Herbert Pembroke, now a clergyman, sat down to arrange the stories, written by Rickie, for possible publication as a book, under the title 'Pan Pipes' because the ten and four stories in their possession "all centre round a Nature theme." And as they were engaged in matters relating to publication a little female child was pampering the leg of Stephen under the table. Stephen "rested his lips on her hair, and carried her, without speaking, until he reached the open down." It was Stephen's daughter—the daughter that would perpetuate his existence, his life! Stephen "bent down reverently and saluted the child"—the child whom he called by her mother's name (section XXXV).

3

DISCUSSION

(i)

This is the first of the two English novels of Forster, the second being *Howards End,* and "is also the most puzzling and complex of Forster's early novels" (Messenger, 80). It is interesting to note that the titles of three of Forster's novels, including the present one, are taken from 'books': "*Where Angels Fear to Tread* quotes Pope's *An Essay on Criticism. The Longest Journey* takes its title from a poem by Shelley, *Epipsychidion. A Passage to India* refers to a poem of the same name written in 1871 by Whitman to celebrate the opening of the Suez Canal" (Edwards, 3). *The Longest Journey* is "the most ostensively tragic and the most truly optimistic of his [Forster's] novels" (Furbank, I, 148). It symbolises Forster's vision of the longest journey that every man undertakes through the highway of life—the highway that ends in utter darkness. It narrates the tragic course of life of its protagonist or hero Frederick Elliot or Rickie Elliot through the dark corridor of the world. It is for this reason that John Sayre Martin has identified this novel as a 'dark novel.' Martin writes: "*The Longest Journey* is [thus] a dark novel—all the darker, in fact, for the number of sudden deaths that occur in it and the air of fatality that surrounds the hero. Born with a lameness derived from his father's side of the family, physically weak besides, and raised by his mother in solitude and loneliness, Rickie seems predestined to failure. His unhappy marriage echoes the unhappiness that subsisted between his mother and father. His daughter's lameness echoes his own. Like Ibsen's Oswald Alving, he becomes haunted by the 'ghosts' of his own prehistory. No other of Forster's novels is so fatalistic; in no other does the hero's unhappiness seem so hopeless" (Martin, 27).

In 1903 Forster, particularly after he returned from his journey to Greece, was very keenly suffering from loss of friendship, intellectual awareness and happiness—all the three that he fully enjoyed to his heart's desire at Cambridge, and all the three whose lack we find in Rickie, the hero of *The Longest Journey,* the novel that Forster was writing in 1904. Naturally, therefore, there is a clear reflection of the state of mind of Forster in the mental state of Rickie. Not only this, the awareness of the loss was perhaps the inspiration or generic cause of the novel. Nicola Beauman writes in this regard. "His [Forster's] month in Greece in the April of 1903 was what turned Cambridge into his lifelong touchstone of friendship, intellectual awareness and happiness. It was at this period in his life that the loss of King's came to be as important as the loss of Melcombe Place, of Battersea Rise, of Rooksnest; and that the idea for *The Longest Journey,* which mourns this loss, first entered his [Forster's] imagination" (Beauman, 131).

The Longest Journey, a novel of some 320 pages, is divided into three Parts, sub-titled Cambridge, Sawston, and Wiltshire. The first Part is the longest and the last Part the shortest. The novel is well planned and is structured as a symphony, the three Parts of it narrating "the three major kinds of experience to which Rickie is exposed in the course of his adult life" (Martin, 32). John Sayre Martin writes about the symphony-like structure of the novel: "*The Longest Journey* is carefully planned. As K.W. Gransden has pointed out, its three major sections are like three parts of a symphony, the first part corresponding to the statement, the second part to the crisis, and the third part to the resolution. The musical analogy can be carried further" (Martin, 42). This musical quality distinguishes *The Longest Journey* from Forster's other novels. In another point also *The Longest Journey* is different from the other novels of Forster. The world *of The Longest Journey,* as the world of his short stories, Forster imaginatively inhabited, but the world of his other novels he perceived with a detached and ironical pair of eyes. Whereas in his other novels Forster was a non-participant, in *The Longest Journey* Rickie's journey of life was, as if, Forster's own journey. Nicola Beauman writes that Forster "inhabited the world of his stories, and to some extent of *The Longest Journey,* imaginatively, whereas the world of his other novel was observed by him with more irony and detachment" (Beauman, 244).

And, consequently, *The Longest Journey,* as has briefly already been pointed out, has obviously been autobiographical. This novel is all the more interesting to us because of its autobiographical elements. Nicola Beauman has very rightly said that the hero of this novel, "Rickie, 'more than any,' represented his creator" (Beauman, 15). Beauman again writes about the autobiographical elements in *The Longest Journey:* "The autobiographical nature of Morgan's [Forster's] second novel was remarked upon by few. Perhaps no one imagined that a writer would voluntarily expose his own weaknesses, or perhaps few believed that a satirical novelist could also be 'a lonely and deformed boy' (*Standard*), 'an anaemic personality'

(*Athenaeum*), 'gauche, timid, incurably naive' (*Revue des Deux Mondes*).... "Morgan put himself into *The Longest Journey,* not only the 'abnormal' Rickie but also his parent's marriage, Tonbridge, Cambridge, Wiltshire, the imagery of the Greeks. There is a good deal of openly expressed bitterness" (Beauman, 194).

There are many autobiographical elements in *The Longest Journey,* some of which are the following. Firstly, Forster, like Rickie, was mother-fixated, and both of them were averse to their respective fathers. Nigel Messenger further writes about the similitude between Forster and Rickie: "Rickie is not Forster but there are some suggestive parallels. Forster never knew his father but both he and his hero share a lonely childhood exclusively with a much loved mother. We know enough about Forster's life to say that both are sensitive and artistic, both labour under a sense of inadequacy, and both are unhappy at school but find friendship and fulfilment at Cambridge" (Messenger, 82). Secondly, Mrs. Elliot of *The Longest Journey* was modelled on Forster's mother, Lily: "Lily, after all, was, like Mrs. Elliot in *The Longest Journey,* 'afraid of intimacy'" (Beauman, 101). Thirdly, Forster's anti-authoritarian attitude has unreservedly been expressed in the novel, where Forster has scathingly satirised Herbert Pembroke for his unflinching aim of correcting the un-Sawstonian behaviour of the day boys of the school where Herbert had been serving as a master. The school, Herbert used to hammer into the heads of the day boys, was "the world in miniature" *(The Longest Journey,* Chapter XVII). All the boys had to highly regard the tradition, had to be "patriotic, athletic, learned, and religious" *(ibid.)*, and they had to prepare themselves for overbearingly administrative positions in future, especially in the colonised countries. In chapters XVI and XVII of the novel, Forster has given us very satirically an idea of the regimentation of the day boys. Nicola Beauman has quoted an appropriate passage from the novel in his *Morgan: A Biography of E.M. Forster* to show the extent of the regimentation and the prurience of Forster's satire thrown at it: "'Like the boarders, they [the day boys] were to be in at 7. 15 p. m....

they, too, must work at fixed hours in the evening., and before breakfast next morning from 7 to 8. Games were compulsory. They must not go to parties in term time. They must keep to bounds. Of course the reform was not complete. It was impossible to control the dieting, though on a printed circular, day-parents were implored to provide simple food. And it is also believed that some mothers disobeyed the rule about preparation, and allowed their sons to do all the work overnight and have a longer sleep in the morning'" (Beauman, 57). Fourthly, Rickie, the hero of the novel, was a creative writer—a writer of short stories like Forster. Fifthly, in a sense, Forster was also 'lame' like Rickie—in the sense that he was not like the hosts of heterosexual persons but was a homosexual, and so always felt somewhat an outcast like Rickie.

Sixthly, as Mike Edwards says, "The opening scene of the novel takes place in Rickie Elliot's room at Cambridge, which is much like Forster's own room when he was a student at King's College" (Edwards, 4). Seventhly, as we have known, Forster was quite doctored by the ethical views of George Moore's *Principia Ethica,* which were also subscribed by Meredith, Ainsworth and Leonard Woolf. "Moore's work allowed Morgan [Forster] and his contemporaries to reject Clapham Sect values without feeling outcast; it allowed them to question religion, the money-making ethic, conventional morals, without feeling impossibly alienated from the society into which they had been born. This is why Cambridge, and later 'Bloomsbury,' mattered so much to Morgan: it became his value system and in this way his family, his background" (Beauman, 84). This value system of Forster shows prevalence in the novel, and with the questioning attitude of the Bloomsbury Group towards the conventional morality and epistemology does the novel begin. In the novel, Stuart Ansell, Rickie's philosopher friend, actually represents the value system of the Bloomsbury Group. However, there are certainly many more autobiographical elements in *The Longest Journey,* but, perhaps, the few that have been stated so far would suffice.

(ii)

The Longest Journey is a philosophical novel, and that it is so is obvious just at the beginning of it where Rickie and his friends are engaged in a radical philosophical question, or, rather, in an epistemological question: is the perceived cow out there existent, or is it an hallucination? Nigel Messenger writes: "Clearly *The Longest Journey* is going to be a philosophical novel and Rickie and his friend Ansell illustrate two contrasting approaches to (this) quest for truth or reality; Rickie is emotional and poetic, Ansell seems more logical and sternly abstract as befits someone training to be a philosopher" (Messenger, 86). Messenger has also termed this novel an 'education' novel, for, according him, the novel deals with how its hero, Rickie Elliot, strived to grow up as a norman human being, how he came to discover himself, and how he tried to control his own destiny. He says that "the subject of this novel seems to be Rickie's quest for some sort of meaning to his life" (Messenger, 82). Nicola Beauman, on the other hand, thinks that the novel is about the antithesis between integrity and falsehood (Beauman, 322). In *The Longest Journey* Forster has also strived to show the importance of passion and the truths underneath the surface that society demonstrates before us. Therefore, the novel does not deal with a single theme but with a multiplicity of inter-related themes.

(iii)

Nigel Messenger, in his book *How to Study an E.M. Forster Novel,* has given a beautiful 'synopsis' of the story of *The Longest Journey,* where the plot and 'pattern' of the novel is obvious. The synopsis runs as follows. "The story opens in Rickie Elliot's undergraduate rooms in Edwardian Cambridge; while he day-dreams, Stuart Ansell and other friends debate the nature of reality; their discussion is interrupted by Agnes Pembroke, invited with her brother Herbert for a visit. Ansell rudely ignores her, declaring later that she doesn't really exist. After the Pembrokes' departure, we learn that Rickie's childhood has been unhappy and lonely. He idealised his mother but his hated father despised both wife and son

(Like his father, Rickie has a club foot). Neither had any chance of a fulfilling life together while he lived, and expectations of better times after his death were cruelly cut short by Rickie's mother's own death a few days later.

"During the Christmas vacation, Rickie visits the Pembrokes at Sawston, a genteel town in the south of England. Herbert teaches at a minor public school there. Agnes is engaged to Gerald Dawes, an athletic bully from Rickie's own schooldays. However, Rickie idealises the lovers when he sees them embrace unaware, and so is able to comfort Agnes when Gerald dies suddenly after a footballing accident. Rickie returns to Cambridge and becomes engaged to Agnes when she visits him during his final term. Ansell is disgusted and warns Rickie against her, prophesying disaster.

"The scene shifts to Cadover, the Wiltshire estate of Mrs. Failing, Rickie's eccentric aunt on his father's side. Rickie and Agnes, prior to their marriage, make a visit there which ends badly. Mrs. Failing has a boorish young retainer called Stephen Wonham who is neither sophisticated nor conventional. In a mischievous moment while out walking in the Cadbury Rings, an ancient Iron Age fortification, Mrs. Failing tells Rickie that Stephen is his illegitimate half-brother. Rickie faints, is revived by Stephen, but is prevented from telling him of their relationship by Agnes. It is agreed that the affair be covered up and Stephen kept in ignorance.

"In order to marry, Rickie gives up trying to write imaginative stories and begins work as a teacher at Sawston School. Herbert is now house master of Dunwood House and Agnes is to act as his housekeeper. Rickie soon becomes entangled in school politics and, dominated by the Pembrokes, grows increasingly unhappy. There is a scandal over the maltreatment of one of the boys and Agnes gives birth to a deformed daughter who quickly dies. Matters are brought to a head by the arrival of Stephen, now an outcast and seeking his brother. The Pembrokes try to buy him off but. Ansell intervenes, telling Rickie that Stephen is his mother's son, not his father's as he had always supposed. Rickie collapses and shortly afterwards leaves Sawston with Stephen to begin a new life.

"But Rickie's life is doomed. On a visit to Cadover he becomes disillusioned with his brother's drinking and dies saving him from an oncoming train. The novel ends sometime later with Stephen now married and reformed character. On an idyllic summer evening, before going out to sleep on the downs with his young daughter, we learn that Rickie's writings live on to give him some posthumous recognition" (Messenger, 81-82).

(iv)

There are six major characters in *The Longest Journey:* Rickie Elliot, Agnes Pembroke, Herbert Pembroke, Stewart Ansell, Stephen Wonham and Mrs. Failing. There are also a handful of minor characters, such as Widdrington, Jackson, Mrs. Orr, Leighton, Gerald Dawes, Mr. Elliot, Mrs. Elliot, etc. Rickie Elliot or Frederick Elliot is the central character or hero of the novel, and he considerably reflects the character of the author, E.M. Forster. Rickie's father, Mr. Elliot, was club-footed, and so was he, and so also was his only daughter by Agnes,—the daughter that died not long after its birth. Because of Rickie's rickety profile, his rude father satirically called him by the name 'Rickie,' which name Rickie took to be a slur on his being, and, consequently, he hated his father all the more. Rickie was 'rather lame,' 'slightly deformed, and so the shoes were not the same size, and one of them had a thick heel to help him towards an even walk.' He also had bleeding nose, and was 'thin.' When he decided to marry Agnes, Stewart Ansell cautioned him not to marry because he was 'unfitted in body' and 'also unfitted in soul.'

Rickie's relation with his father was cool and bitter. His father always behaved superciliously with him. He used to say: "'My father found me a nuisance, and put me through the mills, and I can never forget it—particularly the evenings.'" As Rickie intensely hated his father so he loved his mother intensely. In his room at Cambridge there was a picture of his mother (and none of his father) hung on the wall. Being deformed since birth, Rickie was naturally sensitive, emotional, and loved to read the emotional and romantic poems of such poets as Omar Khayyam, Theocritus, Shelley, Keats and Goethe—Goethe, who said 'the eternal faminine leads us on.' He had had very unhappy days, both at home, in the company of his father, and in the school where he was averse to the drilling methods. Consequently, he always felt lonely and tended to be lugubrious; he was only happy when he went to King's College, Cambridge. But even in Cambridge he would feel pain when Agnes would sometimes obliquely compare him with the athletic Gerald Dawes. He loved friends and friendship very much, and friends to him were like brothers. At the beginning of the novel, we meet Rickie at Cambridge. He was then 20 and in less than two years he was to received his B.A. Rickie's deceased father had been at the Bar, but Rickie would choose a quite different evocation—that of a writer. In fact, he was writing romantic stories even when he was at Cambridge, and only after he was engaged to Agnes he began to write realistic stories. He always kept himself engrossed in a book, especially in a book of poetry: 'Scarcely ever was he without a book.' Rickie was not only emotional but he also valued emotion, because he believed that only through emotion one can be intimate with another. "He valued emotion—not for itself, but because it is the only final path to intimacy." Rickie and his Cambridge friends were both 'scientific and philosophic'.

Rickie loved Cambridge as he loved flowers. In fact, he had 'incurable love for flowers.' He was never enthusiastic about religion, though, unlike his half-brother Stephen he was a believer; and, ofcourse, he never believed in rituals. He was civil, reticent, domesticated, and, to Ansell, he was 'extraordinarily civilised'. Rickie provided an example of the person who did not believe in the traditional system where one person could marry only a single person for life, as Shelley spoke of it in his poem 'Epipsychidion': he believed in universal love. Rickie "believed that life should be in a line—a line of enormous length, full of countless interests and countless figures, all well beloved." "He loved Agnes, not only for herself, but because she was lighting up the human world." He could not be happy after his marriage with Agnes. He, again, could not be happy in the Sawston School, because he could not accept the ideals and practices of it. The Sawston School highly valued tradition and *esprit de corps*—the two things Rickie radically questioned. He was agoraphobic—afraid of open spaces—and felt "nervous at the prospect of confronting the assembled house." His inferiority complex originated in his lameness. "As a teacher he was rather dull." However, one especial feature of his character was that it phenomenally changed in the course of his brief life as the situations of his life changed. He was a romantic and used to write romantic stories, but after his marriage with the realist Agnes, he changed the course of his life and became a realist, as Agnes turned to romanticism. Again, he once believed in liberal humanism, but under the financial constraints of his marital life when he joined Sawston School, he, inspite of himself, 'became a martinet' and he grasped the school regulations, and insisted on prompt obedience to them. He adopted the doctrine of 'collective responsibility.' And lastly, when he first heard from Mrs. Failing that Stephen was his half-brother, he fainted, but it was also for saving the life of this Stephen that he lost his life, as if he sacrificed his life for saving the life of Stephen.

One very deep aspect of Rickie's character is explored by Rae H. Stoll. Stoll says that Rickie was sexually infirm, and was masochistic, and also that he always suppressed his love for his mother. "Rickie, in fact, alternately pursues male and female substitutes for the original object he wishes to possess. In a series of abortive attempts to satisfy desire, he moves from his mother to Gerald to Cambridge and Ansell (the safe *alter mater* and platonic friend) to Agnes and, finally, to Stephen Wonham, who is so intimately linked with both Rickie's ideal self and his mother that the three are conflated at one point in a single Janus-faced image" (Tambling, 38-39). Rae H. Stoll thinks that Rickie pined for ideal love—the sort of love that is to be found not only in Shelley's 'Epipsychidion' but also in Shakespeare's Sonnets nos. 1 to 17. Stoll writes: "... Rickie, like Shelley's speaker [in 'Epipsychidion'] attempts to regain an ideal love .... For the affective centre of *The Longest*

Journey, however, Forster drew not only on Shelley's 'Epipsychidion', but, more profoundly, on the poems of another writer who shared his feelings about continuity and who took as seriously as he the Biblical injunction: 'Be fruitful and multiply.' The language in which Forster explores the nature of the relationship of Rickie, Stephen, and their mother—that is, the nature of Rickie's sexuality and his constitution as a subject—is drawn not from the publicly acknowledged lines of Shelley which appear in the text, but from Shakespeare's Sonnets 1 to 17, the 'procreation sonnets'" (*op. cit.,* 39).

Agnes Pembroke is the second important character in *The Longest Journey.* She was a 'tall young woman' and her nature was kindly. She had a 'brown' 'handsome face.' This French-knowing lady had a peculiar 'freak,' the freak of wearing varied ear-rings. Agnes was 'of the type that pretends to be unconventional and really isn't.' She, particularly before her marriage with Rickie, was a realist or a pragmatist, but after her marriage she, for unknown reasons, turned to be a romantist as Rickie, who had been a romantist, became a realist or a pragmatist after his marriage with her. Widdrington told Ansell that to his cousin Agnes (Mrs. Elliot, wife of Rickie) seemed to be 'Medusa in Arcady.' but Widdrington himself was 'inclined to compare her to an electric light. Click! she's on. Click! she's off. No waste, No flicker.'

At the end of chapter XXIV of *The Longest Journey,* the narrator gives us a picture of the inner world of Agnes after her marriage with Rickie: "But Agnes continued her life, cheerfully beating time. She, too, knew that her marriage was a failure, and in her spare moments regretted it. She wished that her husband was handsomer, more successful, more dictatorial. But she would think, 'No, no; one mustn't grumble. It cant be helped.' Ansell was wrong in supposing she might ever leave Rickie. Spiritual apathy prevented her. Nor would she ever be tempted by a jollier man. Here criticism would willingly alter its tone. For Agnes also has her tragedy. She belonged to the type—not necessarily an elevated one—that loves once and once only. Her love for Gerald had not been a noble passion: no imagination transfigured it. But such as it was, it sprang to embrace him, and he carried it away with him when he died. *Les amours qui suivent sont moins involuntaires:* by an effort of the will she had warmed herself for Rickie. "She is not conscious of her tragedy, and therefore only the gods need weep at it. But it is fair to remember that hitherto she moves as one from whom the inner life has been withdrawn."

Herbert Pembroke was the older brother of Agnes Pembroke, aged 'nearly twenty' and an M.A. Like Agnes, he also knows French, but he was not as handsome as his sister. "But he was not at all the person to knock into a gutter, for though not in orders, he had the air of being on the verge of them, and his features, as well as his clothes, had the critical cut." "His round, rather foolish, face assumed the expression of a conspirator." He was an incurable idealist who could say like Agnes, "Life without an ideal would be like the sky without the sun." Ofcourse, "In practical matters Mr. Pembroke was often a generous man." We come to better understand the character of Herbert Pembroke when, in chapters XVI and XVII of *The Longest Journey,* we see him as a master of Sawston School, where he drowned his idealism in the sea of practicality and squarely conformed himself with the tradition and ideals of the school. His principal charge there was to rein in the 'recalcitrant' day-boys and some of their unobliging parents and to infuse into the day-boys the spirit of *esprit de corps.* "In three years Mr. Pembroke had done much to solidify the day-boys at Sawston School." As a teacher, he respected intellect, as against emotion; atliletics, as against aesthetics; organisation, as against individualism; and patriotism, as against friendship and humanism. To him, the 'school is the world in miniature.' Even so, "Mr. Pembroke was conscientious and romantic, and knew that marriage without love is intolerable. On the other hand, he could not admit that love had vanished from him. To admit this would argue that he had deteriorated. Whereas he knew for a fact that he improved, year by year, each year he grew more moral, more efficient, more learned, more genial. So how could he fail to be more loving?" And, as a proof of his gradual improvement, we learn that even while in the service of the school, he proposed to Mrs. Orr.

Nicola Beauman says that Forster called the character of Stewart Ansell following the name of one of their garden boys. In 1901, Forster wrote that Ansell "'was the third/fourth? of our garden boys—Ray, William, Bible, Ansell, Field, Chalkely were their order, and was the only boy I knew'" (Beauman, 45). Stewart Ansell, a Cambridge friend of Rickie and a realist philosopher, was a participant in the epistemological debate with which *The Longest Journey* begins. At Cambridge he was engaged in writing a dissertation. He came of a low stock: his father was a draper and his uncles were farmers. He got entrance into Cambridge 'just on account of his brains'. "To be born one thing and grow up another—Ansell had accomplished this without weakening one of the ties that bound him to his home." His aim in life was to enter the Civil Service. Rickie did not like him and did not take him for a gentleman. Inspite of all efforts on his part, Ansell failed to get a fellowship at Cambridge. "In many ways Ansell was a conceited man" and "In many ways he was pedantic; but bis pedantry lay close to the vineyards of life—far closer than that fetich experience of the innumerable teacups." Even so, he was an 'unpractical person.' Ansell knew everything of Rickie. He told Widdrington: "'I know not only Rickie but the whole of his history.'" Nicola Beauman says that Ansell symbolises the ideals of George Moore which Forster greatly subscribed—the ideals of friendship, aesthetics, right conduct, etc. He says that to pay homage to Moore's ideals, Forster created Ansell. Beauman writes: "As a person Ansell combines characteristics of Moore, Meredith, Ainsworth and Leonard Woolf; as a symbol, almost an icon, he was one of the few ways Morgan [Forster] could thank Moore for changing his personal philosophy so much for the better" (Beauman, 84).

Stephen Wonham is the half-brother of Rickie Elliot on his mother's side. He was "a powerful boy of twenty, admirably muscular, but rather too broad for his height." People called him 'Podge' until they were dissuaded. Then they called him 'Stephen' or 'Mr. Wonham.' He had 'a straggling blonde moustache' and his face had 'after all a certain beauty.' He had, as Mrs. Failing thought, 'the face of a strong man.' A young man of 22, Stephen was 'built rather heavy' and had an 'ordinary broad face.' The narrator tells us that Stephen's "parents had given him excellent gifts—health, sturdy limbs, and a face not ugly,—gifts that his habits confirmed. They had also given him a cloudless spirit—the spirit of the seventeen days in which he was created." Though he was really not beautiful he thought himself to be so; and in this and other respects he was conceited. Stephen looked exactly like Rickie.

Stephen was the illegitimate son of Mrs. Elliot (Rickie's mother) and a certain Robert, "a young farmer of some education who tried to coax the aged soil of Wiltshire scientifically—[and who] came to Cadover on business and fell in love with Mrs. Elliot." He was born in Sweden, and was adopted by Mrs. Failing who brought him up at Cadover ever since his birth. Mrs. Failing was very fond of him, and "She has always been both father and mother to him." She was to be blamed for Stephen's taking to drinking, because of her 'not being severe enough' with him. It was due to her pampering that Stephen 'has grown up without fixed principles. He has always followed his inclinations.' Mrs. Failing herself once described the behaviour of Stephen to Agnes: "I will describe how he spent yesterday. He rose at eight. From eight to eleven he sang. The song was called, 'Father's boots will soon fit Willie.' He stopped once to say to the footman, 'She'll never finish her book. She idles.' 'She' being I. At eleven he went out, and stood in the rain till four, but had the luck to see a child run over at the level-crossing. By half-past four he had knocked the bottom out of Christianity." Stephen told Rickie: "I'm an atheist." He was a veritable pagan. He had only a smattering of education 'with just a little reading at odd hours.' He was of a philosophical nature, and was averse to women. Agnes heard that Stephen used to lend money to the poor and that he had stolen while at school: "she had heard tales of him lending to the poor and exacting repayment to the uttermost farthing. He had also stolen at school." Stephen was a 'materialist' and 'liked power' and took to drinking heavily at the close of the novel. Astonishingly, inspite of all these, Stewart Ansell said of Stephen to Rickie:

"Stephen is one of the greatest people I have ever met." Rae H. Stoll writes that "Stephen possess those qualities required to make *Rickie* lovable. He is not only Rickie's anti-self, differing from him in 'disposition' and in fairness of form, but Rickie's completed self" (Tambling, 41). Stoll further writes that the character of Stephen is symbolic, and this "explains the unreality of Stephen as an independent character" (*op. cit.,* 43).

Mrs. Failing or Eustace Failing or Emily Failing or Aunt Emily was Rickie's aunt on his father's side. On P.N. Furbank's authority we can say that Forster drew the character of Mrs. Failing basing on one of his uncles, William Howley Forster (1855-1910): "William was the youngest of his Forster uncles: an intelligent, handsome, amusing man, driven slightly crazed by idleness; Forster drew on him in portraying Mrs. Failing in *The Longest Journey*" (Furbank, I, 64). "Her age was between elderly and old, and her forehead was wrinkled with an expression of slight but perpetual pain. But the lines round her mouth indicated that she had laughed a great deal during her life, just as the clean tight skin round her eyes perhaps indicated that she had not often cried." Her one dream was to remain attached to her fond farm, an idyllic pastoral farm about which, one day, she expressed her sentiment to her nephew Stephen Wonham: "'My farm is a mystery to me,' said the lady, stroking her fingers. 'Some day you must really take me to see it. It must be like a Gilbert and Sullivan opera, with a chorus of agitated employers. How is it that I have escaped? Why have I never been summoned to milk the cows, or flay the pigs, or drive the young bullocks to the pasture?'"

Mrs. Failing had a taste for literature, and particularly for poetry. For instance, once in an angry mood she rebuked Stephen thus: "'You distress me. You rob the pastoral of its lingering romance. Is there no poetry and no thought in England? Is there no one, in all these downs, who warbles with eager thought the Doric lay?'" She wrote a charming Introduction to Will Uncle Tony's Essays and read the poems of such poets as Milton. "In the winter she would go to town and frequent the *salons* of the literary." She was not the least interested in philosophy; she hated it. "Mrs. Failing's attitude towards Nature was severely aesthetic—an attitude more sterile than the severely practical. She applied the test of beauty to shadow and odour and sound; they never filled her with reverence or excitement; She never knew them as a resistless trinity that may intoxicate the worshipper with joy. If she liked a ploughed field, it was only a spot of colour—not a hint of the endless strength of the earth." Her literary taste was so intense that she married Mr. Failing only because he was the author of some brilliant books on socialism.

Her concern about religion was peculiar. Ofcourse she used to go to church on Sundays, but "She regaded the church as a sort of sitting-room, and refused even to wear a bonnet there." She was, nevertheless, spiritual at bottom and suffered spiritually. "Finding life dull, she had dropped lies into it, as a chemist drops a new element into a solution, hoping that life would thereby sparkle or turn some beautiful colour. She loved to mislead others, and in the end her private view of false and true was obscured, and she misled herself—her own error had been greater, in as much as it was spiritual entirely."

One Mr. Wonham imposed upon Mrs. failing the charge of bringing up Stephen after his birth in Sweden, and she fondly brought him up till Stephen took to heavy drinking, when she lost her interest in him. Though she could not be termed wise, she sometimes behaved prudently. She well knew the secret of Stephen's birth and she was angry at the affair, but she did not divulge it, considering the row that would have been raised at Cadover. "After all, she was growing old. And therefore, though she had no true regard for Rickie, nor for Agnes, nor for Stephen, nor for Stephen's parents, in whose tragedy she had assisted, yet she did feel that if the scandal revived it would disturb the harmony of Cadover, and therefore tried to retrace her steps."

There are a number of minor characters in *The Longest Journey,* including Widdrington, Maud Ansell, Robert, Mrs. Elliot, Mr. Elliot, Jackson, Mrs. Orr, the Silts, Leighton and Gerald Dawes. Among all these characters, Gerald Dawes and Mrs. Elliot are of the most consequence. Gerald Dawes was of athletic form, was an 'athletic marvel' to whom Agnes Pembroke was heavily drawn. He was Agnes' 'splendid lover.' The narrator, for about half a dozen times, reminds us of the brawny figure of Dawes in the novel. He was a good football player and suddenly died of a hurt received while playing football. Agnes could never forget her 'great moments' with him even after her marriage with Rickie. Mrs. Elliot, Rickie's mother, who was modelled on Forster's mother Lily (Beauman, 101), conceived Stephen Wonham by a certain Robert after her marriage with Mr. Elliot, and gave birth to Stephen in Sweden. Mr. Wonham urged Mrs. Failing to take up the charge of nursing and bringing up the baby, Stephen, and thus the illicit affair was hushed up, and Mrs. Elliot returned to her unsuspecting husband. When Rickie came to learn that Stephen was his half-brother, he suspected his father, Mr. Elliot, and began to hate him all the more, but when he was certain that Stephen was not the son of his father but of his mother, he just excused his mother and forgot everything about Stephen's birth. Rickie was mother-fixated, as we have said, and Mrs. Elliot was also heavily drawn to Rickie, for which reason she would always keep him to herself. "He worshipped his mother, and she was fond of him. But she was dignified and reticent, and pathos, lice tattle, was disgusting to her. She was afraid of intimacy, in case it led to confidences and tears, and so all her life she held her son at a little distance. Her kindness and unselfishness knew no limits, but if he tried to be dramatic and thank her, she told him not to be a little goose."

Mr. Elliot, Rickie's father, was a barrister. "In appearance he resembled his son, being weakly and lame, with hollow little cheeks, a broad white band of forehead, and stiff impoverished hair. His voice, which he did not transmit was very suave, with a fine command of cynical intonation. By altering it ever so little he could make people wince, especially if they were simple or poor. Nor did he transmit his eyes. Their peculiar flatness, as if the soul looked through dirty window-panes, the unkindness of them, the cowardice, the fear in them, were to trouble the world no longer." Mr. Elliot and

Mrs. Elliot 'did not love each other.' Mr. Elliot called his son Rickie because he was rickety, and he 'took pleasure in alluding to his son's deformity, and was sorry that it was not more serious than his own. Mr. Elliot had not one scrap of genius." He was, ofcourse, cruel, but it is not certain whether his cruelty grew out of his extenuating circumstances. The Silts were the poor cousins of Rickie's father; Mrs. Orr was in the staff of Sawston School, and it was to her that Herbert Pembroke proposed; Robert was the illegal father of Stephen; Leighton was 'a kindly, pliable man' and a servant; Widdrington was a cousin of Herbert Pembroke; Maud Ansell was a sister of Stewart Ansell; and Mr. Jackson was a teacher and a 'classical enthusiast' at Sawston School.

(v)

Forster preferred to have introduced fantasies in his novels, as his short stories were themselves fantasies, and *The Longest Journey* shows his preference. In chapter VI of the novel we come across a fantasy for the first time—a fantasy that occurs in a short story of Rickie called "The Bay of the Fifteen Islets'. "There, among spoons and corks and string, he [Rickie] found a fragment of a little story that he had tried to write last term. It was called 'The Bay of the Fifteen Islets,' and the action took place on St John's Eve off the coast of Sicily. A party of tourists land on one of the islands. Suddenly the boatmen become uneasy, and say that the island is not generally there. It was an extra one, and they had better have tea on one of the ordinaries. 'Pooh, volcanic?' says the leading tourist, and the ladies say how interesting. The island begins to rock, and so do the minds of the visitors. They start to quarrel and jabber. Fingers burst up through the sand—black fingers of sea devils. The island tilts. The tourists go mad. But just before the catastrophe one man, *integer vitae scelerisque purus,* sees the truth. Here are no devils. Other muscles, other minds, are pulling the island to its subterranean home. Through the advancing wall of waters he sees no grisly faces, no ghostly medieval limbs, but—"

The second fantasy we read about in chapter XIII of the novel. Mrs. Failing and Agnes went out to the Rings, a Stone Age curiosity, by Mrs. Failing's pony carriage. When they reached there, Mrs. Failing gave Rickie "one of her disquieting smiles, but said pleasantly enough, 'Aren't the Rings a little immense? Agnes and I came here because we wanted an antidote to the morning service.' 'Pang!' said the church bell suddenly; 'pang! pang!' It sounded petty and ludicrous. They all laughed. Rickie blushed, and Agnes, with a glance that said 'apologize' darted away to the entrenchment, as though unable to restrain her curiosity." Mrs. Failing told Rickie that the place was full of 'ghosties.' She asked him to accompany her 'to the tree in the centre.' As they paused at the entrance of the wood, the church bell again sounded, 'Pang!' Rickie asked her what kind of 'ghosties' haunted there, and she told him that they were the Dryads or the tree nymphs who died with the trees they lived in. The third fantasy is to be found in chapter XV of *The Longest Journey*. At the end of their visit to Aunt Emily, Rickie and Agnes were preparing to come back to Sawston. "During the packing he [Rickie] was obliged to go up to the attic to find the Dryad manuscript, which had never been returned. Leighton came too, and for about half an hour they hunted in the flickering light of a candle. It was a strange ghostly place, and Rickie was quite startled when a picture swung towards him, and he saw the Demeter of Cnidus ['an earth goddess of wheat and grain'], shimmering and grey."

Now, is there any prophecy in *The Longest Journey,* to which Forster is driving all the events of it, and all the characters too? There is, and it occurs as is usual in Forster's other novels, at the end of this novel. There is a constant dichotomy in the novel. It begins with an epistemological dichotomy, is there a cow, or no? The Pembrokes and the Elliots are dichotomous—the Pembrokes, like the Wilcoxes of *Howards End,* belonged to the urbane tribe that believed in the Sawstonian philosophy of life. The Pembrokes believed in tradition, mechanisation, *esprit de corps,* money-making and practicality or pragmatism, and consequently they were heartless. On the other hand, the Elliots lacked in urbanity, and so in complexity, and they subscribed to individualism, naturalism and emotionalism. But Rickie Elliot, whose life-story the novel is, changed his stance and subscribed to the philosophy of the Pembrokes since his marriage with Agnes and since he joined the Sawston School under the favour of Herbert Pembroke. At the end of the novel, we find Rickie dying while saving Stephen, and here is the prophecy of the novel. Rickie, with whom the novel was so long concerned, Forster left in the lurch at the end of it, and reverentially took up Stephen, the natural man or the man who was, as if, a part of nature, along with his little angelic daughter to close the novel in a mystically religious atmosphere. Why? The answer is, Forster prophetically upheld any man of Stephen's sort. Mike Edwards points out the contrast between Mr. Pembroke's materialism and Stephen's selflessness, and then writes about the contrast: "It offers, too, a judgement: that Stephen's way is better than Mr. pembroke's, better than Rickie's in so far as Rickie shared Mr. Pembroke's world; that nature is better than any social machinery, however apparently beneficent" (Edwards, 155). This is the prophecy in *The Longest Journey.* Mike Edwards further writes: "When Forster refers to Stephen as 'a man of his sort,' he means basic man, the unaccomodated, poor, bare, forked being Lear envisioned on the heath: archetypal man" (*ibid.*). The prophecy of *The Longest Journey* is the triumph of this archetypal man.

(vi)

Forster always followed a pattern while writing a novel, *apropos* of Henry James. As the central character *of The Longest Journey* is Rickie, the pattern falls principally upon this character. Agnes Pembroke is the other character in which also we find a pattern. The pattern in the cases of these two characters is that of an 'hour glass'—the characters change their places or statuses. Rickie had been romantic, but after his marriage with Agnes he became realistic. Rickie had been a non-conformist and non-traditionalist before joining Sawston School, but after joining it he turned one hundred and eighty degrees about. Agnes, on the other hand, had satirically compared the rickety Rickie with the bully Gerald Dawes, so long as she loved Dawes and Dawes was alive, but after Dawes died she ultimately married Rickie. The novel also progresses along with rhythms: actions or incidents repeat, but sometimes they vary. We move along the narrative line and feel that we are moving through a familiar region, but suddenly we perceive something new. We are not able, for instance, to conceive Rickie as a conformist until we saw him join Sawston School, or we could not think of Agnes' marriage with Rickie till she really married him, though we were being given suggestions of these several times, before. But Peter Burra says that what Forster calls rhythm is not different from *leit-motif* and that in *The Longest Journey* there are several *leit-motifs,* the star Orion being one of them and the level-crossing near Cadover being the other. According to Burra, *leit-motif* is a sort of 'ruse' "whose purpose is to give tightness to the plot itself (Bradbury, 62), and Forster in this novel has very skillfully employed the *leit-motifs* for the purpose of weaving the plot very closely. John Sayre Martin writes about the other *leit-motifs* or 'echoes' in *The Longest Journey:* "As in his other novels, Forster employs numerous 'echoes' or 'leitmotifs' to relate different elements of the story. The imagery of streams and rivers, for example, recurs in various contexts to suggest nature and natural forces, whether beneficent or hostile to man. The chalk, which is so much a part of the Wiltshire soil, also occurs in the dell at Madingley, a fact that helps to connect the two regions with Rickie's sense of the Earth" (Martin, 42).

(vii)

We may think of two contending candidates in *The Longest Journey* to be its hero, Rickie Elliot and Stephen Wonham, for Rickie is a replica of the author of this autobiographical novel, and Stephen is the author's wish fulfillment in so far as Forster confessed to have a wish to sleep in Stephen's arms instead of his baby daughter, in the downs of Wiltshire and under the star-studded sky. Now, so far as the story and the plot of the novel developed keeping Rickie at the centre, Rickie is the legitimate candidate to be the hero of it. Rickie pervades the whole length of the novel from its first chapter to its last, and it is his actions and thoughts and feelings that generally guide the course of the novel. Mike Edwards writes about Rickie: "He is not a simple protagonist. Complex and flawed, anti-heroic and yet very sympathetic, he awakens conflicting feelings in us. Rickie is evidently the central character and we observe much of what happens through his eyes, but we are not limited to his point of view. He is a thread, albeit an important one, in a more complex texture" (Edwards, 10). *The Longest Journey* may be called the road-map of Rickie's education through the maze of conflicting desires and temptations and hopes and frustations that came in his way. So, Rickie should be taken to be the hero of the novel. On the other hand, Stephen's candidature is ofcourse not absolutely null. Peter Burra treats Stephen as a hero besides Gino and George: "Gino, Stephen, George—these are heroes" (Bradbury, 69). Stephen bears the prophecy of the novel that Nature and not the philosophy of Herbert Pembroke would survive. He is the lodestar that would guide the future of mankind. So he was a great bearing in the novel. Nevertheless, Mike Edwards says that he cannot claim to be the hero: "Hard indeed to see him as a hero." Edwards further writes about Stephen: "Forster evidently has no intention of presenting Stephen as a conventional hero.... Stephen is simply a construct of facets that meet the needs of the novel from moment to moment: more than anything, he is the positive that matches various aspects of Rickie's negative; he is brother, warrior or lover as the structure of the novel requires—he is something of an alter ego, indeed.... At the end he seems to embody the principle of natural energy... Stephen is not the vehicle of a resolution, rather he symbolises a principle of moral evolution. Imperfect, he nevertheless exemplifies the human capacity to develop towards perfection, and he is the agent of Rickie's redemption. The triumphal tone of the conclusion [of the novel] celebrates not so much what Stephen has become as what, in Forster's imagination, mankind has the potential to be" (Edwards, 157-58). Therefore, Stephen is not so much a character, a person, really, as a construct, and so he fails to rise up to the stature of a hero.

(viii)

One of Forster's narrative ploys or manoeuvres is that he writes with clues (for the reader) beforehand, which clues foreshadow what is going to happen afterwards, sometimes long afterwards. Sometimes he repeats the clues to prepare the reader for the later happenings. There are at least two instances of using such ploys in *The Longest Journey*. Firstly, only in section XIII of the novel do we learn that Rickie had a brother—Stephen. But long before this Forster has twice given us innuendoes to that effect. In the very first section of the novel there is a faint hint: we are told that to the lonely Rickie his friends were 'more like brothers than anything else'. Again in section II the narrator tells us about Rickie: "And then perhaps he would sob for loneliness, for he would see real people—real brothers, real friends—doing in warm life the things he had pretended. 'Shall I have a friend?' he demanded at the age of twelve. 'I don't see how. They walk too fast. And a brother I shall never have.'"

Secondly, at the fag end of the novel, *i.e.* in section XXXIV, Rickie dies at a level-crossing being run over by a goods train, while trying to save the life of the drunken Stephen from the railway track. But well before that, in section X, Rickie tells Mrs. Failing: "'Another child run over at the Roman crossing. Whish—bang—dead.'" Next, in section XI, we hear from Mrs. failing about Stephen: "'At eleven he went out and stood in the rain till four, but had the luck to see a child run over at the level-crossing.'" In the very next section, *i.e.* in section XII, a certain Mr. Wilbraham tells Rickie "another child dead!" And lastly, in section XV we hear from the narrator about Rickie, and about Stephen who rescued a child from being killed by a train: "As he [Rickie] walked back to the house he met a certain poor woman, whose child Stephen had rescued at the level-crossing." Now, what does Forster gain from such a ploy or manoeuvre? At least one thing he ofcourse gains: belief in what he ultimately tells us after guiding through the clues. The improbability goes and probability appears. Had we been told, for an instance, all on a sudden at the end of *The Longest Journey,* that Rickie died at the level-crossing while trying to save Stephen, we might have thought it hard to believe, to take it as something probable. But in the narrative we have come across several sudden deaths at level-crossings, and this has prepared us to believe in the sudden death of Rickie at a level-crossing.

Sudden deaths (the term is Forster's; see section VI of *The Longest Journey*) are frequent in Forster, and perhaps in *The Longest Journey* these are the most frequent among all his novels. In section II of the novel, the narrator summarily and casually tells us that when Rickie was fifteen, his father died, evidently suddenly, for we do not hear of his long illness, and so also, the narrator again tells us in the same section, died his mother only eleven days afterwards. In section X, Rickie describes to Mrs. Failing how a child was run over at the Roman crossing: "'Whish—bang—dead.'" In the same section we again hear that a child (the same child ofcourse) was killed by a running train. In section XXI, we hear about the sudden death of Rickie's baby daughter: "After a short, painless illness his daughter died." In section XXIX, Robert, Stephen's legal father and his mother's illegal lover, is drowned. In section XXX, the narrator tells us of the (sudden) death of Mr. Failing. And in the penultimate section of the novel, *i.e.* in section XXXIV, we hear of the sudden death of Rickie at the level-crossing.

As we have said, the word 'muddle' and its variations or its synonymous group of words were a pet to Forster, the variations or the synonymous group of words in *The Longest Journey* being 'muddles,' 'muddled,' 'clod of earth,' etc. In about 320 pages of *The Longest Journey* Forster has used the word 'muddle' or its variations at least eleven times. Tea and tea-things are also very beloved objects of Forster, and he uses words like 'tea' and 'tea-things' not sparingly in his creative works. In *The Longest Journey* he has used such words as 'tea,' 'tea-party,' 'tea-things' at least eight times.

Forster, in his novels, rather frequently brings in mythological figures to explicate his ideas or to heighten the emotion or to mystify a particular character or situation. This ploy of his is related to his endeavour of employing fantasy in his novels. The mythological figures that have been used in *The Longest Journey* are: Dryads and Pegasus (sections I and XV); Sibyl (section VI); Fauns (section VII); Demeter (sections XII and XV and XX); Mars, Pan and Erda (section XIII); Artemis (section XX); and Hermes (section XXXI). Dryads were "tree nymphs (also called 'hamadryads') of Greek mythology, especially nymphs of the oak tree (*drys* meaning 'oak' or tree') but later generalised; they died with the trees they lived in" (Lass, 65). Pegasus was the "winged horse that arose from the blood of Medusa when Perseus cut her head off—Because of the association of the winged horse with the Muses (supposedly the Hippocrene spring arose on Mt. Helicon, where the Muses dwelt, at the touch of Pegasus' hoof), 'to mount Pegasus' means to do creative or inspired work" (*op. cit.,* 172). Sibyls were "Prophetesses whose origin was ascribed to the East" (*op. cit.,* 203). "Demeter was the daughter of Kronos and Rhea. She was the goddess of corn, and her cult particularly flourished in the regions where grain was grown: in Sicily, in the region of Eleusis, in Crete, in Thrace and in the Peloponnesus" (Comte, 69). Mars was the Greek god of war; Pan was "the Greek god of nature, fertility, forests, wild animals, and of shepherds and their flocks. He invented the syrinx, a flute of seven reeds. Depicted as half-man and half-goat, he was very playful and lecherous" (Lass, 167). Greek Artemis is identical with Roman Diana. Artemis was the daughter of Zeus and Leto. She was exquisitely beautiful with golden curls, and was equal of any man. She was a huntress. "She was proud of her shape and took great care of it, and because of this she made sure that she kept her virginity" (Comte, 52). Hermes was a Greek god identical with Roman god Mercury. He "was the god of the spoken word—the medium through which exchanges were made, gallantries and amorous raptures were expressed, and knowledge was conveyed. But he was also the god of the lying word, which disguised truth, confused lovers and discredited choices. He was, in addition, the intermediary who went from men to Olympus and from Olympus to Hades" (*op. cit.,* 103). And Faunus was the wild, savage but sympathetic god of agriculture, fertility of plants and the extraordinary energy of living nature.

In no other novel of his has Forster as much adulated Nature as in *The Longest Journey*. The mythological figures that are ralated to Nature frequently appear in the novel—Dryads, Faunus, Demeter, etc. In the last section of the novel we see Mr. Pembroke and Stephen, after the death of Rickie, discussing the possible publication of Rickie's four stories in a volume under the title 'Pan Pipes,' because the stories 'all centre round a Nature theme.' Pan was the Greek god of shepherds, flocks, nature and wild beasts; he was the god of animal instinct too. The title of the novel was taken from Shelley's anti-monogamist poem, 'Epipsychidion' which obliquely refers to Pan, in so far as Pan is the god of animal instinct as well as of Nature. The adulation of Nature is partly expressed through the character of Mrs. Failing who tells Stephen: "'My farm is a mystery to me,' said the lady, stroking her fingers. 'Some day you must really take me to see it. It must be like a Gilbert and Sullivan opera, with a chorus of agitated employers. How is it that I have escaped? Why have I never been summoned to milk the cows, or flay the pigs, or drive the young bullocks to the pasture?'" Peter Burra writes: "We cannot doubt that what is urged upon us in *The Longest Journey* is the return to Nature—what is emphasised is the value of the earth" (Bradbury, 69).

In *The Longest Journey* Forster has used a few very significant symbols. One of the striking symbols occurs just in the beginning section; 'a circle inside a square, inside which was again a square.' The circle and the square represent the two aspects of the reality: the fantastic and the real. The novel begins with a philosophical debate; whether the reality is subjective or objective, whether the reality is dependent on our perception or is independently existing, whether, for instance, the cow is there or no. Rickie wanted an integration of the two mutually opposing aspects of the reality—the square and the circle or the real and the fantastic. He kept himself cocooned in his own fantastic world, in the circle. Ideally, and for a healthy existence, the two mutually opposing aspects of the reality should be integrated, and such an integration he strived to achieve. John Sayre Martin writes: "Consisting of a square within which is a circle, within which is a square, and so on in ever diminishing size, it is a mandala, an age-old symbol of unity and harmony in the material and phenomenal worlds. The circles symbolizing—as in Christian iconography—the celestial and the visionary, and the squares the mundane and the practical, the total configuration points to Rickie's desire for a total, integrated reality (Martin, 29-30).

The picture of Stockholm, that hung on the wall of Rickie's room in Cambridge, is another symbol of importance. The picture bore the imprint of the illicit relationship between Rickie's mother and Robert—the imprint not revealed to Rickie. Stockholm is the place where Robert and Mrs. Elliot met and she conceived Stephen, and it is also the place near which Robert was drowned. Martin writes: "Another significant picture is the portrait of Demeter that hangs in Stephen's room in Cadover. It is 'echoed' in the famous statue of the Cnidian Demeter in the British Museum, which Ansell pauses to admire after leaving the Reading Room" (Martin, 43). Demeter is the goddess of earth. Martin writes about the quality of Forster's symbols or echoes or *leit-motifs:* "Ever sensitive to music, Forster has carefully deployed his echoes in a way that looks back to Wagner and forward to Proust" (*ibid.*).

(ix)

It is only natural that similarities will be found between a few ideas or fragments of expressions or some other things of a particular novel of Forster and those of his other novels and short stories, because in both the cases the writer is the same person. Nicola Beauman tells us that Forster cut off a 'Panic' chapter from the original version of *The Longest Journey,* the chapter that would remind us of his short story, 'The Story of a Panic.' Beauman writes that Forster "told Dent that he had cut a 'Panic' chapter from *The Longest Journey,* in which a

Pan-like Stephen bounds about naked" (Beauman, 193). Beauman has also noticed the similarity between the character of Agnes Pembroke of *The Longest Journey* and that of Adela Quested and the other English women in *A Passage to India.* He writes that Agnes "anticipated the English women in *A Passage to India* both in her egoism, her insensitivity—and in her reliance on the Army & Navy" (*op. cit.,* 251).

(x)

In *The Longest Journey* Forster has clearly idealised physical strength, through adulating the athletic figure and the suggested enormous physical strength of Gerald Dawes and through Agnes Pembroke's romantic love of it. Peter Burra writes: "The one chance which puts the deformed Rickie in the way of salvation is that, he had escaped the sin of despising the physically strong—a sin against which the physically weak must guard. In the person of Stephen physical strength is exalted into the most exciting beauty and the whole novel reminds one constantly of the work which Lawrence produced a few years later" (Bradbury, 67). In all Forster's novels we find a conflict between tradition and freedom, between 'Culture and the Beast,' between civilisation and nature; and in *The Longest Journey* this conflict is a vital ingradient. Peter Burra again writes: "Culture and the Beast are again the conflicting opposites in *The Longest Journey.* Here the clash is between Rickie and Stephen, who eventually find that they are children of one mother—the one educated at Cambridge, the other brought up among shepherds in the Wiltshire downs" (Bradbury, 65). The conflicting opposites were long working in Forster's consciousness till he 'bodied forth' them through the most personal of his novels, *The Longest Journey,* not consciously but unconsciously, not unwillingly but most gladly. Nicola Beauman calls the novel a novel of anguish: "Morgan had in fact written a novel of anguish: his anguish at feeling himself an outsider, beyond the pale of what society considered normality [as regards homosexuality]" (Beauman, 194). And Forster was "'most glad to have written'" this novel. One further element of the novel: in the very first section of it there is a clear reference to Plato's allegory of the Cave (in Plato's *Republic*), which is quite congruent with the on-going epistemological debate among Rickie and his Cambridge friends. Carola M. Kaplan writes in this regard: "The imagery surrounding Rickie's philosopher friends—their shadows reflected on the walls of Rickie's firelit room—recalls Plato's Allegory of the Cave (the allusion to Plato is reinforced by the narrative reference to the group as a 'symposium'" (Tambling, 54).

(xi)

The Longest Journey shows some conspicuous flaws in it, some of which are summarily stated in a single sentence of Carola M. Kaplan: "Indeed, the book [*The Longest Journey*] suffers from a number of problems, among them the author's ambivalence towards the protagonist, the contrivance of the plot, the heavy-handed symbolism, and the gratuitious 'sacrificial' death of the main character" (*op. cit.*, 52). As soon as the novel came out of the press, Forster's 'family' naturally went through it, but, as Nicola Beauman tells us, "his family did not understand *The Longest Journey:* "'it might have been a foreign language as far as they were concerned.'" (Beauman, 189). Appreciations and criticisms were not tardy to come, and Forster was wide awake about them: "'The Longest Journey" published about a month,' wrote Morgan [Forster] in the June of 1907. Critics approve—except the Queen & the World. All say 'jerky,' 'too many deaths.' And that, in his diary, was that. And yet: he [Forster] was being discussed by critics who did not merely 'approve' but applauded rapturously; and who produced over twenty, mostly lengthy, reviews almost united in their praise (*op. cit.*, 191).

Carola M. Kaplan, in the article 'Absent Father, Passive Son: *The Longest Journey*,' says that the narrative of *The Longest Journey* suffers from ambivalences and vacillations: "in short, Forster's narrative is ambivalent and vacillating in three of its primary concerns. The text seeks to dethrone God the Father and to return to ancient and more inclusive conceptions of deity, yet it lacks commitment to this vision. Secondly, it proposes to place friendship rather than marriage at the centre of the narrative; yet the friendship it labours to develop ends in a violent, apparently gratuitous death, which serves to pave the way for a fruitful marriage, whose progeny contain England's future. Finally, it criticises modern industrial development but applauds the business acumen that has produced it and the worthier products of that money-making talent: the breakdown of class barriers, social amelioration, and the patronage of art and intellect" (Tambling, 62-63).

Kaplan finds three other flaws in the novel. "First, there is a strange indeterminacy about Rickie's fate and course of actions. Rickie suffers a strange series of collapses within the narrative, as if not only does he lose confidence in himself but the author loses confidence in him. Accordingly, right after he fails for the first time to tell Stephen about his parentage, we are told: 'The rest of the year was spent by Rickie partly in bed—he had a curious breakdown'(...). After the death of his child: 'Henceforward he deteriorates. Let those who censure him suggest what he should do' (...). Later, when Stephen seeks him out, he at first rejects him but over ten days he experiences a spiritual regeneration—he moves 'from disgust to penitence, from penitence to longing, from a life of horror to a new life' (...)—Rickie is like a motor that keeps losing its generator" (*op. cit.,* 63). "Second, the most important actions and insights are offered not in the form of event and action but in visions, dreams, and symbolic moments. That is, the novel progresses not by linear narration but by pauses or breaks in the narrative" (*ibid.*). And, "Finally, the narrative shows a profound distrust of books and a strong preference for gesture over language. All the characters who author books are unsuccessful in their lifetimes: Ansell's dissertation is twice rejected at Cambridge; Mr. Failing's socialist experiments are unsuccessful during his lifetime and his book is published only posthumously,... and Rickie's stories are rejected during his lifetime and achieve success only after posthumous publication. in general, the novel argues for the supremacy of life over art" (*op. cit.,* 63-64). Therefore, Kaplan decides, *The Longest Journey* "demonstrates not only a distaste for linear narrative, but a mistrust of literature and of language as well" (*op. cit.,* 63).

But before all this, Kaplan is not happy with the narrative itself of *The Longest Journey:* "although primarily linear and orderly, all narrative collapses at times into disorder—into digression, evasion, omission, ambiguity, and contradiction. Some narratives irretrievably founder on the way, either broken on the hard rock of Scylla, the father, or swallowed by the chaos and absorbtion of the mother, Charybdis. *The Longest Journey* is such a narrative. While its unfolding appears to be linear, it is actually circular and repetitious. Finally it collapses upon itself" (*op. cit.,* 51).

Jeremy Tambling says that *The Longest Journey* "has not been regarded as successful" and that it "does not seem to possess a unity of its own" (*op. cit.*, 47). As lately as in 1995, Tambling said that perhaps for its lack of unity the novel "has not yet been filmed" (*ibid.*). As we have already said, the novel conducts us through Rickie's jerky and jaunty life of divers contradictions: mother versus Agnes, tradition versus freedom, licit versus illicit brother, lameness or infirmity versus transcendence, body versus soul, etc. But even after we have walked along the whole course of the novel we do not find even a single contradiction resolved. Rae H. Stoll very perceptively writes: "There is no resolution to Rickie's dilemma within the conceptual-emotional schema of *The Longest Journey*. Rickie's consciousness remains disunified—torn within the system of differences in which he must live but to which he cannot 'adapt.' He is pulled between valuing the life of culture and the small coterie and desiring the vitality of the body and democratic brotherhood; between resentment and love of a woman; between the poles of a complex sexual and social psychology which, although it drives him to pursue his own self-knowledge in a series of Others, finally leads him back to his own infirmity: his sense of incompleteness and his need to seek completion in impossible fantasy rather than in self-acceptance" (*ibid.*).

John Sayre Martin thinks that the 'anaemic' character of Rickie and the 'issue of bastardy' are high hurdles in the way of the novel's being popular. He writes. "Certainly a major bar to the novel's popularity is Rickie himself, who to many readers must seem, as he does to Stephen, an 'anaemic prig.' How can one emphathize with a man who actually faints at the news that he has a bastard brother? And certainly the very issue of bastardy dates the novel" (Martin, 43). Martin's second objection to the novel is that it is 'overladen with incidents': "*The Longest Journey* is also overladen with incidents that add little or nothing to its development of the central theme. As Lionel Trilling has said, there is 'too-much steam that blows up the boiler.' There are too many details relating to Aunt Emily's mismanagement of her estate, too many specimens of her late husband's aphorisms. Stephen's ride with the soldier and its aftermath are recounted at too great a length.... Rickie's mother's affair with Robert seems needlessly detailed" (*op. cit.,* 44). Martin's third objection is that Forster's satire of the public school system has perhaps weakened the novel: "One may also question whether Forster's satire of public school life, effective though it is as satire, does not weaken the novel as a whole" (*ibid.*). We may say that Forster's satire of the public school system could have been removed from the novel without causing any harm to it.

Martin's fourth objection is as follows: "That Forster chose, however, to confront Rickie with a bad school points to what seems to me the novel's greatest flaw, its confusion of aims. It tries to be both realistic and allegorical, and the two aims do not harmonize. Forster in fact betrays the same fault as Rickie: he treats some of the characters as symbols while insisting upon their reality. Stephen, for instance, regarded as a human being, must be one of the least plausible yokels in literature since Wordsworth's *Lyrical Ballads*.... Most of the time, Stephen behaves like a symbol, and not a very compelling one; yet Rickie is asked to accept him as a man, and so, by implication, is the reader" (*op. cit.,* 44-45). The fifth objection of Martin is that the drawing of the character of Herbert is confusing: "Forster's treatment of Herbert pembroke also displays a 'double vision.' On the one hand, he tries to regard him as a mixture of good and bad, a rounded human being; on the other, he sees him as a fool, a hypocrite, and a swindler" (*op. cit.,* 45). The sixth objection of Martin is as regards the characters of Mr. and Mrs. Elliot, Rickie's father and mother: "Rickie's father and mother are also unconvincing, for Forster sees them as Rickie does. They are soap-opera figures, the father urbane, cultivated and cold; the mother insipidly sweet—'beautiful without and within'" (*op. cit.,* 46).

Nigel Messenger says that *The Longest Journey,* the first English novel of Forster (the second being *Howards End*) is 'loose and episodic': "There is no doubt that this is a messy and sprawling tale with none of the elegant balances and formal symmetries of the Italian novels (*Where Angels Fear to Tread* and *A Room with a View*). If the novel has a shape, it seems to be the loose and episodic one of Rickie's life" (Messenger, 82). According to A.S. Collins, the characters of *The Longest Journey* "are not vitally created, but are embodied aspects of good and evil as seen by Forster in (that) fight between the natural and life-giving forces and the conventional and destroying forces which must, in the circumstances of modern bourgeois life, be fought out in the souls of such young people as Rickie" (Collins, 200). G.D. Klingopulos says that in *The Longest Journey* "one cannot avoid the impression that a subject-matter requiring some of Lawrence's powers is, in the end, only very sketchily dealt with. The normal disintegration of Rickie and the fulfilment of Ansell's prophecy that Rickie's marriage would fail are never sharply focused. The novelist, one feels, should have given the marriage more of a chance." (Ford, 250). In the text we hear that after the death of Gerald, Agnes was never to be real again. Klingopulos asks "Why should Agnes not have become real?" and says that "The novel does not provide a satisfactory answer." Klingopulos also says that "the business about inherited deformity in Rickie and his child is an evasion, a feeble symbol for over-civilized decadence" (*ibid.*). Klingopulos goes on further criticising *The Longest Journey:* "The novel gives the impression of having been written out of convictions, feelings, and prejudices—about public school, about townspeople and countrymen and Cambridge—which do not hang together convincingly. The equation between the dead Gerald and the living Stephen as seen by the domineering, disappointed, self-ignorant Agnes, is one of many attempts to 'connect' in Forster which are not quite effective. It is certainly tantalizing. There should have been a deep sense of loss and a tragic song of praise and renewal, but the reader has to guess and invent these for himself because what he is offered is sentimentally vague" (*ibid.*).

However, inspite of all these flaws in *The Longest Journey*, noticed by himself, Klingopulos admitted that "Like everything of Mr. Forster's, *The Longest Journey* is immensely readable" (*op. cit.*, 249-50). Carola M. Kaplan also, inspite of his several points of criticism of this novel, is fascinated by it. He says that the novel "is fascinating, vivid and strange: it has far greater vitality and psychological depth than Forster's more apparently finished novels of his early period, *Where Angels Fear to Tread* and *A Room with a View*" (Tambling, 52). John Sayre Martin's half a dozen points of criticism of *The Longest Journey* have already been stated, but inspite of all those he greatly values the novel particularly for its autobiographical elements: "with all its manifest weaknesses, *The Longest Journey* is uniquely important to an understanding of Forster's mind and his aspirations as a novelist. Rickie's search for 'reality' is also his author's. Like Rickie, Forster is divided in his loyalties—divided between the inner life and the outer, between what Keats called 'the holiness of the heart's affections and the truth of imagination' on the one hand, and the human world in all its rich complexity on the other. More intimately than Forster's other novels, *The Longest Journey* presents his desire to bridge the world of spirit and objective fact" (Martin, 47).

And lastly, one thing has yet to be said: as in other novels of Forster, *The Longest Journey* is also replete with poetic passages, and philosophical observations about life and all that. It is to be noted that Rickie was of poetic disposition and had a great inclination for poets, such as Omar Khayyam, the Persian romantic poet, Theocritus, the pastoral poet and Shelley, the English romantic poet. Poetic passages are strewn throughout the novel. To take one or two instances: after seeing Gerald and Agnes locked in each other's embrace, Rickie questioned himself. 'Do such things actually happen?' and 'he seemed to be looking down coloured valleys.' "Brighter they glowed, till gods of pure flame were born in them, and then he was looking at pinnacles of virgin snow. While Mr. Pembroke talked, the riot of fair images increased. They invaded his being and lit lamps at unsuspected shrines. Their orchestra commenced in that suburban house, where he had to stand aside for the maid to carry in the luncheon. Music flowed past him like a river" (section III). In Cadover Rickie and Agnes were strolling uphill along with Stephen in great solitude: "In this great solitude—more solitary than any Alpine range—he and Agnes were floating alone and for ever, between the shapeless earth and the shapeless clouds. An immense silence seemed to move towards them. A lark stopped singing, and they were glad of it. They were approaching the Throne of God. The silence touched them; the earth and all danger dissolved, but ere they quite vanished Rickie heard himself saying, 'Is it exactly what we intended?'" (section XII). Regarding philosophical observations it can safely be said that among all Forster's novels *The Longest Journey* contains the greatest number of such observations. Instances of philosophical observations freely distributed throughout the novel are the following: "All societies are narrow, but some are good and some are bad—just as one house is beautiful inside and another ugly" (section VII); "no man can be an agnostic who has a sense of humour" (section X); "it is in what we value, not in what we have, that the test of us resides" (section XVII); "those who stay outside their nature invite disaster" (section XXIV); and "'A man wants to love mankind, a woman wants to love one man'" (section XXXIII).

A Room with a View

8

I

INTRODUCTION

This is Forster's third, and his second Italian, novel that was published just one year after *The Longest Journey* came out of the press, i.e., in 1908. *A Room with a View,* a novel of some 223 pages, is much shorter than its predecessor, and "is less ambitious and better controlled than *The Longest Journey,* and most readers like it more. Unlike *The Longest Journey,* it is an overtly romantic novel, a love story whose heroine, after trying from a sense of propriety to ignore her love for a socially questionable young man, finally marries him, and, so far as we can determine, lives happily ever after" (Martin, 89). *A Room with a View* is sometimes referred to as 'Lucy novel' following the name of its heroine Lucy Honeychurch, and the novel Forester dedicated to H.O. Meredith with whom he had deep homosexual relationship. The novel is concerned with 'the undeveloped heart' of the upper middle class, and has been a brilliant social comedy around the institution of marriage.

Nicola Beauman writes about the intention of Forster behind writing *A Room with a View:* "Morgan [Forster] wanted, in a way, to write a romantic novel: not because he wanted the sales (then, as now, literary novels sold far less well than romantic) but because he would have liked to subvert the convention. He would have liked to take the typical marriage plot and mould it into something new; or he would have liked his characters to live together without being married; or he would have liked them to exchange roles ('I hope that for women, too, 'not to work' will soon become as shocking as 'not to be married' was a hundred years ago' declares Margaret Wilcox). It was his continuing fascination with the state of marriage, with the 'glass shade,' that made him want to write about it; since he could not, through lack of firsthand insight, write a 'straight' novel, he chose to write a romantic comedy" (Beauman, 204). The time of writing *A Room with a View* is rather hazy to us, particularly because the novel is partly a reworking of an earlier and fragmentary unpublished novel Forster perhaps would have entitled 'Lucy' and now known as 'New Lucy.' This fragmentary 'Lucy' novel is again itself a reworking of an even earlier draft of a novel now known as 'Old Lucy.' In the summer of 1904, Forster was steadily working on 'New Lucy,' and inspite of his earnest endeavour 'New Lucy' remained less complete than 'Old Lucy.' However, it appears that in the end Forster incorporated most of the fragmentary 'New Lucy' in *A Room with a View*. "Thus the sixty extant sheets of 'New Lucy' (...) begin at Chapter 12 [*of A Room with a View*], and are all set in England, after Lucy has returned from Italy. The likelihood is that the Italian chapters of what was to be *A Room with a View* were written at Kingsley in the new year and early spring of 1904; and that when, in 1907, Morgan came to finish what had by then become *A Room with a View* he only abandoned the second half of 'New Lucy'—what had been written at Drayton Court" (*op. cit.*, 146). As the 'New Lucy' part *of A Room with a View* begins at chapter 12, so perhaps has Forster subtitled chapter 12 of *A Room with a View* as simply and peculiarly 'Twelfth Chapter.' However, *A Room with a View* is certainly an obvious improvement upon 'New Lucy': "in 'New Lucy' Lucy is too shallow and Cecil too unpleasant to be plausible, while George is killed by a falling tree and Lucy resolves that she will never marry. In the finished novel [*A Room with a View*] Lucy and Cecil are far more 'rounded' characters, each with good as well as bad qualities" (*ibid.*).

A Room with a View, may be said to have been drafted thrice; it began as 'Old Lucy,' it was then reconstructed as 'New Lucy,' and ultimately it permanently became what it is now. An early note of Forster on this novel reads as follows (Furbank, I, 91):

> "*Who*? Lucy Beringer. Miss Bartlett, her cousin.
> H.O.M.
> Miss Lavish
> Miss Dorothy & Miss Margaret Alan.
> *Where*? Florence, Pension Bertolini.
> *Doing What*?"

It took for Forster about four years to write the novel, during which period he was spasmodically writing and re-writing the drafts of it. But when he was making the final draft, he had a fast run: he completed it between June 1907 and December of the same year. Nigel Messenger writes about Forster's writing of this novel: "its writing history was a protracted and complex affair. Although the first novel he began, the 'Lucy novel,' as he called it, was redrafted several times and Forster deferred the completion of it twice in order to finish other novels" (Messenger, 53). Forster once before he wrote this novel wanted to call it 'Windy Corner.' In 1905, after the publication of *Where Angels Fear to Tread,* Forster wrote to his mother: "'Should I ever write another book it will be called 'The Longest Journey,' and the one after that 'Windy Corner'" (Furbank, I, 123). 'The Longest Journey' really became *The Longest Journey,* but 'Windy Corner' changed to *A Room with a View*. In any case, we may surmise that the novel was for long being hybernated in the mind of Forster.

A Room with a View has been both dramatised and filmed. S. Tait and K. Allott presented a stage version of this novel at Cambridge in 1950. (Shahane, vi). In 1986, the novel was filmed under the direction of James Ivory (who in 1992 also directed the filming of *Howards End*) In that film, the principal actors and actresses were (Tambling, 220):

> Helena Bonham Carter (who acted in four out of five Forster films): acted as Lucy Honeychurch
> Rupert Graves: acted as Freddy Honeychurch
> Denholm Elliot: acted as Mr Emerson
> Simon Callow: acted as Rev. Arthur Beebe.

The film was "the most generally-lauded" (Tambling, 221) and upto 1995 it earned "US $ 20 million, an extraordinary amount for 'quality' film" (*op. cit.*, 213).

The novel is divided into two Parts: Part I is set in Italy and Part II in England. The major characters in it are:

Lucy Honeychurch (fiancee of Cecil Vyse but later marries George Emerson)
Miss Bartlett (Lucy's chaperone)
Mr Emerson (father of George Emerson)
George Emerson (son of Mr Emerson)
Reverend Arthur Mr Beebe
Miss Lavish (novelist)
Cecil Vyse (cultured and overprotective fiance of Lucy Honeychurch).

There is a very brief summary of the story of *A Room with a View* in *The Wordsworth Companion to Literature in English* which may help us follow the line of the narrative of the novel: "Lucy Honeychurch and her chaperone, the genteel Miss Bartlett, are frustrated in their hopes of obtaining a room with a view at the Pensione Bertolini in Florence. Offered an exchange by Mr Emerson and his son, George, Miss Bartlett's sense of social propriety is offended. She graciously accepts the proposal, however, after being reassured by a respectable acquaintance, the Revd Mr Beebe. Lucy, innocent and impressionable, is shown around Florence by the lady novelist, Miss Lavish, one of the novel's many English 'characters' about whom Forster is gently satirical.

"Venturing out alone, Lucy witnesses a quarrel between two Italians, one of whom is stabbed and dies in front of her. She faints, and recovers to find herself in the arms of George Emerson. Later, a party from the pensione joins an excursion to Fiesole. During the trip Lucy is again rescued, after a fall, by George and impulsively embraced. She and Miss Bartlett are affronted and take themselves off to Rome, then back to Surrey.

"Lucy becomes engaged to the cultured, but shallow and over-protective Cecil Vyse. Her independent spirit is aroused and she eventually rebels. The Emersons, meanwhile, arrive to take up residence nearby. Lucy realizes with some perturbation that she loves George, not Cecil. She extricates herself from the relationship with Cecil, aided by Miss Bartlett, and marries George. The close of the novel finds George and Lucy on their honeymoon in the Pensione Bertolini" (Ousby, 797-98).

2

THE STORY

Miss Lucy Honeychurch and her cousin and chaperone, Miss Charlotte Bartlett, went to Italy and put up in a pensione, Pensione Bertolini, owned by a certain Signora. Lucy lived in a house in England named 'Windy Corner' situated in the parish beside Summer Street in Sussex Weald. The two young women earlier booked two rooms in that pensione and was assured, through letter, by that Signora that they would be allotted two rooms in the southern part of the pensione from where one could have a view of the river Arno (in Central Italy, that flows past Florence and into the Mediterranean). But on coming to the pensione they were frustrated to see that they were allotted rooms not in the southern part but in the northern part of the pensione. Lucy and Bartlett were expressing their disgust and frustration to each other while attending the dinner among other women and men. Suddenly an 'ill-bred' English tourist, Mr Emerson, shouted out at the two women; "'I have a view, I have a view.'" "He was an old man, of heavy build, with a fair, shaven face and large eyes. There was something childish in those eyes, though it was not the childishness of senility." The old man, in unattractive clothes, wanted to get acquainted with the two women, and with this objective he introduced his son, George Emerson, to them. Mr Emerson then, with an air of magnanimity, proposed to Lucy and Charlotte to exchange their rooms—the southern rooms of the Emersons to go to the women and their northern rooms to go to the Emersons. The old Mr Emerson, in support of his proposal, said: "'Women like looking at a view, men don't.'" Both Lucy and Charlotte took the proposal as an instance of impropriety, of violation of civility.

Just at this moment Mr Beebe, a clergyman, barged into the dining hall and immediately got acquainted with Lucy and Charlotte. He told them that next June he was appointed to join the Rectory at Summer Street (where 'Windy Corner' was situated). Mr Beebe asked the two girls, Lucy and Charlotte, to first drive to Fiesole and Settignano, but, Miss Eleanor Lavish, a certain 'clever lady,' hilariously suggested that they should first go to Prato, shaking off 'the trammels of respectability.' Lucy then rose to go, but before going out she gave the Emersons 'a nervous little bow.' The young George Emerson saw it and raising his eyebrows smiled. Now there appeared that Signora, the owner of Pensione Bertolini, accompanied by her little son, Enery, and daughter, Victorier. Miss Charlotte Bartlett told Mr Emerson that she and Lucy could accept his proposal of exchanging the rooms but they must not be under any obligation. Mr Beebe assured them that no harm would be done to them by the Emersons, who were, he said, socialists. He also said that George Emerson was a nice creature and that he had brains.

Lucy liked George because "'He seems to see good in everyone'", and because he was not like a clergyman. She told Charlotte that everyone in the 'Windy Corner', including her mother and her brother Freddy, were 'behind the times, though the 'Windy Corner' was part of the fashionable world just as Tunbridge Wells was of the narrow world. The Signora ultimately succeeded in persuading Lucy and Charlotte to accept Mr Emerson's proposal of exchanging their rooms. Displeased with the rearrangement, Mr Beebe went out only to soon return with George Emerson to announce that the rooms of the Emerson would be ready for the two girls within half an hour or so. Lucy engaged herself in Baedeker's *Handbook to Northern Italy,* for she was determined 'to enjoy herself on the morrow.' Charlotte took the 'largest room' of the younger Emerson because she thought Lucy's mother would not like it went to Lucy. Lucy embraced Charlotte, said 'good night' to her, and entered into her new room where "she opened the window and breathed the clean night air, thinking of the kind old man who had enabled her to see the lights dancing in the Arno and the cypresses of San Miniato, and the foothills of the Apennines, black against the rising moon." Charlotte, on the other hand, on entering her room shut the doors and windows and searched the room to see if there were any outlets or secret entrances. Suddenly she discovered 'an enormous note of interrogation' over the wash-stand. "Meaningless at first, it gradually became menacing, obnoxious, portentous with evil." She did not destroy it as it belonged to the young Emerson, but kept it clean for him, and then went to bed (Part I, chapter I: *The Bertolini*).

The Pensione Bertolini was most attractive with its red floor tiles and painted ceiling "whereon pink griffins and blue amorini sport in a forest of yellow violins and bassons." When the wide windows were opened, the shiny and gurgling Arno came to view. On the bank of Arno people were working with spades, etc. An electric tram passed, the conductor of which spat at the boys gathered on the platform to disperse them. On her first day in Florence, Lucy could go out alone, but Miss Charlotte Bartlett would not leave her alone. Miss Eleanor Lavish "said that she was going to spend a long morning in Santa Croce, and if Lucy would come too, she would be delighted." Miss Lavish told her: "'I will take you by a dear dirty back way, Miss Honeychurch, and if you bring me luck, we shall have an adventure.'" Lucy gratefully agreed to the proposal, and they started for Santa Croce through the streets of Florence. Miss Bartlett kept back in the Pensione Bertolini. Lucy got an offensive smell in the street, whereupon Miss Lavish said that people came to Italy not for niceties but for life: "'Buon giorno! Buon giorno!'" On the street a wine-cart passed and the driver of the wine-cart lecherously stared at the girls. Miss Lavish told Lucy that she was a Radical and so preferred to show a little civility to her inferiors. Lucy told her that she was also a Radical, like her father. The conversation continued around the English politics, in the midst of which Miss Lavish shockingly announced that they had lost their way—the two lone females, Lucy and Miss Lavish. Miss Lavish told Lucy: "'Two lone females in an unknown town. Now, this is what I call an adventure.'" Lucy told her that 'they should ask the way there,' but she would not. She rather would 'simply drift'.

"Accordingly they drifted through a series of those grey-brown streets, neither commodious nor picturesque, in which the eastern quarter of the city abounds.... For one ravishing moment Italy appeared." Lucy "stood in the Square of the Annunziata and saw in the living terracotta those divine babies whom no cheap reproduction can ever stale.... Lucy thought she had never seen anything more beautiful; but Miss lavish, with a shriek of dismay, dragged her forward, declaring that they were out of their path now by at least a mile." They bought some hot chestnut paste out of a little shop. It "tasted partly of the paper in which it was wrapped, partly of hair-oil, partly of the great unknown." They ate of it and drifted to another Piazza where they saw the black-and-white façade of the Santa Croce. When they were about to elegantly enter the church of Santa Croce, Miss Lavish squeaked out: "'There goes my local-colour box! I must have a word with him!'" She speedily walked a little distance and caught an old man with whom she vanished down a side street. Lucy felt befuddled and her eyes filled with tears: how could she return to Pensione Bertolini? Humiliated and depressed she entered the church of Santa Croce.

Alone in the train of visitors, Lucy was watching the frescoes, some of which were done by Giotto and some praised by Ruskin. There were notices hung debarring introduction of dogs and spitting in the church. She saw three Papists anointing 'two he-babies and a she-baby', and she saw one of the he-babies being kicked by a prelate, at which the old Mr Emerson ejaculated 'Hateful bishop!' and cursed the church. The child's legs were broken. Fortunately an Italian lady came to the rescue of the child and helped it somehow walk away. Mr Emerson asked Lucy what she had been doing there. She told him that she was left there by Miss Lavish very badly. George Emerson, who accompanied Mr Emerson, invited Lucy to join them. The Emersons conducted Lucy to the Peruzzi

Chapel; George Emerson felt 'sombre satisfaction' at this. They found in the chapel a lecturer directing visitors how to worship Giotto. They saw the Ascension of St John, and, in the next chapel, the life of St Francis. The lecturer was soon identified as Rev. Cuthbert Eager. The lecture over, people filed out, in the file there being two old ladies of the Pensione Bertolini—Miss Teresa and Miss Catharine Alan.

Lucy liked the Giotto and its 'tactile values', but, she told the old Emerson, she liked babies better than Della Robbia. Suddenly, among other talks, Mr Emerson sprang a surprise for Lucy by telling her that she should learn to understand his son George to learn to understand herself: "'...I don't require you to fall in love with my boy, but I do think you might try and understand him. You are nearer his age, and if you let yourself go I am sure you are sensible. You might help me. He has known so few women, and you have the time. You stop here several weeks, I suppose? But let yourself go. You are inclined to get muddled, if I may judge from last night. Let yourself go. Pull out from the depths those thoughts that you do not understand, and spread them out in the sunlight and know the meaning of them. By understanding George you may learn to understand yourself. It will be good for both of you.'" But immediately Mr Emerson quoted poetry to tell her that 'thing wont fit', that the things of the universe do not really fit, that George would not fit with her, that life is just a knot:

> 'From far, from eve and morning,
>   And yon twelve-winded sky,
> The stuff of life to knit me
>   Blew hither: here am I.'

Mr Emerson said: "'George and I both knew this, but why does it distress him? We know that we come from the winds, and that we shall return to them; that all life is perhaps a knot, a tangle, a blemish in the eternal smoothness. But why should this make us unhappy? Let us rather love one another, and work and rejoice. I don't believe in this world sorrow.'" Lucy laughed, but was touched. At this moment George returned and said that Miss Bartlett was in the nave of the church. She too came and was joined by Lucy with all gladness (Part I, chapter II: *In Santa Croce with no Baedeker*).

Lucy was playing on the piano and Mr Emerson and some others were listening, unnoticed by the player, when Mr Beebe arrived and asked Mr Emerson to introduce him to her. After being introduced to her, Mr Beebe noticed that Lucy "was only a young lady with a quantity of dark hair and a very pretty, pale, undeveloped face." Mr Beebe entered into a conversation with Lucy. Lucy asked if Miss Lavish had been writing a book, and if so what the book was about. Mr Beebe said that it would be a novel, dealing with modern Italy. He believed that he understood Miss Lavish, but not Miss Bartlett who, he believed, "might reveal unknown depths of strangeness, though not, perhaps, of meaning." He questioned himself: "Was Italy deflecting her from the path of prime chaperone, which he had assigned to her at Tunbridge Wells?" All his life Mr Beebe "had loved to study maiden ladies; they were his speciality, and his profession had provided him with ample opportunities for the work. Girls like Lucy were charming to look at, but Mr Beebe was, from rather profound reasons, somewhat chilly in his attitude towards the sex, and preferred to be interested rather than enthralled."

Miss Catherine Alan entered the room with words of praise for Lucy's playing on the piano. She kept herself shut up in her room, because in Italy no one knows what privacy is. "Mr Beebe was not able to tell the ladies of his adventure at Modena, where the chambermaid burst in upon him in his bath." From the chair nearby Miss Alan "extracted a gun-metal cigarette-case, on which were powdered in turquoise the initials 'E.L.'" Mr Beebe declared that the case belonged to Miss Lavish. Miss Alan said that Miss lavish took to smoking 'practically in despair' when she lost a novel of hers in the Grotto of the Calvary at the Capuccini Hotel. She told Mr Beebe that Miss Lavish was a little too 'unwomanly.' Miss Alan then dwelt on Miss Pole's stomach which generated acidity, for which reason Miss Pole used to take lemonade. Mr Beebe warned Miss Pole of her stomach, and Miss Lavish "was positively *attracted* by his mentioning S (short for stomach)." The conversation turned to the early Victorians. After dinner Miss Lavish actually came up and said: "'Miss Alan, I am going into the smoking-room to talk to those two nice men. Come, too.'" The two nice men were Mr Beebe and Mr Emerson. Miss Lavish went alone, but after five minutes slowly returned. But she would not dare to tell what happened and Mr Emerson did not think it worth telling.

Mr Beebe facetiously told Miss Alan that she must say that the Emersons were nice people, particularly after her experience of 'that business of the violets.' But Miss Alan told him: "'I do *not* like the Emersons. They are *not* nice.'" Lucy was of a different opinion. She said that the Emersons were nice. The beautiful evening drew near with 'colours on the trees and hills,' 'streaks of bluish-green clouds,' and 'patches of watery light upon the earth.' Miss Alan thought it too late to go out, but Lucy 'wanted to go round the town in a circular tram.' Miss Alan warned her of the rough Italians. But Lucy did not retrace. She said: "'Perhaps I shall meet someone who reads me through and through!'" (Part I, chapter III: *Music, Violets, and the letter S*).

Lucy was like the medieval lady who used to inspire knights, and she might have been called the Eternal Woman. But in another sense she was not like the medieval lady: she would get annoyed by restrictions imposed upon her. That afternoon, however, she was particularly restive, and "As she might not go on the electric tram, she went to Alinari's shop." From the shop she bought photographs of Botticelli's 'Birth of Venus,' Fra Angelico's 'Coronation,' Giotto's 'Ascension of St. John', etc. and then entered the Piazza Signoria. She was impatient because nothing was happening to her. "The Loggia showed as the triple entrance of a cave, wherein dwelt many a deity, shadowy, but immortal, looking forth upon the arrivals and departures of mankind. It was the hour of unreality—the hour, that is, when unfamiliar things are real. An older person at such an hour and in such a place might think that sufficient was happening to him, and rest content. Lucy desired more." And something more did really happen. "Two Italians by the Loggia had been bickering about a debt. 'Cinque lire,' they had cried, 'cinque lire!' They sparred at each other, and one of them was hit lightly upon the chest. He frowned; he bent towards Lucy with a look of interest, as if he had an important message for her. He opened his lips to deliver it, and a stream of red came out between them and trickled down his unshaven chin." Lucy was feeling dizzy and she fell down, not on the ground but in the arms of George Emerson who had been watching the ghastly drama, and its spectator Lucy, from the other side of the piazza.

Lucy fainted. After a little while, when she was well, she found George's hand extended to her with a view to pull her up. She asked him to gather her newly bought photographs, and as soon as George turned his back to fetch the photographs, "Lucy arose with the cunning of a maniac and stole down the arcade towards the Arno." George called her from behind and asked her to take rest, and she obeyed. He told her that the man whose mouth was oozing blood died. Lucy felt "that she, as well as the dying man, had crossed some spiritual boundary." George enquired of her if the murderer tried to kiss the man he killed, and wondered at the odd behaviour of the Italians. Suddenly he threw Lucy's photographs into the stream. Lucy was not cross at this; rather "Her heart warmed towards him for the first time." Lucy thought that George was 'trustworthy, intelligent, and even kind,' he might even have a high opinion of her. But he lacked chivalry; his thoughts, like his behaviour, would not be modified by awe. It was useless to say to him, 'And would you—' and hope that he would complete the sentence for himself, averting his eyes from her nakedness like the knight in that beautiful picture. She had been in his arms, and he remembered it, just as he remembered the blood on the photographs that she had bought in Alinari's shop." She thought that 'something had happened' between herself and George and that "they had come to a situation where character tells." They were conversing near the parapet of the embankment not far from the pensione. Between them 'eternal comradeship' seemed to glow. "Leaning her elbows on the parapet, she contemplated the River Arno, whose roar was suggesting some unexpected melody to her ears" (Part I, chapter IV: *Fourth Chapter*).

Next morning Lucy, along with Charlotte Bartlett, started off along the Lung' Arno. Charlotte took her to the fateful sight: the Piazza Signoria, where she had a destabilising encounter with George. After the encounter Mr Beebe saw an uncommon sign in the eyes of Lucy, and commented to himself 'Too much Beethoven.' Now, today, Lucy, surveying the Piazza Signoria, "could not have believed that stones, a Loggia, a fountain, a palace tower, would have such significance. For a moment she understood the nature of ghosts." Miss Lavish was just on the spot where the man died on the previous day. She was collecting data for an excellent plot of a novel with the two men quarrelling, not over a five-franc note but over a girl. She was joined by Lucy and Miss Bartlett. Miss Lavish said that the name of the heroine of her story would be Leonora. Her own name was Eleanor. "Love, murder, abduction, revenge, was the plot" of her story to which she would give local colouring. She sternly said that she would not be merciful to the British tourist in her story. Miss Barlett remarked: "'It should be a most pathetic novel.'"

The chaplain Mr Eager, surprised them all by his presence there. He made a suggestion before Miss Bartlett and Lucy: "'I am about to venture a suggestion. Would you and Miss Honeychurch be disposed to join me in a drive some day this week—a drive in the hills? We might go up by Fiesole and back by Settignano. There is a point on that road where we could get down and have an hour's ramble on the hill-side. The view thence of Florence is most beautiful—far better than the hackneyed view from Fiesole. It is the view that Alessio Baldovinetti is fond of introducing into his pictures. That man had a decided feeling for landscape. Decidedly. But who looks at it today? Ah, the world is too much with us.'" Mr Beebe would also accompany them. Both Miss Bartlett and Lucy were delighted. They were talking about various things, one after another—about 'the eternal league of Italy with youth', about the character of the Italians in general, etc. Then the topic was the Emersons, one of them said about the old

Mr Emerson: "'The son of a labourer; I happen to know it for a fact. A mechanic of some sort himself when he was young; then he took to writing for the Socialistic Press. I came across him at Brixton.'" The old Mr Emerson 'made an advantageous marriage,' but 'murdered his wife' in Santa Croce.

Lucy, Miss Bartlett and Mr Eager advanced to the 'English bank'. "They were now in the newspaper-room at the English bank. Lucy stood by the central table, heedless of *Punch* and the *Graphic,* trying to answer, or at all events to formulate the questions rioting in her brain. The well-known world had broken up, and there emerged Florence, a magic city where people thought and did the most extraordinary things." Lucy told Miss Bartlett: "'I don't know what I think, nor what I want.'" Miss Bartlett understood that Lucy was feeling bored, and so she told Lucy: "'I would take you to the ends of the earth tomorrow.'" There were letters for Lucy at the bureau, from one of which she came to know that Mrs Vyse and her son (Cecil Vyse) had gone to Rome from England. "'Charlotte!' cried the girl suddenly. 'Here's an idea. What if we popped off to Rome tomorrow—straight—to the Vyses' hotel? For I do know what I want. I'm sick of Florence. Now, you said you'd go to the ends of the earth! Do! Do!'" Miss Bartlett was equally vivacious to accept the proposal forthwith (Part I, chapter V: *Possibilities of a Pleasant Outing*).

The Reverend Arthur Beebe, the Reverend Cuthbert Eager, Mr Emerson, Mr George Emerson, Miss Eleanar Lavish, Miss Charlotte, and Miss Lucy Honeychurch drove out in two carriages to see a view in Fiesole. The firy youth Phaethon was the driver of one of the two carriages. Phaethon told Persephone that he would pick her up on the way. He gave out to the tourists that Persephone was his sister, and not his beloved. Phaethon picked up the 'tall and slender and pale' Persephone and installing her beside him, slipped his arm round her waist. Elegantly dressed Lucy sat amidst the passengers. "The carriage swept with agonizing jolts up through the Piazza of Fiesole and into the Settignano road." Phaethon had been for long contemplating a kiss to Persephone and only now succeeded. As a bad consequence of his success "the lovers were ordered to disentangle themselves, the boy [Phaethon] was to lose his *pourboire,* the girl [Persephone] was immediately to get down." Mr Emerson "declared that the lovers must on no account be separated, and patted them on the back to signify his approval."

Their carriage reached a place from where the Val d'Arno was visible, and also visible was fifty miles of spring-time budding trees. Mr Eager told Miss Lavish: "'Fifty miles of spring, and we've come up to admire them. Do you suppose there's any difference between spring in nature and spring in man? But there we go, praising the one and condemning the other as improper, ashamed that the same laws work eternally through both.'" Mr Eager ordered the carriage to stop and the tourist party climed up to a promontory that was wet, bushy and virgin—the promontory that caught the fancy of Alessio Baldovinetti nearby five hundred years ago. Soon the tourist party divided into three groups; "Lucy clung to Miss Bartlett and Miss Lavish; the Emersons returned to hold laborious converse with the drivers; while the two clergymen, who were expected to have topics in common, were left to each other."

Miss Bartlett, Miss Lavish and Miss Lucy Honeychurch were conversing. Miss Bartlett said that she heard from George Emerson himself that he was a railway-man. At this Miss Lavish burst out in laughter that signified contempt. She then shyly asked Lucy to go away to a distance, for she said "'We wish to converse on high topics unsuited for your ear.'" Miss Bartlett and Miss Lavish sat on the wet grass to converse and Lucy went away to search for Mr Beebe and Mr Eager. Lucy asked the driver to take her to Dove Buoni uomini and the driver obeyed. Only once did the driver stop and that to collect some great blue violets for Lucy. "She thanked him with real pleasure. In the company of this common man the world was beautiful and direct. For the first time she felt the influence of spring." They reached Dove Buoni uomini and then they proceeded through the thick undergrowth; the driver was occupied with his cigar while Lucy was enjoying her escape from dullness. Suddenly she was perplexed to see Mr Eager there. Mr Eager cried out at her: "'Eccolo!'" "At the same moment the ground gave way, and with a cry she fell out of the wood. Light and beauty enveloped her. She had fallen on to a little open terrace which was covered with violets from end to end." Mr George Emerson was standing six feet above, he saw what happened to Lucy, and cried out: "'Courage and love.'" "George had turned at the sound of her arrival. For a moment he contemplated her as one who had fallen out of heaven. He saw radiant joy in her face, he saw the flowers beat against her dress in blue waves. The bushed above them closed. He stepped quickly forward and kissed her." And, before Lucy could say anything, Miss Bartlett was heard calling out at herself: "'Lucy! Lucy! Lucy!'" "The silence of life had been broken by Miss Bartlett, who stood brown against the view" (Part I, chapter VI: *The Reverend Arthur Beebe, the Reverend Cuthbert Eager, Mr Emerson, Mr George Emerson, Miss Eleanor Lavish, Miss Charlotte Bartlett, and Miss Lucy Honeychurch, Drive out in Carriages to See a View: Italians Drive them*).

In the wood of Dove Buoni Uomini almost everybody lost everyone: "Mr Beebe had lost everyone...Miss Lavish had lost Miss Bartlett. Lucy had lost Mr Eager. Mr Emerson had lost George. Miss Bartlett had lost a mackintosh square, Phaethon had lost the game." The reason of this all was perhaps that "Pan had been amongst them—not the great god Pan, who has been buried these two thousand years, but the little god Pan, who presides over social contretemps and unsuccessful picnics." Meanwhile Phaethon announced that the swift bad weather was approaching, and then sat on the box shivering. And soon "Rain and darkness came on together." The girls were screaming and the men folk were shouting. Amidst the row the two carriages were started. "There was an explosion up the road. The storm had struck the overhead wire of tramline, and one of the great supports had fallen. If they had not stopped perhaps they might have been hurt. They chose to regard it as a miraculous preservation, and the floods of love and sincerity, which might fructify every hour of life, burst forth in tumult. They descended from the carriages; they embraced each other. It was as joyful to be forgiven past unworthiness as to forgive them. For a moment they realized vast possibilities of good." "Mr Eager mumbled a temperate prayer. But the drivers, through miles of dark squalid road, poured out their souls to the dryads and the saints, and Lucy poured out hers to her cousin." Lucy told Miss Bartlett: "'Charlotte, dear Charlotte, kiss me. Kiss me again. Only you can understand me. You warned me to be careful. And I—I thought I was developing.'" Lucy narrated to Miss Bartlett her encounter with George Emerson in the wood: "'He is really—I think he was taken by surprise, just as I was before. But this time I'm not to blame; I do want you to believe that. I simply slipped into those violets. No, I want to be really truthful. I am a little to blame. I had silly thoughts. The sky, you know, was gold, and the ground all blue, and for a moment he looked like someone in a book.'" Lucy meant to say that George looked like heroes, like gods. Miss Bartlett drew Lucy close to herself. "All the way back Lucy's body was shaken by deep sighs which nothing could repress."

The party 're-entered the city,' i.e. the tourists returned to Pensione Bertolini. The rain did not cease yet. "Lucy felt unaccountably sad, though she had long since dried her eyes." As a means of giving solace to Lucy, Miss Bartlett told her about George Emerson: "'My poor dear, did you suppose that this was his first? Come here and listen to me. I am only gathering it from his own remarks. Do you remember that day at lunch when he argued with Miss Alan that liking one person is an extra reason for liking another?'" Miss Bartlett told her that George was 'thoroughly unrefined.' Nevertheless, Lucy said: "'I propose to speak to him.'" At this Miss Bartlett 'uttered a cry of genuine alarm.' She cautioned Lucy about George: "'But we fear him for you, dear. You are so young and inexperienced, you have lived among such nice people, that you cannot realize what men can be—how they can take a brutal pleasure in insulting a woman whom her sex does not protect and rally round. This afternoon, for example, if I had not arrived, what would have happened?'" Miss Bartlett was referring to George's kissing Lucy in the wood. Miss Bartlett at first failed to prevail over Lucy's urge to meet George, but afterwards succeeded in reducing her drive to talk to George.

Nevertheless, Lucy continued to feel that "the world be happier, if she could give and receive some human love." The two girls began to pack for the next morning's journey to Rome. George returned to the pensione and was walking along Lucy's room to reach his own. Miss Bartlett opened the door of her room and told George: "'I wish one word with you in the drawing-room, Mr Emerson, please.'" And then after a little while she said: "'Good night, Mr Emerson.'" Lucy saw all this and cried aloud: "'It isn't true. It can't all be true. I want not to be muddled. I want to grow older quickly.'" Miss Bartlett softly told her: "'Go to bed at once, dear. You need all the rest you can get.'" "In the morning they left for Rome" (Part I, chapter VII: *The Return*)

In the Windy Corner (in England) in August a boy of nineteen and his mother were sitting in a sultry day. The boy was reading an anatomy book and the mother was writing a letter. The boy was Fredd, Lucy's younger brother, and the mother was Mrs Honeychurch, Lucy's mother. Mrs Honeychurch was writing to Mrs Vyse, mother of Cecil Vyse, saying that Cecil had asked her permission to marry Lucy. Mrs Honeychurch was delighted with Cecil's proposal, but Freddy was against the marriage because he thought Cecil would have a bad effect on Lucy. Freddy told his mother about Cecil: "'I don't hate him, but I don't like him. What I mind is that he 'll tell Lucy.'" His mother contradicted him: "'Well, *I* like him,' said Mrs Honeychurch.' I know his mother; he's good, he's clever, he's rich, he's well connected...he has beautiful manners.'" Mrs Honeychurch wrote in her letter: "'Dear Mrs Vyse,—Cecil has just asked my permission about it [his marriage with Lucy], and I should be delighted if Lucy wishes it.'" She added that she had told Lucy about it. While the mother and the son were debating over Lucy's marriage with Cecil, Cecil, in person, appeared before them.

Cecil Vyse "was medieval. Like a Gothic statue. Tall and refined, with shoulders that seemed braced square by an effort of the will, and a head that was tilted a little higher than the usual level of vision, he resembled those fastidious saints who guard the portals of a French cathedral. Well educated, well endowed, and not deficient physically, he remained in the grip of a certain devil whom the modern world knows as self-consciousness, and whom the medieval, with dimmer vision, worshipped as asceticism." Mrs Honeychurch exclaimed at the sight of Cecil: "'Oh, Cecil, do tell me!'" Cecil told her two things: "'I promessi sposi'" and "'She has accepted me'" Mrs Honeychurch was exceedingly glad and Freddy shook hands with Cecil. Both of them wished they knew Italian to freely converse with Cecil. Mrs Honeychurch told Cecil: "'Welcome as one of the family!'" and "'This is indeed a joyous day! I feel sure that you will make dear Lucy happy.'" Cecil assured her: "'I hope so.'"

Lucy smiled at them and departed to the lawn, kissing her mother, as she demanded it. Cecil lit a cigarette and watched Lucy move away and was rehearsing what he would tell her about their marriage. "He had known Lucy for several years, but only as a commonplace girl who happened to be musical. He could still remember his depression that afternoon at Rome, when she and her terrible cousin fell on him out of the blue, and demanded to be taken to St. Peter's. That day she had seemed a typical tourist—shrill, crude, and gaunt with travel. But Italy worked some marvel in her. It her light, and—which he held more precious—it gave her shadow. Soon he detected in her a wonderful reticence. She was like a woman of Leonardo da Vinci's, whom we love not so much for herself as for the things she will not tell us. The things are assuredly not of this life; no woman of Leonardo's could have anything so vulgar as a 'story.' She did develop most wonderfully day by day." George had earlier proposed to her twice. "Already at Rome he [Cecil] had hinted to her that they might be suitable for each other. It had touched him greatly that she had not broken away at the suggestion.... Three months later, on the margin of Italy, among the flower-clad Alps, he had asked her again in bald, traditional language.... He walked home with her unashamed, feeling not at all like a rejected suitor." And "now he had asked her once more, and clear and gentle as ever, she had accepted him, giving no coy reasons for her delay, but simply saying that she loved him and would do her best to make him happy."

Suddenly Mr Beebe arrived and announced that he came to have tea, and Cecil showed him in. Mr Beebe asked Cecil: "'what *is* your profession?'" Cecil answered that he had no profession. At this Mr Beebe quipped that Cecil had the rare opportunity of having 'the possession of leisure'. Their conversation turned to the topic of Miss Lucy Honeychurch. Mr Beebe said: "'I'm not cynical. I'm only thinking of my pet theory about Miss Honeychurch. Does it seem reasonable that she should play so wonderfully, and live so quietly? I suspect that one day she will be wonderful in both. The water-tight compartments in her will break down, and music and life will mingle. Then we shall have her heroically good, heroically bad—too heroic, perhaps, to be good or bad.'" Cecil became interested in Mr Beebe's account of Lucy, and Mr Beebe further said, this time prophetically: "'I could as easily tell you what tune she'll play next. There was simply the sense that she had found wings, and meant to use them. I can show you a beautiful picture in my Italian diary: Miss Honeychurch as a kite. Miss Bartlett holding the string. Picture number two: the string breaks.'"

Cecil was perplexed: "'What do you mean?'" Mr Beebe plainly said that Miss Honeychurch was going to marry him, and not Cecil. Mr Beebe felt that Cecil was disappointed and so his sense of manners urged him to add: "'I am sorry; I must apologize. I had no idea you were intimate with her, or I should never have talked in this flippant, superficial way. Mr Vyse, you ought to have stopped me.'" Cecil "drew down his mouth at the corners." Mr Beebe told him that Miss Honeychurch by then "'has learnt what it is to love: the greatest lesson, some people will tell you, that our earthly life provides.'" By this time Mrs Honeychurch and Freddy came up. Mrs Honeychurch shouted at Mr Beebe: "'Oh, Mr Beebe, have you heard the news?'" Freddy "whistled the wedding march." Mr Beebe said he had heard about the marriage between Cecil and Lucy, and "'I want them all their lives to be supremely good and supremely happy as husband and wife, as father and mother.'" Everybody in Windy Corner was joyous, save Freddy who contemplated scepticism. "Freddy was at his wittiest, referring to Cecil as the 'Fiasco'—family honoured pun on finance" (Part II, chapter VIII: *Medieval*).

"A few days after the engagement was announced Mrs Honeychurch made Lucy and her Fiasco come to a little garden-party in the neighbourhood, for naturally she wanted to show people that her daughter was marrying a presentable man." Cecil was really more than presentable with his slim figure and long face. People congratulated Mrs Honeychurch, which was a 'social blunder.' "At tea a misfortune took place: a cup of coffee was upset over Lucy's figured silk." The party over, Cecil expressed to Lucy his dissatisfaction over the social formalities in the party. However, "The spirit of generations had smiled through them, rejoicing in the engagement of Cecil and Lucy because it promised the continuance of life on earth. To Cecil and Lucy it promised something quite different—personal love."

Sitting in the victoria, Mrs Honeychurch, Lucy and Cecil were talking on divers topic, jumping from one to the other—such as Mr Beebe, the 'fenceless parson,' Mr Eager and the beauty arboreal. Cecil, on the topic of nature, expressed his bivalent attraction: "'When I'm in London I feel I could never live out of it, when I'm in the country I feel the same about the country. After all, I do believe that birds and trees and the sky are the most wonderful things in life, and that the people who live amongst them must be the best.'" Cecil noticed that Lucy, like Mrs Honeychurch, was quite inattentive to his comment on Nature. So he quoted a line of poetry: "'Come down, O maid, from yonder mountain height.'" He recited the line and 'touched her knee with his own.' Lucy flushed and nervously asked: "'What height?'" And then, being stimulated, Cecil added two more lines of poetry to this recitation:

> 'Come down, O maid, from yonder mountain height,
> What pleasure lives in height (the shepherd sang),
> In height and in the Splendour of the hills?'

The victoria by then reached Summer Street, when a certain Sir Harry Otway came near the carriage at the request of Mrs Honeychurch and engaged in a long conversation with her over the architectural patterns of the area, etc. At a point of time, "Cecil pulled Lucy back as she followed her mother." He asked Mrs Honeychurch's leave to walk with Lucy, without herself (Mrs Honeychurch), and Mrs Honeychurch cordially said: "'Certainly!'" Cecil preferred to walk through the woods, but Lucy liked the road. Cecil asked her: "'Why is it, Lucy, that you always say the road? Do you know that you have never once been with me in the fields or the wood since we were engaged?'" Lucy yielded to his fancy, perhaps understanding his meaning, and herself led him through the whispering pines. Cecil told her: "'I had got an idea—I dare say wrongly—that you feel more at home with me in a room.'" He told her: "'I connect you with a view—a certain type of view. Why shouldn't you connect me with a room?'" Cecil conducted her farther into the wood and stopped in a "little clearing among the pines...holding in its bossom a shallow pool." Lucy exclaimed: "'The Sacred Lake!'" At some moment Cecil was overcome by passion. He told Lucy: "'Up to now I have never kissed you.'" She flushed scarlet but yielded to him. She said he could do now.

At that supreme moment he was conscious of nothing but absurdities. Her reply was inadequate. She gave such a business-like lift to her veil. As he approached her he found time to wish that he could recoil. As he touched her, his gold pince-nez became dislodged and was flattened between them.

"Such was the embrace. He considered, with truth, that it had been a failure. Passion should believe itself irresistible. It should forget civility and consideration and all the other curses of a refined nature. Above all, it should never ask for leave where there is a right of way. Why could he not do as any labourer or navvy—*nay*, as any young man behind the counter would have done? He recast the scene. Lucy was standing flower-like by the water; he rushed up and took her in his arms; she rebuked him, permitted him, and revered him ever after for his manliness. For he believed that women revere men for their manliness" (Part II, chapter IX: *Lucy as a Work of Art*).

The surround of Windy Comer, once built by Lucy's deceased solicitor father, has been thoroughly urbanised by new settlers, constructing high-rise buildings. Lucy did not like the change. "A Radical out and out, she learnt to speak with horror of Suburbia. Life, so far as she troubled to conceive it, was a circle of rich, pleasant people, with identical interests and identical foes. In this circle one thought, married, and died. Outside it were poverty and vulgarity, for ever trying to enter, just as the London fog tries to enter the pine-woods, pouring through the gaps in the northern hills. But in Italy, where anyone who chooses may warm himself in equality, as in the sun, this conception of life vanished. Her senses expanded; she felt that there was no one whom she might not get to like, that social barriers were irremovable, doubtless, but not particularly high. You jump over them just as you jump into a peasant's olive-yard in the Apennines, and he is glad to see you. She returned with new eyes." She was completely reformed, and so was Cecil Vyse. His mind, too, was broadened under the impact of the liberal humanism of Italy. Lucy now realised that the soul was the essence of a man, and she "had reached the stage where personal intercourse would alone satisfy her." Now she "desired, not a wider dwelling-room, but equality beside the man she loved. For Italy was offering her the most priceless of all possessions—her own soul."

Lucy was playing bumble-puppy with Minnie Beebe, aged thirteen. It is a game in which tennis balls are struck and they bounce up high and then fall. That day, Lucy's mind was like the *tennis* balls in the game of bumble-puppy. Cecil was not near the game, but Freddy was—Freddy who believed in democracy and in equality of all men. It was reported that certain Emersons were coming as new tenants of Cissie Villa, in the neighbourhood of Windy Corner. Lucy could not imagine that the Emersons, who were coming to Cissie Villa, were the same Emersons she encountered in Italy. Mr Beebe said: "'These particular Emersons consisted of a father and son—the son a goodly, if not a good young man; not a fool, I fancy, but very immature—pessimism, et cetera. Our special joy was his father—such a sentimental darling, and people declared he had murdered his wife.'" From this it was clear to Lucy that the Emersons, who were coming, were the same Emersons she saw in Italy. Cecil also understood this. He therefore thought that the Comic Muse was coming—the Comic Muse that was the cause of Comedy and of Truth. Cecil "perceived that these new tenants might be of value educationally. He would tolerate the father and draw out the son, who was silent. In the interest of the Comic Muse and of Truth, he would bring them to Windy Corner" (Part II, chapter X: *Cecil as a Humorist*).

Mr Beebe planned pleasant moments for the Emersons, the new-comers to Cissie Villa, in Windy Corner. Lucy was at first plunged into despair, but later on she became composed, thinking that it did not matter anything to her. "Now that she was engaged, the Emersons would scarcely insult her and were welcome to come to the neighbourhood. And Cecil was welcome to bring whom he would into the neighbourhood. Therefore Cecil was welcome to bring the Emersons into the neighbourhood." That evening, Lucy called out 'Cecil—Cecil darling' and 'crept into his arms.' "Cecil, too, became demonstrative. He saw that the needful fire had been kindled in Lucy. At last she longed for attention, as a woman should, and looked up to him because he was a man." He asked her: "'So you do love me, little thing?'" And Lucy over-enthusiastically told him: "'Oh, Cecil, I do, I do! I don't know what I should do without you.'"

After this several days passed, and then Lucy received a letter from Miss Bartlett. Miss Bartlett informed Lucy (Lucia) that the Emersons were coming to her neighbourhood, and warned her of the younger Emerson: "'Dear Lucy, I am much worried, and I advise you to make a clean breast of his past behaviour to your mother, Freddy and Mr Vyse, who will forbid him to enter the house, etc.... I am very sorry about it all, and should not feel easy unless I warned you.'" Lucy wrote back: "'Many thanks for your warning. When Mr Emerson forgot himself on the mountain, you made me promise not to tell mother, because you said she would blame you for not being always with me. I have kept the promise, and cannot possibly tell her now. I have said both to her and to Cecil that I met the Emersons at Florence, and that they were respectable people—which I do think—...I like the old father, and look forward to seeing him again. As for the son, I am sorry for *him* when we meet, rather than for myself. They are known to Cecil, who is very well, and spoke of you the other day. We expect to be married in January.'"

Lucy kept her secret ten days longer. In the mean time, Mrs Vyse, Cecil's mother, arranged a dinner-parry of 'grandchildren of famous people,' and Lucy played on the piano in the party. Mrs Vyse emphatically urged Cecil to marry Lucy. She said to Cecil: "'Make Lucy one of us'" and "'Lucy is becoming wonderful—wonderful.'" Cecil said that Lucy's music was always wonderful. Mrs Vyse insinuated to her son that she noticed certain changes in Lucy, and he diagnosed the changes as due to her Italian visit: "'Italy has done it.'" She again told him: "'Cecil, mind you marry her next January. She is one of us already.'" But Cecil pointed out an incongruence: from her/he wanted Beethoven, but she played Schumann. And then he spoke out a dream of his to his mother. "'Do you know, mother, I shall have our children educated just like Lucy. Bring them up among honest country folk for freshness, send them to Italy for subtlety, and then—not till then—let them come to London. I don't believe in these London educations—'" Mrs Vyse once again urged him to marry Lucy, and then proceeded to bed.

As Mrs Vyse was just dozing off, she heard a 'cry of nightmare' from Lucy's room, and straight went to Lucy. Lucy told her that she had bad dreams. Mrs Vyse enquired: "'Bad dreams?'" Lucy replied. "'Just dreams.'" Mrs Vyse kissed her and said: "'You should have heard us talking about you, dear. He admires you more than ever. Dream of that.'" "Lucy returned the kiss, still covering one cheek with her hand. Mrs Vyse recessed to bed. Cecil, whom the cry had not awoken, snored. Darkness enveloped the flat" (Part II, chapter XI: *In Mrs Vyse's Well-appointed Flat*).

It was a Saturday afternoon when Freddy and Mr Beebe playfully decided to annoy the newcomers to Cissie Villa—the Emersons. On entering the sitting room Freddy saw such books as 'A Shropshire Lad,' 'The Way of All Flesh,' books by Gibbon, Schopenhauer, Nietzsche, and so on. Freddy showed Mr Beebe an inscription by an amateur painter: 'Mistrust all enterprises that require new clothes.' The inscription was done by old Mr Emerson. He told the clergyman that Lucy and Cecil were thicker than ever and that Cecil was teaching Lucy Italian. At that moment George ran downstairs and Freddy greeted him with: "'How d'ye do? Come and have a bathe?'" Why he so said was unclear. Perhaps he thought George's face needed washing or perhaps his invitation was 'one of the thunderbolts of youth.' George impassively accepted the invitation, and at this Mr Beebe was much delighted. Mr Emerson also came and was introduced to Freddy and Mr Beebe. Mr Emerson had no objection to George's taking a bath; he asked George to bathe. "George bowed his head, dusty and sombre, exhaling the peculiar smell of one who has handled furniture."

The three enthusiasts, Freddy, Mr Beebe and George, proceeded towards the pond in the pine-woods and bracken, Mr Emerson blowing pragmatic instructions from behind. The three climbed down the slippery bank of the pond, which was not large but its clear water reflected the sky. George sat down on a patch of dry land and 'drearily unlaced his boots,' and Freddy stripped himself. Mr Beebe did not feel like taking a bath. George murmured 'water, water,' and then "Wetting his hair first—a sure sign of apathy—he followed Freddy into the divine, as indifferent as if he were a statue and the pond a pail of soapsuds. It was necessary to use his muscles. It was necessary to keep clean. Mr Beebe watched them, and watched the seed of the willow-herb dance chorically above their heads." George and Freddy began to swim and Mr Beebe began to wonder at the glorious pines, and the blue sky overhead. The clergyman, Mr Beebe, thought: "Water, sky, evergreens, a wind—these things not even the seasons can touch, and surely they lie beyond the intrusion of man?" The 'world of motor-cars and Rural Deans' receded from his consciousness illimitably. Swimming in the pond seemed to Freddy 'swimming in a salad.' By now, Mr Beebe was also in the water. The three now "rotated in the pool breast high, after the fashion of the nymphs in Gotterdammerung.... They began to play. Mr Beebe and Freddy splashed each other. A little deferentially, they splashed George.... He smiled, flung himself at them, splashed them, ducked them, kicked them, muddied them, and drove them out of the pool." George "dirtied his shins, and had to bathe a second time" in the pool—in the 'Sacred Lake.'

"They ran to get dry, they bathed to get cool, they played as being Indians in the willow-herbs and in the bracken, they bathed to get clean. And all the time three little bundles lay discreetly on the sward, proclaiming: "'No. We are what matters. Without us shall no enterprise begin. To us shall all flesh turn in the end.'" Then Freddy made a ball of George's bundle and began to play socker with him. "Clothes flew in all directions." Mr Beebe asked them to stop and dress up. "But the two young men were delirious. Away they twinkled into the trees, Freddy with a clerical waistcoat under his arm, George with a wide-awake hat on his dripping hair." Mr Beebe shouted: "'Hi! Steady on! I see people coming, you fellows!'" and then "'Hi! Hi! *Ladies*!'" "Neither George nor Freddy was truly refined. Still, they did not hear Mr Beebe's last warning or they would have avoided Mrs Honeychurch, Cecil, and Lucy, who were walking down to call on old Mrs Butterworth. Freddy dropped the waistcoat at their feet, and dashed into some bracken. George whooped in their faces, turned, and scudded away down the path to the pond, still clad in Mr Beebe's hat."

Mrs Honeychurch was aghast, perplexed, as was Mr Beebe. Cecil commanded Mrs Honeychurch and Lucy to return towards him. "He led them now towards the bracken where Freddy sat concealed." Lucy thought that Mr Beebe jumped into the pond, because he was not noticeable, and the ladies followed him up the bank. Mrs Honeychurch now discovered Freddy and told him: "'Why not have a comfortable bath at home with hot and cold laid on?'" Mrs Honeychurch asked

Freddy and Lucy to go back with her. She ejaculated at Mr Beebe, "'Oh, poor Mr Beebe!'", for "Mr Beebe was just crawling out of the pond, on whose surface garments of an intimate nature did float; while George, the world-weary George, shouted to Freddy that he had hooked a fish." Freddy shouted back that he had swallowed a fish. George "regarded himself as dressed, barefoot, bare-chested, radiant and personable against the shadowy woods." He called out: "'Hullo, Miss Honeychurch! Hullo!'" Mrs Honeychurch could not recognise whose voice it was, but asked Lucy to bow in the bracken not to be discovered. Both of them bowed (Part II, chapter XII: *Twelfth Chapter*).

Back home, Mrs Honeychurch asked Lucy: "'is anything the matter with Cecil?'" She told her: "'Perhaps he's tired.'" Lucy chose the middle course in her reply: "'perhaps Cecil was a little tired.'" A while later on, she told her mother that she had got a letter from Charlotte while she had been to London. The mother ignored the letter and continued to remind Lucy of the change that occurred to Cecil: "'Since Cecil came back from London, nothing appears to please him. Whenever I speak he winces;—I see him, Lucy, it is useless to contradict me.'" Lucy felt debilitated due to her perception of the clash between the civilization of England and that of Italy: "Something had enfeebled her, and the case for Cecil, which she had mastered so perfectly in London, would not come forth in an effective form. The two civilizations had clashed—Cecil had hinted that they might—and she was dazzled and bewildered, as though the radiance that lies behind all civilization had blinded her eyes. Good taste and bad taste were only catchwords, garments of diverse cut; and music itself dissolved to a whisper through pine trees, where the song is not distinguishable from the comic song." However, at one point Mrs Honeychurch asked Lucy if Charlotte had mentioned "her boiler" in her letter—the boiler in her bath-room. Lucy did not pay attention to her mother's query, and minded her own business.

During dinner Freddy asked Lucy: "'What's Emerson like?'" and "'Is he the clever sort, or is he a decent chap?'"

Lucy did not reply, and asked him to ask Cecil. Cecil said about George Emerson: "'He is the clever sort, like myself.'" Freddy looked at Cecil doubtfully. By then there had been a breach in the relationship between Lucy and Charlotte, and also by then there had been a change in the mind of Lucy, like hydrangeas change their colour at seaside (Part II, chapter XIII: *How Miss Bartlett's Boiler was so Tiresome*).

Lucy, in Windy Corner, expected George Emerson to come to tennis in Summer Street on the Sunday week. "When Cecil brought the Emersons to Summer Street, it had upset her nerves.... She was nervous at night. When she talked to George—they met almost immediately at the Rectory—his voice moved her deeply, and she wished to remain near him." "It is obvious enough for the reader to conclude, 'She loves young Emerson.' A reader in Lucy's place would not find it obvious. Life is easy to chronicle, but bewildering to practise, and we welcome 'nerves' or any other shibboleth that will cloak our personal desire. She loved Cecil; George made her nervous; will the reader explain to her that the phrases should have been reversed?" (Part II, chapter XIV: *How Lucy Faced the External Situation Bravely*).

That Sunday was glorious in all respects. Miss Bartlett had arrived in Windy Corner for the glorious moment. Lucy dressed in cerise, wore a garnet brooch around her throat, and wore a ring set with rubies in her finger—her engagement ring, understandably given by George Emerson. Lucy came upon a deserted novel, 'Under a Loggia,' that was being read by Cecil. She was forgetting things Italian painstakingly taught by Cecil, who noticed it and wondered: "'What you aren't forgetting your Italy already?'" The carriage started for the church after Lucy took her seat. Cecil cried out from behind: "'Good-bye! Be good!'" "Lucy bit her lip, for the tone was sneering." When the carriage reached the church, Lucy saw the Emersons there. Old Mr Emerson expressed his gladness over Lucy's getting married—with Cecil, as he perhaps supposed.

Lucy no more censured Cecil, but anything that George did delighted her. "Perhaps anything that he did would have pleased Lucy, but his awkwardness went straight to her heart:

men were not gods after all, but as human and as clumsy as girls; even men might suffer from unexplained desires, and need help." And Lucy surmised George's weakness towards herself when he threw her photographs into the River Arno. George was that day full of high spirits as Lucy could hardly contain her joy that flowed through her heart that day. She was all the more glad that day because George did not tell old Mr Emerson of the Florence episode, i.e. of her affair with George in Florence, and so Cecil also would not know about it either. "She longed to shout the words: 'It's all right It's a secret between us two for ever. Cecil will never hear.'" What was the real reason of Lucy's averting Cecil, after doing so much with him? It was Cecil's attitude towards her, he took her as a protege. For the only relationship which Cecil conceived was feudal: that of protector and protected. He had no glimpse of the comradeship after which the girl's soul yearned." Before lunch Lucy told Cecil that George Emerson was coming in the evening and that George was an interesting person. After lunch Lucy played on the piano. Meantime, George crept in. Freddy was pressing for playing tennis, but he could not succeed to prolong the play. As told earlier, Cecil had been reading the novel 'Under a Loggia.' The novel was set in Florence and as Cecil was reading part of it aloud, Lucy recognised that it was written by Miss Lavish but was published under somebody else's name.

That day Lucy was not very concerned about Cecil; the ups and downs of his voice were noticeable to her, but they did not affect her. Cecil was reading the novel 'Under a Loggia;' Lucy snatched away the novel. He retrieved the book from her and began to read aloud from it: "'There came from his lips no wordy protestation such as formal lovers use. No eloquence was his, nor did he suffer from the lack of it. He simply enfolded her in his manly arms.'" George and Lucy listened to the reading and remained silent. Then Lucy said: "'Should we go into tea?'" "She led the way up the garden, Cecil following her, George last. She thought a disaster was averted. But when they entered the shrubbery it came. The book [the novel 'Under a Loggia'], as Cecil must go back for it, and George, who loved passionately, must blunder against her in the narrow path." As Cecil went back to search for the book, George enfolded her in his arms and, overruling her protestations, kissed her twice, and then releasing her slipped back. Meantime Cecil returned and he and Lucy 'reached the upper lawn alone' (Part II, chapter XV: *The Disaster Within*).

Lucy began to frequently complain of her nerves, and she began to suppress her emotions. "Remembering that she was engaged to Cecil, she compelled herself to confused remembrances of George: he was nothing to her: he never had been anything: he had behaved abominably, she had never encouraged him." Lucy armed herself with such falsifications. Lucy had sent for her cousin Miss Charlotte Bartlett, and her cousin arrived. Lucy asked her if she had read Miss Lavish's novel ['Under a Loggia'] where there was a scene of love-making between the hero and the heroine. She said: "'Cecil happened to read out the passage aloud to me and to Mr Emerson; it upset Mr Emerson, and he insulted me again. Behind Cecil's back, Ugh! Is it possible that men are such brutes?'"

"George Emerson was coming up the garden with a tennis ball in his hand." He told Lucy that he admired her, and Lucy felt a rush in her blood. George told her: "'You cannot live with Vyse. He's only for an acquaintance. He is for society and cultivated talk. He should know no one intimately, least of all a woman.'" George continued: "'He is the sort who are all right so long as they keep to things—books, pictures—but kill when they come to people.... That is the man all over—playing tricks on people, on the most sacred form of life that he can find. Next, I meet you together, and find him protecting and teaching you and your mother to be shocked, when it was for *you* to settle whether you were shocked or no. Cecil all over again. He cannot let a woman decide. He's the type who's kept Europe back for a thousand years. Every moment of his life he's forming you, telling you what's charming or amusing or ladylike, telling you what a man thinks womanly; and you, you of all women, listen to his voice instead of your own.'"

George concluded by telling Lucy that he loved her and that he settled to fight Cecil.

Lucy told George that he was not much different from Cecil, presumably in as much as he too was a male and so was a brute. George retorted: "'I'm the same kind of brute at bottom. This desire to govern a woman—it lies very deep, and men and women must fight it together before they shall enter the garden. But I do love you—surely in a better way than he does.'" George invited Lucy to get enfolded in his arms: "'Lucy, be quick—there's no time for us to talk now—come to me as you came in the spring, and afterwards I will be gentle and explain. I have cared for you since that man died. I cannot live without you.'" "'And Mr Vyse?' said Lucy, who kept commendably calm. 'Does he not matter? That I love Cecil and shall be his wife shortly? A detail of no importance, I suppose?'" George did not listen to her, but stretched out his hands towards her in the gesticulation of invitation. Lucy thought George was mad. But soon emotion was born in her as she was aware of the autumn. "Cecil's voice came: 'My dear Freddy, I am no athlete. As you well remarked this very morning. "There are some chaps who are not good for anything but books;" I plead guilty to being such a chap, and will not inflict myself on you.'" "The scales fell from Lucy's eyes. How had she stood Cecil for a moment? He was absolutely intolerable, and the same evening she broke her engagement off" (Part II, chapter XVI: *Lying to George*).

Lucy frankly and plainly told Cecil it was not possible for her to marry him. She said: "'I have carefully thought things over. We are too different. I must ask you to release me, and try to forget that there ever was such a foolish girl.'" She produced a reason behind her decision not to marry the fairly educated Cecil: "'I haven't had a really good education, for one thing.'" She elaborated: "'My Italian trip came too late, and I am forgetting all that I learnt there. I shall never be able to talk to your friends, or behave as a wife of yours should.'" And lastly she concluded: "'I cant marry you, and you will thank me for saying so some day.'" Cecil thought Lucy had a headache, she was disturbed. But Lucy continued her arguments as if thinking enough was not pleaded: "'Often before I have wondered if I was fitted for your wife—for instance, in London; and are you fitted to be my husband? I don't think so.'" "But to Cecil, now that he was about to lose her, she seemed each moment more desirable. He looked at her, instead of through her, for the first time since they were engaged. From a Leonardo she had become a living woman, with mysteries and forces of her own, with qualities that even eluded art. His brain recovered from the shock, and, in a burst of genuine devotion, he cried: 'But I love you, and I did think you loved me!'" Lucy responded frustratingly: "'I did not,' she said: 'I thought I did at first. I am sorry, and ought to have refused you this last time, too.'"

Cecil paced up and down a while and then told Lucy: "'You don't love me, evidently. I dare say you are right not to. But it would hurt a little less if I knew why.'" Lucy told him because "'you're the sort who can't know anyone intimately.'" Cecil's look became horrid. Lucy continued.' "'When we were only acquaintances you let me be myself, but now you're always protecting me.'" Lucy's voice swelled; she further said: "'I won't be protected. I will choose for myself what is ladylike and right. To shield me is an insult. Can't I be trusted to face the truth but I must get it second-hand through you? A woman's place! You despise my mother—I know you do—because she's conventional.... Cecil, you're that, for you understand beautiful things, but you don't know how to use them; and you wrap yourself up in art and books and music, and would try to wrap up me. I wont be stifled, not by the most glorious music, for people are more glorious, and you hide them from me. That's why I break off my engagement.'" Cecil did not contradict her, but said: "'It is true'" and "'True, every word. It is a revelation. It is I.'"

Cecil told her: "'You are far too good to me. I shall never forget your insight; and, dear, I only blame you for this: you might have warned me in the early stages, before you felt you wouldn't marry me, and so have given me a chance to improve. I have never known you till this evening. I have just used you as a peg for my silly notions of what a woman should be. But this evening you are a different person: new thoughts—even a new voice—'" Lucy asked what he meant by 'a new voice,' and Cecil said: "'I mean that a new person seems speaking through you.'" At this Lucy lost her balance and cried: "'If you think I am in love with someone else, you are very much mistaken.'" She got infuriated at his supposed notion that whenever a girl would break her engagement it would be assumed that she was in love with somebody else. So Cecil apologized to her, and told her: "'It is a question between ideals, yours and mine—pure abstract ideals, and yours are the nobler. I was bound up in the old vicious notions, and all the time you were splendid and new.'" Cecil's voice broke at this point. But he continued: "'I must actually thank you for what you have done—for showing me what I really am. Solemnly, I thank you for showing me a true woman. Will you shake hands?'" They shook hands and parted (Part II, chapter XVII: *Lying* to *Cecil*).

Mr Beebe told Cecil that he had got a letter from Lucy's friends, Miss Catherine Alan and Miss Teresa Alan, that they were going to Athens and Constantinople. He said that 'Italy is heroic, but Greece is godlike or devilish,' he was not sure which. Freddy came up running and informed Mr Beebe that Lucy was not going to marry Cecil and that Cecil was thereby hard hit. Mr Beebe said: "'It was the one foolish thing she ever did. Oh, what a glorious riddance!'" The house of Windy Corner was "cut off for ever from Cecil's pretentious world." In the drawing-room Lucy was tickling at a Mozart Sonata. Mrs Honeychurch seemed broken down. From Mozart Lucy passed on to Schumann. Mr Beebe told her that he had heard everything about her breaking the engagement, and said: "'I am certain that you have done the right thing.'" Mr Beebe read to Lucy a portion of Miss Alan's letter to him, from which Lucy understood that the Miss Alans were going abroad next week, and she exclaimed: "'Oh, do tell me more about the Miss Alans! How perfectly splendid of them to go abroad!'" Mr Beebe said to Lucy: "'Has Italy filled you with the fever of travel? Perhaps George is right. He says that 'Italy is only an euphuism for Fate.'" Lucy told him she was not so much desirous of going to Italy as of going to Constantinople. She was as if mad for that place, since she broke off her engagement, because she did not find peace at home. She told Mr Beebe: "'I must get away, ever so far. I must know my own mind and where I want to go.'"

Mr Beebe came to Windy Corner to invite Lucy to tea at Beehive Tavern. Lucy, Miss Bartlett and Minnie were also invited. And all went to the Tavern at about five o'clock. Arranging for an opportunity of talking to Miss Bartlett out of Lucy's earshot, Mr Beebe told Miss Bartlett that there was no point in Lucy's joining the Miss Alans in their journey to Athens. But Miss Bartlett told him: "'There I cannot agree with you. In it I spy Lucy's salvation.'" Mr Beebe could not follow the point of Miss Bartlett and so she clarified that Lucy "'wanted to leave Windy Corner.'" Mr Beebe's "belief in celibacy, so reticent, so carefully concealed beneath his tolerance and culture, now came to the surface and expanded like some delicate flower. 'They that marry do well, but they that refrain do better.' So ran his belief, and he never heard that an engagement was broken off but with a slight feeling of pleasure. In the case of Lucy, the feeling was intensified through dislike of Cecil." They came home from the Beehive Tavern, when Mr Beebe asked Mrs Honeychurch if she was offended at Lucy's breaking her engagement. Mrs Honeychurch told him: "'Mr Beebe, I'm thankful—simply thankful.'" Freddy also expressed his satisfaction over Lucy's action.

Mrs Honeychurch could not understand why the Greek scheme was so necessary for Lucy. Moreover, it was an expensive scheme and a dramatic scheme too, and so Mrs Honeychurch loathed the scheme all the more. Mr Beebe was convinced of the futility and the lack of wisdom of the scheme, and he decided to tell Lucy this. As he opened the door he heard Lucy's playing on the piano and singing the lines:

> 'Look not thou on beauty's charming.
> Sit thou still when kings are arming,
> Taste not when the wine-cup glistens—'

Mr Beebe was amazed; he interjected: "'It's a song that Cecil gave her. How odd girls are!'" Along with Mr Beebe, Mrs Honeychurch also entered into Lucy's drawing-room. Mrs Honeychurch now kissed Lucy and told her: "'And you are right, too—Greece will be all right; you can go if Miss Alans will have you.'" Lucy was delighted and thanked her. Freddy was also there listening to Lucy's singing.

"Oddly enough, the group was beautiful. Mr Beebe, who loved the art of the past, was reminded of a favourite theme, the *Santa Conversazione,* in which people who care for one another are painted chatting together about noble things—a theme neither sensual nor sensational, and therefore ignored by the art of today. Why should Lucy want either to marry or to travel when she had such friends at home?" Lucy finished her song:

> 'Vacant heart and hand and eye
> Easy live and quiet die.'

(Part II, chapter XVIII: *Lying to Mr Beebe, Mrs Honeychurch, Freddy, and the Servants*)

The Miss Alans put up in their beloved temperance hotel near Bloomsbury for preparing for the journey to Greece. Lucy, on her part, borrowed a mythological dictionary from Mr Beebe for better understanding Greek Sculpture. She also bought a guide-book. Mrs Honeychurch did not like that Lucy kept her separation from Cecil and her marriage with George secretive: "'You know, Lucy, you and Charlotte and Mr Beebe all tell me I'm stupid, so I suppose I am, but I shall never understand this hole-and-corner work. You've got rid of Cecil—well and good, and I'm thankfull he's gone, though I did feel angry for the minute. But why not announce it? Why this hushing up and tiptoeing?'" Lucy wanted to keep her soul secret. "Lucy had hoped to return to Windy Corner when she escaped from Cecil, but she discovered that her home existed no longer.... She only felt, 'I do not love George; I broke off my engagement because I did not love George; I must go to Greece because I do not love George; it is more important that I should help my mother, everyone else is behaving very badly.'" She wanted freedom, independence. She did not forget her passion in Florence, but independence was her cue.

Lucy and her mother "shopped in silence, spoke little in the train, little again in the carriage, which met them at Dorking Station." The carriage took them to the Rectory and Lucy got out to call for Miss Bartlett who at once came and took Lucy to Mr Beebe's study. There old Mr Emerson was sitting by the fire. He told Lucy: "'Miss Honeychurch, dear, we are so sorry! George is so sorry! He thought he had a right to try. I cannot blame my boy, and yet I wish he had told me first. He ought not to have tried. I know nothing about it at all.'" Mr Emerson continued: "'I taught him 'he quavered,' 'to trust in love. I said: "When love comes, that is reality." I said: "Passion does not blind. No. Passion is sanity, and the woman you love, she is the only person you will ever really understand.'" Mr Emerson appealed to Lucy: "'Miss Honeychurch: you are going to marry the man you love. Do not go out of George's life saying he is abominable.'" Lucy simply said: "'No, of course.'" And then she told him that she had to go to the church where her mother and cousin had already gone. At this point Mr Emerson told Lucy that due to some extremely difficult situations his son, George Emerson, was never baptized. Lucy asked if George was ill. Mr Emerson said: "'George comes down tomorrow, and takes me up to his London rooms. He cant bear to be here, and I must be where he is.'"

Lucy importuned him not to leave his house and go to London. She said she was just going to Greece, meaning she would be returning soon. Mr Emerson told Lucy: "'Greece; but you were to be married this year, I thought'" Lucy told him that she was not going to be married before January. He said: "'I hope that you will enjoy Greece with Mr Vyse.'" Lucy curtly said: "'Thank you.'" Lucy now told Mr Emerson that "Cecil was not her companion to Greece." Mr Emerson asked: "'Why, Miss Honeychurch, why?'" "'Terror came over her, and she lied again. She made the long, convincing speech that she had made to Mr Beebe, and intended to make to the world when she announced that her engagement was no more. He heard her in silence, and then said: 'My dear, I am worried about you. It seems to me'—dreamily; she was not alarmed—that you are in a muddle.'" Lucy admitted she was in a muddle. Mr Emerson sympathetically warned her of muddles in life. He told her: "'Life," wrote a friend of mine, "is a public performance on the violin, in which you must learn the instrument as you go along." I think he puts it well. Man has to pick up the use of his functions as he goes along—especially the function of Love.'" "Then he burst out excitedly: 'That's it, that's what I mean. You love George!' And after his long preamble, the three words burst against Lucy like waves from the open sea." Mr Emerson did not wait for contradiction from the end of Lucy but emphasised his earlier pronouncement: "'You love the body and soul, plainly, directly, as he loves you, and no other word expresses it. You wont marry the other man for his sake.'"

"How dare you! gasped Lucy, with the roaring of waters in her ears. 'Oh, how like a man!—I mean, to suppose that a woman is always thinking about a man.'" Mr Emerson did not lose his ground but with enough confidence retorted that Lucy had surely been thinking of a man, and this forced her to summon 'physical disgust.' Mr Emerson was relentless; he now made his longest emotive speech: "'You're shocked, but I mean to shock you. It's the only hope at times. I can reach you no other way. You must marry, or your life will be wasted. You have gone too far to retreat. I have no time for the tenderness, and the comradeship, and the poetry, and the things that really matter, and *for which* you marry. I know that, with George, you will find them, and that you love him. Then be his wife. He is already part of you. Though you fly to Greece, and never see him again, or forget his very name, George will work in your thoughts till you die. It isn't possible to love and to part. You will wish that it was. You can transmute love, ignore it, muddle it, but you can never pull it out of you. I know by experience that the poets are right: love is eternal.'"

"Lucy began to cry with anger, and though her anger passed away soon, her tears remained." Mr Emerson's voice changed and his pleading became softer: "'I only wish poets would say this too: that love is of the body, not the body, but of the body. Ah! the misery that would be saved if we confessed that! Ah for a little directness to liberate the soul! Your soul, dear Lucy! I hate the word now, because of all the cant with which superstition has wrapped it round. But we have souls. I cannot say how they came nor whither they go, but we have them, and I see you ruining yours. I cannot bear it. It is again the darkness creeping in; it is hell.'" After so much Mr Emerson ceased, but then immediately began once again to persuade Lucy to marry George: "'Dear girl, forgive my prosiness; marry my boy. When I think what life is, and how seldom love is answered by love—Marry him; it is one of the moments for which the world was made.'" Lucy could not understand the meaning of what Mr Emerson told her; and yet she could somehow see the bottom of her soul. "'You've frightened me,' she moaned. 'Cecil—Mr Beebe—the ticket's bought—everything.' She fell, 'sobbing into the chair. I'm caught in the tangle. I must suffer and grow old away from him. I cannot break the whole of life for his sake. They trusted me.'"

A carriage came up. Lucy told Mr Emerson: "'Give George my love—once only. Tell him "muddle."'" Lucy then arranged her veil as tears silently rolled down her cheeks. She bluntly told Mr Emerson that she would not marry George. She was quavering as she said so. Voices from the carriage called out, 'Lucy!' "She turned to Mr Emerson in despair. But his face revived her. It was the face of a saint who understood." Mr Emerson told Lucy: "'Now it is all dark. Now Beauty and Passion seem never to have existed. I know. But remember the mountains over Florence and the view. Ah, dear, if I were George, and gave you one kiss, it would make you brave. You have to go cold into a battle that needs warmth, out into the muddle that you have made yourself; and your mother and your friends will despise you, oh my darling, and rightly, if it is ever right to despise. George still dark, all the tussle and the misery without a word from him. Am I justified?'" Tears gathered in Mr Emerson's eyes. He said: "'Yes, for we fight for more than Love or Pleasure: there is Truth. Truth does count.'" "'You kiss me,' said the girl. 'You kiss me. I will try.'" "He gave her a sense of deities reconciled, a feeling that, in gaining the man she loved, she would gain something for the whole world. Throughout the squalor of her homeward drive—she spoke at once—his salutation remained. He had robbed the body of its taint, the world's taunts of their sting; he had shown her the holiness of direct desire. She 'never exactly understood,' she would say in after years, 'how he managed to strengthen her. It was as if he had made her see the whole of everything at once'" (Part IX, chapter XIX: *Lying to Mr Emerson*).

The Miss Alans did not go to Greece but to Constantinople; on the other hand, George and Lucy put up in the same Pensione Bertolini, where they had stayed one year ago, to celebrate their honeymoon. George said it was his old room; Lucy protested, saying it was George's father's room which she got from his father swapping her own room. George "knelt on the tiled floor, and laid his face in her lap." Lucy said: "'George, you baby, get up.'" George said: "'Why shouldn't I be a baby?'" "Unable to answer the question, Lucy put down George's sock and gazed out through the window. George advanced towards her and naggingly asked her to kiss him, which she did. He strolled to the window and saw the beautiful view below. At one point "He carried her to the window, so that she, too, saw all the view. They sank upon their knees invisible from the road, they hoped, and began to whisper one another's names. Ah! it was worth while; it was the great joy that they had expected, and countless little joys of which they had never dreamt." After a while, they got into a cab and the cabman, Phaethon, drove away singing. Extremely delighted they were when the cab was running along the River Arno. "Youth enwrapped them: the song of Phaethon announced passion requited, love attained. But they were conscious of a love more mysterious than this. The song died away; they heard the river, bearing down the snows of winter into the Mediterranean" (Part II, chapter XX: *The End of the Middle Ages*).

3

DISCUSSION

(i)

A Room with a View is a brilliant social comedy, built on the changing social values during the Edwardian period and shown through Lucy's changed attitude towards George Emerson. The cultured Lucy, with a veneer of Victorian hypocritically suppressive emotional ideology, was highly charged with emotion—with love—when she came into physical contact with the sub-cultured George, and as a result of this her emotion triumphed over her culture and reason. This is of profound importance and this, among some of its other engaging and edifying properties, *A Room with a View* provides us with. The title of this novel Forster had earlier—before completing the writing of it—decided to be 'Windy Corner' where Lucy lived, but for some reason or other this pre-meditated title was changed. In the novel, both the terms in its title have been carefully chosen and emphasised. The word 'view,' in the sense of sight or percept or vision, has been used at least a dozen times in the novel (see 1976 Penguin publication of the novel: pp. 9, 65, 113, 114, 144,145, 151, 163, 268, 270, 206, 217 and 221). Lucy Honeychurch and Miss Bartlett could not find a room in the Pensione Bertolini, which had a view, and ultimately they got such a one from George Emerson by swapping Lucy's room with George's. George's room had a view of the river Arno, which symbolised life ("On the banks of the grey torrent of life, love is the only flower:" *The Longest Journey:* section XXXI) and Lucy was satisfied with this view. The swapping, in course of time, developed into mutual affection that ended in their marriage that was culturally morganatic on the part of Lucy but was hastened by her intense emotion that she always kept in the limbo and that she for the first time in her life irresistibly realised. So the word 'view' in the title bears a great importance and significance. The word 'room' is also important, at least in the sense that each and every one of us does want a 'room' or a house to live in—a 'room' of his own. Throughout his life

Forster was being haunted by his want of a permanent home, and this has reflections in most of his handful of novels, including *A Room with a View* where Lucy and George wanted to have a home of their own. Forster's next novel, *Howards End,* also shows concern for permanent home or room to lead a happy life. 'Room,' therefore, symbolically, presents itself as a part of life, like 'view.' Peter J. Hutchings writes about the expression 'a room with a view' used as the title of the novel: "For Forster, [then,] having a room with a view assumes the same significance as having a room of one's own does for Virginia Woolf. It is the place [the room] from which the writer can resolve the tensions—of modernity and desire—that would otherwise lead to disconnection, disintegration" (Tambling, 216). If we accept Hutchings' explanation of the title of the novel, then we are also to mean by the word 'room' some sort of authority, and by the word 'view' a particular opinion or philosophy.

The substance of the story of *A Room with a View* was, according to Nicola Beauman, 'encapsulated' in Forster's 1904 short story 'The Eternal Moment.' Beauman writes: "Ia a way *A Room with a View* was the culmination of something Morgan [Forster] had first encapsulated in his 1904 story 'The Eternal Moment': Miss Raby believed that the long-ago 'incident upon the mountain had been one of the great moments of her life—perhaps the greatest, enduring'" (Beauman, 207). In *A Room with a View,* the moment when George peremptorily and utterly instinctively kissed Lucy was the greatest moment in her life—the moment when she went beyond all her cultural pretensions. The love, born out of that kiss, was eternal, like Miss Raby's love for the young porter, Feo Ginori.

Forster gestated the novel fragmentarily and from moment to moment for long, but when he sat down to write it he worked the most speedily, and yet the novel has been an excellent work, as regards its structure, characterisation, language, satire, humour, etc. The novel was dedicated to H.O.M. (Hugh Meredith) the delicately beautiful womanish young man with whom Forster had long homosexual relationship, but the novel has nothing to do with homosexuality—it rather deals with a very romantic heterosexual love and marriage. But though Forster overtly dedicated the book to H.O.M, in fact he dedicated it covertly to Edward Carpenter, the homosexual poet and his spiritual mentor. This deception Forster resorted to in order to avoid the displeasure of his mother who could not stand any mentioning of Carpenter. In the novel Mr Emerson is the mouthpiece of Carpenter—Mr Emerson who says, like Carpenter, that 'love is of the body; not the body, but of the body' (Beauman, 209). The novel's hinge-point is 'the underdeveloped heart' of the English upper middle class. Lucy belonged to the upper middle class and was brought up in the 'Sawstonian' cultural atmosphere, as a result of which her heart was atrophied; but when George, who belonged to a relatively lower class and subculture, impulsively kissed, the petals of her heart began to open. The 'underdeveloped heart' of the upper middle class was a great concern for Forster, and in this sense the novel *A Room with a View* is a testament of Forster's view about human heart or about humanity.

(ii)

The theme of the novel is that the shield of pretensions or hypocrisy sustained around one's own self breaks down under the heavy pressure of the instincts or of pure love. After George kissed her, Lucy certainly felt the demands of her instincts, but she chose to resort to hypocrisy, chose to deny the demands of her instincts. But she failed to push her instincts to the limbo and they returned and they engulfed her ultimately setting aside all her cultural and other pretensions. Nicola Beauman writes about the theme of this novel: "The theme of *A Room with a View* is self-deception, using the interwoven leitmotifs of rooms versus views, gloom versus light and lies versus truth. After George has kissed Lucy for the second time she thinks, 'The contest lay not between love and duty. Perhaps there never is such a contest. It lay between the real and the pretended... 'The passage continues, 'Lucy's first aim was to defeat herself.... The armour of falsehood is subtly wrought out of darkness, and hides a man not only from others, but from his own soul. In a few moments Lucy was equipped for battle.' At the end, when Lucy has defeated pretence, she has rejected duty: and this is the other theme of the novel" (Beauman, 204-205).

The plot of the novel is simple like that of Forster's other Italian novel *Where Angels Fear to Tread. A Room with a View* is also a novel of tourism like the other Italian novel. In it Lucy Honeychurch went on a tour to Italy with Miss Charlotte Bartlett as her chaperon and put up in Pensione Bartolini. Earlier, Lucy booked a room with a view, but she was frustrated not to get such a room. However, she got a room with a view from George Emerson through the kind interference of George's father, Mr Emerson. Once, at an opportune moment and at a vantage point George peremptorily and quite instinctively kissed Lucy, which completely changed Lucy's opinion about George. She earlier thought him to be not at all worthy of her attention, but the physical contact between the warm lover and the cold beloved warmed the latter, and love was born in the subconscious mind of Lucy for George. But back home in England, Lucy promptly and silently got engaged to Cecil Vyse, a non-athletic cultured and cold fellow who proposed to Lucy thrice in the past and thrice had been rejected by her. Soon Lucy discovered that Cecil did not love her as much as he loved to possess her. This gave rise to the spirit of independence that so long remained dormant in the soul of Lucy. She, therefore, recoiled from the engagement, married George and, at the fag end of the novel, we find the couple honeymooning in the same Pensione Bartolini. The plot is really simple, but it allowed Forster to introduce two divergent cultures—one, of the English upper middle class, and the other of the liberal humanitarian Italy; or one where cultural hypocricy overruled and the other where the instincts were the highest court of appeal—to show that cultural hypocrisy collapses under the impact of the demands of the natural instincts and under the impact of the promptings of the pure heart. In fact, Forster's objective in the novel was to show that one with an 'underdeveloped heart' was an incomplete man, unnatural man—a man incongruous with the world.

Forster's dexterity as a novelist lies in the fact that in the short plot of *A Room with a View* he has been more than successful in putting forth his points.

(iii)

There are three major characters in *A Room with a View*. Lucy honeychurch, George Emerson and Cecil Vyse. And there are more than half a dozen minor characters, including Mr Eager, Mr Beebe, Mr Emerson, Miss Allan, Miss Teresa, Miss Pole, Freddy, and the Signora of the Pensione Bartolini. Lucy Honeycharch is the heroine of the novel Her name was taken from Forster's great-great-grand mother, Lucy Thornton, in order to pay respect to this lady of great qualities. The word 'Lucy' derived from the Latin word *lux* which means 'light' or a clearing in the woods. In the third chapter of the novel, the narrator describes Lucy thus: Lucy was "a young lady with a quantity of dark hair and very pretty, pale, undeveloped face. She loved going to concerts, she loved stopping with her cousin, she loved iced coffee and meringues." She lived in the house called 'Windy Corner' that was built by her solicitor father in Sussex Weald.

Lucy went to Italy with Baedeker's *Handbook to Northern Italy* along with Miss Charlotte Bartlett as her chaperon, to see the 'real' Italy with her own eyes, as Adella Quested, in *A Passage to India,* went to India to see the 'real' India. She had an 'uneventful childhood.' Her Italian tour, which is the story of the novel, made a sea-change in her career and personality. In chapter 8 of the novel, Mr Beebe tells Cecil Vyse that Lucy learned what love was only in Italy and through Cecil: "'she has learnt what it is to love: the greatest lesson, some people will tell you, that our earthly life provides.'" Lucy was a little daring, undaunted. In Italy she wanted to enjoy a hazardous tram-ride. She said: "'I want to go round the town in the circular tram—on the platform by the driver'" (*A Room with a View,* chapter 3). In chapter 4 of the novel, the narrator tells us that "Lucy never knew her desires so clearly as after music...she wanted something big, and she believed that it would have come to her on the wind-swept platform of an electric tram." In the same chapter, the narrator calls her a 'medieval lady' and tells us that she had 'much that is immortal': "There is much that is immortal in this medieval lady. The dragons have gone, and so have the knights, but still she lingers in our midst.... In her heart also there are springing up strange desires. She too is enamoured of heavy winds, and vast panoramas, and green expanses of the sea. She has marked the kingdom of this world, how full it is of wealth, and beauty, and war—a radiant crust, built around the central fires, spinning towards the receding heavens. Men, declaring that she in spires them to it, move joyfully over the surface, having the most delightful meetings with other men, happy, not because they are masculine, but because they are alive. Before the show breaks up she would like to drop the august title of the Eternal Woman, and go there as her transitory self."

In Italy, the narrator tells us in chapter 8 of the novel, Lucy changed phenomenally, which Cecil marked: "...Italy worked some marvel in her. It gave her light, and—...—it gave her shadow. Soon he detected in her a wonderful reticence. She was like a woman of Leonardo da Vinci's, whom we love not so much for herself as for the things that she will not tell us. The things are assuredly not of this life; no woman of Leonardo's could have anything so vulgar as a 'story.' She did develop most wonderfully day by day." The reason of her development was of course her newly grown awareness of her instinct of love, prompted by the sweet kisses from George. Lucy's psychological metamorphosis in Italy was deftly drawn by Mr Beebe in his diary. Miss Bartlett went to Italy virtually as Lucy's chaperon, but the vigorous change in the mental structure of Lucy prevented Miss Bartlett to discharge her duty. Mr Beebe tells Cecil in chapter 8 of the novel: "'I can show you a beautiful picture in my Italian diary: Miss Honeychurch as a kite, Miss Bartlett holding the string. Picture number two: the string breaks.'"

It may be pointed out here that one may discern a parallelism between Forster and his created character Lucy, and in this sense *A Room with a View* betray autobiographical elements. Forster and Lucy were sexually contrary, but the contrariety did not stand in the way of their being in the similar conditions and having almost identical experiences. Lucy went to Italy symbolically to escape from the tradition and the moral environment of the English upper middle class, which escape was Forster's golden dream. Nicola Beauman writes in this regard that by marrying George, Lucy escaped the Tunbridge Wells mores and that Forster wished the same thing to happen to him, somehow or other. Beauman writes about Lucy and Forster: "She had arrived in Italy as trapped as the rest; but by the end, because her eyes had been opened and because she had married George, she had got away. Lucy's escape from Tunbridge Wells is wish-fulfilment for Morgan [Forster]: and although it has been claimed that as a character she is himself *en travesti* I think this emphasis is wrong. It is not so important that Lucy is Morgan sexually, although she could be him in the guise of a girl; what matters is that her *situation* is his. He had become coerced, imprisoned in a way of life which is usually the lot of women; ...the fact of Lucy's femaleness did not mean that her experiences were so very different from her creator" (Beauman, 102-03).

Though we hear of the Vyes as early as in chapter 5 of the novel, we actually meet Cecil Vyse for the first time only in chapter 8 of it, where the narrator describes him at some length: "Appearing thus late in the story, Cecil must be at once described. He was medieval. Like a Gothic statue, tall and refined, with shoulders that seemed braced square by an effort of the will, and a head that was tilted a little higher than the usual level of vision, he resembled those fastidious saints who guard the portals of a French cathedral. Well educated, well endowed, and not deficient physically, he remained in the grip of a certain devil whom the modern world knows as self-consciousness, and whom the medieval, with dimmer vision, worshipped as asceticism." In the very next chapter, the narrator further describes him: "Cecil was more than presentable; he looked distinguished, and it was very pleasant to see his slim figure keeping step with Lucy, and his long fair face responding when Lucy spoke to him." Cecil was, nevertheless, no athletic figure; he had no profession, and yet he greedily earned money anyhow. He himself told Mr Beebe, in chapter 8 of the novel: "'I know I ought to be getting money out of people'." Such was his instinct of possessiveness that he later applied in the case of Lucy and thus proved a fiasco lover. From chapter 8, we also learn that Cecil "had known Lucy for several years, but only as a commonplace girl who happened to be musical." Italy changed Lucy's view of life, and this changed the view of Lucy, and this changed view of Lucy dazzled the vision of Cecil and ineluctably attracted him to her, so that he proposed to her as many times as thrice, at the last of which—that happened in England—Lucy entered into an engagement with him. But she broke her engagement when she understood that Cecil loved more to posses her than simply to love her, though the free climate of Italy palpably changed him as it changed her.

In chapter 16 of *A Room with a View,* the old Mr Emerson opened a window of Cecil's character before us when he told Lucy about Cecil: "'you cannot live with Vyse. He's only for an acquaintance. He is for society and cultured talk. He should know no one intimately, least of all a woman.'" In the same chapter, Mr Emerson further tells her about Cecil: "'He is the sort who are all right so long as they keep to things—books, pictures—but kill when they come to people...I saw him first in the National Gallery, when he winced because my father mispronounced the names of great painters. Then he brings us here, and we find it is to play some silly trick on a kind neighbour. That is the man all over—playing tricks on people, on the most sacred form of life that he can find. Next, I meet you two together, and find him protecting and teaching you and your mother to be shocked, when it was for you to settle whether you were shocked or no. Cecil all over again. He daren't let a woman decide. He's the type who's kept Europe back for a thousand years. Every moment of his life he's forming you telling you what's charming or amusing or ladylike, telling you what a man thinks womanly; and you, you of all women, listen to his voice instead of to your own.'" And before breaking her engagement with Cecil, we hear in chapter 17 of the novel, Lucy threw the following on to his face: "'conventional, Cecil, you're that, for you may understand beautiful things, but you don't know how to use them; and you wrap yourself up in art and books and music, and would try to wrap up me. I won't be stifled, not by the most glorious music, for people are more glorious, and you hide them from me. That's why I break off my engagement.'"

Lucy's younger brother, Freddy, from the very beginning of her move into an engagement with Cecil understood that the engagement was going to become a flop, and that was why he employed for Cecil the appellation 'Fiasco' instead of 'fiance.' Freddy was prophetic, and so was the incident of Cecil's pince-nez being flattened when he closely hugged Lucy to kiss her. In chapter 9 of the novel, we understand that the relation between Lucy and Cecil adequately warmed, when, once, he told her: "'Up to now I have never kissed you.'" "At that supreme moment he was conscious of nothing but absurdities. Her reply was inadequate. She gave such a business-like lift to her veil. As he approached her he found time to wish that he could recoil. As he touched her, his gold pince-nez became dislodged and was flattened between them."

Nicola Beauman says that the incident of Cecil's kissing Lucy and his pince-nez being flattened reflects Forster's experience of a like incident that occurred between his mother Lily and his tutor Mr Hervey. The widowed Lily 'had had a little flirtation' with Forster's tutor Mr Hervey, for which reason Lily was being criticised. Beauman writes: "It is possible that it was merely Mr Hervey about whom Lily later made hints that she had rejected proposals for Morgan's [Forster's] sake; ...the fact that he [Mr Hervey] had 'eyeglasses and moustache' makes it possible that Morgan [Forster] saw him trying to kiss Lily, and that this was the origin of Cecil's clumsy kiss [on Lucy] in *A Room with a View* when 'his gold pince-nez became dislodged and was flattened between them.' Nor are the names Augustus Hervey and Cecil Vyse quite dissimilar, with their 'V' and 's' sounds" (Beauman, 102 f.n.).

If Lucy Honeychurch is the heroine of *A Room with a View,* George Emerson may be taken to be its hero. Nicola Beauman says that 'George' means 'farmer' or 'husband' and also "saviour because St George slew a dragon and saved a stranded maiden" (Beauman, 102, f. n.). In the novel, in a sense, George Emerson saved Lucy from the conventional English upper middle class morality, and from the possessive instinct of Cecil Vyse, standing as a viable and better alternative to him as Lucy's object of romantic love. George was a railway man and a clever fellow. In the beginning chapter of the novel, we hear from Mr Beebe that George had 'brains' and that he was a socialist, like his father. In chapter 5 of the novel, Mr Eager tells Miss Bartlett about George's father, the old Mr Emerson: "'The son of a labourer; I happen to know it for a fact. A mechanic of some sort himself when he was young; then he took to writing for the Socialistic Press.'" So, presumably, George grew up in a socialistic atmosphere, and consequently he himself subscribed socialism.

In chapter 12, we come to know George to be quite naive and silly, lacking in all sorts of pretensions that are called culture. Here we find Mr Beebe, Freddy and George impulsively jump into a pool in the woods and swim and splash water at each other, thus creating a mockery of culture sacred to the upper crust of the society: "They began to play. Mr Beebe and Freddy splashed each other. A little deferentially, they splashed George. He was quiet: they feared they had offended him. Then all the forces of youth burst out. He smiled, flung himself at them, splashed them, ducked them, kicked them, muddied them, and drove them out of the pool." Such queer humour of George did not end there but continued to work till they returned from the woods. George was also extremely impulsive. In section 4 of the novel, we see Lucy faint in Piazza Signoria at the sight of blood gushing out of a man stabbed by another. Before she was about to fall to the ground, George passionately held her up in his arms, as a consequence of which "Her heart warmed towards him for the first time." Next, George kissed her twice very impulsively, and this completely changed Lucy's vision of life. She discovered that George was 'trustworthy, intelligent, and even kind,' but, of course, 'he lacked chivalry.' In section 10 of the novel, we hear from Mr Beebe about George Emerson. Mr Beebe says about George: "'the son a goodly, if not a good young man; not a fool, I fancy, but very immature—pessimism, et cetera.'"

George was quite contrary to Cecil: Cecil was intellectual, George passionate; Cecil was conventional, George liberal; Cecil was urbane and cultured, George suburban and naive; Cecil was devoted to 'things,' George to persons; Cecil was possessive while George believed in individualism; and, lastly, Cecil drifted away from life whereas George "held the key to life" (Beauman, 206). Italy completely changed Lucy's view of life—the view that she received from the upper middle class of the English society, and this change of view was initiated by George's holding her in his arms in Piazza Signoria. The reformed Lucy therefore broke her engagement with Cecil and married George, and thus showed the triumph of passion over convention and culture. Cecil, therefore, is only a foil to George, and George happens to be within the central focus of the novel.

Of the several minor characters of *A Room with a View,* Mr Emerson (George's father) and Miss Eleanor Lavish are the most interesting. Mr Emerson, old and an widower and the 'unconventional' father of George, was falsely arrogated by people as being the murderer of his wife. In chapter 5 of the novel we hear from Mr Beebe about Mr Emerson: "'The son of a labourer; I happen to know it for a fact. A mechanic of some sort himself when he was young; then he took to writing for the Socialistic Press.'" In chapter 1 of the novel, when Miss Bartlett first saw Mr Emerson, her impression of him was that he was 'ill-bred.' In the same chapter, the narrator tells us about Mr Emerson: "He was an old man of heavy build, with a fair, shaven face and large eyes. There was something childish in those eyes, though it was not the childishness of senility." Again in the same section we further learn about Mr Emerson that 'he is a type one disagrees with rather than deplores' and that he was a Socialist and also that to the estimation of Lucy he was 'nice' and unlike a clergyman—meaning, he was not humourless. Also in the first chapter of the novel Signora Bertolini, the owner of Pensione Bertolini, tells Miss Bartlett about Mr Emerson: "'About old Mr Emerson—I hardly know. No, he is not tactful; yet, have you noticed that there are people who do things which are most indelicate, and yet at the same time—beautiful?'"

Long afterwards, in chapter 19, we learn that it was Mr Emerson, the 'unconventional' father of George, who himself very earnestly persuaded Lucy to marry his son George, because he knew that she loved him from the innermost circle of her soul and because, as he believed, 'love is eternal'. Mr Emerson told Lucy: "'You must marry, or your life will be wasted. You have gone too far to retreat. I have no time for the tenderness, and the comradeship, and the poetry, and the things that really matter, and *for which* you marry. I know that with George you will find them, and that you love him. Then be his wife. He is already part of you. Though you fly to Greece, and never see him again, or forget his very name, George will work in your thoughts till you die. It isn't possible to love and to part...I know by experience that the poets are right: love is eternal.'" (ch. 19) Immediately afterwards, we hear Mr Emerson define love and further persuade Lucy: "'I only wish poets would say this too: that love is of the body; not the body, but of the body. Ah! the misery that would be saved if we confessed that! Ah for a little directness to liberate the soul!... Dear girl, forgive my prosiness; marry my boy. When I think what life is, and how seldom love is answered by love—Marry him; it is one of the moments for which the world was made.'" (ch. 19)

According to Nicola Beauman, Mr Emerson is the representative of Edward Carpenter, a homosexual and the author of the influential homosexual pamphlet *Love's Coming of Age* (1896). Beauman writes: "'The mouthpiece for Carpenter in *A Room with a View* is Mr Emerson. He is the representative of the natural life, in which emotions are freely expressed; and he is set against the forces of Sawstonian respectability. He is a socialist; and in 'New Lucy' [the second draft *of A Room with a View*] he, like Carpenter, was a mathematician" (Beauman, 209).

We first meet Miss Eleanor Lavish, "who was partly modelled on a real novelist called Miss Spender whom the Forsters [E.M. Forster and his mother] met at Perugia" (Beauman, 105), in chapter 2 of *A Room with a View* and learn that she was an adventurous and 'clever' lady. In the next chapter of the novel, we hear from Mr Beebe that she had been writing a novel 'dealing with modern Italy.' She "had four brothers, all University men, except one who was in the army." In the same chapter Miss Alan tells Mr Beebe about Miss Lavish that "'she is a little too—I hardly like to say unwomanly.'" In chapter 5, we hear that the name of the heroine of the novel that Miss Lavish had been writing was Leonora which suggested or reminded the name of the novelist herself—Eleanor. In the same chapter the narrator tells us about the plot of Miss Lavish's novel: "Love, murder, abduction, revenge, was the plot. Out it all came while the fountain plashed to the satyrs in the morning sun." Miss Lavish said: "'There will be a deal of local colouring, descriptions of Florence and the neighbourhood, and I shall also introduce some humorous characters. And let me give you all fair warning: I intend to be unmerciful to the British tourist.'" She confessed about her novel: "'I confess that in Italy my sympathies are not with my own countrymen. It is the neglected Italians who attract me, and whose lives I am going to paint so far as I can....'" Long afterwards, in chapter 15, we learn that Miss Lavish's novel was published anonymously with the title 'Under a Loggia.'

In chapter 6 of the novel we learn more about Miss Lavish. Here she told Lucy Honeychurch that she used to undertake journeys "'as a student of human nature,'" and she told Mr Eager that she "'had always flown in the face of the conventions all my life. This is what I call an adventure.'" Miss Lavish's character is perhaps questionable, as may be evident in chapter 6 of the novel. The reverend Arthur Beebe, the Reverend Cuthbert Eager, Mr Emerson, Mr George Emerson, Miss Lavish, Miss Bartlett and Miss Honeychurch—three relatively young and an old males and three relatively young females—drove out to see a view around Val d' Arno. At one point of their sight-seeing, Miss Lavish tried to persuade Lucy to go to Mr Eager and leave her behind so that she could converse with Mr Beebe. Miss Lavish was feeling discontented in the company of only females, and she was hungry for immodest talks with the males. Miss Lavish disgruntedly told Lucy: "'it's like a school feast; the boys have got separated from the girls. Miss Lucy, you are to go. We wish to converse on high topics unsuited for your ear.'"

From chapter 9 of *A Room with a View* we know that the Reverend Cuthbert Eager, 'the English chaplian at Florence', 'was a snob, and so conceited'. The narrator describes Mr Eager mostly in chapter 5 of the novel. He writes about Mr Eager: "...Mr Eager was no commonplace chaplain. He was a member of the residential colony who had made Florence their home. He knew the people who never walked about with Baedekers, who had learnt to take a siesta after lunch, who took drives the pensione tourists had never heard of, and saw by private influence galleries which were closed to them." The narrator tells us that Mr Eager was dark, but his face was beautiful: "dark, handsome face". He was an M.A. of the University of Oxford, the narrator tells us at the very beginning of chapter one of the novel. Like Mr Eager, Mr Beebe was also a clergyman, or what in Italian called *dove bouni uomini.* Mr Beebe was 'smaller' than Mr Eager and used to wear 'ruddy whiskers'. This we know from chapters 6 and 19 of the novel. In chapter 12 of the novel, Mr Beebe displays a sort of behaviour that is quite silly and childish. Here we find him jump into a pool in the woods, along with Freddy and George, and swim and splash water about—a sort of behaviour extremely incongruous with his vocation.

Miss Charlotte Bartlett, cousin of Lucy, went to Italy as a sort of chaperon of hers. In the beginning chapter of *A Room with a View,* she herself says this: "'I am, as it were,' she concluded, 'The chaperon of my young cousin, Lucy'." She always tried to protect Lucy during their Italian tour. Charlotte was full of energy, and was extremely unselfish. In the beginning chapter of the novel, the narrator tells us: "Charlotte's energy! And her unselfishness! She had been thus all her life, but really, on this Italian tour, she was surpassing herself." P.N. Furbank says that Forster modelled Charlotte Bartlett, in *A Room with a View,* on Aunt Emily, wife of his uncle William Howley (1855-1910) (Furbank, I, 65). Freddy was Lucy's younger brother. In chapter 9 of the novel, the narrator says: "Freddy was neither clever, nor subtle, nor beautiful, and what prevented Cecil from saying, any minute, 'it would be wrong not to loathe Freddy'?" It was Freddy who could correctly prognosticate that the love between Lucy and Cecil would not end in a marriage but in a fiasco. In chapter 10 of the novel, Forster tells us that Freddy "was democratic. Like his sister, and like most young people, he was naturally attracted by the idea of equality." In chapter 12, Forster also says that Freddy, like George, was not refined: "Neither George nor Freddy was truly refined." And this is quite clear from the behaviour of Freddy in the pool in the woods in association with George and Mr Beebe. It may be pointed out here that 'Freddy' is the corruption of 'Frederick.' However, the about half a dozen other minor characters are almost inconsequential in the novel. Some of such minor characters are: Miss Teresa, Miss Pole, Mrs Vyse, Miss Alan and Mrs Honeychurch.

(iv)

Forster valued the use of fantasies in novels, and himself used these in his novels, not excepting *A Room with a View.* Fantasy, Forster tells us in his *Aspects of the Novel,* is a sort of side show in an exhibition, is something 'extra' for the reader to be had almost gratis. Fantasies, he further tells us, are related to mythologies, to mythological creatures, and also to human beings behaving as mythological creatures. However, *A Room with a View* has a good number of mythological figures, such as Satyrs (gods of the forest with bodies of human beings but with legs and feet of goats, having hair over the whole bodies and horns on the heads), Pan (the Greek god of nature, fertility and flocks), Dryads (the tree nymphs), Neptune (the Roman god of the sea), Eros (the god of romantic love), Psyche (the mortal girl loved by Eros and symbol of the human soul), Perseus (the son Zeus), Judith (the widow who saved her people by destroying the beastly Babylonian general Holofernes), and Hercules (the same as Greek Heracles, known for his fabulous physical strength, good nature and compassion). In *A Room with a View,* Forster has also used human beings as fantastic creatures. In chapter 12 of the novel, the bathing episode where Freddy, George and Mr Beebe jump into the pool in the woods and swim and splash water at each other is really fantastical, quite out of the common. Again, the love-affairs of Phaethon (the name reminds one of Phaeton, the son of Apollo. 'His reckless driving of the chariot of the sun posed a threat to heaven and earth.'), the driver, and Persephone (the name recalls the daughter of Zeus and Demeter abducted by Hades), his beloved, in chapter 6 of the novel is also fantastical.

Prophecy, according to Forster, 'is a tone of voice.' It is quite opposite of fantasy, in the sense that it is serious and humourless, which fantasy is not. Prophesy may be called inspired moral edification that subsists in the heart of a novel, or, may we say, in the nave of all the woven episodes. The prophesy of a novel is deeper than all the experiences the novelist tells about. In *A Room with a View,* Freddy had a prophetic voice; he knew, through intuition, that the seeming love between Lucy and Cecil ('Fiasco') would not fructify into marriage, into a permanent comradeship, and this really happened. Another prophetic voice we find in the old Mr Emerson, when we hear him tell Lucy in chapter 19 of the novel that she could not anyhow part with George, and that 'love is eternal.' At the fag end of the novel, i.e. in chapter 20, we find that the prophesy of the old Mr Emerson came exactly true.

There is a pattern in the plot of any good novel, says Forster. A pattern is a sort of shape of the plot of a novel. In the pattern, again, there is repetition and there is variation, like in music. In *A Room with a View,* there is a love-triangle among George, Cecil and Lucy. Lucy's dormant love instinct was first stimulated by George's kissing her, but she ignored her attraction towards him. Next. Cecil intruded into the life of Lucy, as he got fascinated by the changed air of Lucy while in the liberating atmosphere of Italy. He twice proposed to her in Italy, but, like George, was rejected by her. But coming back to England. Lucy felt the insurmountable demands of her instinct of love and accepted the third proposal from Cecil, and entered into an engagement with him. Mr Emerson had been repeatedly persuading Lucy to get married to his son George. Lucy ultimately yielded to Mr Emerson's persuasion, and, moreover, she now realised that she really did love George and not Cecil. The consequence: she broke her engagement with Cecil and married George. This is the pattern of the plot, with accompanying repetitions and variations of episodes.

(v)

It is an obvious peculiarity of any novel of Forster that there must be multiple tea-parties (or coffee-parties), some picnic, reference to *genius locus,* and frequent uses of the word 'muddle' or its variants. In *A Room with a View,* we hear of tea or coffee parties at least for thirteen times, of picnic once, and come across the word 'muddle' or its variants at least fifteen times (the length of the novel is some 223 pages). The *genius locus* is the spirit of Piazza Signoria of which we read at the end of chapter 5 of the novel: "The Piazza Signoria is too stony to be brilliant. It has no grass, no flowers, no frescoes, no glittering walls of marble or comforting patches of ruddy brick. By an odd chance—unless we believe in presiding genius of places—the statues that relieve its severity suggest, not the innocence of childhood, nor the glorious bewilderment of youth, but the conscious achievements of maturity. Here, not only in the solitude of Nature, might a hero meet a goddess, or a heroine a god." Yet another peculiarity of Forster's novels is that in each one of them some one dies or some persons die very suddenly. In *A Room with a View* (chapter 4), a man is stabbed by another in Piazza Signoria and instantly dies.

Forster is a difficult novelist to follow, no doubt, but, as a critic has pointed out, he writes with clues, which help us a lot to follow his narrative, by providing fore-shadows, or insinuations of what is going to happen sometime afterwards.

One example of clue in *A Room with a View* is Freddy's referring to Cecil as the 'Fiasco'—'family honoured pun on fiance' at the end of chapter 8 of the novel. Freddy's 'prophetic' utterance came to be true afterwards when Cecil was finally rejected by Lucy as her husband. Another example of clue occurs just at the beginning of chapter 9 of the novel. That the engagement of Lucy with Cecil was going to prove a flop is insinuated through a 'misfortune' that took place in the little garden-party. The narrator tells us: "At tea a misfortune took place: a cup of coffee was upset over Lucy's figured silk." Cecil, who was present in the party, felt much disturbed at the untoward incident.

(vi)

In both his Italian novels—*Where Angels Fear to Tread* and *A Room with a View*—Forster has painted a sketchy picture of Italy and the Italians, through occasional and casual comments and very brief descriptions. For instance, in chapter 5 of the novel, we see Lucy and Mr Eager 'in the newspaper-room at the English bank.' "Lucy stood by the central table, heedless of *Punch* and the *Graphic,* trying to answer, or at all events to formulate the questions rioting in her brain. The well-known world had broken up, and there emerged Florence, a magic city where people thought and did the most extraordinary things. Murder, accusations of murder, a lady clinging to one man and being rude to another—were these the daily incidents of her streets? Was there more in her frank beauty than met the eye—the power, perhaps, to evoke passions, good and bad, and to bring them speedily to a fulfilment?" All of Lucy's questions were to be answered in the positive. Before this, but in the same chapter, the narrator told us that the spirit of Italy was the spirit of youth: "the eternal league of Italy with youth."

The Italians were nasty: their rooms smelt. In the beginning chapter of the novel, Lucy said, "'our rooms smell'" and so "'We dread going to bed.'" In the next chapter Miss Lavish meant to tell Lucy that Italy was not a nice place and that most Italians were lecherous, but, of course, they were full of vivacity, full of the rhythms of life. Miss Lavish told Lucy: "'One doesn't come to Italy for niceness,' was the retort; 'one comes for life. Buon giorno! Buon giorno!' bowing right and left. 'Look at that adorable wine-cart! How the driver stares at us, dear, simple soul!'" In chapter 3, Miss Alan told Lucy that the Italians did not respect anyone's privacy: "'No one has the least idea of privacy in this country. And one person catches it from another.'" At the same place of the novel, the narrator tells us that Mr Beebe could not tell Lucy and Miss Alan for shame how once at Modena a certain 'chambermaid burst in upon him in his bath.' But Mr Beebe told them that "'The Italians are a most unpleasant people. They pry everywhere, they see everything, and they know what we want before we know it ourselves.... Yet in their heart of hearts they are—how superficial! They have no conception of the intellectual life.'" At the end of chapter 5 of the novel, we are told that Miss Charlotte Bartlett was warned about carrying money in Italy; she was told that money should be carried like a nose-bag and that "this was the only safe way to carry money in Italy." It may be pointed out here that inspite of all these drawbacks or negative aspects of Italy, Forster was always almost idolatrous of that country.

(vii)

A Room with a View is full of adulating references to the beauty of nature and to the joy of pastorality. It pleads for the country and against the town. It upholds simplicity and naturalness and denounces complexity and artificiality. It persuades us to escape the sin of all social pretensions authorised by tradition and enjoy life in the sunshine of the liberal atmosphere of Italy. In chapter 5 of the novel, Mr Eager, a chaplain though he was, was attracted by the beauty of Florence and its hill-side. He suggested a drive up to Fiesole to Lucy and Miss Bartlett for a view of Florence and its landscape. He regretted, like William Wordsworth in his sonnet 'The World is too much with us', that due to the 'sick hurry' of the modern world people hardly found time to appreciate the beauty of nature. He asked Miss Bartlett: "'would you and

Miss Honeychurch be disposed to join me in a drive some day this week—a drive in the hills? We might go up by Fiesole and back by Settignano. There is a point on that road where we could get down and have an hour's ramble on the hillside. The view thence of Florence is most beautiful—far better than the hackneyed view from Fiesole. It is the view that Alessio Baldovinetti is fond of introducing into his pictures. That man had a decided feeling for landscape. Decidedly. But who looks at it today? Ah, the world is too much with us.'" In the same chapter of the novel, again, Mr Eager praises the countryside, though to him the town is more beautiful than the village, because in the village there is purity. He said: "'In these days of toil and tumult one has great needs of the country and its message of purity... Ah! the town! Beautiful as it is, it is the town.'" In chapter 9 of the novel, we find Cecil fondling Lucy, while quoting from poetry that spoke of the exquisite beauty of the hills:

> 'Come down, O maid, from yonder mountain height,
> What pleasure lives in height (the shepherd sang),
> In height and in the splendour of the hills?'

Chapter 12 of *A Room with a View* is, so to say, orgiastic as regards the enjoyment of the bounteous pleasures of nature, as it is full of sexual overtones. Here we find the pristine instinctual nature of man when he is away from the tentacles of inhibitory social conventions codified by civilisation. Here we see Freddy, George and Mr Beebe, all of them stripped, swim and splash water at each other in a pool in the wood in an autumn afternoon. To Mr Beebe, the clergyman, the arboreous ambience of the pool seemed the garden of Eden. He told Freddy: "'I believed in a return to Nature once. But how can we return to Nature when we have never been with her? Today, I believe that we must discover Nature. After many conquests we shall attain simplicity. It is our heritage.'" While swimming across the tranquil water of the pool, the three naturalists could feel that 'water's wonderful.' Mr Beebe, perhaps conscious of his ecclesiastical obligations, "could detect no parishioners except the pine-trees, rising up steeply on all sides, and gesturing to each other against the blue. How glorious it was! The world of motor-cars and Rural Deans receded illimitably. Water, sky, evergreens, a wind—these things not even the seasons can touch, and surely they lie beyond the intrusion of man?" The narrator closes the chapter by making the following remark on the influence of the nature of the particular spot on the three: "It had been a call to the blood and to the relaxed will, a passing benediction whose influence did not pass, a holiness, a spell, a momentary chalice for youth."

A Room with a View is also replete with poetic passages, four of which may be cited below. In chapter 3, when Lucy and Mr Beebe were chatting, the particular evening waxed exquisitely beautiful: "Evening approached while they chatted; the air became brighter; the colours on the trees and hills were purified, and the Arno lost its muddy solidity and began to twinkle, there were a few streaks of bluish-green among the clouds, a few patches of watery light upon the earth, and then the dripping facade of San Miniato shone brightly in the declining sun." The second passage occurs in chapter 7. The party of Mr Beebe, Mr Eager, Miss Lavish and others were returning after seeing a view, and on their way back they faced a fierce storm: "There was an explosion up the road. The storm had struck the overhead wire of the tramline, and one of the great supports had fallen. If they had not stopped perhaps they might have been hurt. They chose to regard it as a miraculous preservation, and the floods of love and sincerity, which might fructify every hour of life, burst forth in tumult. They descended from the carriages; they embraced each other. It was as joyful to be forgiven past unworthinesses as to forgive them. For a moment they realized vast possibilities of good." The third we come across at the end of chapter 16. Lucy was ambivalent towards Cecil while she was walking with Miss Bartlett. "But, once in the open air, she paused. Some emotion—pity, terror, love, but the emotion was strong—seized her, and she was aware of autumn. Summer was ending, and the evening brought her odours of decay, the more pathetic because they were reminiscent of spring. That something or other mattered intellectually? A leaf violently agitated, danced past her, while other leaves lay motionless. That the earth was hastening to re-enter darkness, and the shadows of those trees to creep over Windy Corner?" Lastly, the fourth poetic passage occurs in chapter 18. Mr Beebe and Miss Bartlett walked up a summit and then paused to see the following: "The sky had grown wilder...Grey clouds were charging across tissues of white, which stretched and shredded and tore slowly, until through their final layers gleamed a hint of the disappearing blue. Summer was retreating. The wind roared, the trees groaned, yet the noise seemed insufficient for those vast operations in heaven. The weather was breaking up, breaking, broken, and it is a sense of the fit rather than of the supernatural that equips such crisis with the salvos of angelic artillery."

(viii)

Nicola Beauman says that *A Room with a View* is full of sexual imagery, and we may add that it is also replete with subtle sexual insinuations. About *A Room with a View,* Beauman writes: "Sexual fulfilment, Morgan was openly declaring in his [this] novel, is the greatest gift life has to offer because with this fulfilment come all the other aspects of life that matter so much: intimacy, unvarnished truth, the rejection of purely intellectual values. What Cecil fails to realise about Lucy is 'that if she was too great for this society she was too great for all society, and had reached the stage where personal intercourse would alone satisfy her'; what George realises—and this is made immediately clear in the uninhibited and undifferential way he kisses her, twice—is that she is not too great, i.e. sexual, for this society, but that she can only survive in it within a sexual and loving relationship—'personal intercourse'" (Beauman, 206). Beauman further writes: "...Morgan [Forster], by allowing Lucy and George to marry, would display his passionate belief in love's potential for good and in the importance of sexual passion for happiness. *A Room with a View* is therefore imbued with sexual imagery: Lucy, for example, when she goes on her own into the Piazza Signoria, metaphorically loses her virginity: 'The Loggia showed as the triple entrance of a cave...the tower of the palace, which rose out of the lower darkness like a pillar of roughened gold...seemed...some unattainable treasure throbbing in the tranquil sky...as she caught sight of him he grew dim; the palace itself grew dim, swayed above her, fell onto her softly, slowly, noiselessly, and the sky fell with it'" (Beauman, 146).

There are, further, sexual insinuations at many places in the novel. In chapter 3 of the novel, for instance, the narrator tells us: "Mr Beebe was not able to tell the ladies of his adventure at Modena, where the chambermaid burst in upon him in his bath, exclaiming cheerfully, 'Fa niente, sono vecchia.'" In *A Room with a View,* mention of such things as *The Decameron* (chapter 6) and 'A Shropshire Lad' and 'The Way of All Flesh' (chapter 12) certainly insinuates fleshiness. Curiously, Forster sometimes uses blood as a symbol of sexuality. In chapter 4 of the novel, Lucy entered the Piazza Signoria where she fainted after seeing blood gushing out of a man stabbed by another man, and she fell into the warm embrace of George. This was the occasion in which Lucy was first sexually attracted to George: "Her heart warmed towards him for the first time." And chapter 12 of it is, may we say, blatantly sexual in its insinuations. Here we see, as has already been said, Freddy, George and Mr Beebe swim in the pool—each one stark naked and each one gesticulating, after coming out of the pool, sexually meaningfully. Jeremy Tambling calls this particular chapter carnivalesque. He says that the fact that this chapter has been "significantly only called 'Twelfth Chapter,' keeping it anonymous, suggests that there are positive aspects to Forster's sense of homoerotic and homosocial bondings" (Tambling, 5) in this chapter.

(ix)

John Sayre Martin says about *A Room with a View* that "More than Forster's other four novels, it recalls Jane Austen" (Martin, 89). But, all the same, he says that in at least two respects, Forster, in this novel, went beyond the limited novelistic domain of Austen. Martin writes: Yet *A Room with a View* is wider in scope than any of Jane Austen's novels. Its heroine Lucy Honeychurch travels to Italy where she encounters a spirit totally new to her. Wilder and freer than the spirit of Summer Street and her home Windy Corner, it embraces beauty, passion, violence, and love; and it makes an indelible impression on Lucy. Not only does she acquire a new view of the world, she becomes involved in a new life. The result is that try as she does to return to the old view and the old life, she cannot. They no longer fulfil her needs, and she cannot be happy until she accepts the new. "In another respect, too, the novel goes beyond one of Jane Austen's for it reaches out beyond Lucy and her social environment toward the unseen and the infinite. It pits the genteel pretensions of village life against the mystery of life itself. Envisioning man in a disjointed, inexplicable universe, it implicitly searches for some means of gaining a sense of wholeness and harmony, a sense that the inner life and the outer can be attained" (*op. cit.*, 89-90).

The central issue of *A Room with a View* is Lucy's dilemmatic status—should she keep close to the English upper middle class tradition of sexually inhibitory morality or to accept the new view of life that flouted that tradition and would do justice to the demands of Lucy's instincts of love and sex aroused by George. Lucy, after rather prolonged dilatory moves, decided to quoit her tradition and accept the new way of life that she discovered in Italy, being inspired by the 'unadorning', natural and manly kisses of George. She realised that the cold, mechanical and perfunctory love of Cecil, who was devoted to the inhibitory moral tradition of the Summer Street, of Windy Corner, was incompatible with her inner voice, and so she rejected him. John Sayre Martin says that thus Lucy was saved, and that her being saved was due to two forces: one, her inner voice; and two, her 'good luck.' Her good luck was, ironically, brought in by Cecil Vyse. It was Cecil who managed for the Emersons a rented house in Summer Street, where Lucy found occasion to be once again stimulated by the memories of George's amorous adventures on herself, and so to reconsider her engagement with Cecil. And, her inner voice of rebellion grew out of her new experiences of liberal humanism in Italy, spearheaded by

George's osculation. It is in this sense that Martin is justified when he says that Lucy's salvation depended "at least as much on good luck as on her own character" (Martin, 100).

Lucy was salvaged, but she was only partially happy, because by accepting her new Italian experiences as authentic, she also, at the same time, rejected her old, past experiences as null and void, and thus rejected her own family and its long tradition. But, before this she experienced a moral ambiguity and a tension between her happiness, for accepting the new view of life, and her regret, for losing her old. She perceived, as if, a space of 'unreality' where both light and shade played crisscrossing. Martin says that light and darkness are in fact inseparable in life, as good and evil are so in it. Martin writes about the chiaroscuro in Lucy's moral life in *A Room with a View:* "The moral ambiguity—the mixture of light and darkness—that can surround an event is nowhere more pointedly shown than in the scene in the piazza where Lucy witnesses the murder. Coming into the square, she sees it in shadow. The figure of Neptune is 'unsubstantial in the twilight,' the Loggia shows like a cave, its statues 'shadowy but immortal.' It is the hour, Forster remarks, 'of unreality.' Only upon the tower of the palazzo does the sun still shine. Suggestive of Lucy's still unexpressed sexual yearnings, it seems 'no longer a tower, no longer supported by earth, but some unattainable treasure throbbing in the tranquil sky. Its brightness mesmerized her...' (...). The pattern of light and shade is emblamatic of the ensuing event—of a passionate outburst leading to the death of one human being and the salvation of two others" (Martin, 107).

(x)

Immediately after *A Room with a View* was published in October, 1908, the *Daily Mail* effusively praised the novel, and the *Spectator* found in it a better novel of Forster than his earlier ones. But the *Outlook* was 'seriously rude' about the novel, saying: "'The heroin is one of those uncomfortable girls who cannot make up their minds. She is kissed on all possible occasions, and without provocation, by the uncouth

George Emerson, and these osculatory overtures often unsettle her intentions. We do not share the disquiet of her family when at last she decides to marry George; indeed we are grateful to the young man for taking her off our hands'" (Furbank, I, 170). Among Forster's acquaintances, Dent denounced the novel, but Malcolm Darling "wrote praising the novel to the skies" (*op. cit.,* 171).

However, John Sayre Martin says that the novel is a 'tightly controlled book' in which the episodes or incidents are very skilfully interwoven around the central problem of the diversity and compatibility and incompatibility of the different views of a multiplicity of characters. Martin writes: "*A Room with a View* is a tightly controlled book, and one of the ways in which Forster shows his control is in his careful deployment of 'views.' Key characters can be measured by the kinds of views they respond to. Indeed the ability to respond to views at all separates the saveable from the dammed; for only those who respond to some kind of view, the novel suggests, are able to love. The views that Lucy responds to in Florence and from the terrace at Windy Corner are vital and natural; they are scenic reminders of the course that she must follow. Cecil, on the other hand, chiefly responds to art. Conceiving Lucy as a work of art, he views her in his mind against a Leonardo-like background of flower-clad mountains and shadowy rocks (...). His views are aesthetic and clearly to be connected with his indifference to people and dislike of sport. Lucy connects George with the view from Fiesole, but Cecil she can only connect with a viewless drawing-room (...). Charlotte, loveless and self-encased, responds to no views at all. Entering her room at the pension, she immediately fastens the shutters (...); and staying at Windy Corner, she begs to be given 'an inferior spare room—something with no view, anything' (...). When she intrudes on Lucy and George at Fiesole, it is entirely in keeping with her nature that she should block in view; her very presence, in fact, gives Lucy 'the sensation of a fog' (...). Finally, in complete contrast to Charlotte, the Emersons respond most intensely to views of the open sky, for like their famous American namesake they are transcendentally minded.

'My father,' remarks George approvingly, 'says that there is one perfect view—the view of the sky straight over our heads, and that all these views on earth are but bungled copies of it.' (...) Taken together the novel's 'views' serve to enforce its theme and structure and to provide a measure of character" (Martin, 107-108).

Lastly, Martin points out the deeper significance of *A Room with a View* in the following words: "Forster's third novel, then, is a romantic one, concerned with a simpler, more conventional society than our own. But its romance and outmoded conventionalism need not blind one to the fact that it also explores with subtlety and intelligence a perennial problem: the difficulty of being true to oneself and to others in a precarious world largely governed by chance—a world in which good and bad, clarity and muddle, violence and love are inextricably intertwined and as much a part of the nature of things as time and change themselves" (Martin, 108).

Howards End

9

1

INTRODUCTION

Howards End, Forster's second English novel (the-first being *The Longest Journey*), is a novel of realistic domestic theme, and its setting is the early twentieth century England. The novel deals with two classes of people: one class cultured and intellectual (represented in the novel by the Schlegels), and the other class pragmatic and bent upon amassing money not for any ulterior motive but just for the pleasure of doing so (represented in the novel by the Wilcoxes). The two classes, though not antagonistic, are incompatible with each other. Forster believed that no one of the two classes is a conglomeration of fully grown or fully formed human beings, who are supposed to be both cultured and pragmatic, intellectual and emotional; and that each of them needs some properties or essential qualities of the other; and also that the two classes can come closer to each other only through mutually fraternal sympathy. The famous epigrammatic expression of the novel, 'Only connect!,' that occurs in section XXII of it, means just this fraternal sympathy that is needed to cement two apparently incongruous classes. Forster, in the novel, advocated a marriage between the two views or philosophies of life—a marriage between the 'prose' and the 'passion' of life. In the novel, he persuades us to connect instinct and intellect, or emotion and intellect. The whole man, and not the fragmentary man, is ideally a combination of intellect and emotion. And only a marriage between intellect and emotion can fetch for man his much needed salvation.

This is the 'sermon' of Margaret that we read in section XXII of *Howards End:* "Only connect! That was the whole of her sermon. Only connect the prose and the passion, and both will be exalted, and human love will be seen at its highest. Live in fragments no longer. Only connect, and the beast and the monk, robbed of their isolation that is life to either, will die." And, consequently, Forster probably means to conclude, man will shine with all his glory. He, therefore, wanted the development of the head *pari passu* with the development of the heart.

Forster could never stand the bourgeois mentality of ceaselessly endeavouring to make money and amassing property, for no proximate or distant honest motive, but simply for the mindless pleasure of doing so (though he himself was the proprietor of a considerable amount of money). He once wrote in this regard: "'...The parts of Communism and of Christianity that interest me are *not* their boring egalitarianisms, but their attempt to cut out money. I do think money is dangerous, and I know more about its dangers than you suppose, for my great grandfather was quite a famous banker, and some of the canniness runs in my blood, and tempts me to prefer money to the things it buys'" (Beauman, 236). It was this monetary philosophy of Forster that formed a part of the central focus of *Howards End.*

As regards its literary credentials, *Howards End* is generally adjudged second only to *A Passage to India,* among all the novels of Forster. Forster, in his Commonplace Book, wrote about the novel: "'my best novel and approaching a very good novel'" (*op. cit.,* 369). The 'germ' of *Howards End,* according to P.N. Furbank, was Forster's meeting with a very charming and cultivated lady. Furbank writes that in 1906 Forster met Mr Poston's new wife, "and the sight of this charming, cultivated woman...seems to have supplied the germ of *Howards End*" (Furbank, I, 142). The episode of Forster's meeting with the Postons happened like this. In 1906, Forster went to Rooksnest, the house where he and Lily once lived, and stopped there for some time. The house, called Highfield, was situated nearby. In Highfield there lived Charles Poston, senior, (the first) Mrs Poston, and their little son, Charles Poston, junior, and their daughter. Lily, being rather asocial, did not like Forster mixed with people freely, but she allowed him to mix with a few persons, and the Postons were among those few. The Postons came to Highfield in 1886 (and left it in 1913). For six years, while he had been at Rooksnest, Forster remained a friend to the Postons. When in 1906 Forster went to Highfield, he found that Charles Poston, senior, had married for the second time after the death of his first wife. But Forster saw no sign of any change whatsoever in Highfield inspite of the second Mrs Poston's occupying the place of the first Mrs Poston. He, therefore, thought that to the Poston family only the house, Highfield, mattered, and the Mrs Postons were of no consequence.

This thought Forster translated into the plot of *Howards End*. Nicola Beauman writes about Forster's experiences in the Poston family, showing some parallels between what Forster saw in Highfield and what happen in *Howards End*: "It was in 1886 that the first Mr and Mrs Poston had moved there [in Highfield] and for Morgan's remaining six years at Rooksnest he had been friends with them and with their son and daughter, the former being called Charles like his father and like the Wilcoxes' son in *Howards End*. When Charles Poston senior re-married the menage went on in equal harmony in the same house: which must have made Morgan [Forster] ponder the state of being a second wife, especially one who continued life in the same house as her predecessor, almost as if it was the house that was the stability and the harmony not a particular wife. Although it was the first Mrs Poston and the first Mrs Wilcox who seemed at one with their houses, their successors were as well: as if the strength and the spirit of the house transcended individuality. It was this theme, with the Postons transposed to Howards End, that Morgan [Forster] would explore; so that Clementine Poston [the second Mrs Poston] and what she stood for was in his mind throughout the book, up until the last chapter when it is August and the hay is being cut and Margaret, the second wife, has in her turn become part of Howards End" (Beauman, 186). And, all at the same time,

Beauman adds, Forster "continued to ponder the mysterious, unknown state of marriage" (*ibid.*), and wrote down what it all appeared to him to be in *Howards End.* It may be pointed out here that the little of the novel derives from the name of the house Howards End, situated in Hertfordshire, from which—very sad it was—Forster and Lily were, for reasons unknown to us, turned out by the landlord (Furbank, II, 204).

Forster wrote *Howards End* during 1908-1910, mostly in Weybridge. During the summer of 1909, particularly, he was working hard on the preparation of the manuscript of the novel, and after making a draft of thirty chapters of the novel (the novel contains a total of 44 sections or chapters), he sent them to Edward Arnold, the publisher, for his perusal and comments, in March 1910, and Arnold "greeted it with great enthusiasm. He had, however, not liked the part about Helen's seduction and asked Forster to consider altering it, to which Forster replied that he knew it was faulty, but it was too late for change—the offending part was intrinsic to the plot" (Furbank, I, 185). Arnold advanced Forster 130 Pounds (equivalent to approximately 6,000 Pounds in 1993). Curious it is that neither in his diary nor in his letters that he wrote during the period of making the manuscript of this novel, did Forster make any mention that he had been writing *Howards End.* However, by July 1910, the final draft of the novel was completed, and in the same year it was published. It was priced 6 shillings a copy (equivalent to approximately 15 Pounds in 1993). In the year 1910 the novel sold 7,662 copies and by 1913 it sold 9,959 copies, and with a royalty of 10 per cent Forster received from all these sales a total of 280 Pounds (equivalent to approximately 13, 000 Pounds in 1993). Besides these sales, by 1946, *Howards End* sold fabulous 250,000 copies in Penguin (Beauman, 281). Two reprints of the novel were released in just just next year. From all this, one can easily surmise the popularity of this novel of 300 odd pages.

And this popularity of the novel was the reason of its being both dramatised and filmed. The dramatisation of *Howards End* was done by Lance Sieveking and Richard Cotrell, following the dramatisation of *A Room with a View* by S. Tail and K. Allot in 1950 (Shahane, vi). In 1992, *Howards End* was also filmed under the direction of James Ivory (who directed the filming of *A Room with a View* in 1986). In the film version of the novel, directed by James Ivory, the following actors and actresses, among others, performed the following roles (Tambling, 220-221):

i. Helena Bouham Carter (who acted in four out of five Forster films) played the role of Helen Schlegel.
ii. Crispin Bouham Carter played the role of Colonel Fussell.
iii. James Wilby played the role of Charles Wilcox.
iv. Venessa Redgrave played the role of Mrs Wilco.

The principal characters of *Howards End* are the following:

i. Henry Wilcox (a British businessman, and father of Charles and Paul).
ii. Ruth Wilcox (first wife of Henry Wilcox).
iii. Charles Wilcox (elder son of Henry Wilcox).
iv. Paul Wilcox (younger son of Henry Wilcox).
v. Margaret Schlegel (elder sister of Helen and the second wife of Henry Wilcox).
vi. Helen Schlegel (younger sister of Margaret).
vii. Theobald Schlegel (Margaret's brother; nickname: Tibby).
viii. Leonard Bast (a poor young man).
ix. Jacky Bast (Leonard's wife).

In *Master Plots* (15 vols.), edited by Frank N. Magill, there is a beautiful resumé of the story of *Howards End* which may help us better understand the plot and follow the narrative of the novel, and so we are quoting below the resumé, in full.

"The Wilcox family met Margaret Schlegel and her sister Helen while both families were vacationing in Germany. Neither group expected the chance acquaintance to amount to anything more, but later, after all had returned to England, Helen Schlegel was invited to visit Wilcox family at Howards End, their country home near London. While there, Helen fell in love with Paul Wilcox. Both families disapproved of the match, and after hard words on both sides it was broken off.

"A few months later the Wilcoxes rented a town flat across the street from the Schlegel home. Both young people were out of the country. Mrs Wilcox and Margaret Schlegel met and became friends.

"Also acquainted with the Schlegels was a young man named Leonard Bast, a seedy fellow whose umbrella had been accidentally taken by Helen at a concert. The young man had interested the girls and their brother by his conversation when he called to reclaim his umbrella. They did not know that he had an exceedingly frowsy wife, a woman some years older than he who had trapped him into a distasteful marriage.

"Some months after the acquaintance between Mrs Wilcox and Margaret Schlegel had ripened into friendship, Mrs Wilcox became ill and died. Much to her husband's and son's surprise, she left a note, in addition to her will, leaving Howards End to Margaret. In their anger at the prospect of letting the house go out of the family, the Wilcoxes disregarded the note, since it was not a part of the official will.

"Margaret Schlegel, knowing nothing of the bequest, was really glad that the tie between herself and the Wilcox family had been broken, for she was afraid that her sister was still in love with Paul Wilcox and suffered when she came into contact with other members of the family.

"One evening, long after Mrs Wilcox's death, Margaret and her sister were sitting in the park. There they met Mr Wilcox, who told them that the firm for which Leonard Bast worked was unreliable. Acting on that information, the girls advised the young man to change jobs. He did so. They did not know that Mr Wilcox, in love with Margaret, had given them bad advice in order to get rid of the young man he saw as a possible rival for Margaret's love.

"A few weeks later the long-term lease on the Schlegels' house was up and they were forced to move. Although they searched a long time, they found nothing suitable. Mr Wilcox, hearing of their predicament, sent a letter to Margaret offering to lease them his house in London. Margaret went with him to look at the house. While they were there, Mr Wilcox declared his love. Margaret, who was well into her thirties, was surprised, but without embarrassment or shock. She asked only for a few days to think over the rental of the house and the proposal of marriage. After considering both problems, she agreed to marry Mr Wilcox, thus making any decision about the rental unnecessary.

"Before Margaret's marriage to Mr Wilcox, his daughter was also married at a house owned by the Wilcoxes near Wales. Shortly after the daughter's wedding Helen Schlegel, who had disapproved of Margaret's approaching marriage, appeared at the house with Leonard Bast and his wife. Helen had learned that through their bad advice Bast had lost everything he had, including his job. Helen thought that Mr Wilcox ought to recompense the young man. When Mrs Bast was discovered, rather tipsy, on the lawn, she revealed to Mr Wilcox and Margaret that she had been Mr Wilcox's mistress many years before. Margaret was willing to forgive Mr Wilcox, but she resolved not to help the Basts. Under the circumstances, she felt it was unnecessary and in poor taste to do so.

"Helen, who had unwittingly fallen in love with Bast, felt sorry for him. She spent part of one night with him and then remorsefully left England. She tried to give Bast five thousand pounds, most of her fortune, but he refused to accept her aid.

"The relationship between her sister and Leonard Bast was unknown to Margaret, who went ahead with her marriage to Mr Wilcox, despite the fact that his sons did not approve of their father's second marriage. Helen's refusal to return for the ceremony did not surprise her sister. Eight months went by, Helen still not returned, and Margaret began to worry about her sister.

"Helen finally came back to England and sent word that she wanted some books stored in the house at Howards End. She acted so mysteriously that Margaret and Mr Wilcox planned to encounter her at the house. Because she refused to see them directly, Margaret, worried, thought that Helen might need mental treatment. When Margaret saw Helen, however, the reason for the mystery was plain: Helen was pregnant as the result of the night she spent with Leonard Bast. Helen asked to be permitted to spend one night with her sister in the unoccupied house at Howards End. Mr Wilcox refused to allow Margaret to do so.

"The two sisters stayed in the house inspite of Mr Wilcox's refusal. The following morning Mr Wilcox's older son, Charles, went to the house to get them out. A minute or two after his arrival Leonard Bast came to the house in search of Margaret, from whom he hoped to get money. As soon as he saw him, Charles seized a saber that hung on the wall and struck Bast on the shoulders with the flat of the weapon several times. The shock of seeing Helen and the beating were too much for Bast's weak heart. He died suddenly.

"Charles was tried for manslaughter and sentenced to three years in prison. The disgrace was too great for his father, who became an invalid. Margaret moved her husband and her sister into the house at Howards End, where Helen's child was born. Mr Wilcox came to love the baby during his illness and convalescence, and so Helen and the child, much to the displeasure of other Wilcoxes, were permitted to remain. A few months before Charles' release from prison, Mr Wilcox called a family conference. He had made a new will giving all his money to the children by his first marriage, but the house at Howards End was to go to Margaret and after her death to Helen's illegitimate child. Thus the mansion, which had played so great a part in all their lives, eventually came to Margaret Schlegel as the first Mrs Wilcox had wished before her death" (Magill, vol. 6, 1648-1650).

2

THE STORY

Forster begins the novel with the rather peculiar and brief sentence, "One may as well begin with Helen's letters to her sister." Miss Helen Schlegel wrote three closely consecutive letters from Howards End: the first one on Tuesday, the second on Friday, and the third on Sunday. In the third letter she confessed that she had fallen in love with Paul Wilcox (section 1). Margaret and Aunt Juley were at the breakfast table, in the house at Wickham Place. Margaret told Aunt Juley that she and Helen had met the Wilcoxes "on the awful expedition that we made from Heidelberg to Speyer." The Wilcoxes liked Helen and invited her to Speyer where they were stopping, and Helen went there alone. Aunt Juley (Mrs Munt) told Margaret that they (Margaret and Helen) were "'English to the backbone.'" Aunt Juley cautioned Margaret that she should think seriously about the Wilcoxes, because the Wilcoxes did not care for art and literature—the two very important things.

Margaret did not approve Helen's supposed engagement with Paul Wilcox, and so she thought the engagement had to be broken somehow and slowly. Mrs Munt (Aunt Juley) thought that Helen should have thought about the age and the financial capability of Paul to satisfy her and make her happy before entering into an engagement with him. Margaret now told Mrs Munt that she would be near Helen in her crisis, i.e., in her love of Paul, and for the reason of this she must go to Howards End, the home of the Wilcoxes. But impulsive and restless as she was, Margaret changed her mind under the impact of Mrs Munt's arguments, and ultimately decided not to go there herself but to send Mrs Munt to Howards End, where Helen had been staying. Margaret's revised decision was very much prompted by her brother Tibby's acute illness. Margaret sent Mrs Munt (Aunt Juley) to Helen at Howards End with a letter. She accompanied Mrs Munt upto King's Cross railway station and after Mrs Munt's train left the station, she returned to Wickham Place, where she received the following telegram from Helen: *All over. Wish I had never written. Tell no more—Helen.* But Mrs Munt (Aunt Juley) had already started for Howards End (section II).

Margaret was 13 and Helen 5 when their brother Tibby was born and their mother Emily Schlegel died almost immediately after giving birth to Tibby. Emily Schlegel's death was followed by her husband Mr Schlegel's death 5 years afterwards. However, the train of Mrs Munt reached Hilton station, near London, which was the station for Howards End. There in the Hilton station Charles Wilcox went for collecting a parcel. Mrs Munt introduced herself to Charles and told him that she wanted to meet Helen at Howards End. Mrs Munt asked Charles if he was the young Wilcox. Charles said he was, and from this Mrs Munt presumed that he was Paul Wilcox. The narrator describes Charles thus: "To a feminine eye there was nothing amiss in the sharp depression at the corners of his mouth, nor in the rather box-like construction of his forehead. He was dark, clean-shaven, and seemed accustomed to command." Charles told Mrs Munt that she could avail of his car that he had brought there for collecting a parcel. He put petrol into his motor cab, loaded it with a parcel and whirred away towards Howards End, Mrs Munt sitting docile inside the cab and Charles driving fast wearing gloves and spectacles. As told earlier, Mrs Munt mistook Charles for Paul and so the conversation between Mrs Munt and Charles on the point of the love between Helen and Paul continued to be very enjoyably humorous until at last Charles revealed to her his identity. In fact, Mrs Munt had asked Charles if he was the younger Wilcox and Charles said he was. Charles thought he was younger Wilcox in relation to his deceased father, but Mrs Munt understood only Paul Wilcox by the appellation 'younger Wilcox,' because Paul was younger to Charles.

Mrs Munt at first wished to champion the lovers—Helen and Paul. But seeing that Charles was irritated at this, now betrayed to him her true mind and planned objective—the breaking up of the supposed engagement between Helen and Paul. When Mrs Munt was telling Charles about the love between Helen and Paul, Charles became infuriated and clenching his fists once shouted out at Paul: "'The idiot, the idiot, the little fool!'" At this Mrs Munt found a bed-rock to stand on and began to plead her point. She told Charles: "'I quite agree, sir. The thing [the engagement between Helen and Paul] *is* impossible, and I *will* come up and stop it. My niece is a very exceptional person, and I am not inclined to sit still while she throws herself away on those who will not appreciate her.'" She told him that Helen and Paul met only for a brief period, about a week, by which she meant that their love was immature.

Charles told Mrs Munt that "'Paul hasn't a penny'" and so the engagement was impossible, and she, on her part, assured him that she would scold Helen for her rashness, once they were back in London. After this, Mrs Munt and Charles engaged themselves in a sort of quarrel as to whether the Schlegels were better than the Wilcoxes or the Wilcoxes were better than the Schlegels. Meantime, the cab reached Howards End and Helen , who was 'looking very pale,' came out of the house to receive her aunt Mrs Munt and told her "'it's over.'" She asked her aunt not to tell anybody that she was so silly: "'Don't let them know I've been so silly. It wasn't anything.'" Charles called out "'Paul! Paul!'" and a "very young man" came out. Also came out Mrs (Ruth) Wilcox, with a wisp of hay in her hands. She was an aristocrat and worshipped the past (tradition). She asked Helen to conduct Mrs Munt to her own room or to Helen's room in order to propitiate both Mrs Munt and Charles who were till then bearing animus for each other that resulted from Mrs Munt's overbearing attitude and Charles' blatant neglect of it (section III).

Helen and her aunt, Mrs Munt, returned to Wickham Place (the house of the Schlegels near London), but Helen's attachment to Howards End did not end, for she had "fallen in love, not with an individual but with a family [the family of the Wilcoxes]." Helen became, so to say, converted to the Wilcoxes' philosophy and manners of life: "The energy of the Wilcoxes had fascinated her, had created new images of beauty in her responsive mind. To be all day with them in the open air, to sleep at night under their roof, had seemed the supreme joy of life, and had led her to that abandonment of personality that is a possible prelude to love. She had *liked* giving in to Mr Wilcox, or Evie, or Charles; she had *liked* being told that her notions of life were sheltered or academic; that Equality was nonsense, Votes for Women nonsense, Socialism nonsense,

Art and Literature, except when conducive to strengthening the character, nonsense. One by one the Schlegel fetishes had been overthrown, and, though professing to defend them, she had rejoiced."

Paul Wilcox became enamoured of Helen in this way. Paul would talk of his 'approaching exile in Nigeria,' and when Helen would hear of this, her bosom would heave, and "the heave of her bosom flattered him. Passion was possible, and he became passionate." "It is easy to talk of 'passing emotion,' and to forget how vivid the emotion was ere it passed. Our impulse to sneer, to forget, is at root a good one. We recognize that emotion is not enough, and that men and women are personalities capable of sustained relations, not mere opportunities for an electrical discharge. Yet we rate the impulse too highly. We do not admit that by collisions of this trivial sort the doors of heaven may be shaken open. To Helen, at all events, her life was to bring nothing more intense than the embrace of this boy [Paul] who played no part in it. He had drawn her out of the house, where there was danger of surprise and light; he had led her by a path he knew, until they stood under the column of the vast wych-elm. A man in the darkness, he had whispered 'I love you' when she was desiring love. In time his slender personality faded, the scene that he had evoked endured. In all the variable years that followed she never saw the like of it again."

But when Helen said about her love of Paul "'It was over at once'", Margaret asked how. Helen told her that one day Charles was talking to Paul about Stocks and Shares, and then Paul 'looked frightened.' From this Helen understood that "'the whole Wilcox family was a fraud, just a wall of newspapers and motor-cars and golf-clubs, and that if it fell I should find nothing behind it but panic and emptiness.'" But Margaret protested, saying: "'The Wilcoxes struck me as being genuine people, particularly the wife [Mrs Ruth Wilcox].'" Margaret further told Helen: "'The truth is that there is a great outer life that you and I have never touched—a life in which telegrams and anger count. Personal relations, that we think supreme, are not supreme there. There love means marriage settlements; death, death duties.... This outer life, though obviously horrid, often seems the real one—there's grit in it. It does breed character.'" Helen did not agree with her. She said: "'I know that personal relations are the real life, for ever and ever.'" The Schlegels understood temperance, tolerance and sexual equality, but they did not understand the British Empire's Forward Policy in Tibet. "Not out of them are the shows of history erected: the world would be a gray, bloodless place were it entirely composed of Miss Schlegels. But, the world being what it is, perhaps they shine out in it like stars." However, the father of the two girls—Margaret and Helen—"had obtained work in one of our [English] provincial universities, and there married Poor Emily (or *Die Englanderin,* as the case may be), and as she had money they proceeded to London, and came to know a good many people."

The Germans (and Margaret and Helen were of German extraction), the narrator tells us, only care about those things which they can use, "and therefore [they] arrange them in the following order: money, supremely useful; intellect, rather useful; imagination, of no use at all." The Pan-German movement is no more imaginative than the Imperialist Britain. The narrator tells us about the German origin of the Schlegel sisters: "A word on their origin. They were not 'English to the backbone,' as their aunt had piously asserted. But, on the other hand, they were not 'Germans of the dreadful sort.'" Both the sisters, after the death of their father, ruled Wickham Place. They were great talkers, and attracted great numbers of their admirers. Of the two sisters, Helen was more pretty than Margaret. The two sisters had their lone brother, Tibby, who was "an intelligent man of sixteen, but dispeptic and difficile" (section IV).

Beethoven's Fifth Symphony was being played in the Queen's Hall in London. The andante or the music in slow, even movement began. Helen was rather more attentive to the image of the 'attenuated Cupids who encircle the ceiling of the Queen's Hall' than to the andante, and Margaret was preoccupied with 'her new young man' (Leonard Bast). The andante came to its conclusion and a great applause followed.

Helen left Queen's Hall in the middle of the programme, and then Margaret's 'new young man' (Leonard Bast) told her that Helen had quite inadvertently took away his umbrella. Margaret requested her 'new young man' to give her his address so that she could return his umbrella, but he did not oblige. So Margaret gave him her address (Wickham Place) and invited him to come to her address to take back his umbrella. Aunt Juley and Tibby also went to the Queen's Hall along with Margaret and Helen. When the umbrella of the 'new young man' was found missing. Aunt Juley told Margaret that Fraulein Mosebach had "'left her beautiful little bag behind her on the seat.'"

After the whole musical programme was over, Margaret told the 'new young man:' "'We live quite near; I am going there now. Could you walk round with me, and we'll find your umbrella?'" He obliged. When she was returning home along with Mrs Munt, Tibby, and of course the 'new young man,' Margaret was wishing to invite the 'new young man' to tea. All the way back home, she was demonstrating her superior culture, particularly in music. When at last they reached Wickham Place at dusk, she called out at Helen who had been inside the house. When Helen appeared, Margaret told her that she had taken away the gentleman's (of the 'new young man') umbrella. Helen, not the least ashamed, admitted: "'I do nothing but steal umbrella.'" Helen disclosed that Margaret '"stole an old gentleman's silk top-hat.'" As night fell, light was turned on and the 'new young man' identified his umbrella from holes along the seams of it. The 'new young man' then went away with his pathetic umbrella without leaving his address behind. Helen asked Margaret for a cigarette, and the 'little incident' passed away. The 'little incident' proved that "all is not for the best in the best of all possible worlds, and that beneath these superstructures of wealth and art there wanders an ill-fed boy, who has recovered his umbrella indeed, but who has left no address behind him, and no name" (section V).

Leonard Bast, with his retrieved poor umbrella, was walking back home, thinking that Helen and Margaret were no better than thieves. On his way he first met Mr Dealtry, a fellow clerk, and then Mr Cunningham. Reaching home, which was in a semi-basement, he occupied a chair, drank a little tea and ate dusty crumbs of a cake, and then "went back to the sitting room, settled himself anew, and began to read a volume of Puskin" whom he understood "to be the greatest master of English Prose." Leonard heard a noise, opened the door, and Jacky barged into the room. The narrator describes Jacky thus: "it is simplest to say that she was not respectable. Her appearance was awesome. She seemed all strings and bell-pulls—ribbons, chains bead necklaces that clinked and caught—and a boa of azure feathers hung round her neck, with the ends uneven. Her throat was bare, wound with a double row of pearls, her arms were bare to the elbows, and might again be detected at the shoulder, through cheap lace. Her hat which was flowery, resembled those punnets, covered with flannel, which we sowed with mustard and cress in our childhood, and which germinated here yes, and there no. She wore it on the back of her head. As for her hair, or rather hairs, they are too complicated to describe, but one system went down her back, lying in a thick pad there, while another, created for a lighter destiny, rippled around her forehead. The face—the face does not signify. It was the face of the photograph, but older, and the teeth were not so numerous as the photographer had suggested, and certainly not so white. Yes, Jacky was past her prime, whatever that prime may have been. She was descending quicker than most women into the colourless years, and the look in her eyes confessed it."

Jacky "sat down on Leonard's (Bast's) knee, and began to fondle him. She was now a massive woman of thirty-three and her weight hurt him, but he could not very well say anything." She very naggingly asked Leonard if and when actually he would marry her. Leonard told her that he would certainly keep his word of marrying her when he would become twenty-one of age. He told Jacky that he "'pretended to the people here that you're my wife.'" He further informed her: "'I've bought you the ring to wear.'" Leonard had prepared dinner, and they ate it. Then Jacky again sat on Leonard's knee and smoked. Smoking over, Leonard brought the piano, and badly played a little Grieg for some time while Jacky went to bed, from where she called him several times. But he remained absorbed in reading Ruskin's *Stones of Venice* (section VI).

Next morning Aunt Juley informed Margaret very worriedly that the Wilcoxes had taken a flat opposite the house of the Schlegel family. "Margaret received the information calmly, and did not agree that it would throw a cloud over poor Helen's life." Nevertheless, Aunt Juley cautioned her that Helen must be careful. But Helen told Mrs Munt (Aunt Juley) a little crassly: "'It is that you and Meg [Margaret] are so absurdly grave about it, when there's nothing to be grave at all.'" However, once Mrs Munt, by the bye, said that Mr Wilcox was copper-coloured, and at this Margaret was understandably a little hurt and quipped: "'He [Mr Wilcox] has a remarkably good complexion for a man of his age.'" Mrs Munt, apparently very irrationally, was apprehensive of something about the closeness of the residence of the Wilcoxes to that of the Schlegels, but Margaret assured her that '"there's never any great risk as long as you have money.'" Margaret further told her: "'You and I and the Wilcoxes stand upon money as upon islands. It is so firm beneath our feet that we forget its very existence. It's only when we see someone near us tottering that we realize all that an independent income means. Last night when we were talking up here round the fire, I began to think that the very soul of the world is economic, and that the lowest abyss is not the absence of love, but the absence of coin.'" Mrs Munt seemed cynical.

Margaret did not stop there on the economic policy, but further told Mrs Munt: "'The poor cannot always reach those whom they want to love, and they can hardly ever escape from those whom they love no longer. We rich can.'" Mrs Munt suspiciously commented that Margaret's speech smacked of socialism. Margaret continued her lecture: "'Call it what you like. I call it going through life with one's hand spread open on the table. I'm tired of those rich people who pretend to be poor, and think it shows a nice mind to ignore the piles of money that keep their feet above the waves. I stand each year upon six hundred pounds, and Helen upon the same, and Tibby will stand upon eight, and as fast as our pounds crumble away into the sea they are renewed—from the sea, yes, from the sea. And all our thoughts are the thoughts of six-hundred-pounders, and all our speeches; and because we don't want to steal umbrellas ourselves we forget that below the sea people do want to steal them, and do steal them sometimes, and that what's a joke up here is down there reality—'" Helen surveyed the flat of the Wilcoxes with her eyes but she "swore that never, nowhere and nohow would she again fall in love with any of the Wilcox family, down to its remotest collaterals" (section VII).

The friendship between Margaret and Mrs Wilcox grew fast. To wipe off the memory of the Helen-Paul affair from Mrs Wilcox's mind, Margaret sent a letter to her by the post, and in the letter Margaret assured her that the affair had already been absolutely over: "'*As far as I know, she* [Helen] *no longer occupies her thoughts with your son* [Paul].'" The very next morning Margaret received the reply to her letter from Mrs Wilcox, by hand. Mrs (Ruth) Wilcox wrote to Margaret: *You should not have written me such a letter. I called to tell you that Paul has gone abroad.* Ashamed, Margaret straight went to Mrs Wilcox and apologised. Margaret told her that she knew that Paul had gone to India, but Mrs Wilcox corrected her and said that Paul had gone to Nigeria. Then Margaret informed Mrs Wilcox that Helen had gone to Germany. Thus the nimbus of doubt about the love between Paul and Helen was swept away from the minds of both Margaret and Mrs Wilcox. Mrs Wilcox told Margaret that Paul was ephemerally attracted by Helen because he was momentarily subject to his instincts, and that she was alarmed of this. From her Margaret came to know that her elder son, Charles, was married. The two women talked for some time as two very close friends, though Margaret was twenty-nine and Mrs Wilcox fifty-one.

Margaret arranged a luncheon party in honour of Mrs Wilcox, and some other persons were invited to the luncheon party. But the party was not a success, particularly because the guests could not naturally blend with Mrs Wilcox, and this was due to some faults in her: "Her tastes were simple, her knowledge of culture slight, and she was not interested in the New English Art Club, nor in the dividing-line between Journalism and Literature, which was started as a conversational hare." "Mrs Wilcox, whose life had been spent in the service of husband and sons, had little to say to strangers who had never shared it, and whose age was half her own. Clever talk alarmed her, and withered her delicate imaginings; it was the social counterpart of a motor-car, all jerks, and she was a wisp of hay, a flower." The conversation soon veered towards the Continent, particularly towards Germany. Margaret said that her sister Helen was in Germany, and she emphatically pleaded that the Germans had tastes for beauty and poetry. As expected, Mrs Wilcox kept herself aloof from the boisterous conversation among the other guests and Miss Margaret. She was not intellectual and so she was not interested in the fashionable and *avant garde* conversation. "There was no bitterness in Mrs Wilcox; there was not even criticism; she was lovable, and no ungracious or uncharitable word had passed her lips. Yet she and daily life were out of focus: one or the other must show blurred. And at lunch she seemed more out of focus than usual, and nearer the line that divides daily life from a life that may be of greater importance." The guests were so much interested in matters of 'greater importance'—in arts, literature, etc.—that they comfortably remained quite oblivious of the worldly life, which only interested Mrs Wilcox. However, the lunch over, the guests departed, dismissing Mrs Wilcox as 'uninteresting' (section IX).

One fine morning, several days afterwards, Mrs Wilcox and Margaret Schlegel went out for Christmas shopping, in a brougham. The relation between the two was "singular but not intimate." During the time, the Schlegels were leaving the rented house at Wickham Place after the expiry of the lease. Knowing this, Mrs Wilcox asked Margaret: "'But couldn't you get it renewed?'" The proprietor of the house at Wickham Place wanted to pull it down to create place for building flats like those of Mrs Wilcox. Hearing this, Mrs Wilcox was greatly annoyed. The Schlegels were living in the Wickham Place for long; even their father had been living there. Why then should they leave it? The urgent question was Mrs Wilcox's. She was greatly disturbed: "'It is monstrous, Miss Schlegel; it isn't right. I had no idea that this was hanging over you. I do pity you from the bottom of my heart. To be parted from your house, your father's house—it oughtn't to be allowed. It is worse than dying. I would rather die than—oh, poor girls. Can what they call civilization be right, if people mayn't die in the room where they were born? My dear, I am so sorry—'" Mrs Wilcox tried hard to persuade Margaret to go with her to Howards End and see things there, but Margaret told her that she would go there sometime afterwards. Then Margaret ordered her brougham to proceed towards Wickham Place while Mrs Wilcox left for Howards End thanking Margaret very kindly: "'A thousand thanks, Miss Schlegel, for all your help.'" Mrs Wilcox told her: "'My husband and Evie will be back the day after tomorrow. This is why I dragged you out shopping today.'" Back home, Margaret felt fidgety, and so took a hansom and went to King's Cross to catch the train to go to Hilton in five minutes. Unexpectedly, there at the platform Margaret again met Mrs Wilcox. Soon Evie came out of the cloakroom and met Mrs Wilcox, who was also immediately joined by her husband Mr Wilcox. Mrs Wilcox then returned home along with her husband and her daughter Evie (section X).

Mrs Wilcox suddenly died, and her 'funeral was over'. Mr Wilcox "remembered his wife's even goodness during thirty years. Not anything in detail—not courtship or early ruptures—but just the unvarying virtue, that seemed to him a woman's noblest quality. So many women are capricious, breaking into odd flaws of passion or frivolity. Not so his wife. Year after year, summer and winter, as bride and mother, she had been the same, he had always trusted her. Her tenderness! Her innocence! The wonderful innocence that was hers by the gift of God. Ruth [Mrs Wilcox] knew no more of worldly wickedness and wisdom than did the flowers in her garden, or in the grass in her field." Mr Wilcox lovingly recalled Mrs Wilcox's simple, innocent and naive ideas about politics and religion. Mr Wilcox was 'in appearance a steady man.' "His face was not as square as his son's, and indeed the chin, though firm enough in outline, retreated a little, and the lips, ambiguous, were curtained by a moustache. But there was no external hint of weakness. The eyes, if capable of kindness and good-fellowship, if ruddy for the moment with tears, were the eyes of one who could not be driven. The forehead, too, was like Charles's. High and straight, brown and polished, merging abruptly into temples and skull, it had the effect of a bastion that protected his head from the world. At times it had the effect of a blank wall. He had dwelt behind it, intact and happy, for fifty years."

Charles prepared to go out with his wife Dolly for a pleasure drive when he was informed by her that their house Howards End was going to be owned by Margaret Schlegel. Charles, at first, did not quite listen to what she said. He rather "put his arm round her waist and pressed her against him. All his affection and half his attention—it was what he granted her throughout their happy married life." At that moment Evie, Charles' sister, came over there and informed them that Mr Wilcox was annoyed with a letter 'that's too awful.' Charles was actually given two letters—rather two notes—, both of which were written by his deceased mother, Mrs Wilcox. In one of the letters, "She had written: 'To my husband: I should like Miss Schlegel (Margaret) to have Howards End.'" This letter was accompanied by a *note* also written by the deceased Mrs Wilcox from the nursing-home, and the two letters were sent to Mr Wilcox through the emissary of a matron. This accompanying letter only meant that the other letter, inside it, was for Mr Wilcox.

Dolly excitedly said: "'But I say that note isn't legal. Houses ought to be done by a lawyer, Charles, surely.'" Charles "worked his jaw severely" and Dolly wanted to see the letters with her own eyes. Mr Wilcox gave the letters to Dolly, and she found that the letters were written in pencil. She found a strong ground for denying the legal value of the letters in their being written in pencil, and so exclaimed: "'Why, it's only in pencil! I said so. Pencil never counts.'" Mr Wilcox dittoed Dolly: "'We know that it is not legally binding.'" He said he "'should be justified in tearing it up and throwing it into fire.'" But he asked her not to interfere into the matter. Charles doubted that Margaret had had some undue influence on his invalid mother before her death. He also doubted that the letters were really in his mother's hand. Therefore he asked his father to consult a legal expert.

At this point of the narrative, the narrator very unusually makes his own judgement on the legal status of the two letters and on the spirit of the bequeath of Mrs Wilcox through those two letters, as regards Howards End. He tells us that the letters could cerainly be torn up and thrown into the fire, as a practical moralist would think fit, but he points out the important thing that the letter bore a 'personal appeal' of a deceased person, where legality or morality may not count, but of course sentiment does count. However, the incident made a great impact on all of the Wilcox family. "Yesterday they had lamented: 'She [Mrs Wilcox] was a dear mother, a true wife; in our absence she neglected her health and died.' Today they thought: 'She was not true, as dear as we supposed.'" And ultimately their final, shattering and unkind verdict was that Mrs Wilcox was 'treacherous in bequeathing Howards End to Margaret Schlegel. Miss Schlegel had her own house, and so they could not understand why should Mrs Wilcox have given Howards End to her. Nevertheless, Mr Wilcox expressed the opinion that he could deal evenly with the matter with Margaret if she did once come to Howards End, but he knew she wouldn't. Charles pointed out that Margaret would not come because of the Paul-Helen business. Mr Wilcox did not say anything about that business; he only said about Margaret that after all "'upon my soul she's honest'" (section XI).

After Mrs Wilcox's demise, Margaret was winding herself away from the Wilcox family. But Margaret had her 'grim secret' as regards the Wilcox family. "She had told a little of her grim secret to her friends, but not too much; she had shut up her heart—almost but not entirely." The "Wilcoxes continued to play a considerable part in her thoughts.... They were not 'her sort,' they were often suspicious and stupid, and deficient where she excelled; but collision with them stimulated her, and she felt an interest that verged into liking, even for Charles. She desired to protect them, and often felt that they would protect her, excelling where she was deficient.... They led a life that she could not attain to—the outer life of 'telegrams and anger'.... To Margaret this life [of 'telegrams and anger'] was to remain a real force. She could not despise it, as Helen and Tibby affected to do. It fostered such virtues as neatness, decision and obedience, virtues of the second rank, no doubt, but they have formed our civilization. They form character, too; Margaret could not doubt it: they keep the soul from becoming sloppy. How dare Schlegels despise Wilcoxes, when it takes all sorts to make a world?" "'Don't brood too much,' she wrote to Helen, 'on the superiority of the unseen to the seen. It's true, but to brood on it is medieval. Our business is not to contrast the two but to reconcile them.'"

Helen did not bother much about what her sister advised her to do or not to do; she was busy herself. "She and the Mosebachs had gone tobogganing on the only hill that Pomerania boasted." Tibby, on the other hand, "had just been up to try for a scholarship at Oxford." As to Margaret, she was bewildered at the chaotic nature of the real life. "Looking back on the past six months, Margaret realized the chaotic nature of our daily life, and its difference from the orderly sequence that has been fabricated by historians. Actual life is full of false clues and signposts that lead nowhere. With infinite effort we nerve ourselves for a crisis that never comes. The most successful career must show a waste of strength that might have removed mountains, and the most unsuccessful is not that of the man who is taken unprepared, but of him who has prepared and is never taken.... Life is indeed dangerous, but not in the way mortality would have us believe. It is indeed unmanageable, but the essence of it is not a battle. It is unmanageable because it is a romance, and its essence is romantic beauty." Perhaps because she understood that life is romantic in its essence, "Margaret hoped that for the future she would be less cautious, not more cautious, than she had been in the past" (section XII).

"Over two years passed, and the Schlegel household continued to lead its life of cultured but not ignoble ease, still swimming gracefully on the gray tides of London." The city of London was then Georgian and fashionable. "One visualizes it as a tract of quivering gray, intelligent without purpose, and excitable without love; as a spirit that has altered before it can be chronicled; as a heart that certainly beats, but with no pulsation of humanity." Mr Wilcox, the 'particular millionaire,' desired to pull down Wickham Place and erect 'babylonian flats' upon it. Tibby was then in his second year at Oxford. One day Tibby asked Margaret why she was not getting married. Margaret told him: "'...I would if I got the chance.'" Tibby jokingly asked her to tell him about her choice of a husband—about her loved ones: "'Tell me about your ninnies, then.'" Margaret only told him that she preferred the Wilcoxes: "'Look at the Wilcoxes, look at Mr Pembroke. With all their defects of temper and understanding, such men give me more pleasure than many who are better equipped, and I think it is because they have worked regularly and honestly.'" To Margaret, people like the Wilcoxes or like Mr Pembroke were 'the right sort.' She commented: "'A nation who can produce men of that sort may well be proud. No wonder England has become an Empire.'" Tibby was arsy-versy to Margaret: she dreamt of a civilisation vibrant with activities while he wanted a 'civilization without activity.'

While Margaret and Tibby were thus debating, Helen barged into the room and told them in a state of excitement: "'A woman's been here asking me for her husband.'" Helen said: "'A perfectly delightful experience...she asked for a husband as if he was an umbrella.'" A light conversation ensued among the three, and at last Margaret expressed her concern about finding a residence from next September: "'Tibby and I have again been wondering where we'll live next September,' she said at last" (section XIII).

Next day Leonard Bast arrived at Wickham Place, and he was cheerfully welcomed by Helen, Margaret and Tibby. Bast "was a clerk in the employment of the Porphyrion Fire Insurance Company." He was "a young man, colourless, toneless, who had already the mournful eyes above drooping moustache that are so common in London, and that haunt some streets of the city like accusing presences. One guessed him as the third generation, grandson to the shepherd or ploughboy whom civilization had sucked into the town; as one of the thousands who have lost the life of the body and failed to reach the life of the spirit. Hints of robustness survived in him, more than a hint of primitive good looks." Helen asked Bast where she did see him last and Bast replied that it was in the Queen's Hall. Bast, in his turn, asked Helen if it was she who had inadvertently taken away his umbrella and she said that she it was and that she was used to stealing umbrellas: "'I steal umbrellas even oftener than I hear Beethoven.'"

Then there followed demonstrations of personal levels of culture and literary excellence among the Schlegels and Leonard Bast, at the end of which the door-bell rang, which meant that a hansom had arrived to take the Schlegels to the appointed evening party. Now the Miss Schlegels were to part with Bast. Helen importuned him: "'do, do come round again and have a talk.'" Margaret almost echoed those words of Helen for him. The two sisters were presumably much impressed by the conversation and cultural awareness of Bast. Now, "London was beginning to illuminate herself against the night. Electric lights sizzled and jagged in the main thoroughfares, gas lamps in the side-streets glimmered a canary gold or green." Leonard Bast was returning home through the nocturnal elegance and romance of London. Really, today he talked with the Schlegels keeping aside his reticence, and he talked very intimately. "To the Schlegels,...he was an interesting creature, of whom they wanted to see more. But they to him were denizens of Romance, who must keep to the corner he had assigned them, pictures that must not walk out of their frames."

The visiting card that Margaret had given Bast when he had been returning from the Beetoven symphony in the Queen's Hall, he used as a flag for a book by Ruskin, that he had been reading, and the card was discovered by his wife Jacky in his absence. When he returned home, Jacky asked him: '"Len [Leonard], who's Miss Schlegel?'" Leonard Bast replied: "'A lady took my umbrella, another gave me this that I might call for my umbrella.'" Mutual misunderstanding between him and her followed. But Bast had some consolation. "That the Schlegels had not thought him foolish became a permanent joy. He was at his best when he thought of them. It buoyed him as he journeyed home beneath fading heavens. Somehow the barriers of wealth [between the Schlegels and himself] had fallen, and there had been—he could not phrase it—a general assertion of the wonder of the world. 'My conviction,' says the mystic, 'gains infinitely the moment another soul will believe in it,' and they had agreed that there was something beyond life's daily gray" (section XIV).

The Schlegels attended the evening party for which that hansom came. The party was organised in a club. The dinner over, an economics-sociological Paper was read out. The reading of the Paper was followed by a debate on the Paper. One speaker in the debate said: "'give people cash, for it is the warp of civilization, whatever the woof may be. The imagination ought to play upon money and realize it vividly, for it's the—the second most important thing in the world.'" He further said that "'independent thoughts are in nine cases out of ten the result of independent means.'" The party came to a close and Helen and Margaret walked a distance, 'arguing copiously all the way.' Once they reached their house, Wickham Place, Helen asked Margaret: if money was the warp of the world, what was the woof of it? Margaret replied that the woof was something that was not money. Their conversation now veered round Wickham Place which they were soon to leave. Margaret now began to think that the woof of the world—the second most important thing in life—was a place of dwelling. She told Helen that for the deceased Mrs Wilcox the woof was certainly Howards End. A moment afterwards Margaret told Helen: "'It is sad to suppose that places may ever be more important than people.'"

The Schlegel sisters were sitting out on Chelsea Embankment, and as they were thus talking, Mr Wilcox came there. "His tone were protective. He implied that one ought not sit out on Chelsea Embankment without a male escort." Margaret was much inspired to see Mr Wilcox; Helen was lukewarm. Margaret said: "'What an age it is since I've seen you, Mr Wilcox.'" Mr Wilcox asked them to tell their news, whereat Helen said: "'We belong to a kind of club that reads pepers, Margaret and I—all women, but there is a discussion after. This evening it was on how one ought to leave one's money—whether to one's family, or to the poor, and if so how—oh, most interesting.'" Mr Wilcox, the 'man of business,' smiled. "Since his wife's death he had almost doubled his income. He was an important figure at last, a reassuring name on company business prospectuses, and life had treated him very well. The world seemed in his grasp as he listened to the river Thames, which still flowed inland from the sea." Mr Wilcox sat between the two sisters. "With a good dinner inside him and an amiable but academic woman on either flank, he felt that his hands were on all the ropes of life." The topic of Leonard Bast was evoked by Margaret. She told Mr Wilcox that Bast was 'evidently very poor,' liked reading books, was adventurous, and had a wife. She asked Mr Wilcox whether it was right to help the poor by advancing a moderate amount of money, or whether the poor would thereby become more poor. And then she asked him point blank: "'Imagine that you were a millionaire and wanted to help the poor. What would you do?'" Mr Wilcox did an Olimpian laugh and said that the poor fellow (Leonard Bast) should immediately leave the concern he had been working in—the Porphyrion Fire Insurance Company—because it was going to sink. But Mr Wilcox did not advise anything about how that poor fellow could find an alternative job, in case he left his present one.

As Mr Wilcox was about to leave the place, Margaret, wishing to change the subject of discussion, asked him: "'And how's Howards End looking?'" He said that they had moved away from that house and it was let out, about a week ago, because it was 'impossibly small' and because there were 'Endless drawbacks' there. Margaret did not agree with him: "'As far as the house, never.'" Mr Wilcox explained why the house had many faults: "'Well, Howards End is one of those converted farms. They don't really do, spend what you will on them.'" Margaret exclaimed: "'What a change!'" She told him: "'I can't imagine Howards End or Hilton without you.'" He said that Charles was then at Hilton and not in Howards End. Margaret was sorry for the house, and she told Mr Wilcox: "'When you moved out of Howards End, I should have moved Mr Charles Wilcox into it. I should have kept so remarkable a place in the family.'" Mr Wilcox told her that Howards End was let out to Hamar Bryce, an invalid, and that he had no intention of selling it. They shook hands, and Mr Wilcox was about to depart when Margaret informed him that they (the Schlegels) were also leaving Wickham Place and moving to somewhere else. Helen also shook hands with him, but with a sense of disgust at him: "'What a prosperous vulgarian Mr Wilcox has grown!'" But she recalled Mr Wilcox's advice for Bast, and she told Margaret that they should write to Bast about Mr Wilcox's advice. She added: "'Let's ask him to tea'" (section XV).

"Leonard (Bast) accepted the invitation to tea next Saturday. But he was right: the visit proved a conspicuous failure." The narrator describes Leonard thus: "As a lady's lap-dog Leonard did not excel. He was not an Indian, still less a Frenchman, in whose blood there runs the very spirit of persiflage and of gracious repartee. His wit was the Cockney's; it opened no doors into imagination." Leonard went to the Schlegels' and was at the tea-table. The Schlegel sisters "were Romance, and so was the room to which he had at last penetrated, with the queer sketches of people bathing upon its walks, and so were the very teacups, with their delicate borders of wild straw-berries. But he would not let Romance interfere with his life." Helen told Leonard Bast that she heard that the Porphyrion, where he worked, was going to sink. Margaret told him that one friend of theirs told them that the Company was not 'sufficiently reinsured.' Bast replied to Margaret with an air of disgust: he told her that she could tell their friend that he was wrong. Nevertheless, Helen told Bast that their friend was also a businessman and that he advised Bast to clear out of Porphyrion. Helen looked more beautiful and lively than Margaret, but the two sisters seemed 'a composite Indian god.' Bast wished to talk about books during that romantic hour, but the two sisters only discussed reinsurance. Just at this moment Mr Wilcox and Miss Wilcox (Evie) arrived 'preceded by two prancing puppies,' Ahab and Jezebel. Leonard's gorge rose and he contemptuously expressed his objection to the presence of Mr Wilcox. Helen tried to persuade him to understand that Mr Wilcox might be of some help to him. At this Leonard burst out: "I don't want your patronage. I don't want your tea. I was quite happy. Why do you want to unsettle me for?'" Margaret tried to propitiate him by saying that she and Helen only wanted to help him, and not to provide him with charity. She told him that they invited him to tea to enjoy with him natural beauty and some freedom from the pressure of life: "'What is the good of your stars and trees, your sunrise and the wind, if they do not enter your daily lives?... haven't we all to struggle against life's grayness, against pettiness, against mechanical cheerfulness, against suspicion?'" Leonard said if there was any misunderstanding, he could better leave the place, and actually he went away.

Mr Wilcox advised the Miss Schlegels to keep away from persons like Leonard Bast, and he expected that they did not like him. But Margaret told him that both she and Helen liked him: "'I do (like Bast). Firstly, because he cares for physical adventure, just as you do. Yes, you go motoring and shooting; he would like to go camping out. Secondly, he cares for something special in adventure. It is quickest to call that special something poetry—.'" Mr Wilcox was told that Bast's wife (Jacky) was a bore, and that for the reason of that Bast needed 'outside interests.' As Margaret was saying all this, Mr Wilcox was emotionally touched by her: "As she spoke their eyes met, and it was as if Mr Wilcox's defences fell. She saw back to the real man in him. Unwittingly she had touched his emotions. A woman and two men—they had formed the magic triangle of sex, and the male was thrilled to jealous, in case the female was attracted by another male. Love, say the ascetics, reveals our shameful kinship with the beasts." The woman was Margaret and the two males were Mr Wilcox and Bast. Now, Mr Wilcox drove away with his dark-eyed, firm-lipped daughter Evie who was soon to get married to Mr Percy Cahill, an uncle of the wife of Charles Wilcox (section XVI).

As expected Wickham Place was pulled down and flats were built on its site by the owner of the house, and, consequently, the Schlegels became nomadic. They were desperately searching for a house. "Margaret grew depressed; she was anxious to settle on a house before they left town to pay their annual visit to Mrs Munt." Mrs Munt lived at Swanage, a dull but stable countryside. Meantime, Margaret received a note from Evie: she and her husband Mr Cahill desired the pleasure of taking lunch with the Schlegels in Simpson's restaurant. During lunch, Margaret said that she wanted a new home by September next. As she was talking to Mr Percy Cahill about her necessity of immediately finding a new home, Margaret pointed out Cahill's 'beautiful aura.' The conversation now veered from a rented house to supernatural phenomena, such as astral planes, astral bodies, and aura. Soon Margaret changed the subject, as it failed to evoke much interest from Cahill, and asked him if he could turn out present tenant of Howards End and let it to them—to the Schlegels. Cahill avoided the point of letting out Howards End to them, but assured Margaret of trying to help them in their search for a house. Margaret told him: "'It's the houses that are mesmerizing me. I've no control over the saucy things. Houses are alive. No?'" Margaret pointed out the unwanted division between the rich and the poor, as she had a socialistic turn of mind. But Cahill told her that the divide between the two classes was irremovable: "'if wealth was divided up equally, in a few years there would be rich and poor again just the same. The hardworking man would come to the top, the wastrel sink to the bottom.'" The lunch over, Margaret took leave, and the Schlegels parted away. "Next morning the

Schlegels left for Swanage. They had not succeeded in finding a new home" (section XVII).

In the country house of Mrs Munt (Aunt Juley), at Swanage at The Bays, the Schlegels and their aunt were sitting at the breakfast-table, all enjoying the view of the bay, when a letter for Margaret came from Mr Wilcox and 'threw her into perturbation.' Mr Wilcox wrote that due to Evie's marriage he had changed his plans. Now he wanted to let his house in Ducie Street on a yearly tenancy. So, if Margaret were interested in that house, she should come to him *at once* (the two words were underlined in the letter), if not 'a wire would oblige.' On reading this, Margaret thought that the letter might be a maneuver of Mr Wilcox of proposing marriage to her. But she was never certain about it, and yet she decided to meet Mr Wilcox. Both Helen and Tibby were against her decision, and so was their aunt Mrs Munt. They did not like the idea of changing houses. Among them, Helen was more vociferous. But Margaret told her: "'I was thinking of father. How could he settle to leave Germany as he did, when he had fought for it as a young man, and all his feelings and friends were Prussian? How could he break loose with patriotism and begin aiming at something else? It would have killed me. When he was nearly forty he could change countries and ideals—and we, at our age, can't change houses. It's humiliating.'"

However, unexpectedly, Mr Wilcox himself met Margaret at Waterloo, without waiting for her coming to him. He told her: "'I've got my work all day—indeed, a great deal too much of it—but when I came home in the evening, I tell you, I can't stand the house.'" Margaret also expressed her grief: "'In my absurd way, I'm lonely too,' Margaret replied. It's heartbreaking to leave one's old home. I scarcely remember anything before Wickham Place, and Helen and Tibby were born there. Helen says—.'" Mr Wilcox wondered that Margaret, too felt lonely. But she refused the offer of the tenancy of a house from him: "'It's no fun helping us, Mr Wilcox, I assure you.'" "Yet she liked being with him. He was not a rebuke, but a stimulus, and banished morbidity. Some twenty years her senior, he preserved a gift that she supposed herself to have already lost—

not youth's creative power, but its self-confidence and optimism. He was sure that it was a very pleasant world. His complexion was robust, his hair had receded but not thinned, the thick moustache and the eyes that Helen had compared to brandy-balls had an agreeable menace in them, whether they were turned towards the slums or towards the stars. Some day—in the millennium—there may be no need for this type. At present, homage is due to it from those who think themselves superior, and who possibly are."

Inspite of Margaret's refusal to accept his offer, Mr Wilcox was not offended. "'At all events you responded to my telegram promptly,' he remarked." He suddenly made another rather off-the-track remark: "'Self denial is all very well as a means of strengthening the character. But I can't stand those people who run down comforts.'" To this remark of Mr Wilcox, Margaret said that comforts were of two kinds: "'those we can share with others, like fire, weather, or music; and those we can't—food, for instance. It depends.'" Mr Wilcox said that he meant reasonable comforts, and when he said this he was about to kiss her. "He did not kiss her, for the hour was half past twelve, and the car was passing by the stables of Buckingham Palace." Margaret was so much charged with emotion at this action of Mr Wilcox that "people only seemed to exist on her account." After a moment Margaret told him that she would talk with Helen and Tibby about his offer of the house when she would get back to Swanage and then wire him 'yes or no'.

They now entered the over-furnished dining-room, where Mr Wilcox told her: "'It's all rubbish not making oneself comfortable.'" Margaret almost agreed with him: "'Ye-es. Semi-rubbish.'" The drawing-room too was very big and heavily decorated, and the bigness and gorgeousness of the room raised in the head of Margaret the question: 'Had Mrs Wilcox's drawing-room looked thus at Howards End?' "Just as this thought entered Margaret's brain, Mr Wilcox did ask her to be his wife, and the knowledge that she had been right [in comparing the two drawing-rooms] so overcome her that she nearly fainted." Mr Wilcox renewed his proposal: "'I am asking you to be my wife.'" "So deep already was her sympathy, that when he said, 'I am asking you to be my wife,' she made herself give a little start. She must show surprise if he expected it. An immense joy came over her." Mr Wilcox asked her: "'You aren't offended. Miss Schlegel?'" Margaret said good-bye to him, and told him that she would send him a letter after going back to Swanage the next day.

"They parted without shaking hands; she had kept the interview, for his sake, in tints of quietest gray. Yet she thrilled with happiness ere she reached her own house. Others had loved her in the past, if one may apply to their brief desires so grave a word, but those others had been 'ninnies'—young men who had nothing to do, old men who could find nobody better. And she had often 'loved,' too, but only so far as the facts of sex demanded: mere yearnings for the masculine, to be dismissed for what they were worth, with a smile. Never before had her personality been touched. She was not young or very rich, and it amazed her that a man of any standing should take her seriously. As she sat trying to do accounts in her empty house, amidst beautiful pictures and noble books, waves of emotion broke, as if a tide of passion was flowing through the night air. She shook her head, tried to concentrate her attention, and failed. In vain did she repeat: 'But I've been through this sort of thing before.' She had never been through it; the big machinery, as opposed to the little, had been set in motion, and the idea that Mr Wilcox loved obsessed her before she came to love him in return." But Margaret did not come to any final decision as to Mr Wilcox's love for her. "She must examine more closely her own nature and his; she must talk it over judicially with Helen." And only then would she take the final decision. But, before she could reach the ultimate decision, "Mrs [Ruth] Wilcox strayed in and out, ever a welcome ghost; surveying the scene, thought Margaret, without one hint of bitterness" (section XVIII).

Frieda Mosebach, now Frau Architect Liesecke, Mrs Munt and Helen climbed up the Purbeck hills to see the beauty of the surround: the valley of the Frome, Clearbury Ring, Bournemouth, Poole Swanage, the valley of Stour, glorious downs, etc.—some with physical eyes and some with the eyes of imagination. Suddenly Helen cried out "'Aunt Juley, wouldn't that be Meg's [Margaret's] train?'" Really, Margaret was returning from Waterloo by that train, along with Tibby. After sometime, Margaret and Tibby were found escaping from within a pony-cart. All the three sight-seeing women shouted at Margaret: "'Have you got the house?'" Before Margaret said anything, Tibby quipped "'Some mystery'" and "'We are to be enlightened presently.'" Margaret came close to Helen and "whispered that she had had a proposal of marriage from Mr Wilcox." Helen was overly glad and remarked about Mr Wilcox that he did something expected of an honest widower and that it was quite right that he had selected as his wife one of his first wife's friends. But almost immediately afterwards Helen burst into tears, and Margaret became stupefied. Helen told her not to marry him: "'Don't, don't do such a thing! I tell you not to—don't! I know—don't!'" Margaret asked: "'What do you know?'" "'Panic and emptiness,' sobbed Helen. 'Don't!'"

Margaret thought that Helen was selfish in asking her not to marry Mr Wilcox. She told Helen that it was just stupidity not to marry him. Helen stopped sobbing, smiled a little, and then asked Margaret: "'Then you love him?'" In reply Margaret told her that Mr Wilcox was a 'real man' who cared for her, and that "'I've known and liked him steadily for nearly three years.'" She asked Helen what her objections were as to her marriage with Mr Wilcox. Helen told her that she abhorred the philosophy of life of the Wilcoxes that she particularly saw in Paul on that very revealing day—the philosophy of counting only the outer life in which 'personal relations' do not matter and in which what matter are money, comfort, telegrams and anger, all sans morality. Margaret did not budge from her stand. She told Helen: "'That's foolish. In the first place, I disagree about the outer life.... The real point is that there is the widest gulf between my love-making and yours. Yours was romance; mine will be prose. I'm not running it down—a very good kind of prose, but well considered, well thought out. For instance, I know all Mr Wilcox's faults. He's afraid of emotion. He cares too much about success, too little about the past. His sympathy lacks poetry, and so isn't sympathy really.'" Margaret concluded: "'spiritually, he's not as honest as I am. Doesn't that satisfy you?'" Helen said it did not satisfy her: "'It makes me feel worse and worse. You must be mad.'" Margaret knew that there were 'heaps of things' in Mr Wilcox that he would not under any pressure divulge before her, but, contrarily, he possessed some 'public qualities' which Helen despised. In support of Mr Wilcox, Margaret continued to argue further before Helen: " 'If Wilcoxes hadn't worked and died in England for thousands of years, you and I couldn't sit here without having our throats cut. There would be no trains, no ships to carry us literary people about in, no fields even. Just savagery. No—perhaps not even that. Without their spirit life might never have moved out of protoplasm'" (section XIX).

Love fructifies into matrimony only after getting clearance from Property, Propriety, Family Pride and Theology. Before getting married, Margaret expected disturbances from these four things, but, she was not irritated. Good humour and not Romance, and confirmation of old relation rather than revealing new ones was to dominate the conjugal life of Margaret and Mr Henry (the narrator cites this name for the first time only at this stage) Wilcox. On these two conditions she promised to marry him. However, Mr Henry Wilcox brought the engagement ring to Swanage to the most joy of both Margaret and her aunt Mrs Munt. This was Margaret's first ever love scene, and she had had a novel experience: "Love was so unlike the article served up in books; the joy, though genuine, was different; the mystery an unexpected mystery. For one thing, Mr Wilcox still seemed a stranger." However, Margaret and Henry Wilcox talked about divers things: about Calamata, the currant farm where they could possibly go for honeymoon; about Evie's proposed marriage with Dolly's uncle Percy Cahill; about Charles' possessing Howards End in course of time; about how much was Henry's income; about how Henry was going to distribute his wealth among his sons and daughter and wife; etc. Then Margaret suggested that after their marriage they might live in Howards End, but Henry told her that the house had already been let to Hamar Bryce last March on a three years' agreement.

Mr Henry Wilcox was behaving masterly with Margaret, but that did not result in any jarring between the two. "A younger woman might have resented his masterly ways, but Margaret had too firm a grip on life to make a fuss. She was, in her own way, as masterly." She was rather "penetrating to the depths of his soul, and approving of what she found there." "And if insight were sufficient, if the inner life were the whole of life, their happiness had been assured." They were now walking up by the side path. Suddenly Mr Wilcox threw down his cigar, and "took her in his arms." "She was startled, and nearly screamed, but recovered herself at once, and kissed with genuine love the lips that were pressed against her own. It was their first kiss, and when it was over he saw her safely to the door and rang the bell for her, but disappeared into the night before the maid answered it. On looking back, the incident displeased her. It was so isolated. Nothing in their previous conversation had heralded it, and, worse still, no tenderness had ensued. If a man cannot lead up to passion he can at all events lead down from it, and she had hoped, after her complaisance, for some interchange of gentle words. But he had hurried away as if ashamed, and for an instant she was reminded of Helen and Paul" (section XX).

The news that Margaret and Mr Wilcox are going to get married to each other had reached Charles and Dolly at their home in Hilton, but not Paul. Charles thought that as long as Evie was there to look after his father, his father would not even dream of marrying the second time. He told Dolly, who was fondling her baby: "'Miss Schlegel [Margaret] always meant to get hold of Howards End, and, thanks to you, she's got it.'" Charles wrongly believed that Dolly was to some extent instrumental in making the match. He, therefore, scolded her: "'Who asked him [Mr Wilcox] while I was away? Who asked my sister down to meet him? Who sent them out in the motor day after day?'" Charles simply fumed at Margaret: "'I could simply scratch that woman's eyes out, and to say it's my fault is most unfair.'" He thundered: "'Taking my mother's place! Heaven knows what poor old Paul will say when the news reaches him'" (section XXI).

The day after the day on which Charles expressed his uncontainable anger against Mr Wilcox, Margaret greeted her future husband with 'peculiar tenderness.' She thought that she would be able to connect the prose of Mr Wilcox and her passion with a 'rainbow bridge.' Without such a connecting bridge between prose and passion "we are meaningless fragments, half monks, half beasts, unconnected arches that have never joined into a man. With it love is born, and alights on the highest curve, glowing against the gray, sober against the fire. Happy the man who sees from either aspect the glory of those outspread wings. The roads of his soul lie clear, and he and his friends shall find easy going." But the road of the soul of Mr Wilcox was not clear, and he did never look inside his soul—he rather believed that 'bodily passion is bad.' "He could not be as the saints and love the Infinite with a seraphic ardour, but he could be a little ashamed of loving a wife.... And it was here that Margaret hoped to help him." And "It did not seem so difficult. She needed trouble him with no gift of her own. She would only point out the salvation that was latent in his own soul, and in the soul of every man. Only connect! That was the whole of her sermon. Only connect the prose and the passion, and both will be exalted, and human love will be seen at its highest. Live in fragments no longer. Only connect, and the beast and the monk, robbed of their isolation that is life to either, will die."

But Margaret failed in her endeavour, in her objective, just due to Mr Wilcox's 'obtuseness.' He told her: "'My motto is Concentrate. I've no intention of frittering away my strength on that sort of thing.'" Margaret protested: she said that instead of concentrating one should enlarge his space by connecting prose with passion. But Mr Wilcox stuck to his stand. Now Helen appeared before them; she had been ominously quiet since Margaret settled to marry Mr Wilcox. Margaret told him that Helen had got a nice letter from Bast, but as Margaret was now ready to marry him, he was quite indifferent to Bast—"the triangle of sex was broken for ever." Mr Wilcox said that Bryce, who was the tenant of Howards End, was ordered abroad and so was leaving Howards End, and that in the circumstance he had been thinking of letting the house anew. Mr Wilcox proposed to Margaret to go to Charles' house and take lunch with his family. Margaret heard of a prejudice about the wych-elm near the house: "'Aren't there pig's teeth in the wych-elm?'" She heard that if one did chew the bark of the wych-elm with pig's teeth nailed into it he would get relief from toothache. Mr Wilcox quited off her notion as a 'rum notion.' But she was not to part with her prejudices: "'Perhaps I have confused it with some other tree. There are still a great number of sacred trees in England, it seems.'"

Helen asked if the Porphyrion Fire Insurance Company was really going to be smashed, and Mr Wilcox told her that it was not. Helen again asked if in that case Bast should not have left it, and got the reply that he should not. She tried to make him understand that Bast had been a poor clerk, and his unsympathetic response was that life was a battle and so the poor clerk should fight in it. Helen now became hard and told him that the poor were so because of the rich like them. Mr Wilcox actually could not recall Bast, and so Helen said: "'We have told you about the fellow [Bast] twice already.'" She said: "'You have even met the fellow. He is very poor and his wife is an extravagant imbecile. He is capable of better things. We—we, the upper classes—thought we would help him from the height of our superior knowledge—and here's the result!'" Mr Wilcox told Helen: "'A word of advice. Don't take up that sentimental attitude over the poor. See she doesn't, Margaret. The poor are poor, and one's sorry for them, but there it is. As civilization moves forward, the shoe is bound to pinch in places, and it's absurd to pretend that anyone is responsible personally. Neither you, nor I, nor my informant, nor the man who informed him, nor the directors of the Porphyrion, are to blame for this clerk's [Bast's] loss of salary. It's just the shoe pinching—no one can help it; and it might easily have been worse.'" Helen was quivering with indignation, and, yet Mr Wilcox continued: "'By all means subscribe to charities—subscribe to them largely—but don't get carried away by absurd schemes of Social Reform. I see a good deal behind the scenes, and you can take it from me that there is no Social Question—except for a few journalists who try to get a living out of the phrase. There are just rich and poor, as there always have been and always will be.'" He also told her that the division between the rich and the poor was done by 'impersonal forces' and that 'the tendency of civilization has on the whole been upward.' Helen sneeringly said that all that was due to God, perhaps. She told him: "'You grab the dollars. God does the rest.'"

Helen was speaking of God 'in that neurotic modern way.' Margaret asked her not to discuss political economy with Mr Henry Wilcox. But Helen could not contain herself; she continued to talk political economy. She said about Mr Wilcox and the poor like Bast: "'I don't like those men. They are scientific themselves, and talk of the survival of the fittest, and cut down the salaries of their clerks, and stunt the independence of all who may menace their comfort, but yet they believe that somehow good—it is always that sloppy 'somehow'—will be the outcome, and that in some mystic way the Mr Basts of the future will benefit because the Mr Basts of today are in pain.'" Margaret and Helen were to see the family of Charles and so to leave Swanage early next week. Mrs Munt knew this from Margaret. After so much of political economy, Mr Wilcox joined Margaret. "A wave of tenderness came over her. "She put a hand on either shoulder of Mr Wilcox and looked deeply into his black, bright eyes, and gazed at the 'competent stare' of his eyes. "What was behind their competent stare? She knew, but was not disquieted" (section XXII).

The evening before she left Swanage, Margaret scolded Helen not for disapproving her marriage with Mr Wilcox "but for throwing over her disapproval a veil of mystery." "Helen in those days was over interested in the subconscious self. She exaggerated the Punch and Judy aspect of life and spoke of mankind as puppets, whom an invisible showman twitches into love and war." After the scolding, the irate Helen told

Margaret: "'Go on and marry him.'" Helen told her that there had certainly been an affair between herself and Paul, but she said: "'I can only entice and be enticed.... If I marry, it will either be a man who's strong enough to boss me or whom I'm strong enough to boss. So I shan't marry, for there aren't such men.... But you, you're different; you're a heroine.'" Margaret wandered. Helen did not stop but continued: "'Henceforward I'm going my own way...I mean to dislike your husband, and to tell him so...I mean to love *you* more than ever. Yes, I do. You and I have built up something real, because it is purely spiritual. There's no veil of mystery over us. Unreality and mystery begin as soon as on touches the body. The popular view is, as usual, exactly the wrong one. Our bothers are over tangible things—money, husband, house-hunting.'" Helen was perhaps right: "The businessman who assumes that this life is everything, and the mystic who asserts that it is nothing, fail, on this side and on that, to hit the truth." Margaret had to do her packing, and so Helen calmed down and assured Margaret that though she disliked Mr Wilcox, she would do everything she could for him. Margaret was contented.

Next morning, at eleven o'clock, Margaret presented herself before Mr Wilcox in his Imperial and West African Rubber Company office in London. She enjoyed her being there and for the first time felt shy. Mr Wilcox had earlier called Charles by ringing the bell to meet his future stepmother and Charles obeyed. After some time Mr Wilcox boarded a car with Margaret and ordered Crane, the chauffeur to go to Mr Wilcox's house in Hilton, in the meditative Hertfordshire. Dolly, dressed upto the nines, had been standing at the gate to receive them. During lunch they discussed Bryce, the outgoing tenant of Howards End, with all derision, and after lunch Mr Wilcox asked Margaret to kiss the two kids of Dolly, but she did not, as she did not like children. After all this, they—Margaret and Mr Wilcox—again took the car and Crane drove it to a country house of Mr Wilcox, but the house was locked. Mr Wilcox forgot to bring with him the key, and so he told Margaret to wait there in the dry, as it was raining heavily, and that he would be back in a huff with the key. The car again moved away, and a very beautiful pastoral panorama opened before the eyes of Margaret, which Helen once described to her. A cow was menacing her, and so she went near the door of the house and laid her hand on it, and the door opened—it was, in fact, not locked.

There was no human response, obviously because Mr Bryce, the tenant, left the house without any intimation to Mr Wilcox. Margaret took a fancy to enter into the house—Howards End—and she entered into it. She was greeted by five empty rooms and a drawing-room and a dining-room. There were a flowering garden in the backyard and a 'hint of the meadow' in the little distance. "She remembered again that ten square miles are not ten times as wonderful as one square mile, that a thousand square miles are not practically the same as heaven. The phantom of bigness, which London encourages, was laid for ever when she paced from the hall at Howards End to its kitchen and heard the rains run this way and that where the watershed of the roof divided them." As she was pacing, the house reverberated, and Margaret enquired: "'Is that you, Honey?'" There was none to answer: imagination was working on her—"starved imagination, not the well-nourished." She now opened the door to the stairs, and an intense noise seemed to deafen her, and she saw an old woman descending, and the old woman exclaimed at herself: "'Oh! Well, I took you for Ruth Wilcox.'" "Margaret stammered: "'I—Mrs Wilcox—I?'" "'In fancy, of course—in fancy. You had her way of walking. Good day.'" "And the old woman passed out into the rain" (section XXIII)

Mr Wilcox came back, and hearing everything told Margaret that the old woman was 'silly old Miss Avery', one of the crew of his farm, who frightened her. Margaret said she only startled her. Dolly asked Margaret if she took Avery for a spook, and Margaret said, "'Not exactly.'" Howards End got its name from Tom Howard—the last of the Howards. Dolly, therefore, cried: "'I say! Howards End—Howards Ended!'" Mr Wilcox said that he had to be back in London by seven, and so Margaret, once again, lost her sense of space and regained her sense of flux that dwelt in London and in

Wickham Place. She was now to forget, at the least for a time, the bucolic beauty of the surround of Howards End.

Before she was to lose all these things of her desire that was newly born in her, by going back to London with her future husband, her future husband showed the different corners and aspects of his property there. Mr Wilcox, her future husband, grumbled that more money had not been invested in the property and so it had not increased four or five times in valuation. Margaret "saw two women as he [Mr Wilcox] spoke, one old, the other young, watching their inheritance melt away. She saw them greet him as a deliverer." Mr Wilcox explained to her that the days of small farms had been over, and that "'nothing pays on a small scale.'" In the nearby Common oaks had been being ruined, but Mr Wilcox saved the remaining oaks 'without fine feelings or deep insight.' He said that when he acquired more control over Howards End, he made structural changes in it. They entered the garden, and to Mr Wilcox's surprise, there was really pig's teeth in the bark of the wych-elm tree. He asked Margaret: "'Who told you?'" "'I heard of it one winter in London,' was her answer, for she, too, avoided mentioning Mrs Wilcox by name" (section XXIV).

Evie was also offended at her father's decision to marry Margaret, and thought of baulking the marriage, for, she thought, it was an "insult to their mother's memory." She, being only eighteen, childlikely thought of "returning Mrs Wilcox's lace and jewellery 'as a protest'." Dolly suggested that Evie and Uncle Percy "should pretend to break off their engagement, and then perhaps Mr Wilcox would quarrel with Miss Schlegel, and break off his." But as no scheme of theirs in the end materialised, Evie's banns were duly published in the church. Evie wanted her marriage to be held not in the town but in the country, preferably at Oniton. Invitation letters were sent. Helen refused the invitation, and Tibby did not even respond to the invitation. However, Margaret took the Great Western express to reach Mr Wilcox's house, which had been a castle, at Oniton. With her were also other guests of Evie's wedding, such as Mrs Warrington, her daughter Myra,

Mr Fussell, Albert and Angelo. On the way to Oniton, she landed at Shropshire and was received by Charles. Charles took the guests in his car and drove away, but as the car moved about a hundred yards it dashed against a dog. Margaret got angry and demanded she be taken back, but Charles took no notice of her protest and continued to drive away. She, angered more than before, stood up in the car and jumped out of it, as the car was moving slowly. "She fell on her knees, cut her gloves, shook her hat over her ear. Cries of alarm followed her. 'You've hurt yourself,' exclaimed Charles, jumping after her." He told her: "'Your hand's bleeding.'" Margaret curtly said: "'I know.'" In the hotel at Oniton, Mr Wilcox, in evening dress, was waiting to welcome the guests. When Charles' car reached the hotel, Mr Wilcox accompanied Margaret inside the hotel and asked her to change.

In the evening, which was inordinately exquisite, Charles had been thinking that Margaret would disgrace his father and so he was depressed. To ward off his depression, he "strolled out on to the castle mound to think the matter over." There he saw Margaret walking on to the nearby meadow and "thought that she was in love with him, and had come out to tempt him." But, he was wrong. Margaret accosted Charles and, laughing in the darkness, told him: "I love this place, I love Shropshire. I hate London. I am glad that this will be my home." And, walking back to the castle, ejaculated: "'what a comfort to have arrived!'" (section XXV).

Next morning the weather was fine and the outline of the castle mound grew clearer, and Margaret noticed this and was thrilled. "Margaret was fascinated by Oniton. She had said that she loved it, but it was rather its romantic tension that held her.... The house was insignificant, but the prospect from it would be an eternal joy, and she thought of all the friends she would have to stop in it, and of the conversion of Henry himself to a rural life." Margaret was day-dreaming about her happy life with Henry (Wilcox) in Oniton: "Love is the best, and the more she let herself love him the more chance was there that he would set his soul in order.... Each lift of his eyes, each parting of the thatched lip from the clean-shaven, must prelude the tenderness that kills the monk and the beast at a single blow. Disappointed a hundred times, she still hoped. She loved him with too clear a vision to fear his cloudiness. Whether he droned trivialities,... or sprang kisses on her in the twilight, she could pardon him, she could respond." The 'genuine country house' that Oniton was attracted her insuperably.

Margaret dressed up to witness the marriage ceremony of Evie. The ceremony seemed a small affair. "Everything went like one o'clock. Mr Cahill materialised out of space, and was waiting for his bride at the church door. No one dropped the ring or mispronounced the responses, or trod on Evie's train, or cried. In a few minutes the clergymen performed their duty, the register was signed, and they were back in their carriages, negotiating the dangerous curve by the lych-gate. Margaret was convinced that they had not been married at all, and that the Norman church had been intent all the time on other business." After the ceremony was over, the bride and bridegroom drove off, and 'Henry who was more tired than he owned, came up to her [Margaret] in the castle meadow, and, in tones of unusual softness, said that he was pleased." Margaret told him: "'Let's be married from off Curzon Street.'"

Margaret saw a group of persons approaching them, among which was Helen. Helen shouted out that all of the family of Leonard Bast were starving, and pointed her accusing finger towards Margaret and Mr Wilcox. She told about Bast: "'He has lost his place. He has been turned out of his bank. Yes, he's done for. We upper classes have ruined him, and I suppose you'll tell me it's the battle of life. Starving. His wife is ill. Starving. She fainted in the train.'" Margaret said: "'Helen, are you mad?'" But Helen did not cease: "'Perhaps. Yes. If you like, I'm mad. But I have brought them. I'll stand injustice no longer. I'll show up the wretchedness that lies under this luxury, this talk of impersonal forces, this cant about God doing what we're too slack to do ourselves.'" Helen had brought Bast and his wife Jacky from London to Shropshire to show Margaret and Mr Wilcox their very wretched condition after Bast left his job at the bank under the apparently friendly advice of Mr Wilcox. Bast and Jacky shook hands with Margaret and Mr Wilcox. Jacky was as stupid and shy as her husband. Helen told Mr Wilcox and Margaret that Bast was penniless and that for that "'we and our informant [who had told us that the bank, Dempster's Bank, in which Bast had been serving had been going to crash] are directly to blame.'"

Margaret's advice to Bast at that moment was simply cruel: "'I can only advise you to go at once. My sister has put you in a false position, and it is kindest to tell you so. It's too late to get to town, but you'll find a comfortable hotel in Oniton, where Mrs Bast can rest, and I hope you'll be my guests there.'" Bast told her: "'That isn't what I want'," and Helen told her that he only needed work. Margaret then very conventionally told Bast that they would like to find some work for him, and again told him to go to a hotel and take rest. Bast said that rich people might find new jobs once their jobs are lost, but the poor, like him, were unfortunate. He added: "'There always will be rich and poor.'" Margaret suddenly changed and told her sister: "'Helen, I like Mr Bast. I agree that he is worth helping. I agree that we are directly responsible.'" Margaret assured her that she would try to convince Mr Wilcox to come out to help Bast. Helen told her that it was a duty on the part of Mr Wilcox to help Bast. Margaret then met her Henry (Wilcox) and pleaded for Bast, and Henry promptly gave her word that he would try for Bast. Margaret won over Mr Wilcox 'by the method of the harem'.

Mrs Bast was still in the garden, as she was left there by her husband and Helen. Margaret and Henry Wilcox went there and met her. Margaret found her repellent; perhaps Mrs Bast was drunk. Now that Margaret was going to marry him, Henry 'discountenanced risque conversations' with Mrs Bast. He went to Mrs Bast, who "raised her face, which gleamed in the twilight like a puff-ball." Mr Wilcox addressed Mrs Bast as 'Madam,' and she called him by his first name—Henry—for which Mr Wilcox felt much annoyed and was about to go away when, from behind, Mrs Bast (Jacky) called him: "'Hen, don't go. You do love me, dear, don't you?'" Margaret was beside herself in astonishment and exclaimed: "'Bless us, what a person!'" But Jacky, i.e. Mrs Bast remained unfezzed, and, yawning, told Mr Wilcox: "'You're a nice boy, you are'" and "'There now I love you.'" Margaret told Mr Wilcox: "'Henry, I am awfully sorry.'" She asked him: "'Why does she call you "Hen"?'" She also asked him whether Mrs Bast had ever before seen him. Before Wilcox could say anything, Jacky hinted to Margaret that many women had earlier known him. Margaret was frightened and Henry "saw his whole life crumbling."

Mr Wilcox was trying to wash his hands of all blames related to Jacky by using a ploy. He said that Margaret used this trick to trap him, but she told him that it was actually Helen who was behind this drama. But, ultimately, Mr Wilcox gave in to Margaret. He told her: "'You are quite right—it was necessary. I am a man, and have lived a man's past. I have the honour to release you from your engagement.'" All the guests of Evie's marriage ceremony returned home. And then Margaret asked Mr Wilcox: "'So that woman has been your mistress?'" and "'When, please?'" Mr Wilcox curtly replied: "'Ten years ago.'" "She left him without a word. For it was not her tragedy: it was Mr Wilcox's" (section XXVI).

Helen and Bast were left in the Shropshire hotel for the night. She told him that the Wilcoxes were on the wrong tack, surely. She said: "'There's a nightmare of a theory that says a special race is being born which will rule the rest of us in the future just because it lacks the little thing that says "I".'" Bast could not follow her, and so she further said: "'there are two kinds of people—our kind, who live straight from the middle of their heads, and the other kind who can't, because their heads have no middle.... They can't say "I." They *aren't* in fact, and so they are supermen.'" Bast suggested that such people must be egoists apropos of Nietzsche's philosophy. But Helen said that they were never supermen. She said: "'No superman ever said "I want," because "I want" must lead to the question, "Who am I?" and so to Pity and to Justice. He only says "want." "Want Europe" if he's Napoleon; "want wives" if he's Bluebeard; "want Botticelli" if he's Pierpont Morgan. Never the "I;" and if you could pierce through him you'd find panic and emptiness in the middle.'" Bast asked her: '"May I take it, Miss Schlegel, that you and I are both the sort that say "I"?'" Helen said: "'Of course.'" Bast further asked of her if Margaret too was of that sort and Helen said that Margaret also was of that sort.

Helen then changed the subject of their conversation by asking him what kind of woman his wife was. Bast blushed and she understood. She told him: "'Don't pretend your marriage has been a happy one. You and she can have nothing in common.'" Bast told her about his relation with his wife: "'I needn't have married her, but as I have I must stick to her and keep her.'" Helen knew from him that he married his wife, Jacky, nearly three years ago. She also learnt from him that "His parents, who were dead, had been in trade; his sisters married commercial travellers; his brother was a lay-reader." Bast's grandparents, he said shamefacedly, were 'agricultural labourers and that sort.' Helen did not blame Jacky for Bast's poverty but the society. Bast told her that he now fairly understood that money was *sine qua non* of life—'one must have money.' He told her that "'the real thing's money, and all the rest is a dream.'" Helen was rather irritated at this remark of his. She said that money was not everything because there was Death too, and she justified the phenomenon of Death, because Death destroys the overlordship of money and reveals the truth that the soul depends upon nothing else but on itself, that we are what we are: "'Injustice and greed would be the real things if we lived for ever. As it is, we must hold to other things, because Death is coming.... Death and money are the eternal foes. Not Death and Life. Never mind what lies behind Death. Mr Bast, but be sure that the poet and the musician and the tramp will be happier in it than the man who has never learned to say: "I am I."'" Helen meant to say that only those people who identify themselves with money or wealth are so much afraid of death. "'Death destroys man; the idea of Death saves him.' Behind the coffins and the skeletons that stay the vulgar mind lies something so immense that all that is great in us responds to it. Men of the world may recoil from the charnel house that they will enter, but Love knows better. Death is his foe, but his peer, and in their age-long struggle the thews of Love have been strengthened, and his vision cleared, until there is no one who can stand against him." Therefore Helen asked Bast not to 'give in' but to stand erect, because "the Invisible lodges against the Visible." Bast was imbued with the unearthly spirit provided by Helen. "Presently the waitress entered and gave her a letter from Margaret. Another note, addressed to Leonard, was inside. They read them, listening to the murmurings of the river" (section XXVII).

The matter of Mr Wilcox's relation with Jacky, i.e. Mrs Bast, so disturbed Margaret that she could do nothing for a couple of hours. Then she tried to write a letter or note to Mr Wilcox but she did not succeed because of the contrariness within her mind: once she thought that Mr Wilcox degraded himself by yielding to the temptation of that lowly woman—Jacky; but the next moment she thought that men must be different from womenfolk, with their particular code of morality. "Are the sexes really races, each with its own code of morality, and their mutual love a mere device of Nature's to keep things going? Strip human intercourse of the properties, and is it reduced to this? Her judgement told her no. She knew that out of Nature's device we have built a magic that will win us immortality. Far more mysterious than the call of sex to sex is the tenderness that we throw into that call.... We are evolving, in ways that Science cannot measure, to ends that Theology dares not contemplate." For the moment Margaret thought of Evie's marriage with Mr Cahill as a 'carnival of fools' and thought of her own imminent marriage as 'too miserable.' She then tore up the letter, and wrote up the following one:

Dear Mr Bast,

I have spoken to Mr Wilcox about you, as I promised, and am sorry to say that he has no vacancy for you.

Yours truly,

M.J. Schlegel.

And in a note, accompanying the letter, Margaret wrote to Helen: *Give him* [Bast] *this* [letter]. *The Basts are no good. Henry found the woman drunk on the lawn.... The Basts are not at all the type we should trouble about.*

Margaret could not easily wipe off the images where Mrs Bast (Jacky) and Henry were conjoined. She thought that Henry laid bare before Jacky "his intellectual confusion, his obtuseness to personal influence, his strong but furtive passions. Should she refuse him because his outer life corresponded?" She struggled against herself, but "Pity was at the bottom of her actions all through this crisis." Ultimately she decided that "Henry must be forgiven, and made better by love; nothing else mattered." And sticking to this decision, she went to sleep (section XXVIII).

When in her spare moment Margaret met Mr Wilcox, he frankly repeated that he had released her from her engagement with him, because, he told her, he was not worthy of her. Margaret kissed his hand, but he jerked it from her and told her that she, being a woman, could hardly "guess the temptations that lie round a man." She said that it was certainly difficult to guess the temptations of a man, but in case a woman was going to marry him, she must guess. Margaret "knew that Henry was not so much confessing his soul as pointing out the gulf between the male soul and the female." After a while, Henry "came and sat down near her, improvising emotion. She could not bear to listen to him." Henry told her that even the strongest man at least once in his life time comes to grief, like himself. He told her: "'If you knew all, you would excuse me. I was far from good influences—far even from England. I was very, very lonely, and longed for a woman's voice. That's enough. I have told you too much already for you to forgive me now.'" And then bit by bit he told her the story of his corruption, and then Margaret told him: "'I have already forgiven you, Henry.'" At this moment the butler came to clear the breakfast table. "Margaret looked intently at the butler. He, as a handsome young man, was faintly attractive to her as a woman—an attraction so faint as scarcely to be perceptible, yet the skies would have fallen if she had mentioned it to Henry."

Henry asked her: "'Would you like one turn in the garden?'" She consented and took his arm, when the beautiful weather soothed her. He now told her: "'I am far from a saint—in fact, the reverse—but you have taken me, for better or worse. Bygones must be bygones. You have promised to forgive me. Margaret, a promise is a promise. Never mention that woman again.'" He asked her not to worry about the matter as "'This is a man's business.'" And Margaret forgave him. Her only worry now was, though Charles, Evie and Paul were not in the know of it, her sister Helen had heard something of the matter of Henry and Mrs Bast (Jacky) (section XXIX).

Tibby "was now approaching his last year at Oxford." He did never show any interest in economic classes, like Helen, but engrossed himself in modern literature, and Chinese, particularly, to qualify as a Student Interpreter. Helen made a bee-line from Oniton to Tibby at Oxford, immediately after knowing about Mr Wilcox's relation with Mrs Bast and receiving Margaret's letter to herself to the effect that Mr Wilcox was not doing anything for Leonard Bast. She told Tibby that she was overly annoyed and exasperated, and that therefore she was going either to Munich or to Bonn. Helen burst into tears and told Tibby about Mr Wilcox whom Margaret (Meg) was going to marry: "Meg cannot have heard it yet. But I cannot face her and tell her that the man she is going to marry has misconducted himself" Tibby guessed the man had a mistress. Helen told him that the man (Mr Wilcox) had gone to Cyprus 'to get rich' and there he fell into the trap of the loose woman, Jacky. Jacky, as it generally happens to such woman, later on button-holed Bast to marry her. Helen also told Tibby that Mr Bast should be compensated for the ill luck that had been brought over him. Informing Tibby of all these, she asked for his opinion. Tibby told her: "'Let them (Margaret and Mr Wilcox) marry. There remains the question of compensation.'"

Helen took it upon herself to do the compensation; she decided to give the Basts five hundred pounds, of which one hundred pounds were to be sent immediately without telling anybody about this. And then she went abroad. The cheque that Tibby had sent to Bast was returned, and then Tibby sent the unaccepted cheque to Helen's foreign address, "adding in the fullness of his heart that Leonard Bast seemed somewhat a monumental person after all." She frantically wrote to him to go to Bast immediately and tell him that she 'commanded' him (Bast) to accept the money given him by her. During this time, Helen reinvested her money and, "owing to the good advice of her stockbrokers, became rather richer than she had been before" (section XXX).

Having been constrained to leave Wickham Place, the Schlegels were offered Howards End, which was cleared after the death of its incumbent tenant Mr Bryce abroad, by Mr Wilcox. "Until he re-let the house, the Schlegels were welcome to stack their furniture in the garage and lower rooms. Margaret demurred, but Tibby accepted the offer gladly; it saved him from coming to any decision about the future." "Shortly before the move, our hero and heroine [Margaret and Mr. Wilcox] were married." They were married quietly; only Charles and Mr Cahill, among the near ones, were present. Paul only sent a cablegram. "In a few minutes, and without the aid of music, the clergyman made them man and wife." "She, a monogamist, regretted the cessation of some of life's innocent odours; he, whose instincts were polygamous, felt morally braced by the change, and less liable to the temptations that had assailed him in the past."

Their honeymoon was observed near Innsbruck. There Margaret thought of meeting Helen, but Helen showed only apathy to them, and this inflicted pain in her heart. Yet, Margaret wrote to her pointing out "the need of charity in sexual matters." However, Margaret proved to be lively, intelligent and submissive, and Mr Wilcox "kept himself worthier of her." He had, besides the Jacky episode, another germane episode which took place in the days of his bachelorhood. And for these two cursed episodes he was 'heartily sorry.' Poor Ruth Wilcox, alas, could not delve deep into the reality of Mr Wilcox's character! However, Mr Wilcox's "affection for his present wife grew steadily. Her cleverness gave him no trouble, and, indeed, he liked to see her reading poetry or something about social questions; it distinguished her from the wives of other men." At times he would enjoy fighting mock battles with her—verbal battles or other things like those.

During the honeymoon, Mr Wilcox told her that Oniton Grange was let out, and this displeased her. She had been searching for a permanent home of her own. Even marriage "had not saved her from the sense of flux." She now hated London which gave her a taste of the nomadic civilization; she now liked the country, and loved nature, that moulds character. Mr Wilcox suggested to her putting up in the house in Ducie Street during the winter, and think of somewhere else in the spring. Margaret became impatient. She told him: "'If possible, something permanent. I can't be as young as I was, for these alterations don't suit me.'" In the end, Ducie Street was her first fate after marriage—'a pleasant enough fate', the house being a little larger than Wickham Place. Margaret did not altogether forget the Basts, and she even liked to help them, but being Mr Wilcox's wife she preferred to help someone else. After her marriage she certainly changed a lot; and "perhaps some deep instinct did warn her not to travel further from her husband than was inevitable" (section XXXI).

One day, the following spring, Margaret was looking at the plans of their house to be built in Sussex when Dolly, i.e. Mrs Charles Wilcox, who went to meet her, was announced. Margaret warmly greeted her, and from her learnt that Helen had been staying in the Continent for eight months then and that she left for the Continent just after Evie's marriage. Margaret came to know from Dolly that the family of Charles Wilcox was in a financially straitened condition with Dolly giving birth to a number of kids. Dolly told her that Miss Avery had been unpacking Margaret's packing-cases that she left with the Charleses at the time of leaving Wickham Place. Margaret did not like that her packing-cases were unpacked, particularly lest Tibby's books were harmed. So "With Henry's permission, she wrote a pleasant note to Miss Avery, asking her to leave the cases untouched." Then at her first convenient opportunity she herself went down to Howards End to repack her belongings. "So, for the second time in her life, she entered the house [Howards End] alone" (section XXXII).

"The day of her visit was exquisite, and the last of unclouded happiness that she was to have for many months. Her anxiety about Helen's extraordinary absence was still dormant, and as for a possible brush with Miss Avery—that only gave zest to the expedition." Margaret first went to the low brick farm house, not far from Howards End, and there she was received by Miss Avery's niece who told her to accompany her to Howards End and then went inside to bring her hat. Standing there on the outskirt of the farm, Margaret fully felt the beauty of the countryside—the beauty that she never enjoyed in the town. The narrator here tries to show us the salubrity of the English countryside: "In these English farms, if anywhere, one might see life steadily and see it whole, group in one vision its transitoriness and its eternal youth, connect—connect without bitterness until all men are brothers."

Along with Miss Avery's niece, Margaret reached Howards End, which its tenant Mr Bryce left behind before dying on a foreign shore and which was being looked after by Miss Avery. After calling Miss Avery several times from without, Margaret was introduced inside the house by Miss Avery herself. Margaret was appalled finding her bookcases used as items of decoration of the inside of the house. Miss Avery told her that the deceased Mrs Wilcox did never allow the house to remain empty and so she filled the house with her bookcases. Margaret commented that the deceased Mrs Wilcox's brain must have been poor and decaying for that. Margaret told her: "'We have settled to build a new home for ourselves in Sussex, and part of this furniture—my part—will go down there presently.'" But Miss Avery told her: "'You think that you won't come back to live here, Mrs Wilcox, but you will'" (section XXXIII).

Aunt Juley's (Mrs Munt's) health sharply deteriorated and soon she succumbed to death. Helen had been apprised of the critical health of Aunt Juley and had been asked to come to Swanage to see her aunt perhaps for the last time, but she had written back from Munich that she would not be able to stop for long at Swanage but would be back to Germany at the earliest. Margaret was offended as well as depressed at this reaction of Helen. Henry discovered the growth of morbidity in Margaret, and she fancied that she could trace the growth of her morbidity in the unexpected and wayward changes in Helen's life during four years in the recent past: "The flight from Oniton; the unbalanced patronage of the Basts; the explosion of grief up on the downs—all connected with Paul [Wilcox], an insignificant boy whose lips had kissed hers for a fraction of time." Margaret and Mrs Wilcox had suspected that they might kiss again.

Helen did not come to Swanage to see her aunt, instead a letter of hers arrived from Munich: *Dearest Meg, Give Helen's love to Aunt Juley. Tell her that I love and have loved her ever since I can remember.... My address will be care of the bankers...write or wire to me there and give me detailed news...you must not think it odd if I do not come.... I am living abroad at present, and want to get back as quickly as possible. Will you please tell me where my furniture is. I should like to take out one or two books; the rest are for you.* Margaret was highly annoyed by this letter and consulted Henry about Helen's madness, Charles keeping at a bay from their concerns. At last, under the advice of Henry, Margaret planned to lay a bait before Helen for catching her. She wrote a letter, full of falsehood, to Helen. She wrote that "the furniture was all at Howards End, but could be seen on Monday next at 3.0 p.m., when a charwoman would be in attendance." "Helen would think she was offended. And on Monday next she [Margaret] and Henry were to lunch with Dolly, and then ambush themselves in the garden." Margaret's plan was apt: Helen might have come back, for her share of the furniture, if not to herself then to Howards End—to Charles and Dolly—where she might catch hold of her (section XXXIV).

Helen really came back to Howards End, which was under locks and keys, and the keys of the house were in the hand of Margaret. The arrival of Helen was reported to Margaret, who took a car and went to Howards End with Henry. As she could not enter Howards End, because it was locked, Helen was sitting in the porch with her back to the road. Margaret and Henry got down from the car and approached Helen. The most important thing that Margaret heard from Helen was that she was carrying. Margaret then whispered to her: "'Oh, my darling—'" She was not displeased (section XXXV).

Henry had earlier brought in a doctor for Helen (who had been carrying a child of Bast—the child that was the result of her sleeping with him for only one night), thinking that she was not quite well, but, as Margaret saw no need of a doctor for her, she asked the doctor to please go away. The doctor apprehended nervous breakdown in Helen, inspite of Margaret's observation, and told her about this. Displeased with the doctor at this she asked him to retire: "'I beg your pardon, but it is nothing of the sort. You are not qualified to attend my sister, Mr Mansbridge. If we require your services, we will let you know.'" Helen was 'many weeks from her confinement' and so Margaret told Henry: "'Well, Henry, send your doctor away. What possible use is he now?'" Margaret's affection for Helen this time increased phenomenally (section XXXVI).

Margaret bolted the door from inside as if to protect Helen from the notices of men and from their possible undigestible comments upon her. Helen told her: "'I am going to have a child in June, and in the first place conversations, discussions, excitement, are not good for me.... In the second place I have no right to trouble people. I cannot fit in with England as I know it. I have done something that the English never pardon. It would not be right for them to pardon it. So I must live where I am not known.'" Helen also told her that she had taken a flat in Munich and was living in it with

Monica, an Italian girl who lived by journalism and who was "'much the best person to see me through.'" Monica was 'extraordinarily sensible' with Helen. She was of the type they named: 'Italiano inglesiato'—"the crude feminist of the South, whom one respects but avoids." "And Helen had turned to it in her need!" Changing the subject of their conversation Margaret told her that the house, Howards End, seemed dead to her—the house that earlier her husband lent to them on some conditions. Margaret told Helen that she was unkind to her to hate Henry, but Helen told her that she did no more hate Henry, and that she only hated 'English life.' Earlier Margaret was afraid that Helen might have been displeased with her for her 'treachery'—for her dishonesty or falsehood of writing to her that Aunt Juley had expired. Margaret wrote this to her in order of bringing her to Swanage. However, Helen was not at all offended by Margaret's innocently dishonest letter. She told Margaret: "'I am still Helen, I hope.'"

Helen enquired of Margaret's married life: "'your marriage has been happy, Meg?'" Margaret's reply was cryptic: "'Yes, but I don't feel inclined to talk.'" "Something had come between them. Perhaps it was society, which hence forward would exclude Helen. Perhaps it was a third life, already potent as a spirit. They would find no meeting-place. Both suffered acutely, and were not comforted by the knowledge that affection survived." Helen was about to depart; she told Margaret: "'Give my love to Aunt Juley and Tibby, and take more yourself than I can say. Promise to come and see me in Munich later.'" Helen was about to leave the house when a note from Henry was handed down to Margaret by the driver of Helen's car, as she unbolted the door for Helen, and so she was detained, somehow. Helen "remained in the hall, going from bookcase to table. She grew more like the old Helen, irresponsible and charming." She asked Margaret if Howards End belonged to Mr Wilcox and Margaret said it did. But Helen said: "'But it seems to be ours now.'" Helen found items of the furniture of Wickham Place—a sword, a piano, her mother's chiffonier, etc.—displayed at places of Howards End.

Within moments Helen became quite natural and at home, and the two sisters recalled memories of some past pleasantries and both shared the joys of them.

The bell rang and a little boy (Tom) entered and told them: "'Please, I am the milk.'" The boy wanted a can from them to pour some milk for them in it. The two sisters then engaged in a pleasant conversation with the boy. Margaret asked the boy:

> "'Did Miss Avery send you?'"
> "'Yes, please.'"
> "'Then take it back and say we require no milk.'"
> "'But I like milk,' cried Helen. 'Why send it away?'"
> "'Do you? Oh, very well. But we have nothing to put it in, and he wants the can.'"
> "'Please, I'm to call in the morning for the can,' said the boy."
> "'The house will be locked up then.'"
> "'In the morning would I bring eggs, too?'"
> "'Are you the boy whom I saw playing in the slacks last week?'"
> "The child hung his head."

Margaret then commanded the boy: "'Well, run away and do it again.'" Helen was delighted to see the boy, and whispered to Margaret: "'Nice little boy.'" She asked him to tell his name and the boy said: "'Tom.'" The little boy, who was probably the son of the dreadful Madge, brought milk for the Schlegels, who drank of it.

Earlier Margaret had told Helen that Howards End had seemed to be dead to her, and now she said that the house was not dead, really, but she herself was so. Helen rather contradicted her; she said that Wickham Place was 'a grave.' They went upstairs and opened all the windows, and then the inside of the house was rustling to the spring. Helen proposed they two would spend a night in the house: "'It would give me so much pleasure to have one night here with you. It will be something to look back on. Oh, Meg, lovely, do let's!'" Margaret told her that for that Henry's permission would be required and to seek for his permission they were to go Ducie Street, "'but you said yourself that you couldn't visit at Ducie Street now'." Helen told her: "'Ducie Street is his house. This is ours. Our furniture, our sort of people coming to the door. Do let us camp out just one night, and Tom shall feed us on eggs and milk. Why not? It's a moon.'"

Margaret told her that she thought Henry might not object to their staying in the house together but Charles would not like it, because Charles "'feels it's his mother's house. He loves it in rather an untaking way.'" Margaret said she could persuade Henry, but she could not but sympathise with Charles. Helen was impatient; she said: "'We know this is our house, because it feels ours. Oh, they may take the title-deeds and the door-keys, but for this one night we are at home.'" Margaret was also glad to have her with herself for that night, of course with leave from Henry, 'a loyal wife' as she was (section XXXVII).

When Margaret went to Henry for his leave to let Helen stop at Howards End for that night, he asked her point blank: "'Was your sister wearing a wedding-ring?'" Margaret stammed a 'No.' Henry's next enquiry was: "'I am now obliged to ask for the name of her seducer.'" Margaret said she did not know the name of the 'seducer' of Helen. Henry now told Margaret: "'Next you must tell me whether you have gathered anything. I have often noticed your insight, dear. I only wish my own was as good. You have guessed something, even though your sister said nothing. The slightest hint would help us.'" By 'us' Henry meant himself and Charles. Margaret told him that the news (of Helen's wedding) should not be broken before Charles, since "'This news will give Charles disproportionate pain.'" Henry told her that he and Charles were gentlemen and so they were doing what they were doing only for saving Helen's honour.

At this point Margaret first hit out at Henry: "'Are we to make her seducer marry her?'"

"'If possible. Yes.'

"'But, Henry, suppose he turned out to be married already? One has heard of such cases.'"

"'In that case he must pay heavily for his misconduct, and be thrashed within an inch of his life.'"

Margaret backed away from casuistry and once more appealed to Henry to let Helen stop at Howards End for a single night. Henry did not oblige her; he said the hotel would be more comfortable for Helen than the damp house, Howards End. Helen's old furniture was at Howards End as was that of Margaret, and Helen was sentimentally attached to her furniture, and this Margaret now used as a plea for Helen's wish to stay at Howards End for the night. But, yet, Henry was not softened. He told her: "'a house in which one has once lived becomes in a sort of way sacred. I don't know why. Associations and so on. Now Helen has no associations with Howards End, though I and Charles and Evie have. I do not see why she wants to stay the night there. She will only catch cold.'" Henry told her "'Helen commands my sympathy'" and yet he further told her: "'As your husband, I shall do all for her that I can, and I have no doubt that she will prove more sinned against than sinning. But I cannot treat her as if nothing has happened. I should be false to my position in society if I did.'" Margaret repeated her request: she asked him to grant the prayer of 'an unhappy girl' that Helen was, to let her sleep only for one night, for Helen would go back to Germany on the morrow.

Henry was inflexible; he told Margaret that he might seem to be 'unaccomodating' but "'I have my children and the memory of my dear wife to consider. I am sorry, but see that she leaves my house at once.'"

"'You have mentioned Mrs Wilcox.'"

"'I beg your pardon?'"

"'A rare occurrence. I reply, may I mention Mrs Bast?'" Henry flew into a sharp rage. "Margaret rushed at him and seized both his hands. She was transfigured." And then she harangued at him: "'You have a mistress—I forgave you. My sister has a lover—you drive her from the house. Do you see the connection? Stupid, hypocritical, cruel—oh, contemptible!—a man who insults his wife when she's alive and cants with her memory when she's dead. A man who ruins a woman for his pleasure, and casts her off to ruin other men. And gives bad financial advice, and then says he is not responsible. These men are you. You can't recognize them, because you cannot connect. I've had enough of your unweeded kindness. I've spoilt you long enough. All your life you have been spoilt. Mrs Wilcox spoiled you. No one has ever told you what you are—muddled, criminally muddled. Men like you use repentance as a blind, so don't repent. Only say to yourself: 'What Helen has done, I've done.'" Henry said: "'The two cases are different.'" The irate Margaret quipped: "'In what way different? You have betrayed Mrs Wilcox, Helen only herself. You remain in society, Helen can't. You have had only pleasure, she may die. You have the insolence to talk to me of differences, Henry?'" Henry told her: "'I perceive you are attempting blackmail. It is scarcely a pretty weapon for a wife to use against her husband. My rule through life has been never to pay the least attention to threats, and I can only repeat what I said before: I do not give you and your sister leave to sleep at, Howards End'" (section XXXVIII).

Tibby was staying at Ducie Street, where Charles went to talk with him about Helen. Charles now deemed Helen to be the foe of his family. He thought about Helen: "the girl must be got out of the way before she disgraced them further. If occasion offered she might be married to a villain or, possibly, to a fool." Charles suspected that Helen's ultimate motive was to possess Howards End. But "though he disliked the house, was determined to defend it." Tibby was contrary to Charles: whereas Charles was under the conventional morality, Tibby was above it, though to be above it was difficult enough. "Unlike Charles, Tibby had money enough; his ancestors had earned it for him.... He was the leisure without sympathy—an attitude as fatal as the strenuous; a little cold culture may be raised on it, but no art." The contrariety between the two persons failed their interview, because "the gulf between them was economic as well as spiritual." But Charles could achieve at least this that he pointed out before Tibby that it had been his duty to protect his sister Helen from the evil intention of her corruptor (Bast). When Charles asked him if he suspected anybody as the corruptor, Tibby said he suspected none. "Involuntarily he [Tibby] blushed. He remembered the scene in his Oxford rooms." Charles then thunderingly asked: "'When you saw her [Helen] last, did she mention anyone's name? Yes or no!'" Tibby replied: "'In my rooms she mentioned some friends called the Basts—'" (section XXXIX).

That moonlit evening Margaret and Helen were taking stocks of their tragic conditions, when to them "Leonard [Bast] seemed not a man, but a cause." Helen was asking herself whether "she ever loved in the noblest way, where man and woman, having lost themselves in sex, desire to lose sex itself in comradeship." Margaret, on her part, could not blame Helen for what she had done: "Not even to herself dare she blame Helen. She could not assess her trespass by any moral code; it was everything or nothing. Morality can tell us that murder is worse than stealing, and group most sins in an order all must approve, but it cannot group Helen. The surer its pronouncements on this point, the surer may we be that morality is not speaking. Christ was evasive when they questioned Him. It is those that cannot connect who hasten to cast the first stone." Helen told her that she was trying to save Bast even ignoring justice, if necessary. She confessed that it was she who drew Bast to herself and not the other way round: "'I drew him to me...I felt very lonely myself. He is not to blame. He would go on worshipping me. I want never to see him again, though it sounds appalling.'" Helen laid her face against the wych-elm with pig's teeth in its bark—the bark that gave one anodyne. Margaret was also wandering about the tree that also gave one peace.

Helen told Margaret that she did no more hate Mr Wilcox and that she knew how Margaret married him and also that Margaret "'will now be very happy.'" The memory of Mrs Wilcox returned to Margaret who to Helen suddenly made a cryptic appreciation about the deceased Mrs Wilcox: "'I feel that you and I and Henry are only fragments of that woman's mind. She knows everything. She is everything. She is the house, and the tree that leans over it. People have their own deaths as well as their own lives, and even if there is nothing beyond death we shall differ in our nothingness. I cannot believe that knowledge such as her will perish with knowledge such as mine. She knew about realities. She knew when people were in love, though she was not in the room. I don't doubt that she knew when Henry deceived her.'"

The Schlegel sisters, inspite of everything, felt like tourists—perpetual tourists. Margaret felt no strong pull from the end of Henry and fancied she could fly with Helen to Germany and get on with Monica. "The present flowed by them like a stream. The tree rustled. It had made music before they were born, and would continue after their deaths, but its song was of the moment. The moment had passed. The tree rustled again. Their senses were sharpened, and they seemed to apprehend life. Life passed. The tree rustled again." Margaret and Helen had been stalking; they now came back home, "passed upstairs, kissed, and amidst the endless iterations fell asleep." After a while, "Margaret awoke and looked into the garden." How incomprehensible that Leonard Bast should have won her this night of peace! Was he also part of Mrs Wilcox's mind?" (section XL).

"Far different was Leonard's development. The months after Oniton, whatever minor troubles they might bring him, were all overshadowed by remorse. When Helen looked back she could philosophise, or she could look into the future and plan for her child. But the father [Leonard] saw nothing beyond his own sin." He became a split personality; one half of him cursed the other half. Even Jacky noticed the change that occurred in him. He suffered inconceivably, and yet he could not blame Helen for his pathetic plight. She gave him five thousand pounds but that could not save him from becoming a virtual beggar. His sisters—Blanche and Laura—helped as much they could in all possible ways, but peace he could not come across: Laura censured him for his 'immoral marriage' and his brother, the lay-reader, did not even answer his urgent and eager letter. His life was full of horror, and darkness that had only two bright spots: one, he did not voluntarily end his life, though the consciousness of his sinfulness remained with him; and two, he still maintained his tenderness for Jacky.

One day Leonard Bast "caught sight of Margaret and her brother" near St Paul's, and yearned to confess to her his sin and thus save himself from his yearning for suicide and gain peace of mind. He now wanted her hardness and her cold, intellectual nature. He was not in the know of anything about Margaret's marriage with Mr Wilcox. He saw new flats rising on the site of Wickham Place and wondered if the Schlegel sisters had been turned out of Wickham Place because of his immoral doings. Leonard decided to meet Margaret and confess before her his misconduct with Helen, and he wanted to meet her in Howards End in the village of Hilton in Hertfordshire. His mind was, at that time, seething with bizarre images, such as those of 'a clenched fist' and double snakes, which mightily disturbed his sleep. He took train.

As soon as the train drew up at Hilton, the beauty of the village revealed before him and he saw the people of all sorts of the village—the people who were 'England's hope.' Here at Hilton, Leonard's remorse 'had become beautiful' too. Near the village was a chalk-pit where, in the ambience of the township, he saw another type of people, the 'imperial people,' who were healthy and ever in motion. These people wanted to 'inherit the earth' and carried the country's [England's] virtues overseas. "But the Imperialist is not what he thinks or seems. He is a destroyer. He prepares the way for cosmopolitanism, and though his ambitions may be fulfilled the earth that he inherits will be gray." However, at Hilton, though Leonard was preoccupied with the confession of his sin, optimism invaded his mind, and also goodness. Even death showed itself as hope: "Death destroys man, but the idea of death saves him." Tragedy too lost its proper meaning: "Squalor and tragedy can beckon to all that is great in us, and strengthen the wings of love." Such notions presently comforted Leonard in his gathering tragedy.

As Leonard approached Howards End, he heard several human voices over-toned with anxiety and ire. Among the voices were Margaret's and another unseen person's. Leonard was waiting in the outer room of the house, which he entered into through an open door. He heard the unseen person shout out: "'Oh, is he there? I am not surprised. I now thrash him within an inch of his life.'" The shout was intended for Leonard.

> 'Mrs Wilcox,' said Leonard, 'I have done wrong.'
> The man [the unseen person, i.e., Charles] took him by the collar and cried, 'Bring me a stick.' Women were screaming. A stick, very bright descended. It hurt him, not where it descended, but in the heart. Books fell over him in a shower. Nothing had sense.
> "'Get some water,' commanded Charles, who had all through kept very calk. 'He's shamming. Of course I only used the blade. Here, carry him into the air.'"
> Thinking that he understood these things, Margaret obeyed him. They laid Leonard, who was dead, on the gravel; Helen poured water over him.
> "'That's enough,'" said Charles.
> "'Yes, murder's enough,' said Miss Avery, coming out of the house with the sword" (section XLI).

Charles had returned home from Ducie Street by the first train and was astonished to learn that Margaret had not yet returned from the same place. Mr Wilcox was vexed at this and had confided to Charles: "'I cannot let this kind of thing continue without comment. I am morally certain that she [Margaret] is with her sister at Howards End. The house is mine—and, Charles, it will be yours—and when I say that no one is to live there I mean that no one is to live there.'" He further told him: "'To my mind this question is connected with something far greater, the rights of property itself.'" Mr Wilcox, in fact, was not inimical either to Margaret or to Helen, but, nevertheless, he wanted that they did "'clear out of the house at once'" to settle the matter. Charles said that he would go to Howards End at eight next morning. Mr Wilcox had cautioned him not to use violence. And, on the morrow, even leaving Leonard dead on the gravel, it did not occur to Charles that he did anything violent. He, rather, on his way back home, himself informed the police that Leonard had died of heart-disease. Returning home Charles told his father about his heroic deed and broke the news to him that Margaret was going to Germany along with her sister that very evening. Mr Wilcox became anxious about the future on two counts: there would be instituted an inquest by the police, in which case Margaret and Helen would be detained by them, and there might be a separation between Margaret and himself. The news of the inquest soon reached the father and the son. Charles said that he had expected it and that he would "'naturally be the most important witness'" in the case (section XLII).

Leonard lay in his grave, but death was not everything, for besides death there were 'beauty and adventure' and "there was hope this side of the grave; there were truer relationships beyond the limits that fetter us now." Helen was dumb with fright due to the murder drama, but kept herself calm thinking of her yet unborn child. The excitement and turbulence consequent upon the inquest died down, and "the time for telegrams and anger was over," but nothing could shake Helen's belief in the 'eternity of beauty.' The police questioned Charles and others, and the doctor was satisfied that Leonard died of heart-disease. And yet Margaret decided to go to Germany along with Helen. No message came to her from Mr Wilcox. Perhaps he expected her to apologize, but she would not do that. She rather "neither forgave him for his behaviour nor wished to forgive him." This action of hers was "a protest against the inner darkness in high places that comes with a commercial age"—against the inner darkness of Mr Wilcox. Margaret thought about her husband: "Though he would build up his life without her, she would not apologize. He had refused to connect, on the clearest issue that can be laid before a man, and their love must take the consequences." Mr Henry Wilcox faded away as the reality emerged before her vision, and "only her love for him should remain clear, stamped with his image like the cameos we rescue out of dreams."

Margaret had been contemplating on her husband's future: "He would grow into a rich, jolly old man, at times a little sentimental about women, but emptying his glass with anyone. Tenacious of power, he would keep Charles and the rest dependent, and retire from business reluctantly and at an advanced age.... What next? The inevitable word. The release of the soul to its appropriate Heaven." She believed in immortality and so did Henry, in his own particular way. She was thinking if their two notions of immortality would ultimately prove to be identical, if they would meet beyond their graves. While Margaret was thus meditating, she was summoned by Henry through his chauffeur. She thought Henry "would probably sell the place [Howards End] now." She locked the house and soon presented herself before Henry. She told him: "'I am going to Germany with my sister. I must tell you now that I shall make it [Germany] my permanent home... I am unable to forgive you and am leaving you.'" She tossed the keys of Howards End to him and said: "'Here are your keys.'"

Henry wanted to tell her something, softly, but she would not hear. She, rather, told him: "'My sister is going to be ill. My life is going to be with her now. We must manage to build up something, she and I and her child.'" Henry told her that Charles had been convicted of manslaughter and was sentenced to three years' imprisonment. "Then Henry's fortress gave way. He could bear no one but his wife, he shambled up to Margaret afterwards and asked her to do what she could with him. She did what seemed easiest—she took him down to recruit at Howards End" (section XLIII).

The father of six years old Tom was cutting the big meadow near Howards End while Helen was negotiating with the boy. Tom was enquiring of her if her fourteen months old baby could play with him. Margaret was sitting beside her. She suddenly told Margaret: "'Meg, may I tell you something? I like Henry.'" Margaret told her: "'You'd be odd if you didn't.'" Helen looked into the abyss of the past: Leonard was dead and Charles had two years yet in prison. Helen said she liked Henry because he 'does worry'; and Margaret said Henry liked Helen because she did not worry. Helen said: "'everything is peaceful now; I seem cured...I used to be so dreamy about a man's love as a girl, and think that for good or evil love must be the great thing. But it hasn't been; it has been itself a dream.'" "'I ought to remember Leonard as my lover,' said Helen." She said: "I tempted him, and killed him, and it is surely the least I can do. I would like to throw out all my heart to Leonard on such an afternoon as this. But I cannot. It is no good pretending. I am forgetting him." Helen's eyes filled with tears.

Margaret tried to sooth her: "'Don't fret yourself, Helen. Develop what you have; love your child. I do not love children. I am thankful to have none. I can play with their beauty and charm, but that is all—nothing real, not one scrap of what there ought to be. And others—others go further still, and move outside humanity altogether. A place, as well as a person, may catch the glow. Don't you see that all this leads to comfort in the end? It is part of the battle against sameness. Differences—eternal differences, planted by God in a single family, so that there may always be colour; sorrow perhaps, but colour in the daily gray. Then I can't have you worrying about Leonard. Don't drag in the personal when it will not come. Forget him.'"

Helen told Margaret that her life had been 'heroic,' for it was she who did everything: it was she who "'picked up the pieces, and made us a home'" and it was she who managed the affairs after the arrest of Charles. Helen expected that the home (Howards End) that Margaret had provided her with, somehow or other, would be their permanent home. Margaret said: "'I think so. There are moments when I feel Howards End peculiarly our own.'"

Paul suddenly Berged into their midst, wearing 'heavy blank moustache,' and told Margaret: "'My father has asked for you'." She followed him and met her husband. "Her husband was lying in a great leather chair in the dining-room, and by his side, holding his hand rather ostentatiously, was

Evie. Dolly, dressed in purple, sat near the window." It was six o'clock in the evening. Margaret said nothing. Mr Wilcox told Paul that he wanted to give the house, Howards End, to him, but Paul, who was scratching his hand, declined the offer: "'as I've given up the outdoor life that suited me, and have come home to look after the business, it's no good my settling down here,' he said at last. 'It's not really the country, and it's not the town.'" The house was earlier declined by Charles as well. Now Mr Wilcox declared amidst the assemblage of the family members: "'Then I leave Howards End to my wife absolutely.'" He added: "'And let everyone understand that; and after I am dead let there be no jealousy and no surprise.'" "Margaret did not answer. There was something uncanny in her triumph. She, who had never expected to conquer anyone, had charged straight through these Wilcoxes and broken up their lives."

To allay the anger of the others, perhaps, Mr Wilcox said that he would give his money to them, which was also the wish of Margaret, and that Margaret would distribute a great deal of her money amongst them. He said that "'She intends to diminish her income by half during the next ten years; she intends when she dies to leave the house [Howards End] to her—to her nephew, down in the field.'" The business of Mr Wilcox being over, all the visitors—his family members who assembled there—one by one, took leave of him and departed. The ultimate visitor to take leave was Dolly, who said: "'Good-bye, Mr Wilcox. It does seem curious that Mrs Wilcox should have left Margaret Howards End, and yet she get it, after all.'"

Margaret saw their visitors to the gate. Then she returned to her husband and laid her head in his hands. He was pitiably tired. But Dolly's remark had interested her. At last she said: 'Could you tell me, Henry, what was that about Mrs Wilcox having left me Howards End?'

Tranquilly he replied: 'Yes, she did. But that is a very old story. When she was ill and you were so kind to her she wanted to make you some return, and, not being herself at the time, scribbled "Howards End" on a piece of paper. I went into it thoroughly, and, as it was clearly fanciful, I set it aside, little knowing what my Margaret would be to me in the future.'

"Margaret was silent. Something shook her life in its inmost recesses, and she shivered."

"'I didn't do wrong, did I?'" he asked, bending down.

"'You didn't, darling. Nothing has been done wrong.'

"From the garden came laughter. 'Here they are at last!" exclaimed Henry, disengaging himself with a smile. Helen rushed into the gloom, holding Tom by one hand and carrying her baby on the other. There were shouts of infectious joy.

"'The field's cut!' Helen cried excitedly—'The big meadow! We've seen to the very end, and it'll be such a crop of hay as never!'"

3

DISCUSSION

(i)

It is interesting to know that perhaps there is no novel (or are very few) where the title of the novel has been so frequently used throughout the text as in *Howards End,* in which the title has been used throughout the text of around 314 pages as many times as not less than seventy-three times. The house, 'Howards End,' the central locus of the novel, was modelled on the house, 'Rooksnest,' to which both Forster and his mother Lily were emotionally attached. Unfortunately, they were, almost literally, turned out from the house—the house in which Forster lived till he was fourteen. Rae H. Stoll writes: "In the early thirties [nineteen thirties] Forster gave a paper on memory to the Bloomsbury Memoir Club which related how the owner had turned his mother and himself out of 'Rooksnest,' their beloved home in Hertfordshire and the model for 'Howards End,' where he lived until he was fourteen. He concluded his recollection with a remarkable statement: 'If I had been allowed to stop on there I should have become a different person, married, and fought in the war'" (Tambling, 42). 'Howards End' was also actually the name of a house. Paul Delany writes: "In 1907, the year before he [Forster] began *Howards End,* the Georgian mansion of the Thornton family [on the side of Forster's paternal grandmother], 'Battersea Rise,' had been torn down and its site 'completely covered with very small two-story houses.' Forster had given money to campaign to save the house and garden, but nothing could be done. *Howards End* is named after a house which is saved" (*op. cit.,* 75).

The history of the creation of *Howards End* began in 1906, in which year Forster went to Stevenage and there met with a certain Mr Poston's new wife, and "the sight of this charming, cultivated woman...seems to have supplied the germ of *Howards End*" (Furbank, I, 142). This was one source of the novel. The other source, perhaps, "was provided by Uncle Philip Whichelo, who came to Weybridge bringing 'squalid stories of flat-life'" (*op. cit.,* I, 165). Forster had heard from Uncle Philip Whichelo the 'squalid stories of flat-life' and the disagreeable effect of the stories are discernable in *Howards End.* However, on 28 June, 1908, Forster 'jotted down a first sketch' of *Howards End* as follows: "'Idea for another novel shaping, and may do well to write it down. In a prelude Helen goes to stop with the Wilcoxes, gets engaged to the son & breaks it off immediately, for her instinct sees the spiritual cleavage between the families. Mrs Wilcox dies, and some years later Margaret gets engaged to the widower, a man impeccable publicly. They are accosted by a prostitute M. Because she understands and is great, marries him. The wrong thing to do. He, because he is little, cannot bear to be understood, and goes to the bad. He is frank, kind, and attractive. But he dreads ideas'" (*ibid.*). The novel certainly differs from this sketch to some extent, particularly from the latter part of it, but the main line of the novel does not go very far away from the general course of it.

(ii)

The novel has a motto: 'Only connect!' In section XXII of the novel, Forster elaborates on this motto: "Only connect!... Only connect the prose and the passion, and both will be exalted and human love will be seen at its highest. Live in fragments no longer. Only connect, and the beast and the monk, robbed of the isolation that life is to either, will die." Mr Henry Wilcox was the prose, he being the representative of the merely rational-minded commercial class, and Helen was the passion, she being the representative of the singularly emotional pastoral people. Both of them were fragmented persons, incomplete in their individual beings. They were contradictory to each other, one rasping against the other: Helen hated Henry, and Henry could not bear with Helen. Margaret was the compromise formula, and she effected a marriage between the prose and the passion by marrying Henry. Margaret, too, had been passionate like Helen, but she could realise the necessity of prose that life requires as well, and she inculcated rationality within herself, and thus struck a balance between the two properties of life, of nature. She was successful in connecting prose and passion, and consequently could make Howards End a happy home, with Helen beginning to like Henry and Henry beginning to accommodate Helen, and, after all, Margaret and Henry beginning to show as an enviable couple.

The theme of the novel echoes, and expatiates on, the motto of it. The theme underlines Forster's life-long belief in the great importance of personal relationship, honesty, and feeling (or emotion, or passion) in growing up as a whole, unfragmented human being. A person who is absolutely rational, lacking in the other human quality of passion, is as fragmentary as another who is just the opposite. To be a whole man, a complete man, one must hold a balance within himself between the two cardinal human properties: rationality and passion. The bi-variant man may thus become an integrated whole.

These two antagonistic properties of man has given birth to two contrary cultures: the urban commercial-culture, dependent upon cool rationality with misgivings for passion; and the passionate culture of the countryside that is funky about frigid rationality. In *Howards End,* the former culture has been represented by Henry Wilcox, and the latter culture by Helen Schlegel. A marriage between these two antagonistic cultures has been effected by Margaret Schlegel, who harbours within herself as much passion as Helen has but who has been able to understand, through her exotic experiences, the necessity of calculating rationality as well. Margaret (who is the mouthpiece of Forster) has realised the futility of Helen's and Henry's overly tilting tendency towards one of the two-some cardinal human spiritual qualities: rationality and passion. She could realise that persons, like Henry and Helen, could achieve salvation not through personal antagonism but through 'personal intercourse,' and she retrieved both of them by herself marrying Henry. By marrying Henry she could transfigure both Henry and Helen, could connect their two divergent cultures, and thus could establish a happy concord. This is clear from the fact that after her marriage with Henry, Helen no more hated Henry and Henry condescended to accommodate Helen. Therefore, the theme of *Howards End* is that salvation is possible and so should be achieved, through 'personal intercourse,' because life is not a battle, but a romance.

The plot of *Howards End* has been given at the beginning of this chapter from Frank N. Magill's *Master Plots* (vol. 6). It is rather simple. There are three groups of characters, and the interactions of the three economically and culturally divergent groups form the warp and woof of the plot. The first group comprises two passionate and intellectual Schlegel sisters—Margaret and Helen—and their aesthetic and lukewarm brother Tibby; the second group consists of the hard-core businessman Henry Wilcox and his two sons and a daughter—Charles, Paul and Evie; and the third group includes Leonard Bast and his wife Jacky. The first two groups belong to the affluent upper middle class while the third group comprises the poor Basts. The interactions among the three groups began with Helen briefly falling in love with Paul Wilcox, and Margaret briefly striking a shallow friendship with Leonard Bast and developing a deep friendship with Mrs Ruth Wilcox, wife of Henry Wilcox.

Mr Wilcox became jealous of Leonard Bast seeing Margaret, to whom he was attracted, liking Leonard, and by a rule got him cashiered out of his job and thus reduced to a virtual beggar. Leonard, next, is enticed by Jacky into a nuptial tie with her. Before this, Helen was once impulsively drawn to Leonard on the spur of the moment and got pregnant. Seeing the financially straitened condition of the Basts, consequent upon the malicious trickery of Mr Wilcox with Leonard, Helen conducted the Basts straight to Mr Wilcox during the marriage ceremony of Evie, and demanded compensation for the Basts. It was revealed that Mr Wilcox and Jacky had become lovers after the death of Mrs Ruth Wilcox. Margaret, who was by then engaged to Mr Wilcox, did not break her engagement; she rather forgave his misconduct, because through her exotic experiences she came to understand that life was composed not only of passion but also of rationality. She maintained her sangfroid and married him.

The pregnant Helen had fled to Munich to save her face, but came back hearing of her aunt Mrs Munt's illness. Charles, who was so long in the dark about Leonard adultering Helen, killed him when the crime was revealed to him, and went into the prison for a term of three years. The cool and calculating Mr Wilcox emotionally broke down for Charles' prison term, and for the first time felt the touch of nostalgic passion for his deceased wife Mrs Ruth Wilcox, and according to her last wish made Margaret the owner of Howards End—the house to which Margaret and Helen were emotionally attached but from which Mr Wilcox always strived to keep them placated off. By the time Helen's child was born, and the Schlegel sisters began to happily live in Howards End. When Mr Wilcox handed over Howards End to Margaret, he decided that after Margaret's death the house was to go to her nephew—to the child of Helen. Thus a part of the wealth of the rich Wilcoxes went to the poor Basts, and thus Margaret (Forster's mouthpiece) worked as a bridge between the rational Wilcoxes and the passionate Schlegels. John Sayre Martin writes about the plot of the novel: "The plot of *Howards End* is contrived to effect a partial synthesis of its antithetical elements. Margaret is to marry Henry, Helen to have a child by Leonard; then, in the final chapter, will settle at Howards End, of which Margaret becomes the acknowledged mistress" (Martin, 117).

(iii)

In *Howards End* there are, as has been said, nine major characters: Henry Wilcox, Ruth Wilcox, Charles Wilcox, Paul Wilcox, Margaret Schlegel, Helen Schlegel, Theobald Schlegel, Leonard Bast and Jacky Bast. Margaret, as in section XXXI of the novel Forster tells us, is the heroine. The Schlegels were of German extraction, in so far as their father had left Germany at the age of forty (section XVIII) and "obtained work in one of our [English] provincial universities and there married Poor Emily" (section IV), Emily having a considerable amount of money. Margaret was 29 when the novel begins. She was quite intellectual and emotional (section IV); impulsive and, at times, even hysterical (section II). She loved money (section VII), which was one of the reasons of her falling in love with the widower, Mr Henry Wilcox. Her cold intellectual nature debarred her from being pragmatic, in spite of her love of money. Margaret believed in such queer supernatural phenomena as aura and astral plane (section XVII), and in immortality (section XLIII). She and Helen "were alike as little girls" (section IV); of course Helen was pretty while she "was not a female of the encouraging type" (section V). There was a great difference between the two Schlegel girls as regards their attitudes towards political economics: Margaret, the elder sister, was bourgeois in inclination while Helen, the younger sister, was an out and out socialist (sections VII and XXII).

Both the Schlegel sisters believed in personal relations, i.e., they believed that we can get everything from personal relations, even happiness and salvation (in the worldly sense of the term). They looked for the inner light of human beings, and did not believe that there is, beside the inner life of a man, an outer life—the 'public life' or the 'social life' which is always turbulent with 'telegrams and anger.' Margaret once told Helen: "'The truth is that there is a great outer life that you and I have never touched—a life in which telegrams and anger count. Personal relations, that we think supreme, are not supreme there. There love means marriage settlements; death, death duties.... This outer life, though obviously horrid, often seems the real one'" (section IV). In section XVI of the novel, the narrator tells us that Leonard Bast failed to distinguish between the two Schlegel sisters. So similar were they that to Leonard they sometimes seemed 'a composite Indian god:' "he [Leonard] scarcely distinguished between the two sisters. One [Helen] was more beautiful and more lively, but 'the Miss Schlegels' still remained a composite Indian god, whose waving arms and contradictory speeches were the product of a single mind." Margaret, like Helen, was 'amiable but academic' (section XV). Mr Wilcox, after marrying her, "liked to see her reading poetry or something about social questions" (section XXXI). She had much affection for Helen; and she became much concerned when she saw signs of morbidity in Helen, particularly after her affairs with Leonard Bast, (section XXXIV). Her deep concern for Helen is evident from her Amazonian determination to save the honour of Helen after her pregnancy (section XXXVI).

Margaret was briefly and romantically drawn to Leonard Bast. She told Helen why she liked him—"'Let me explain exactly why we like this man, and want to see him again.'" She produces two reasons: "'Firstly, because he cares for physical adventures, just as you do. Yes, you go camping out. Secondly, he cares for something special in adventure. It is quickest to call that special something poetry—'" (section XVI). But the Leonard Bast episode soon fizzled out and Margaret inclined towards Mr Henry Wilcox, particularly after he became a widower. Opportunities of coming closer to Mr Wilcox was rather wide, because earlier Margaret and Mrs Ruth Wilcox had struck a deep friendship between themselves. Some twenty years older than Margaret (section XVIII), Mr Wilcox appeared to her physically attractive. She told her aunt Mrs Munt about Mr Wilcox: "'He has a remarkably good complexion for a man of his age'" (section VII). Her personality was for the first time 'touched' by Mr Wilcox: "Others had loved her in the past, if one may apply to their brief desires so grave a word, but those others had been 'ninnies'—young men who had nothing to do, old men who could find nobody better. And she [Margaret] had often 'loved,' too, but only so far as the facts of sex demanded: mere yearnings for the masculine, to be dismissed for what they were worth, with a smile. Never before had her personality been touched. She was not young or very rich, and it amazed her that a man of any standing [i.e., Mr Wilcox] should take her seriously" (section XVIII).

After her marriage with Mr Wilcox, Margaret's mental structure changed phenomenally: "Her conscience pricked her a little about the Basts [who had become impoverished chiefly due to the cozenage of Mr Wilcox]; she was sorry to have lost sight of them. No doubt Leonard was worth helping, but being Henry's wife she preferred to help someone else. As for theatres and discussion societies, they attracted her less and less. She began to 'miss' new movements, and to spend her spare time rereading or thinking, rather to the concern of her Chelsea friends. They attributed the change to her marriage, and perhaps some deep instinct did warn her not to travel further from her husband than was inevitable. Yet the main cause lay deeper still; she had outgrown stimulants, and was passing from words to things" (section XXXI). She also rose above her earlier bourgeois turn of mind; after Henry made her the sole owner of Howards End, she felt triumphant. At the fag end of the novel, the narrator tells us that "There was something uncanny in her triumph. She, who had never expected to conquer anyone, had charged straight through these Wilcoxes and broken up their lives" (section XLIV). And we hear from Mr Wilcox that Margaret "'is giving away a great deal of money. She intends to diminish her income by half during the next ten years'" (section XLIV). Really, Helen was not amiss when she told Margaret: "'your life has been heroic'" (section XLIV).

Elizabeth Langland, in her essay '*Howards End:* Gender, Form, Language,' writes that Margaret transcends the traditional femininity: "Whereas Henry Wilcox remains inscribed in a made mode of discourse, set within masculine imagery of dominance and conquest, Forster's descriptions of Margaret transcend the traditionally feminine and reinscribe her within a rhetoric of reconciliation and connection. Through Margaret Schlegel, the traditional terms of masculinity and femininity are scrutinised and subjected to the demands of higher integration. Margaret's point of view, then, is ultimately not representative of a view we might code as essentially female or feminine. Forster is sensitive both to essentialist conceptions of the female and to the social coding of the feminine. He subverts both in his characterisation of Margaret Schlegel, who can calmly state, for example, 'I do not love children. I am thankful to have none' (...), thus debunking ideas of a natural, maternal female" (Tambling, 86). The character of Margaret is doubly important in the novel, for as Elizabeth Langland says, "the most moving scene occurs between two women, Helen and Margaret" (*op. cit.,* 88), and it is Margaret who connects Helen and Henry, which has been the objective of Forster in it. The 'most moving scene,' referred to by Elizabeth Langland is that where the pregnant Helen met Margaret and where the antagonism between the two sisters melted down into deep affection: "'Helen, still smiling, came up to her sister. She said: 'It is always Meg.' They looked into each other's eyes. The inner life had paid'" (*op. cit.,* 89). And it was Margaret who connected the impulse of Helen and the cool rationality of Henry, which followed the motto of the novel: 'Only connect!'

John Sayre martin also says that Margaret is the heroine of *Howards End,* agreeing with Helen that her 'life has been heroic' (section XLIV). Comparing between the two Schlegel sisters, Martin writes that "Margaret, too, is impulsive, but less so than Helen, and much more balanced in outlook. Whereas Helen declares an exclusive commitment to the inner life ('I know that personal relations are the real life, for ever and ever'), Margaret sees that the outer life also has claims" (Martin, 112-113). Martin writes: "More keenly than Helen, she sees the extent to which their comfortable, cultured existence is tied to business by an economic umbilical cord" (*op. cit.,* 113). Martin further writes about Margaret: "her regard for the outer life is prompted by more than a sense of economic responsibility. It also contains an emotional, even, perhaps, a sexual, element. Sheltered, inhibited, and yet curious, like an Ibsen heroine, Margaret is simultaneously repelled by the masculine world of business and attracted to it. On the one hand, it is 'obviously horrid;' on the other, it somehow seems 'real.' Business people like the Wilcoxes get things done; they are virile and strong, and their household would seem to complement the too-feminine character of her own. 'Ours is a female house,' she declares, with a touch of regret. Howards End is 'irrevocably masculine'" (*ibid.*)

Forster himself said that the two Schlegel sisters were modelled on "the three sisters of Goldsworthy Lowes Dickinson," but Elizabeth Langland writes that critics, like Wilfred Stone and Elizabeth Heine, "have pointed to Virginia [later Woolf] and Vanessa Stephen as models for the Schlegel sisters" (Tambling, 98 f.n.). However, Martin very perceptively writes that "Throughout the novel, Margaret is often the mouthpiece for Forster's views" (Martin J. 14). P.N. Furbank agrees with Martin: "Margaret was Forster himself; her views are certainly his" (Furbank, I, 173).

Helen Schlegel was the younger sister of Margaret Schlegel, and so was of German extraction. In section IV of the novel, Forster writes about the two sisters' German origin: "They were not 'English to the backbone,' as their aunt had piously asserted. But, on the other hand, they were not 'Germans of the dreadful sort.' Their father had belonged to a type that was more prominent in Germany fifty years ago than now.... If one classed him at all it would be as the countryman of Hegel and Kant, as the idealist, inclined to be dreamy, whose Imperialism was the Imperialism of the air... He had obtained work in one of our provincial universities, and there married Poor Emily." Helen was the 'charming sister' (section IX) of Margaret and was a 'tremendous talker' (section V) like her elder sister, Margaret, and sometimes seemed hysterical (section XXX). Helen was 'pretty' (section V) and "Musical, literary, artistic...—a very 'charming girl" (section XXXV), but she was 'irresponsible' (section XXXVII) and 'silly' (section III). Like her elder sister before her marriage, Helen was quite intellectual, lacking in emotion. Forster tells us: "the world would be a gray, bloodless place were it entirely composed of Miss Schlegels. But, the world being what it is, perhaps they shine out in it like stars" (section IV).

As has already been said, the two Schlegel sisters were almost alike in disposition and mental frame, though they considerably differed in their attractiveness, Helen being much prettier than Margaret. Both the sisters were, of course, 'amiable but academic' (section XV). The freak difference between the two sisters was in their social attitude: Margaret was a virtual bourgeois while Helen was a confirmed socialist. Helen hated Henry particularly for his bourgeois attitude, and it was especially for her socialistic bent of mind that she deliberately conducted the impoverished Leonard and Jacky Bast in front of Mr Wilcox during Evie's marriage ceremony to demand compensation from him for his cozenage due to which Leonard was cashiered out of his job in the Porphyrion. Mr Wilcox believed that life was a battlefield where the theory of 'survival of the fittest' applied, but Helen was of the opinion that the poor were so because of the rich. Mr Wilcox believed that affluence or poverty of men depended on 'impersonal forces, or on God, but Helen believed that poverty is induced by the rich. Seeing Helen had dragged the starving and ill Basts before Mr Wilcox, Margaret called her 'mad', and Helen fleeing into a rage retorted: "'Perhaps. Yes. If you like, I'm mad. But I've brought them. I'll stand injustice no longer. I'll show up the wretchedness that lies under this luxury, this talk of impersonal forces, this cant about God doing what we're too slack to do ourselves'" (section XXVI).

Both Margaret and Helen believed in the great importance of personal relations in life, but whereas, later on, Margaret could realise the existence of an 'impersonal' sphere beside the sphere of personal relations, could realise that there was an 'outer world' in addition to the 'inner world' of personal relations, Helen always failed to see that outer world. Helen blandly told Margaret: "'I know that personal relations are the real life, for ever and ever'" (section IV). Helen's notion of personal relation and its great importance in human life reminds us of the same notion of the philosopher G.E. Moore who had been Forster's mentor in the sphere of morality. But, inspite of her sense of responsibility, very queer it is that she admittedly frequently used to steal umbrellas. In the concert at the Queen's Hall, she took away Leonard Bast's umbrella, not inadvertently but consciously. She, not shamefacedly though, confessed before Margaret: "'I steal umbrellas even oftener than I hear Beethoven.'"

Her impulsiveness was abundantly manifested in her falling in love consecutively with two not-so-desirable candidates—Paul Wilcox and Leonard Bast. In fact she fell in love of Paul very peremptorily while she, along with the other Schlegels, was living in Howards End rented out by the Wilcoxes. In her third letter to Margaret (the novel begins with three letters of hers to Margaret), which is but a chit, she confessed: "'Paul and I are in love—the younger son [of Mr Wilcox] who only came here Wednesday.'" Helen wrote this letter on Sunday, which means she took only three to four days to love Paul unforgettably, for she did never forget him ever after, not withstanding her Leonard affair later on. Paul and she were about the same age, he being a "very young man" (section III). Round Paul, "she began to throw the halo of Romance, to irradiate him with all the splendour of those happy days, to feel that in him she would draw nearest to the robust ideal" (section IV). She certainly loved Paul for reasons of his, but it was also true that she loved him for the family to which he belonged: "The truth is that she had fallen in love, not with an individual, but with a family. "Before Paul arrived she had, as it were, been turned up into his key. The energy of the Wilcoxes had fascinated her, had created new images of beauty in her responsive mind. To be all day with them in the open air, to sleep at night under their roof, had seemed the supreme joy of life, and had led to that abandonment of personality that is a possible prelude to love. She had *liked* giving in to Mr Wilcox, or Evie, or Charles; she had *liked* being told that her notions of life were sheltered or academic; that Equality was nonsense, Votes for Women nonsense, Socialism nonsense, Art and Literature, except when conducive to strengthening the character, nonsense. One by one the Schlegel fetishes had been overthrown, and, though professing to defend them, she had rejoiced" (section IV).

Helen's next amorous adventure was with Leonard Bast. It was she who tempted him, not the other way round. After Leonard was jugulated by Charles, Helen repented for him and arrogated to herself the cause of his death: "'I ought to remember Leonard as my lover,' said Helen, stepping down into the field. 'I tempted him, and killed him... I would like to throw out all my heart to Leonard.... But I cannot. It is no good pretending. I am forgetting him.' Her eyes filled with tears" (section XLIV). Helen was drawn to Leonard especially being moved by his most pathetic financial plight after he was duped into resigning his job at the Porphyrion by Mr Wilcox. She never could forgive Mr Wilcox for his downright ruse employed on Leonard until Margaret's becoming the sole owner of Howards End, according to the wish of Mr Wilcox. She conceived by lying with Leonard "perhaps for half an hour" under the spell of "the magic of Oniton under darkness" (section XLI), and she compensated him for his moral improbity with an offer of five thousand pounds. Elizabeth Langland writes about Helen's role in their unlawful union: "Helen has a sexual relationship with Leonard—a woman's classic offering of her body in sympathy—and then arrogantly seeks to compensate him with cash, admitting that 'I want never to see him again, though it sounds appalling. I wanted to give him money and feel finished'" (Tambling, 85). But why did Helen only love Paul and Leonard but not marry any one of them, or even thought of doing that? She explained to Margaret why she did not marry: "'I can only entice and be enticed. I can't, and won't, attempt difficult relations. If I marry, it will either be a man who's strong enough to boss me or whom I'm strong enough to boss. So I shan't marry, for there aren't such men. And heaven help anyone whom I do marry, for I shall certainly run away from him before you can say Jack Robinson'" (section XXIII).

Elizabeth Langland, in her essay '*Howards End.* Gender, Form, Language,' contrasts between Helen and Margaret thus: "Helen Schlegel, in contrast to Margaret, is emotional, impulsive, impatient of logic, impatient of all restraint on her generous impulses. She scoffs moderation and is incapable of balance; she is first seduced by the Wilcox men and then violently rejects them. She extols the 'inner life' and, unlike Margaret, refuses to acknowledge the value of Wilcox energy, which has created a civilised world in which her sensibilities and the inner life can have free play" (Tambling, 87). And John Sayre martin writes about Helen: "Helen is a romantic idealist. Truth and justice, she believes, are absolute, and she finds it hard to compromise with the world as it is" (Martin, 111). We hear that Helen loved Paul and Leonard, one after the other, but Martin tells us that she really loved none of the two as individuals but only as symbols: "Neither man did she really love. Both to her were symbols, Paul of romantic virility, Leonard of the poor and exploited. 'Did Leonard,' she wonders, 'grow out of Paul?' (...) The answer, obviously, is yes" (*op. cit.,* 112).

In section XXXI of the novel, Forster himself has dubbed Mr Henry Wilcox as the 'hero' of the story. How far Forster is facetious here is of course a question, but if Margaret is the acknowledged heroine, there should be no objection to Henry's claim to be the hero. He was a "kind gentleman" (section XI) and "an elderly man with a moustache and a copper-coloured face" (section VII). His moustache must have been prominent, for the narrator repeats his reference to it in section XXVI, "the thatched lip." In section XI of the novel, Forster has given us a graphic description of the physical features of Henry Wilcox: "His face was not as square as his son's [Charles'], and indeed the chin, though firm enough in outline, retreated a little, and the lips, ambiguous, were curtained by a moustache. But there was no external hint of weakness. The eyes, if capable of kindness and good-fellowship, if ruddy for the moment with tears, were the eyes of one who could not be driven. The forehead, too, was like Charles.' High and straight, brown and polished, merging abruptly into temples and skull, it had the effect of a bastion that protected his head from the world. At times it had the effect of a blank wall. He had dwelt behind it, intact and happy, for fifty years" (section XI).

Henry enjoyed a happy married life for thirty years with Ruth Wilcox before she died and then married Margaret. After the death of Ruth, he would recall the sweet memories of his association with her as well as her uncommon virtues: "He remembered his wife's even goodness during thirty years. Not anything in detail—not courtship or early raptures—but just the unvarying virtue, that seemed to him a woman's noblest quality. So many women are capricious, breaking into odd flaws of passion or frivolity. Not so his wife...he had always trusted her. Her tenderness! Her innocence! The wonderful innocence that was hers by the gift of God. Ruth knew no more of worldly wickedness and wisdom than did the flowers in her garden, or the grass in her field" (section XI).

Henry was a "man of business," and was a successful businessman: "Since his wife's death he had almost doubled his income. He was an important figure at last, a reassuring name on company prospectuses, and life had treated him very well. The world seemed in his grasp" (section XV). As a good businessman ought to be, Henry was "Always a good judge of character for business purposes" (section XVIII). He had his share of flaws, and Margaret knew them. She told Helen about his faults: "'I know Mr Wilcox's faults. He's afraid of emotion. He cares too much about success, too little about the past. His sympathy lacks poetry, and so isn't sympathy really. I'd even say...that, spiritually, he's not as honest as I am'" (section XIX). In section XXII of the novel, Forster describes an aspect of Mr Wilcox's soul or inner world: "It was hard going in the roads of Mr Wilcox's soul. From boyhood he had neglected them. 'I am not a fellow who bothers about my own inside.' Outwardly he was cheerful, reliable and brave; but within, all had reverted to chaos, ruled, so far as it was ruled at all, by an incomplete asceticism. Whether as boy, husband or widower, he had always the sneaking belief that bodily passion is bad, a belief that is desirable only when held passionately. Religion had confirmed him.... He could not be as the saints and love the Infinite with a seraphic ardour, but he could be a little ashamed of loving a wife" (section XXII).

Henry, a "good average Englishman," (section XII) but "the avatar of colonialist capitalism" (Tambling, 221), first met Jacky, the future wife of Leonard Bast, in Cyprus, and fell into the seine of this woman who had then been a pimp (section XIII). He had had carnal relation with her, but afterwards had forgotten her altogether, and yet could shamefully recognise her when she was taken by Helen before him, along with Leonard, to demand from him compensation for Leonard.

Henry was a clear contrast to Helen: Helen was a devoted socialist but Henry thought socialism to be an absurd idea. He told Helen in the manner of an advice: "By all means subscribe to charities—subscribe to them [the poor] largely—but don't get carried away by absurd schemes of Social Reform. I see a good deal behind the scenes, and you can take it from me that there is no Social Question—except for a few journalists who try to get a living out of the phrase. There are just rich and poor, as there always have been and always will be. Point me out a time when men have been equal—" (section XXII). Henry showed not even a little sympathy for Leonard Bast who had been reduced to a veritable beggar for his own cozenage, and was of the opinion that the rich would have to bear with, from time to time, the 'unjust' and nagging demands of the poor, if the rich wanted to keep their mental peace. He told Helen: "'A word of advice. Don't take up that sentimental attitude over the poor, one's sorry for them, but there it is. As civilization moves forward, the shoe is bound to pinch in places, and it's absurd to pretend that anyone is responsible personally.'" Hearing this, true to her nature, "Helen quivered with indignation" (section XXII). Henry believed only in the 'prose' of life and never in the 'poetry' of it, he believed only in reason and never in passion, and so he failed to 'connect' the prose with the poetry, or reason with passion, and, consequently, he had been suffering from his 'inner darkness'—his was a 'fragmented' life.

To Henry sex-difference was a fact, and equality between the sexes was a myth. Henry believed that "Man is for war, woman for the recreation of the warrior" (section XXXI).

Elizabeth Langland writes in this regard: "In contrast to Helen, Henry is associated with an imagery of war, battle, and self defence. When Margaret discovers that Jacky Bast was Henry's mistress, the narrator claims that, 'Expelled from his old fortress, Mr Wilcox was building a new one'.... At the end of the novel, in the crisis over Helen, Henry speaks 'straight from his fortress'.... It is only when 'Henry's fortress [gives] way' that Margaret can initiate the process that leads to the integration, the connection" (Tambling, 88). Henry's preference for masculine virility is obvious from all these, and his notion of feminine weakness is only a matter of influence. Nonetheless, Henry was fond of the womankind. He was never misogynist: he was drawn to Jacky, he loved—genuinely loved—both his wives, past and present. He recalled the sweet memories of Ruth and he would enjoy the 'show of fight' from Margaret. Not only this, he was inordinately reformed by Margaret, his new wife, and was almost totally converted into her bucolic philosophy which she herself adopted after her marriage with him, rejecting her earlier suburban philosophy. Margaret once did not detest the urban life, but, after her marriage, she was hankering after the green and quietude of the country, and Mr Wilcox only acquiesced.

However, John Sayre Martin writes about the character of Henry Wilcox: "Henry is the novel's chief flaw. A caricature of a businessman, he is stiff, easily muddled, utterly imperceptive about himself and others, and without a grain of redeeming wit and humour. Forster's dislike for the man comes through again and again. We learn of Henry's 'Olympian laugh' (...), his 'patronizing tone,' and his feeling that 'what he did not know could not be worth knowing'" (Martin 115). Forster, as if, for a moment comes out of the bound of his fictional world to personally despise Henry, or men like him, through his mouthpiece, Margaret, when it was exposed that he had a mistress even while he had a wife, and an ideal one at that. In section XXXVIII of the novel, Margaret bitterly vituperates Henry: "'Stupid, hypocritical, cruel—oh, contemptible!—a man who insults his wife when she's alive and cants with her memory when she's dead. A man who ruins a woman for his pleasure, and casts her off to ruin other men. And gives bad financial advice, and then says he is not responsible. These, man, are you. You can't recognize them, because you cannot connect. I've had enough of your unweeded kindness, I've spoilt you long enough. All your life you have been spoiled. Mrs Wilcox spoiled you. No one has ever told you what you are—muddled, criminally muddled. Men like you use repentance as a blind, so don't repent. Only say to yourself, "'What Helen has done, I've done.'" The dark inside and the bright outside of the character of Henry is quite revealed here. Of course Henry had a few redeeming qualities, otherwise Margaret could not have fallen in love of him and eventually marry him. These qualities are 'charm,' 'kindness', 'strength of character' and inexhaustible energy. These qualities attracted Margaret to Henry who was some twenty years older than herself, and, through him, to the outer world.

As Mr Wilcox deserves our hatred so Mrs Ruth Wilcox deserves our love and respect. She may be called an ingenue, showing attachment to nature, and possessing innocence, simplicity and love of simple and open hearts, like that of Margaret Schlegel. Ruth Wilcox, a lady of fifty-one years (section VIII) struck a deep and enduring friendship with Margaret Schlegel who was only twenty-nine. This proves that she loved the heart irrespective age. "Her tastes were simple, her knowledge of culture slight, and she was not interested in the New English Art Club, nor in the dividing-line between Journalism and Literature." Mrs Wilcox's "life had been spent in the service of husband and sons." "She was not intellectual, nor even alert.... There was no bitterness in Mrs Wilcox;...; she was lovable, and no ungracious or uncharitable word had passed her lips." "Clever talk alarmed her, and withered her delicate imaginings" (section IX). The only one passion of this 'tall' lady was her house (section X). She was aristocratic and worshipped the past (section III).

Mrs Wilcox died thirty years after her marriage with Mr Wilcox, who, plainly, cheated her by associating himself with Jacky as his mistress for some time, keeping Mrs Wilcox, the most simple and unsuspicious lady, quite in the dark.

Innocent love perhaps pays, for after Mrs Wilcox's death Mr Wilcox, who cheated her during her lifetime, "remembered his wife's goodness during thirty years." Mr Wilcox recalled the uncommon virtues of Mrs Wilcox: "Not anything in detail—not courtship or early raptures—but just the unvarying virtue, that seemed to him a woman's noblest quality. So many women are capricious, breaking into odd flaws of passion or frivolity. Not so his wife. Year after year, summer and winter, as bride and mother, she had been the same, he had always trusted her. Her tenderness! Her Innocence! The wonderful innocence that was hers by the gift of God. Ruth knew no more of worldly wickedness and wisdom than did the flowers in her garden, or the grass in her field." Mrs Wilcox's idea of politics was utterly naive. As regards religion, "She came of Quaker stock" and desired more of 'inward light' than of anything else, (section XI). If Mrs Wilcox had less intelligence and practical knowledge, she had enough of intuitive faculty; she could know, she could perceive through her sixth sense—with her inner eyes. At the end of the novel, Margaret was perhaps not amiss when she told Helen about Mrs Wilcox: "'She knows everything...I don't doubt that she knew when Henry deceived her'" (section XL).

Mrs Wilcox could sacrifice everything for 'personal intercourse,' for friendship. Her world was the 'inner world,' the world of feeling and intuition, as against Mr Wilcox's 'outer world'—the world of 'telegrams and anger.' That she valued 'personal intercourse' or friendship the most is evident from the fact that she bequeathed her most beloved property, Howards End, to none else than Margaret, with whom she developed a brief but the most deep friendship as with none else. It may be noted here that she did not bequeath Howards End to anyone of her three issues, which was only natural. Mrs Wilcox, who belonged to the 'inner world' could very successfully lead a married life for long thirty years with a man who utterly belonged to the 'outer world,' with Henry Wilcox. She knew the magic of connecting, more perfectly perhaps than Margaret.

Mrs Wilcox was, after all, more a symbol than a character, and this is explicit in what Margaret tells Helen about her in section XL of the novel: "I feel that you and I and Henry are only fragments of that woman's [Mrs Wilcox] mind. She knows everything. She is everything. She is the house, and the tree that leans over it.... I cannot believe that knowledge such as hers will perish with knowledge such as mine. She knew about realities. '...I don't doubt that she knew when Henry deceived her.'" The narrator suspects that not only the house and the tree are parts of Mrs Wilcox but also Leonard Bast: "Was he [Leonard Bast] also part of Mrs Wilcox's mind?" (section XL) That she is rather a symbol than a character is explicit also in what Stephen Spender writes about her: "Mrs Wilcox represents—or rather she incarnates—the English past in a particular meadow of Hertfordshire where there is still the house which is to her a shrine, but which is doomed to be submitted to the 'improvements' made at the command of her husband and the vulgar Wilcox clan.... She stands for values more deeply rooted than the Fabian socialist enthusiasms of Margaret and Helen or the brutalities and shabbiness of the 'Wilcox clan'" (Spender, 225). In her being a symbol, she is a parallel to Mrs Moore of *A Passage to India,* and very much foreshadows her: Mrs Wilcox is as intuitive, mystical and indefinable as Mrs Moore.

Leonel Trilling writes about the character of Mrs Ruth Wilcox: "As a character Ruth Wilcox is remarkably—and perhaps surprisingly—successful. Her 'reality' is of a strange kind and consists in her having no reality in the ordinary sense—she does not have, that is, the reality of personality, of idiosyncrasy or even of power. Her strength comes exactly from her lack of force, her distinction from her lack of distinguishing traits. She suggests Shakespeare's 'gentle' woman, the Countess of *All's Well* or an older Imogene; or she has a touch of Chaucer's Griselda. It is appropriate that we should find her kind in the past, for she represents England's past. But for all her lack of contemporary 'reality,' she is more successful as a real person than as a symbol; she must be seen to be believed and when she dies and becomes the brooding ghost of the story [like

Mrs Moore of *A Passage to India]*, she becomes a little trying, as perhaps all such symbolic spirits in novels do" (Trilling, 104-105). And John Sayre Martin writes about Mrs Wilcox: "Only Ruth Wilcox stands out from the rest of the [Wilcox] family. One of Forster's wise old woman, she incarnates the spirit of Howards End. An enigmatic, quasi-symbolic figure, less developed than Mrs Moore [of *A Passage to India*], whom she somewhat resembles, she values the past and the unseen, is intuitive rather than intellectual, and illustrates, by virtue of her successful marriage to Henry, the possibility of integrating past and present, the inner life and the outer" (Martin, 116).

Charles Wilcox was the elder son of Henry and Ruth, was happily married to Dolly, and to some extent resembled his father in terms of physical features. His physical features are as follows: "He seemed a gentleman...To a feminine eye there was nothing amiss in the sharp depressions at the corners of his mouth, nor in the rather box-like construction of his forehead. He was dark, cleanshaven, and seemed accustomed to command." Such was Mrs Munt's impression of Charles when she first met him at the station (section III). Charles was a conventional person, unlike Tibby. The "gulf between them was economic and spiritual" (section XXXIX). Paul Wilcox was Charles' younger brother, and was handsomer than Charles. Paul was about the age of Helen towards whom he was once passionately drawn and then kissed her: "But the heave of her bosom flattered him. Passion was possible, and he became passionate. Deep down in him something whispered: 'This girl would let you kiss her; you might not have such a chance again'" (section IV). Helen did never forget Paul's kiss ever afterwards, inspite of her Bast episode. Paul was a "very young man" (section III) with "heavy black moustache" (section XLIV).

Tibby is Theobald Schlegel (section XXV). He was sixteen and was "dyspeptic and diffident" (section XXVI). He was a lonely scholar at Oxford, having no friends there. "Tibby, for all his defects, had a genuine personality." His ideal was a society of sinecures or 'lotus-eaters' not to be found in England, but elsewhere: "'And I,' said Tibby, 'want civilization without activity, which, I expect, is what we shall find in the other place'" (section XII). Unlike his sister Helen, Tibby was quite insouciant about social or political matters, but, then, he was not inhumane. In section XXX of the novel, the narrator describes Tibby's nature and his socio-political ideal: "Tibby neither wished to strengthen the position of the rich nor to improve that of the poor, and was well content to watch the elms nodding behind the mildly embattled parapets of Magdalen. There are worse lives. Though selfish, he was never cruel; though affected in manner, he never posed. Like Margaret, he disdained the heroic equipment, and it was only after many visits that men discovered [Tibby] Schlegel to possess a character and a brain." In the later years of his Oxford career, there occurred a change in the personality of Tibby. "Mellowing rapidly, he was a pleasanter companion than before. Oxford had done much for him. He had lost his peevishness, and could hide his indifference to people and his interest in food. But he had not grown more human. The years between eighteen and twenty-two, so magical for most, were leading him gently from boyhood to middle age. He had never known young manliness, that quality which warms the heart till death...his was frigid—through no fault of his own, and without cruelty" (section XXXIV). Tibby was also unlike Charles, because, whereas Charles respected conventions, Tibby "stood above the conventions" (section XXXIX). Paul Delany, in his article 'Rentier Culture in *Howards End*,' writes about Tibby: "The Schlegels' younger brother Tibby is stigmatised, but for emotional rather than physical laziness. As his name suggests, he is a rather epicene young man, who warms the teapot 'almost too deftly' (...). He is also a surrogate for Forster himself; as with Rickie in *The Longest Journey,* the author passes a stern sentence on those whose deficiencies are closest to his own. Tibby's languid existence contrasts with the striving Wilcoxes, but morally he is no better than them" (Tambling, 74).

We come across Leonard Bast for the first time in section V of the novel, where we see him enjoying, or he seems to be enjoying, a Beethoven concert in the Queen's Hall, where both

Margaret and Helen also went. Helen stole Leonard's umbrella and thus he came into the warp and woof of the story. At the beginning of section VI, the narrator describes him as follows: "He knew that he was poor, and would admit it; he would have died sooner than confess any inferiority to the rich. This may be splendid of him. But he was inferior to most rich people, there is not the least doubt of it. He was not as courteous as the average rich man, nor as intelligent, nor as healthy, nor as lovable. His mind and his body had been alike underfed, because he was poor." In section XVI, the narrator further tells us about Leonard: "As a lady's lap-dog Leonard did not excel. He was not an Italian, still less a Frenchman, in whose blood there runs the very spirit of persiflage and of gracious repartee. His wit was the Cockney's; it opened no doors into imagination." In the same section, Margaret tells Mr Wilcox why she liked Leonard: "'Firstly, because he cares for physical adventure, just as you do. Yes, you go motoring and shooting; he would like to go camping out. Secondly, he cares for something special in adventure. It is quickest to call that special something poetry—.'"

Leonard was 'a clerk in the employment of the Porphyrion Fire Insurance Company.' He was "a young man, colourless, toneless, who had already the mournful eyes above a drooping moustache that are so common in London, and that haunt some streets of the city like accusing presences. One guessed him as the third generation, grandson to the shepherd or ploughboy whom civilization had sucked into the town; as one of the thousands who have lost the life of the body and failed to reach the life of the spirit. Hints of robustness survived him, more than a hint of primitive good looks, and Margaret, noting the spine that might have been straight, and the chest that might have broadened, wondered whether it paid to give up the glory of the animal for a tailcoat and a couple of ideas" (section XIV). He was 'handsome' and well-read as well as cultured. He liked reading books and doing adventures, and believed and told Helen that "'the real thing's money, and all the rest is a dream'" (section XXVII). Nicola Beauman says that Forster probably had chosen the title 'Bast' to mean 'spiritual bastard' (Beauman, 215 f. n.) and perhaps Leonard Bast was so, but, nonetheless, to Tibby, "Leonard Bast seemed somewhat a monumental person after all" (section XXX). And, in the eyes of Margaret and Helen, Leonard appeared to be the "'real man, who cared for adventure and beauty'" (Tambling, 84).

He quite unwillingly fell into the carnal drag-net of Jacky when he was not yet twenty-one and she, a massive woman, thirty-three, and got married to her. Before his intimacy with Jacky developed, he was amorously enticed by Helen who got impregnated by him. In section XV, Mr Wilcox tells Margaret about Leonard's relation with Jacky, and about his life after marriage: "'He is married to a wife whom he doesn't seem to care for much. He likes books, and what one may roughly call adventure.... He lives a life where all the money is apt to go on nonsense and clothes. One is afraid that circumstances will be too strong for him and that he will sink.'" Leonard's relation with Jacky may be clear from the following lines of the narrative in section XIV: "All the Friday Leonard had refused to speak to her [Jacky], and he had spent the evening observing the stars. On the Saturday he went up, as usual, to town, but he came not back Saturday night, nor Sunday morning, nor Sunday afternoon. The inconvenience grew intolerable, and though she was now of a retiring habit, and shy of women, she went up to Wickham Place. Leonard returned in her absence."

Leonard's parents and kins were very humble: "His parents, who were dead, had been in trade; his sisters had married commercial travellers; his brother was a lay-reader." His grandparents were "'agricultural labourers and that sort.'" Though his married life was not happy, he was dutiful enough to his wife. He said: "'I needn't have married her, but as I have I must stick to her and keep her'" (section XXVII). Leonard was the victim of the jealousy of Mr Wilcox around Leonard's fictive love for Margaret, and consequently he was reduced to a virtual beggar, and yet he did not harbour in himself any animus against Mr Wilcox. To Helen, "Leonard seemed not a man, but a cause" (section XL)—Leonard represented the exploited poor for whom the socialist Helen fought. Whatever faults may have invaded the character of Leonard, according to the narrator, there were in him 'two bright spots.' Firstly, "He never confused the past." He believed in the philosophy: "And if I drink oblivion of a day, /So shorten I the stature of my soul." And the other bright spot yet was his tenderness for Jacky" (section XLI).

John Sayre Martin writes about the character of Leonard Bast: "For all their differences, the Schlegels and Wilcoxes are rich. Leonard Bast, the novel's other key character, is poor. A young clerk, who lives in a squalid London flat with his mistress—later his wife—Jacky, he tries to relieve the tedium of existence by going to concerts and reading Ruskin and other 'improving' writers.... Victimized by the outer life, Leonard cannot give more than sporadic attention to the inner. Spiritually he is in no-man's-land, a fragmented being who will never be whole" (Martin, 116). Martin thinks that the character of Leonard has not been successfully drawn by Forster: "like Henry Wilcox, Leonard is one of the novel's failures, for Forster had no firsthand knowledge of what it feels like to be poor and ambitious" (*op. cit.*, 117).

Jacky Bast was a disreputable woman before her marriage with Leonard, having had immoral relationship with Mr Wilcox in the Cyprus island. In section VII, Forster describes her at some length, as he does no other character in the novel: "A woman entered, of whom it is simplest to say that she was not respectable. Her appearance was awesome. She seemed all strings and bell-pulls—ribbons, chains, bead necklaces that clinked and caught—and a boa of azure feathers hung round her neck, with the ends uneven. Her throat was bare, wound with a double row of pearls, her arms were bare to the elbows, and might again be detected at the shoulder, through cheap lace. Her hat, which was flowery, resembled those punnets, covered with flannel, which we sowed with mustard and cress in our childhood, and which germinated here yes, there no. She wore it on the back of her head. As for her hair, or rather hairs, they are too complicated to describe, but one system went down her back, lying in a thick pad there, while another, created for a lighter destiny, rippled around her forehead. The face—the face does not signify. It was the face of the photograph, but older, and the teeth were not so numerous as the photographer had suggested, and certainly not so white. Yes, Jacky was past her prime, whatever that prime may have been. She was descending quicker than most women into the colourless years, and the look in her eyes confessed it." This caricaturistic description of her externalities is eloquent enough to suggest what sort of a mind dwelt in herself. Jacky was a "massive woman of thirty-three" (section VI) when she enticed Leonard into marrying her. She was "bestially stupid" (section XXVI). Margaret could not tolerate her, but Helen was rather sympathetic to her, inspite of her improbity, particularly because she was, as Helen understood, a victim of aggressive patriarchy, of Mr Wilcox's ill treatment of her, not only in Cyprus but also afterwards.

(iv)

As expected, Forster has employed fantasy also in *Howards End:* he has referred to such mythological figures as Cupid (section V and VI); Pan (section XIII); Isis, Sabrina and Leo (section XXIII) and Erinyes (section XLI). Cupid and Pan we have already discussed. The Erinys were the Furies; Isis "was goddess of the rainbow and messenger of the gods" (Lass, 110). The myth that has been dealt with a little elaborately is that of pig's teeth in the bark of the wych-elm near Howards End. In section VIII, we first hear of the myth of pig's teeth from Margaret who tells Mr Wilcox: "'There are pig's teeth stuck into the trunk, about four feet from the ground. The country people put them in long ago, and they think that if they chew a piece of the bark it will cure the toothache.'" We hear of pig's teeth in wych-elm once again in section XXII, where we learn that such trees are sacred and that chewing their bark dispels toothache. In section XXXIII, Forster pines for more mythology in England: "Why has not England a great mythology? Our folklore has never advanced beyond daintiness, and the greater melodies about our countryside have all issued through the pipes of Greece. Deep and true as the native imagination can be, it seems to have failed here. It has stopped with the witches and the fairies. It cannot vivify one fraction of a summer field, or give names to half a dozen stars. England still waits for the supreme moment of her literature—for the great poet who shall voice her, or, better still, for the thousand little poets whose voices shall pass into our common talk."

The prophesy of *Howards End* may be found in its epigram 'Only connect!' The novel's especial concern is human relationship. The novel is dialectical in nature, in so far as it deals with the conflict between the two economic classes, in so far as it deals with the discrepancies between the township and the countryside, in so far as it deals with the relation between the sexes, and, lastly, in so far as it deals with the conflict between reason and passion—between prose and poetry. And the novel suggests that all the conflicts can be overcome or averted only if we can connect the two conflicting poles. In section XXXIII, Forster's prophetic vision reflects England's past—the England that comprised only of the countryside and consisted only of the English farms. But the Georgian England, in which the novel was created, was very much suburban. The old England represented 'eternal youth' and the contemporary Edwardian England represented life's 'transitoriness.' England's salvation, according to the prophesy lies in connecting the two aspects of her Life is, in a sense, both transitory and eternal—and these two aspects of life must be connected if one wants to make it a whole. In the same section, Forster persuades us to connect all the opposing poles of life, everywhere, so that life could be made worth living: "In these English farms, if anywhere, one might see life steadily and see it whole, group in one vision its transitoriness and its eternal youth, connect—connect without bitterness until all men are brothers."

In all his novels, Forster's style is the same: he follows almost the same pattern and always moves forward rhythmically. At least three major characters of *Howards End* change their 'positions' in the plot, i.e., are reformed: the two Schlegel sisters and Mr Wilcox. The Schlegel sisters at the end of the novel are not what they had been in the early part of it, and this is equally true also of Mr Wilcox. The rhythmical movement of the narrative is manifested in the almost repetitive actions of the major characters with occasional divergencies, conditional to situations newly arisen as a result of interactions of the characters.

(v)

As normal in any other Forster's novel, sudden deaths are there also in *Howards End;* there are three sudden deaths in it—Mrs Wilcox dies in section XI, Mr Bryce dies in section XXXI, and Leonard Bast dies in section XLI. Forster treats of all the three deaths very casually, as if death is one of the daily events of life, and his duty it is only to report to us that those who died duly passed through the 'Great Gate' (section XXXIV). Another Forsterian caprice—the frequent use of the word 'muddle' and its variants—is also to be noticed in this novel: the word 'muddle' and its variants occur at least nine times throughout this novel of some 314 pages.

In his novels, Forster always tends to be poetical whenever the occasion arises. In *Howards End* there are many brief passages where his narrative has verged into poetry. Four such poetic passages may be cited as examples. In section XIV, we come across the following very beautiful description of an evening when Leonard Bast was going away after a tryst with Schlegel sisters: "London was beginning to illuminate herself against the night. Electric lights sizzled and jogged in the main thoroughfares, gas lamps in the side-streets glimmered a canary gold or green. The sky was a crimson battlefield of spring, but London was not afraid. Her smoke mitigated the splendour, and the clouds down Oxford Street were a delicately painted ceiling, which adorned while it did not distract. She has never known the clear-cut armies of the purer air. Leonard hurried through her tinted corridors, very much part of the picture. His was a gray life, and to brighten it he had ruled off a few corners for Romance." In section XV, Forster describes the city of London at a particular moment thus: "As Margaret and Helen sat down, the city behind them seemed to be a vast theatre, an opera-house in which some endless trilogy was performing, and they themselves a pair of satisfied subscribers, who did not mind losing a little of the second act." Then, in section XIX, we read: "England was alive, throbbing through all her estuaries, crying for joy through the mouths of all her gulls, and the north wind, with contrary motion, blew stronger against her rising seas. What did it mean? For what end her fair complexities, her changes of soil, her sinuous coast? Does she belong to those who have moulded her and made her feared by other lands, or to those who have added nothing to her power, but have somehow seen her, seen the whole island at once, lying as a jewel in a silver sea, sailing as a ship of souls, with all the brave world's fleet accompanying her towards eternity?"

And, lastly, at the end of section XL, the following: They were silent for a little. It was Helen's evening.

The present flowed by them like a stream. The tree rustled. It had made music before they were born, and would continue after their deaths, but its song was of the moment. The moment had passed. The tree rustled again. Their senses were sharpened, and they seemed to apprehend life. Life passed. The tree rustled again.

'Sleep now,' said Margaret.

"The peace of the country was entering into her. It has no commerce with memory, and little with hope. Least of all is it concerned with the hopes of the next five minutes. It is the peace of the present, which passes understanding. Its murmur came 'now,' and 'now' once more as they trod the gravel, and 'now' as the moonlight fell upon their father's sword. They passed upstairs, kissed, and amidst the endless iterations fell asleep. The house had enshadowed the tree at first, but as the moon rose higher the two disentangled, and were clear for a few moments at midnight. Margaret awoke and looked into the garden. How incomprehensible that Leonard Bast should have own her this night of peace! Was he also part of Mrs Wilcox's mind?"

Forster is always delighted by the even beauty of nature—of pastures, of farms, of the moonlit sky, of gurgling streams, etc. and his joy of such things unawares intrudes his fictions. Though he was not virulently anti-science, like Robert Frost or

Wordsworth, he was a lover of nature and as such was lukewarm about the prospects that humanity may derive from the éclat of science. Forster's story 'The Machine Stops' was a protest against contemporary scientific credo, upheld by such writers as H.G. Wells. In 1908, it was reported that 'a man had flown an air machine for one and a half minutes' and Forster wrote the following: "'It's coming quickly, and if I live to be old I shall see the sky as pestilential as the roads. It really *is* a new civilization. I have been born at the end of the age of peace and can't expect to feel anything but despair. Science, instead of freeing man—the Greeks nearly freed him by right feeling—is enslaving him to machines. Nationality will go, but the brotherhood of man will not come'" (Beauman, 214). Nicola Beauman writes: "This entry was a direct prefiguration of *Howards End,* in its impassioned feeling for the English countryside ('in these English farms, if anywhere, one might see life steadily and see it whole'), in its loathing of the kind of scene that may be observed all over London, whatever the locality—bricks and mortar rising and falling with the restlessness of the water in a fountain, as the city receives more and more men upon her soil,' and in its vision of a landscape destroyed by the motor car ('month by month the roads smelt more strongly of petrol')" (*ibid.*).

The narrative of *Howards End* is studded with stochastic, sketchy, but exquisite descriptions of the salubrius nature, espicially in the English countryside. Only a few of these descriptions are being cited here. In section XXIII, we come across the description of a patch of nature: "There were the greengage trees that Helen had once described, there the tennis lawn, there the hedge that would be glorious with dog-roses in June, but the vision now was of black and palest green. Down the dell-hole more vivid colours were awakening, and Lent lilies stood sentinel on its margin, or advanced in battalions over the grass. Tulips were a tray of jewels. She could not see the wych-elm tree, but a branch of the celebrated vine, studded with velvet knobs, had covered the porch." In the same section, after a few lines, Forster compares the beauty of the small patch of green countryside with the metropolis of

London. Helen saw the little beautiful garden at the back of Howards End and compared it with the grey vastness of London: "The garden at the back was full of flowering cherries and plums. Further on were hints of the meadow and a black cliff of pines. Yes, the meadow was beautiful. "Penned in by the desolate weather, she recaptured the sense of space which the motor had tried to rob from her. She remembered again that ten square miles are not ten times as wonderful as one square mile, that a thousand square miles are not practically the same as heaven." Before this, in section XXXI, Margaret compared the influence of the countryside and that of the metropolis, such as London, on human beings: "London was but a foretaste of (this) nomadic civilization which is altering human nature so profoundly, and throws upon personal relations a stress greater than they have ever borne before. Under cosmopolitanism, if it comes, we shall receive no help from the earth. Trees and meadows and mountains will only be a spectacle, and the binding force that they once exercised on character must be entrusted to Love alone. May Love be equal to the task!"

(vi)

Lionel Trilling says that "*Howards End* is undoubtedly Forster's masterpiece; it develops to their full the themes and attitudes of the early books [previous novels of Forster] and throws back upon them a new and enhancing light. It justifies these attitudes by connecting them with a more mature sense of responsibility" (Trilling, 99). Trilling further writes: "*Howards End* is a work of full responsibility. Its theme is 'Only connect the prose and the passion,' and it shows how almost hopelessly difficult it is to make this connection. That the insights of Forster's earlier novels could have come to face this difficulty is their justification" (*op. cit.,* 102). John Sayre Martin says that "*Howards End,* Forster's fourth novel, has a wider social range than his previous fiction [or, fictions?]. In addition to the society of the cultivated and well-to-do, it deals with the world of business and that of shabby gentility" (Martin, 109). Trilling and Martin are at variance as to the subject matter of *Howards End.* While Trilling says that "*Howards End* is a novel about England's fate" (Trilling, 102), Martin writes that the novel is not about England's fate, "for it leaves too much of England out of account" (Martin, 109). But Martin admits that in one respect the novel is concerned about England. He writes: "Nevertheless, in one important respect, the world of *Howards End* does resemble our own [the world of England]: socially and spiritually it is fragmented. Except in their formal dealings, the various classes of society scarcely communicate with one another. There is a gulf between rich and poor, and a subtler, but nonetheless insidous one, between men and women. Public life is divorced from private, the outer world from the inner" (*ibid.*).

The title of the novel is taken from the name of a rural house that was situated in Hilton in Herfordshire and belonged to Mr Wilcox. In section XXIV of the novel, Forster tells us that the house was called Howards End because it earlier belonged to Tom Howard—the last of the Howards—before it was owned by Mrs Wilcox. It is for this reason that when Dolly first heard of the peculiar nomenclature of the house, she cried out: "'Howards End—Howards Ended!'" (section XXIV). As we have said in the novel of some 314 pages, the name of the house, Howards End, appears at least seventy-four times. The reason of this is that Howards End is not simply a house, it is the central locus of the major events of the novel, and it is the symbol of the bucolic past of England—one of the major concerns of the novel. Howards End was Ruth Wilcox's ancestral home, where she, along with her husband Henry Wilcox and three grown up children—Charles, Paul and Evie,—lived.

Martin has pointed out that the novel is allegorical and thrives upon contraries: "Forster's fictive imagination tends to work allegorically, and nowhere more obviously so than in *Howards End*. The novel's world is composed of contraries—of antithetical places and people, embodying antithetical values" (Martin, 110). There is the city of London and there is the village of Hilton, adjoining Howards End; there is the masculine household of the Wilcoxes and there is the feminine household of the Schlegels (among the Wilcoxes the males outnumber the females, and among the Schlegels, the females outnumber the males); and there is the rich class, consisting of both the Wilcoxes and the Schlegels (the rentier class) and there is the poor class, consisting of the Basts. Further contraries are also there in the novel. "Superficially Margaret and Helen are similar, both being liberal, cultivated, intelligent, and, compared to almost any modern girl of their class, unbelievably sheltered and ignorant of the world. Yet the antitheses that help to define the novel's structure also distinguish Helen from Margaret" (*op. cit.,* 111). "Helen is a romantic idealist. Truth and justice, she believes, are absolute, and she finds it hard to compromise with the world as it is" (*ibid.*). She was an extremist, she could not, and did not want to, 'connect' the poetry with the prose, or the reason with the passion, but Margaret could and did—she 'connected' Mr Wilcox's rationality with the passion of Helen. Further, Margaret was a realist while Helen was for the most part a symbolist. Both Paul and Leonard were, for instance, symbols to Helen: "Neither man did she really love. Both to her were symbols, Paul of romantic virility, Leonard of the poor and exploited" (*op. cit.,* 112).

Margaret is the heroine of the novel and is Forster's mouth-piece, and she is the heroine because she is the mouth-piece. Martin writes: "Margaret, not Helen, is the heroine, because it is only Margaret who, when the three connected crises of the novel occurs—the disclosure of Helen's adultery, of Helen's pregnancy, and of Leonard's death—demonstrates the love, compassion, and the sense of proportion needed to establish harmony. Disdaining 'the heroic equipment' (...), she nevertheless performs heroically" (*op. cit.,* 120). According to Martin, Helen cannot claim to be the heroine. Martin writes that she "tries to be heroic and fails. Taking up Leonard's cause in the name of Truth and Justice by melodramatically bringing him and Jacky to Evie Wilcox's wedding-party, she inadvertently paves the way for Leonard's death. Her action recalls Harriet Herriton's even brasher attempt to secure 'justice' for Gino's baby by kidnapping the child, in *Where Angels Fear to Tread*. Such extremism, both novels suggest, can be disastrous. Forster, who claims to distrust Great Men and the radical social surgery they frequently advocate, puts more faith in the less spectacular, mediating force of people like Margaret" (*op. cit,* 120-121). But Leonel Trilling does not agree with Martin; according to him, both Margaret and Helen are heroines of *Howards End,* "one the heroine of the practical life, the other of the ideal life" (Trilling, 116) However, Trilling says that, as there are double heroines in the novel, so there in it Henry Wilcox and Leonard Bast "together, the practical man and the seeker after experience, make up the composite hero" (*ibid.*).

(vii)

Howards End had had its immediate and immense success as very few novels may have had. P.N. Furbank writes (and let us quote at some length): "*Howards End* was published on 18 October 1910, and the press, almost unanimously, treated the occasion as marking Forster's 'arrival.' The book hit the note of the time. Even *Punch* said that anything could be forgiven an author who introduced us to the great Wilcox family. 'For the Wilcoxes *are* England; they contain more of the essence of England even than Sunday afternoon, or Lords, or Sir WILLIAM BULL.' For the first time, the word 'great' was bandied about; Archibald Marshall, in the *Daily Mail,* hailed it as 'The Season's Great Novel,' and the *Daily Telegraph* went so far as to begin: 'There is no doubt about it whatever, Mr. E.M. Forster is one of the great novelists.' Frank Harris's *Saturday Review* said that, to express his genius in using everyday speech to betray 'cunning shadowings' of personality, the term 'Forsterian' was now a necessity. There was another development, too. Hitherto, reviewers had all been confident, as reviewers are, that his true talent all lay in one single direction—though, to be sure, they had different views as to what this was; some thought social satire, some thought character-creation, some visionary profundity. Now one or two reviewers acknowledged, what seems plainer to us now, that his genius lay in a peculiar amalgam of talents and aims. R.A. Scott-James, by now an entire convert to Forster, saw this, and in his review in the *Daily Mail,* laid all his emphasis on coherence and 'connectedness'.... Forster's method, he said, was a sort of bridge between that of Conrad and that of Galsworthy: Conrad began with an incident from life and moved out from it towards a meaning, while Galsworthy started with a generalization and searched round for facts to illustrate it. 'But who could say of *Howards End* that the one method or the other had been adopted? The novel rises like a piece of architecture full-grown before us. It is all bricks and timber, but it is mystery, idealism, a far-reaching symbol.'" (Furbank, I, 188-189). Forster's own evaluation of *Howards End,* it may be pointed out here, was highly appreciative. Forty years after the publication of the book, he wrote about it: "'*Howards End* [and not *A Passage to India*] is my best novel and approaching a good novel. Very elaborate and all pervading plot that is seldom tiresome or forced, range of characters, social sense, wit, wisdom, colour'" (*op. cit.,* I, 190).

But all were not happy with *Howards End;* there were a few critics who could not at all appreciate the novel. P.N. Furbank writes: "One of the book's [Howards End's] few enemies was Edmund Gosse. He had been sent it by Edward Marsh and wrote to Marsh (27 December 1910) that he could 'hardly remember such a disappointment.' 'I try to analyse why, when *Where Angels Fear to Tread* was so very promising, and when *A Room with a View* seemed to advance that promise, *Howards End* makes one fear that no good thing will come of these anticipations. I think it is due to the author's having listened to the people who (may have) said that he should give more 'story,' and that he should be coarse in morals, and that he should coruscate in style. But these three things are not native to him, and so the man who gave us before such delicate and faithful studies of character, and who wrote so simply, now produces a book (which has many details of merit, but) which, taken as a whole, is sensational and dirty and affected'" (*op. cit.,* I, 189).

Among the later critics, Virginia Woolf only "disapproved of Helen's pregnancy in *Howards End*" (Beauman, 203) and D.H. Lawrence only "accused Morgan [Forster] of making 'a nearly deadly mistake glorifying those *business* people' [the

Wilcoxes]'" (*op. cit.,* 222). But John Sayre Martin has found many flaws in the novel: "*Howards End* has many weaknesses. Besides the poorly conceived characters...and a sometimes crudely managed plot, there is a good deal of coy or sentimental authorial comment, much of which attempts to control the reader's response to characters. Margaret's view, for example, that the portals of King's Cross Station suggest infinity is undercut with a facetious apology: 'If you think this ridiculous, remember that it is not Margaret who is telling you about it.' (...) Suspecting that Leonard's account of his nocturnal walk may not impress the reader, Forster tries to fortify it with a comment so ill-judged as to guarantee the reverse. 'You may laugh at him, you who have slept nights out on the veldt, with your rifle beside you and all the atmosphere of adventure pat. And you also may laugh who think adventures silly. But do not be surprised if Leonard is shy whenever he meets you, and if the Schlegels rather than Jacky hear about the dawn.'... These and other such remarks indicate not merely a failure of technique; they are symptomatic of Forster's inability to control his vision. They suggest that he is trying to force both himself and the reader to take seriously characters and values that he inwardly sees as ineffective or false" (Martin, 125-126).

Nicola Beauman is quite appreciative of *Howards End* for more reasons than one. He writes that "One of the most remarkable aspects *of Howards End* is its modernity. This is not just modernity of tone of voice, as in the Clough-influenced *Where Angels Fear to Tread,* but modernity of theme. It is still, to my mind, *the* great twentieth-century novel about London; and is perfectly contemporary for today in its contrasting of Thatcherism with liberal values. Margaret Thatcher is a direct descendant of Henry Wilcox, preaching the competitive instinct, the pay-your-way mentality, the work ethic; as opposed to liberal kindliness, loyalty to the individual, self-fulfilment. When Mr Wilcox says that 'one sound man of business did more good to the world than a dozen of your social reformers' and when we are told that he cares about 'neatness, obedience and decision'; and when the Schlegel sisters declare, famously, that 'personal relations are the important thing for ever and ever, and not this outer life of telegrams and anger' and when Margaret tries to help Mr Wilcox to achieve 'the building of the rainbow bridge that should connect the prose in us with the passion'; then we are reading about capitalist values and the liberal, intellectual classes that are opposed to them" (Beauman, 221). Nicola Beauman speaks of "the enormous success of *Howards End,* with reviewers almost unanimously recognising it as a great novel" (*op. cit.,* 241). He further says: "*Howards End* and *A Passage to India* are among the great novels of the [20th] century—but only for those who can see that lightness of touch, humour, domestic observation and psychological perception do not preclude insight into the weightiest, the most crucial aspects of our society" (*op. cit.,* 212). Beauman's opinion is fully shared by Leonel Trilling when he declares that "*Howards End* is undoubtedly Forster's masterpiece" (Trilling, 99).

Maurice

10

(i)

Forster published his fourth novel, *Howards End,* in 1910, and his sixth and last, *A Passage to India,* in 1924; then what did he do in the literary sphere during the intervening fourteen years or so? Yes, his literary production during the intervening period was small and comparatively unimportant. The reason is not one, but there are more than one reasons. Firstly, in 1911 he unsuccessfully tried his hand at play-writing and published the same year his only play *The Heart of Bosnia* which by his own account, was not good, and which has never been produced or published (Trilling, 117). Secondly, in 1912, Forster sail for India along with Dickinson and R.C. Trevelyan, and it was during this his first Indian visit that he was much preoccupied meeting Masood and the Maharajah of Dewas, sighting historical places, mixing with divers people, and through all these, collecting materials for his projected novel, *A Passage to India.* And thirdly, the breaking out of the First World War disturbed him much and threw him into a sort of mental chaos.

Nevertheless, it was even during the intervening period, from 1910 to 1924, that Forster, among some other minor things, not only wrote his only play *The Heart of Bosnia* (written in 1919) but also his only blatantly homosexual novel *Maurice.* We have not been sure as to when exactly did he write this novel, yet, on the authority of Nicola Beauman, we may say that it was written between 1910 and 1912 or 1913 (Beauman, 234). But we definitely know that it was posthumously published in 1971. P.N. Furbank agrees with Beauman as to when the novel was written, but according to

The Wordsworth Companion to Literature in English, Maurice was "written in 1913-14 and circulated privately, but not published until 1971, after the writer's death" (Ousby, 606). Forster also wrote another homosexual story during this long intervening period: 1910 to 1924. The story, 'The Life to Come', was written in 1922: "The story began merely as one of his 'indecencies,' but turned into something very different. It concerns a handsome young missionary who once sleeps with a young native chieftain, with the result that the chieftain takes their love to be that 'love of God' which is spoken of by Christians and promptly announces the conversion of his tribe. The missionary is appalled but is too prudent to give up this brilliant conversion, so he cheats his uncomprehending disciple, who wishes to enjoy more such love, with shadowy promises. Years pass, and the chieftain, broken-hearted at the postponement, and finding himself robbed not only of his religion but of his lands and royal authority, falls mortally ill. The missionary, now dried-up and middle-aged, comes to visit him on his deathbed, finding him lying alone and naked on his house-roof. He feels it safe now to venture a Christian embrace and tells the dying Vithobai of the joys of the life to come. 'And will there be love?' asks Vithobai. 'In the real and true sense, there will,' answers the missionary. 'The life to come,' shouts Vithobai. 'Life, life, eternal life. Wait for me in it'; and he stabs the missionary through the heart and hurls himself, victoriously, over the parapet" (Furbank, II, 114-115).

The origin of *Maurice* was somewhat mysterious. Edward Carpenter, the poet and proponent of homosexualism and the author of *The Intermediate Sex* (1908), "was a healer, who worked through personal and physical contact: he had what Forster later spoke of as 'the influence which used to be called magnetic'" (*op. cit.*, I, 257). He openly lived in his Millthorpe household with his young male lover George Merrill of the slums of Sheffield. Merrill also healed people by touching them. Forster himself felt the healing touch of Carpenter. In 1913, he visited Carpenter at Millthorpe and felt his healing touch. "He had never before felt such power in another man, and he put it down to Carpenter's breadth of humanity: 'He touched everyone everywhere.' Forster liked George Merrill too, in a mild sort of way, though he doubted if he were as devoted to wholesome toil as Carpenter believed, and Merrill also touched people—in his case, usually on the behind. He did so to Forster on this occasion [of his meeting with Carpenter and Merrill]; and his touch, or pinch, had momentous results. 'The sensation was unusual,' Forster wrote years later [in his Terminal Note of 1960 to *Maurice*], 'and I still remember it, as I remember the position of a long vanished tooth. It was as much psychological as physical. It seemed to go straight through the small of my back into my ideas, without involving my thoughts. If it really did this, it would have acted in strict accordance with Carpenter's yogified mysticism, and would prove that at that precise moment I had conceived.' "What he [Forster] had conceived was a novel about homosexual love—the novel *Maurice* in fact. The entire outline, the three main characters and the happy ending rushed into his mind, vivid and complete. He went back to Harrogate in a state of exaltation, feeling that the fog had cleared from his life. It was *this* he had been needing, he decided, to cure his sterility; and he sat down to work at once (It was the only occasion that he would write a novel in this manner, without lengthy planning and premeditation). In the intervals of writing, he read Samuel Butler's *Life and Habit,* which with its praise of instinct as the basis of right conduct, lent a kind of support to Carpenter's teaching" (*op. cit.,* I, 257-258). Forster "had no intentions of publishing the novel; so long as he lived with his mother he thought it out of the question; and for the moment [in 1913] he did not even plan to show it to anyone. What was necessary, he told himself, was simply to write it" (*op. cit.,* I, 258).

A brief summary of the story of *Maurice* is being given below from *The Wordsworth Companion to Literature in English* (edited by Ian Ousby): "Maurice Hall, aged 14, is to attend public school. The senior prep school master acquaints the boy with 'the mystery of sex,' an avarice idealization of relations between the sexes. Maturing, Maurice experiences homosexual tendencies but represses them to avoid conflict with the prevailing sexual ethos. Cambridge too is 'hell,' but Maurice, now entering his twenties, meets Clive Durham. After an agonizing and protracted flirtation, first Clive and then Maurice declare their love and a clandestine relationship ensures. Maurice leaves Cambridge for clerical work, Clive qualifies as a barrister. "Whilst in Greece, Clive decides to 'become normal, and breaks off their relationship. Maurice is heartbroken when Clive marries, and suffers acute isolation. However, during a visit to the newly-weds he meets Alec Scudder, Clive's gamekeeper. Alec is about to emigrate, but approaches Maurice in search of love. The latter responds, then is suspicious of Alec's motives and inhibited by class prejudice. They reach an understanding and spends Alec's last night in England together. Alec leaves for Southampton. Maurice, watching the boat sail, learns that Alec has decided to stay and proceeds triumphantly to join his lover" (606-7).

Nigel Messenger summarises the story of *Maurice* as follows. "Maurice Hall is the only son of a respectable Edwardian family. His home for most of the novel is middle-class, London suburbia where he lives with his widowed mother and his two sisters. After public school and Cambridge, he seems destined for an unexceptional life as a stockbroker in the family firm. However, though to outer appearances an entirely conventional business man whose career does indeed take the predictable route, Maurice is a homosexual. Most of the novel explores his slow discovery of this fact, the effect that it has on his private life, and how, finally, it transforms his existence. "After briefly following Maurice through his school days, the substance of the novel examines his relationship with two contrasting lovers. Maurice meets Clive Durham, a young squire, at Cambridge; they fall in love and have an intense, lyrical, platonic relationship that lasts for three years. Then, quite suddenly, Clive experiences an emotional change and reverts to 'normal' sexual feeling. He marries and takes up his role as pillar of the local community. Maurice is devastated. Full of sexual guilt and emotional self-loathing, he seeks a cure for his condition without any success. Matters are brought to a crisis on a visit Maurice makes to Penge, Clive's country house. He has a sexual liaison with Alex [Alec] Scudder, a gamekeeper on the estate. After the initial revulsion, fear and consequent antagonism between this socially ill-matched pair, Maurice persuades Alex to give up his plans to emigrate and live with him outside respectable society. The book ends with Maurice telling Clive of his new love before beginning his life as a social outlaw" (Messenger, 8-9).

Nicola Beauman has presented the plot of *Maurice* as follows: "The plot of the novel is simple. Maurice, a child of the suburbs, leaves his public school and goes to Cambridge. In his second year he meets Clive Durham, who has understood his own homosexual inclinations for a long time. Indeed 'His sixteenth year was ceaseless torture. He told no one, and finally broke down and had to be removed from school.'... Clive and Maurice realise they love one another; their love is chaste.... After two years of idyllic friendship Clive goes on holiday on his own to Greece. He determines to be 'normal' and tells Maurice as much; the following year, in the spring, he announces his engagement. Initially Maurice contemplates suicide. Then he tries to change his nature for, after all, 'He wanted a woman to secure him socially and diminish his lust and bear children.' He tries hypnosis; but at the Durham's house encounters a gamekeeper named Alec. Alec climbs into Maurice's bedroom and they make love: 'By pleasing the body Maurice had confirmed—the very word was used in the final verdict—he had confirmed his spirit in its perversion, and cut himself off from the congregation of normal man'" (Beauman, 231-232).

(ii)

Maurice has three major characters: Maurice Hall, Clive Durham and Alec Scudder. The word 'Maurice' derives from the Latin word 'Morris' which means 'Moorish' or 'dark-coloured.' Maurice, the protagonist of *Maurice,* is certainly not dark-coloured, but he is dark in the sense that, as a homosexual, he is a social outcast. The name of the character of Maurice and the title of the novel as well may have been taken from the name of the founder of the Working Men's College, which Forster joined in 1909: John Frederick Denison Maurice (1805-1872). The college was founded by F.D. Maurice to try to bridge the gulf between the upper class and the lower class by means of 'culture' awareness. P.N. Furbank writes about the Working Men's College: "It was in many ways a remarkable institution, very important during its first fifty years or so—that is, from the 1850s onwards—though by the time Forster joined it, it had been overtaken by newer types of adult education (in particular the Workers' Educational Association). It had been founded by F.D. Maunce in 1854, in the period—just after the defeat of Chartism and the year of revolutions—when there was a concerted effort of intellectuals, and the 'clericy' general, to heal the class-war by means of 'culture.' ('We came forward to help the working man that we might help ourselves,' said Maurice.)" (Furbank, I, 174). Maurice was a clergyman and a leader of Christian Socialism. He was Professor of English Literature and History at King's College, London, and also Professor of Theology in the same college. He expressed his views in favour of religious unity and socialism through his following books: *The Kingdom of Christ, The Religions of the World, Social Morality, Moral and Metaphysical Philosophy* and *Theological Essays.*

Associating Christian practice with the need for social reform, Maurice held that 'a true socialism is the necessary result of a sound Christianity.' The belief led to the formation of the Christian Socialist group and his connection with J.M.F. Ludlow, Thomas Hughes and Charles Kingsley. *Theological Essays* (1853) brought Maurice into conflict with authority (once more) by questioning the accepted doctrine of eternal punishment. He was dismissed from King's College, an event which prompted Tennyson's lyric, 'To the Rev. F.D. Maurice' (1855). In 1866 he became Professor of Moral Philosophy at Cambridge. Maurice's lasting memorial is The Working Men's College, London, which arose from the organization of evening classes and was firmly established in 1858" (Ousby, 607). In that lyric, Tennyson has paid homage to Maurice in glorious terms. The lyric begins with the following four lines, in which the poet has called Maurice 'Godfather:'

> Come, when no graver cares employ,
> Godfather, come and see your boy:
> Your presence will be sun in winter,
> Making the little one leap for joy.

In 1987, *Maurice* was filmed by James Ivory who in 1986 directed *A Room with a View* and in 1992 directed *Howards End*. In that film of *Maurice,* the following stars appeared (Tambling, 220):

i. James Wilby as Maurice
ii. Rupert Graves as Alec Scudder
iii. Helena Bonham Carter (who acted in four out of five Forster films) as 'lady at cricket match.'

(iii)

In *Maurice* there are both fleshy and platonic homosexual relationships, and through the tension between the two opposing relationships Maurice grew up, failed to attain a compromise formula between the two, and succumbed to his carnal homosexual tendency and showed himself as an outlaw. Robert K. Martin, in his learned article 'Edward Carpenter and the Double Structure of *Maurice,'* has very perceptively analysed the novel. Martin, in that article writes that "The novel is divided into roughly equal parts, each of which is then again divided in two, to provide the four parts identified by Forster. The first half of the book is devoted to the Maurice-Clive relationship, to suburban life, and to Cambridge. Similarly, the second half of the book is devoted to the Maurice-Alec relationship, to the opposition of gentry and servants, and to the country house, Penge. The first is dominated by Plato and, indirectly, by John Addington Symonds [1840-93: poet, homosexual, and supporter of sexual inversion] and the apologists for 'Greek love,' the second is dominated by Edward Carpenter and his translation of the ideas of Walt Whitman. The two sections run almost exactly parallel: Part I ends with Maurice entering Clive's window in response to his call;

Part III concludes with Alec entering Maurice's room in response to a similar call. Part II concludes with dawn, the hope-for light that ironically brings the death of the love between Maurice and Clive; Part IV ends with sunset, the apparent darkness that ironically brings life and the survival of the love of Maurice and Alec" (Tambling, 101).

In the same article, next, Martin shows us the stages in Maurice's development. He writes: "The novel (thus) depicts three stages in Maurice's development. In the first, Maurice comes to accept homosexuality as an idealised friendship, as the expression of a pure and spiritual love. In the second he moves toward the acceptance of lust in the physical expression of homosexuality. In the final stage he begins to accept the social and political consequences of homosexuality. In this final stage he realises that the outlawed state of the homosexual provides the privilege of a radical perspective on society. By creating a hero who is completely unexceptional, Forster calls attention to the possibility that homosexuality may provide growth for even the most conventional" (*op. cit.,* 108-109). The basic propositions of the novel are mostly dependent on Edward Carpenter's view of homosexuality, which view Carpenter mostly derived from Walt Whitman. Martin writes that "Forster's visit to Carpenter and his reading of him and Whitman, provided the basis for a novel [*Maurice*] that would attempt not to analyse the passage of a man from confused or repressed homosexuality to a blissful ideal homosexuality, but to juxtapose that development with another, much more significant one from the homosexuality of the *fin de siecle* aesthetes to the robust political homosexuality of Whitman and Carpenter" (*op. cit.,* 109).

Martin writes, in the same article, once again, that Carpenter exerted an immense influence on Forster in conceiving his *Maurice.* Martin says that a brief examination of Carpenter's *Love's Coming of Age* will make the point clear: "A brief examination of *Love's Coming of Age* will shed some light on the role Carpenter played in the conception of *Maurice.* Carpenter's essay 'Man the Ungrown' seems particularly pertinent. In it he concerns himself with 'the men of the

English-speaking well-to-do class' whose learning stops after public school. These men are, in Carpenter's analysis, permanent schoolboys who continue to run society by the rules of their school days. These men see no reason for equality in marriage, since for them, according to Carpenter, 'it seems quite natural that our marriage and social institutions should lumber along over the bodies of women, as our commercial institutions grind over the bodies of the poor and our "imperial" enterprise over the bodies of barbarian races.' The character of Clive is particularly influenced by Carpenter's analysis. He is Forster's illustration of the 'ungrown' man, who has never learned to question any of the values of his class. Clive's marriage in *Maurice* is an illustration of the marriage of such a man. The novel's final words '[he] returned to the house, to correct his proofs and to devise some method of concealing the truth from Anne' (...), illustrate not the failure of marriage, but the failure of such a marriage, based on inequality and ignorance.... The novel clearly rejects the idea of the superiority of homosexuality, and idea that is specifically Clive's and derived from Plato [Plato's *Symposium*], while keeping the idea that homosexuality may provide the occasion for a growth in spiritual awareness. It is not, of course, that heterosexuals are denied the possibility of such growth; it is that they lack the impulse toward it, and that the institutions of heterosexuality, such as marriage, specifically work against growth. Marriage in Carpenter's view is linked to property, whereas homosexuality exists outside of class and ownership. Maurice's realisation. 'They must live outside class, without relations or money; they must work and stick to each other till death' (...), is pure Carpenter—and, in turn, pure Whitman: recall the closing stanza of 'Song of the Open Road'.

> Camerade, I give you my hand!
> I give you my love more precious than money,
> I give you myself before preaching or law;
> Will you give me yourself? will you come travel with me?
> Shall we stick by each other as long as we live?"
>
> (Tambling, 109-110).

A few words about Edward Carpenter (1844-1929) at this point may not be *outre*. Carpenter, poet and socialist reformer, was educated at Cambridge. "In 1874 he abandoned the church to pursue his own brand of primitive communism, much influenced by the writings of Whitman and Thoreau. Among the English writers, he was indebted to Ruskin and William Morris. He eventually settled at Millthorpe, near Chesterfield, where he earned his living as a lecturer, farmer and controversial author in support of numerius progressive causes (sexual reform, women's rights, vegetarianism) aimed at subverting middle-class convention. He attracted a considerable number of admirers, notably E.M. Forster, for his overt homosexuality; and he was an early influence on D.H. Lawrence. "Carpenter's best-known prose works were *England's Ideal* (1887), *Civilization: Its Cause and Cure* (1889) and *Love's Coming of Age* (1896). Collections of his poetry included *Narcissus* (1873), *Towards Democracy* (1883-1902), along poem, published in four parts, which reflected his Whitmanic sense of 'cosmic consciousness' and 'spiritual democracy,' and *Sketches from Life in Town and Country* (1908). His autobiography, *My Days and Dreams,* was published in 1916" (Ousby, 156).

(iv)

As told earlier, Forster did not want to publish *Maurice* at all, or, at the least, not to let it be published during his life-time; but he wanted it privately circulated among his close friends. In 1915, he sent the novel to his friends Lytton Strachey, biographer and essayist, and Forrest Reid, the Irish novelist. Strachey's reaction was positive. He wrote to Forster: "'I enjoyed it [*Maurice*] very much indeed—I think really more than the others...'" Qua story, first—I thought it seemed to go off at the end to some extent. The beginning—especially up to the successful combination of Maurice and Clive—I liked very much: it appeared solid and advanced properly from point to point. The psychology of both excellent. The Maurice-Alec affair didn't strike me as so successful. For one thing, the class question is another red herring, I think. One suddenly learns that Maurice is exaggeratedly upper-classish—one wouldn't at all have expected it on the face of things—and then when the change comes, it seems to need more explanation. No doubt his falling in love with Alec was possible, but it's certainly queer as it happens—partly because the ground isn't enough prepared: and Alec's feelings I don't quite seize. As you describe it, I should be inclined to diagnose Maurice's state as simply lust and sentiment—a very wobbly affair; I should have prophesied a rupture after 6 months—chiefly as a result of lack of common interests owing to class differences—I believe even such a simple-minded fellow as Maurice would have felt this—and so your Sherwood Forest ending appears to me slightly mythical.... "'This is my main criticism of the story—I wonder if you'll see anything in it. A minor point is that I find it very difficult to believe that Maurice would have remained chaste during those 2 years with Clive. He was a strong healthy youth, and you say that, unless Clive had restrained him 'he would have surfeited passion (chap. XV). But how the Dickens could Clive restrain him?'" (Furbank, II, 15). But, for all these, Lytton Strachy found enough to praise the novel: "'I admire the cleverness [of the novel] very much. The opening scene with Mr Ducie is very good, and his reappearance 10 years later. The upper class conversations and that awful household in the country—how can you do it? Then the ingenuity of the machinery—e. g. the piano-moving incident—seems to me...'supreme!' I like enormously Alec's letters'" (*op. cit.*, II, 15-16).

Forrest Reid, on the other hand, could not at all stand *Maurice,* particularly for 'the physical love-making in the novel.' Forster felt the necessity of defending his novel, and he wrote to Reid, among other things, the following. "'I do want to raise these subjects out of the mists of theology: Male and Female created He not them. Ruling out underdeveloped people like Clive—or your youth, whom you advised most rightly—one is left with 'perverts' (an absurd word, because it assumes they were given a choice, but let's use it). Are these 'perverts' good or bad like normal men, their disproportionate tendency to badness (which I admit) being due to the criminal blindness of Society? Or are they inherently bad? You answer, as I do, that they are the former, but you answer with reluctance. I want you to answer vehemently! The man in my book is, roughly speaking, good, but Society nearly destroys him, he nearly slinks through his life furtive and afraid, and burdened with a sense of sin. You say 'if he had not met another man like him, what then?' What indeed? But blame Society not Maurice, and be thankful even in a novel when a man is left to lead the best life he is capable of leading!'" (*op. cit.*, II, 14).

John Sayre Martin's approach to *Maurice* is even, balanced: he is scathingly critical as well as frankly appreciative. On the side of his criticism of the novel, he writes: "For all its sensitivity and perceptiveness, *Maurice* is the most patently flawed of Forster's novels. For one thing, its construction is weak. In an attempt, presumably, to broaden the novel's range, Forster dwells too much on some of the minor characters—for example, Maurice's sisters, Clive's sister and her fiance Archie London, and the shadowy guests at Penge—none of whom are interesting in their own right. But the character who does most to throw the novel off balance is Clive Durham. In the Cambridge section, Forster devotes so much attention to Clive and his background that, reading *Maurice* for the first time, one might easily assume that the novel was to be centrally concerned with not one, but two, homosexuals of contrasting pamperment" (Martin, 136). Martin's second criticism of *Maurice* is that in it Forster is uncertain about the character of its hero, Maurice: he sometimes identifies himself with Maurice and sometimes does not, as a result of which the character lacks in high resolution. Martin says that Forster has less control than is necessary over the whole structure of *Maurice,* particularly over the drawing of the character of Maurice. Martin writes: "Forster's uncertain control is also evident in his conception of Maurice and in his attitude towards him. He cannot really decide what kind of man his protagonist is. 'In Maurice,' he writes, 'I tried to create a character who was completely unlike myself or what I supposed myself to be: someone handsome, healthy, bodily attractive, mentally torpid, not a bad business man and rather a snob.'... "Too often, however, he identifies himself with his hero [Maurice]" (*op. cit.,* 136-137). The result of Forster's vacillation has been disastrous—the character of Maurice is muddled.

But, as has been said, Martin has words of praise for *Maurice,* too. He says that how much so ever flawed the conception and writing of the novel may be, it betrays Forster's basic motive behind writing the kind of novels he has done. Martin writes: "Despite its flaws, *Maurice,* as Forster's only homosexual novel, has a special importance: it suggests the extent to which certain recurrent themes and incidents in his fiction are connected with his homosexual concerns. The journey theme, for example, which takes the traveller from a world of middle-class values and expectations to a new order of experience, would seem to have some basis in Forster's discovery of his own homosexuality—a discovery that Maurice's journey projects. Moreover, the fact that so many of Forster's travellers become involved, like Maurice, in tabooed relationships, leading in some cases to scandalous revelations, can hardly be unconnected with Forster's awareness of the perils of being a homosexual" (*op. cit.,* 139).

Maurice was the first ever novelistic plea for homosexuality, male homosexuality to be exact. It came into being much before its right time, and so it was contretemps, and so it received scant notice of critics and was neglected and vituperated by the reading public. Time has, perhaps, changed as is apparent from the very recent changes in the part of the legal system that relates to homosexuality in the western hemisphere, and this being so, *Maurice,* in the time present and in the time future, may have had sympathetic readings and unopinionated criticisms and appraisements.